HER SAVAGE PROTECTOR

Stunned silence filled the cavern. Ariana's heart thudded so loudly that the sound seemed to fill her ears. Then, slowly, her protector rose to his feet. He lifted his broken staff above his head, and from his throat came the most terrifying, barbaric howl of conquest that Ariana had ever imagined. It echoed and filled the cavern; it shuddered through Ariana's heart and she trembled, then backed away, edging from the jagged cliffs, away from *him*.

He saw her, and he smiled. Not the tender smile of a boy, but the smile of a hunter who has cornered his prey. His agility intact, he bounded down the rock face, then caught Ariana by her arm. He pulled her back up the mount to its pinnacle, then lifted Ariana's arm above her head, just as his vanquished foe had done. Again, he shouted words she did not know—but she knew what he said: "Mine!"

As one, the people of the cavern shouted, chanting, and the drums rolled again. They heralded this blood-soaked victory. She also knew instinctively that this man wasn't just claiming leadership of this dark cavern and all this world. He was claiming *her*.

STOBIE PIEL

LORD OF THE DARK SUN

LOVE SPELL   NEW YORK CITY

LOVE SPELL®

December 2002

Published by

Dorchester Publishing Co., Inc.
276 Fifth Avenue
New York, NY 10001

ISBN 0-505-52505-4

When I was thirteen, I read J.R.R. Tolkien's *Lord of the Rings* twenty-two times. I recited Elvish poems and tried to walk on the snow without leaving any imprint. Middle Earth became a home to me, and inspired me to create my own.

This year, I found myself once again inside that beautiful, poignant world, thanks to Peter Jackson's wonderful film *Fellowship of the Ring*, which I have seen thirteen times and counting. I dedicate this book to the memory of a master of fantasy, J.R.R. Tolkien, and to Peter Jackson and the cast and crew of *Fellowship of the Ring*, who brought that magical story to life. Thank you.

Frodo lives!

LORD
OF THE
DARK SUN

Part One

The Caverns
of the Dark Sun

*"In the barbarian, a
prince . . ."*

Chapter One

The sound wasn't human, but it was speech. Ariana fought upward against a thick fog of sleep, battling for a consciousness she wasn't ready to face. Her mind flitted through her recent memory: a wild trip with her friends beyond the safe confines of Intersystem space; exotic outposts; dark, seamy taverns; dancers on tables; races of beings she'd never seen before; revelry she'd never imagined. . . . Ariana opened one eye and saw a towering figure above her—it clearly was not a person. For an instant she stared, then blinked as if to give life to the dark figure. It moved, but not by nature. It spoke, but not with voice.

"What are you?" She wasn't sure whom she was asking, and the figure took no apparent notice of her. Ariana struggled to sit up, but a casing that resembled an ancient burial wrap bound her legs and lower body. Frustrated, she spoke up again. "Who are you?"

Slowly the figure turned. It didn't see her, but it somehow perceived her. A series of mechanical noises emanated from somewhere inside its shell. Some flitted by like snippets of languages she had heard but never learned, like sitting in at an Intersystem Council session while her father quietly presided over the many representatives of numerous races. The figure made a sound resembling the Intersystem translator devices, but much quicker, as if all language had been sped to a rate beyond living transmission.

"Captive One-twenty-one speaking Language Four. Maintain silence until distribution." It seemed to be speaking to her, but she had no idea what it meant. The voice indicated no personality, no feeling, thought, or opinion. It was no living creature.

Ariana recognized it as an Automon, but one so perfectly crafted as to betray no working parts, no mechanical apparatus. Its shell was a deep matte black crafted in the shape of a humanoid figure with a small oval head, a slender metallic torso, and two straight legs jointed in the area of the knees. The Automon was slightly taller than an average human, as if once it might have been made to encase a man-sized being. It sensors resembled eyes, and a speaker could have been mistaken for a mouth.

Whoever designed this thing had modeled it on the human form, but without love or sense of beauty. It was functional. Ariana perceived, as if glimpsing the mind of its creator, that the creature was designed in human form not for love or admiration of the shape, but because it was meant to walk, operate, and function wherever humans might.

And yet, a curious sorrow emanated from the Automon, as if it were fueled not by mechanical energy, but by the depths of a great soul's pain. Ariana shook her head. It had to be her own pain and fear she felt. Certainly not the Automon's.

The Automon seemed to study her for a while, then turned its head toward a wall speaker. "Captive One-twenty-one logged. Evaluation complete." The thing paused, and a sound came as if from a message received from some distant source. The Automon responded. "It lives."

It. . . . "It" was her, Ariana. The Automon moved away, and Ariana struggled to move her head, to see where she was. *A space ship.* Painful memories flooded through her. Ariana's vessel had been attacked by unknown assailants. They'd come out of nowhere, from the depths of uncharted space. They'd fired on Ariana's small journeying ship, docked alongside her disabled vessel, and boarded her craft. Before Ariana had seen who—or what—attacked them, a strange gas flooded her ship and she remembered no more.

In those last dim moments of consciousness, she had expected death, but instead, she found herself a captive. Several young women lay in ordered rows, nearby Ariana, bound as she was, like the ancient encased dead—but living. Only one she knew well—Lissa of Lower Nirvahda. None but Ariana was conscious.

The Automon moved around the room, logging each of the women. Ariana's group was held captive in a rectangular room, empty except for control panels along the wall and a closed exit at one end. Along one side appeared to be bins, now closed, but Ariana couldn't guess their purpose. The walls were dark gray with black and red flecks, crafted of a rich, unfathomable metal. There were no odors other than a faint metallic scent, and no sounds other than those made by the Automon and the low hum of a ship's engine, louder and more powerful than the engine of even the best Intersystem vessels. It seemed likely that this ship was moving at a speed unmatched by the vessels Ariana knew.

She furrowed her brow. These ships might be faster than those of the Intersystem, but her Academy training had prepared her for anything. If she could regain control, she would be able to pilot this ship back to Intersystem space, to safety. Ariana fixed on this resolve, then pinned her gaze on the Automon as it went from one captive to the next. It paused over a dark-skinned girl who had accompanied her boyfriend on Ariana's expedition into the lawless territory outside the Intersystem. The girl didn't move when the Automon prodded her, and her head lolled to one side. Her blank eyes slid open. Ariana's chest clenched. The girl was

5

dead. The Automon emitted a sound, and two squat figures appeared, like the first Automon but shorter, with less detail. They seized the girl's lifeless body, opened one of the sleek bins, then placed her body in a tube in the ship's hull. The Automon pulled a lever. With a loud rush and a horrible noise, the tube expelled the girl from the ship.

"Cull released." The Automon returned to its task, but the loud noise of the body's ejection into space woke those captives strong enough to hear it.

Beside Ariana, Lissa stirred, then woke with a plaintive cry. She looked around wildly, her large eyes bright with panic. She spotted Ariana and her trembling increased. "Ariana . . . What happened? Where are we?"

The sight of Lissa's familiar face offered less reassurance than burden. Lissa wasn't the strongest in Ariana's group of friends, or the brightest. But wherever Ariana went, Lissa seemed to follow, and Ariana felt responsible for her. "I don't know where we are. We were attacked and our ship disabled. That's all I remember."

Lissa eyed the Automon as it proceeded methodically around the room. "What are those things?"

Ariana fought the desire to shout, *How am I supposed to know?* "Some kind of Automon, obviously, but I've never heard of any so perfectly crafted."

"What do they want with us?" Lissa shuddered as if fearing some personal assault.

Ariana studied the Automon. "I doubt they *want* anything. But they have some purpose, that is clear. There must be some life, some mentality behind them. Someone created them. Someone alive must be directing them."

"What does it matter who made them? Ariana, we aren't on a class field trip! What are you going to do to save us?"

Ariana didn't answer. She glanced at her own bound body. *Save us?*

"Ariana . . ." Lissa gasped for breath, but she was gaining strength. "You have to do something." The Automon moved toward them, probably to record Lissa's condition. Lissa nodded vigorously. "Tell him who you are!"

Ariana eyed her doubtfully. "I doubt that thing will care."

"Of course he will!" Lissa paused, a thoughtful look in her eye. "It's probably because of you we were abducted. Not that I'm blaming you, of course. You're the best of us. You always have been. But they're probably using us to get at your father."

Ariana repressed an irritated sigh. Lissa hadn't said it outright, but Ariana heard her implication: *It's you they want, not us.* If so, then it was Ariana's duty to give herself up to save the others. *It's up to me, and I will do what I can.* Ariana struggled again and managed to sit up, though her legs had numbed from their casing, and her torso was bound so tightly that bending caused pain.

Her voice shook, but her words came out clearly. "I am Ariana of Valenwood, daughter of Arnoth, King of the Ellowan, Prime Representative of the Intersystem Council. You will release us now, or face the wrath of the entire Intersystem fleet!"

Lissa shrunk away as if Ariana had said too much, but Ariana faced her grim captor without wavering. The Automon made no response, nor did it seem to understand.

Lissa struggled to sit up, too. "Don't you know who she is? Her father is the most powerful man in the galaxy! He is a king, as well as the head of the Intersystem Council! Ariana is a princess!"

Ariana frowned: Lissa had always made too much of her heritage. If Lissa hoped the Automon were after a ransom, Ariana suspected she would be sorely disappointed.

The Automon ignored her, and Ariana lay back, staring at the ceiling. "I don't think it cares, Lissa. We are far outside the Intersystem now."

"Then why? Why have they taken us?"

Ariana didn't answer. In celebration of their graduation from the prestigious Intersystem Academy, Ariana had talked a group of her friends into venturing to the infamous outpost of Lodder Vale at the outskirts of the Border Territory. Only her closest friend, Hakon, son of the Intersystem Sage, hadn't been able to come. Hakon had recently

7

joined the Intersystem's elite pilot force, and his new duties prevented him from the fun they'd once shared. Ariana closed her eyes. At least Hakon was safe. Though her group had kept their destination a secret from their parents, Hakon knew where they'd gone. He would come after her. Her father would send the whole Intersystem fleet after her.

But what then? She had no idea where they were, and the space beyond the Intersystem boundaries wasn't well known. The black ships came from a region known as Dark Sun Space. No one knew who piloted them, or where their home world was, but quietly, slowly, they had become a presence, and a dread. The Intersystem Council had tried to learn more, but the black ships appeared like assassins, then disappeared as quickly as they'd arrived. They had never struck so close to Intersystem space before, but their reach appeared to be expanding dangerously. Apparently, they had captured only the six women from her ship this time—what had become of the others, she had no idea.

The ship that carried them jerked, then lowered rapidly. For a moment, Ariana feared they were crashing. Lissa screamed, then covered her face. But the Automon gave no indication of danger. Their landing was handled with no more grace, and the ship's metal walls groaned as if scratched by rock. The ship stilled, and for a long moment, only small robotic noises came from the ship's core.

A bell rang, and activity began at once. Several short, square Automon models entered and stood near the rear hull. Gears turned, and doors ground open. The black Automon positioned itself by the open door, waiting silently and motionless. Footsteps, too even for life, echoed up a long hallway, and six more of the larger Automon appeared, identical to the first. Their creaking, jointed necks turned in unison as they in-tuned themselves with the first Automon.

"Group One speaking Language Four. Engaged for distribution," the Automon reported. "Five living, one culled."

The new Automon positioned themselves near the captives, waiting. With vacant sensors, which Ariana couldn't help humanizing to "eyes," they stared straight ahead, uninterested in the terrified young women who lay helpless beneath them. It seemed to Ariana that raging madmen couldn't have been worse. Something in the cold disregard, the nothingness, was more terrifying than any living foe.

Despite their emptiness, their hollow black shells, Ariana sensed some consciousness—not within the Automon, but around them. A force of life directed them somehow. Though they were lifeless, the method that drove them was not.

The smaller Automon bustled more quickly, but with the same methodical precision, the same mindless purpose, as they removed the captives' casings. Ariana's legs went cold and she trembled, but she moved to sit up. Before she could rise, a tall Automon seized her by the hair and pulled her to her feet. She struggled, but the Automon didn't react. With the others behind, it dragged her along an empty, narrow hall, lit with hidden red bulbs. Terror built in her heart, as she stumbled behind the Automon on half-numb legs, and she heard Lissa weeping, while the others cried and pleaded for mercy.

Ariana remained silent, not out of courage but because fear had always rendered her still. Hakon had said that he could tell when she was scared—because it was the only time she didn't talk. The Automon stopped abruptly, and Ariana tripped. Air, cold yet filled with a hot scent of burning, reached her awareness. She could feel the exit ahead rather than see it. Perhaps it was night. Or maybe in this distant world there was no day.

Two short Automon of a third type met them. These were almost square, less humanlike, with several appendages resembling arms. They carried a stout machine with prongs like teeth. Ariana bit back a cry—it seemed a likely device for murder. She fought her fear. If they had meant to kill them, there would have been no need to transport them anywhere. Before she could guess at the device's purpose, the Automon shoved her head toward it. The device screamed into activity. Ariana couldn't see, facedown, but her lifeless captor yanked at her hair, pulling it outward. In one motion, the short Automon shaved her head, and her long dark hair fell at her feet in a thick pile of waves.

Ariana screamed as she had never screamed before. It wasn't fear or vanity or any emotion she recognized. But as the Automon ripped this part of her away, she knew what she hadn't understood until now. She was nothing, no one. Nothing she had been, nothing she had dreamed or studied, nothing she had learned or loved, had any meaning here. She was a slave to some uncertain purpose—it didn't matter what, for it didn't involve *her* at all. She was naked despite her light clothing, unprotected, and all she had thought real and sure were gone.

The task done, the Automon pushed her forward, in line for the next. Ariana trembled, her shaved head cold in the dark ashen wind. She watched, horrified, as each girl's head was shaved, as they emerged shocked, and bewildered. Stunned, Ariana caught Lissa's eye, desperate for a friend's comfort and the knowledge she wasn't alone. A strange glint flickered in Lissa's eyes as she looked at Ariana, and Lissa's wide mouth curled in the slightest of smiles—but not in comfort. It was almost as if Ariana's devastation had instilled a new sense of power in Lissa, regardless of her own fate.

Ariana turned quickly away, but her heart beat in odd little jerks. When the mask was stripped away, what remained? If she didn't truly know Lissa, did she know herself any better?

The seven larger Automon moved them into a transport vehicle. Ariana saw little outside to differentiate it from the ship. If it was night, there was no sun anywhere, and there were no stars. A thick cloud of smoke obliterated the sky. A strangely familiar scent tinged the air. At first, she couldn't place it, but then an image of a classroom filled her mind. Of all things! She closed her eyes. . . . *Malloreum fuel, rare and untested, but promising. Might be the next great advancement in space travel, if it could be found and mined in great enough quantities. Deep in rocks, but so far only detected via probes.* From far beyond Intersystem space it was found in worlds that revolved around Dark Suns, rare volcanic planets whose unique evolution produced rocks that when crushed could be turned into the most potent fuel ever discovered—and those rocks could be mined only by human hands.

As if to verify her unspoken guess, the first Automon spoke into a receiver as soon as the transport vehicle stopped. "Female Group One distributed to Mining Colony Fifteen." The rest of the Automon shoved the women toward a door. Ariana heard the mechanical voice as she fell forward into ashen darkness, and it echoed with brutal finality. "Group One disengaged."

11

Chapter Two

Something pushed Ariana from behind, but she saw no one as she crashed downward. She steadied herself, but kept sliding down a slick, unseen surface. Hot, noxious air filled her senses, but it was breathable. It didn't mean death, and soon she was blind to its potency. Behind her, the other captives tumbled down, some screaming, some crying. Ariana reached to brace herself, but the surface revealed no cracks, no bumps, and she continued to fall.

She guessed they had been shoved into a tunnel. The air grew hotter, but not unbearable. Below, the tunnel dipped, then glowed with a golden-red light. The end burst open with a suddenness that startled her, but the yelps and shouts that met her ears astonished her even more. For these sounds *were* human, though more primitive and barbaric than anything she'd heard before.

Ariana's group slid out onto a rough earthen floor. The tunnel closed behind them with a dull clang. Ariana blinked in what seemed a bright light, but she realized it was instead a dark red, the color of flame or molten lava. Great clusters of crystal points covered the cavern walls, shining from nooks and crannies, rising from narrow crevices on the ground. They reflected the red lava almost like lanterns.

The other captives assembled around her, some weeping, some shaking with fear. But Ariana shoved herself up and stood. Hot ash and pungent air stung her eyes, and she blinked, fighting to see her surroundings. All seemed clouded in an ashen cloud of dust from the tunnel. The dust settled and shadowy forms appeared in the midst of the cavern. They were not alone.

The dark forms moved toward them, but without the methodical, precise movements of the Automon. These creatures crept nearer, hesitant but vigilant like hunters. The shapes came clearer as they drew near. They were men. But men like none Ariana had ever seen. More like specimens of a history lesson, they grunted and yelped like creatures born of some long-forgotten race, like animals.

Ariana stared, astounded, as the creatures drew closer. Behind them, she could see a larger group gathering in interest, but still holding back. A mark had been scarred into each man's chest—a brand, perhaps indicating a number. Most were bearded, though they looked young, clothed in rough leather strips that covered little more than their loins. Some wore collars adorned with crystal, some with what looked like bone.

One man stood taller than the rest. He was large boned, with hair hanging past his shoulders—it might have been black or dark red, and it lay matted and decorated with what looked like crystal shards. This apparent leader carried a large stave, handcrafted of roots and decorated with primitive carvings. He stood before the others, who positioned themselves around him, eager and wary at the same time. As they came closer to Ariana's group, she saw that they were indeed young, much younger than she'd imagined when they first appeared. She glanced around and saw no one in the room who looked older than twenty and no one younger than fourteen.

Perhaps they were captives, too. Maybe they, too, had

been taken by the cold Automon, perhaps as slaves in a mining operation, which this apparently was. She knew from that far-off classroom that the rare fuel malloreum came from volcanic worlds that provided a unique mix of rock and gases, and was obtainable only by hand because no metallic equipment could maneuver in its delicate pursuit.

Ariana swallowed hard, then cleared her throat. "I am Ariana of Valenwood. . . ." Before she finished, the leader laughed and shouted. The other young men echoed his sound, guttural, without real words, but still with some rudimentary language. Only one, younger than the leader but almost as tall, made no sound. He just stared at Ariana, wonder shining in his dark eyes. His straight hair was long and black, and a single crystal point hung around his neck on a leather cord. She saw marks carved into the stone, symbols wrought with some meaning, but she couldn't make out the design. He leaned toward her as if spellbound, and the gentleness in his gaze tugged at her wariness. He reached his hand toward her. He had long fingers—powerful, stained, but elegant. They reminded her of Ellowan hands, her father's race—hands of healing, of the galaxy's greatest art, and of its greatest music.

The leader noticed the other's attention, and his face darkened. He glanced back and forth between the younger man and Ariana, and his lips formed a grin that was as much a snarl. He shoved the younger man back, then tossed his head. He thumped his chest. Ariana didn't need to understand his primitive language. He meant, "Mine."

The younger man didn't fight, but neither did he back away. The leader seemed to swell with arrogance and pride, but Ariana recognized bravado. Despite his laugh and posture, he considered the younger man a threat. The leader had assessed the women as a group, but his young rival had directed his attention at Ariana—so it was Ariana the leader now claimed.

Ariana shook her head, then held up her hand. "You do not understand. We were taken captive by the Automon, too." It was hopeless. Her words were received with no more understanding than the singing of birds. Already, the group of men jostled near their leader, nodding toward the women, reaching with greedy hands. The leader struck one back with his stave and laughed when the boy yelped. He grunted a command, and again, Ariana recognized his meaning: "Me first."

Lissa moved closer to Ariana. "What are they? What do they want?"

Ariana eyed Lissa doubtfully. "I think they want us."

"Us? No!" Lissa gasped in horror, but Ariana ignored her. She had to think, to reason. . . . *How do I reason with animals?*

Ariana tried to smile, but she was shaking. "We don't mean you any harm." She kept her voice calm, but it quavered, and she knew they heard her fear, even if they didn't understand her words. The leader paid no attention. He thumped his chest and moved himself in front of the others. She guessed her group wasn't the first dumped in upon these pathetic creatures—she could see a few women in the background, cowering and subdued. There weren't many. One or two appeared pregnant, but she saw no children. Perhaps the Automon required new blood to keep their race of mining slaves. But why, then, were there no elder people in the colony?

Lissa's attention shifted from the leader to his younger rival, and then she clutched at Ariana's arm. "Give him what he wants, Ariana." Before Ariana could reply, Lissa's grip tightened. "You have no choice. If you don't submit to their leader, he'll kill us all."

Ariana fixed her gaze on the leader. "I have a choice." A sharp hiss escaped Lissa's lips, as though Ariana had doomed them all by her selfishness. But in this dark cavern where she faced the end of her self, all her former good intentions were stripped away. She spoke again, her voice deep and rich with emotion. "I have a choice!"

The brazen leader stepped toward her, his muscles rippling as he flexed. It seemed a display of power meant to

15

impress his followers more than the new women. He grabbed Ariana's arm and yanked her forward. Holding her arm up, he yelped loudly, like a chant, as she recoiled. The others, the older boys who seemed like the guards of a barbarian king, joined the chant, broken with guttural laughter. *I will not fall this way, I will not.* . . . Wild fury woke in her heart, and Ariana fought, beyond thought or reason. She bit and kicked, used all the power in her body . . . and nothing worked. The leader seemed to enjoy her spirit. He bent her arm in a brutal lock behind her back. With his hunter's eye fixed on her, he twisted her arm until she slowly sank before him. Ariana's gaze never faltered. Her lip bled—she didn't know how she'd cut it. He cranked her arm until it neared breaking, but she refused to yield. He laughed again, liking her fight, and he yanked. Ariana screamed and crumpled to her knees.

With his free hand, he pulled back his loincloth, but the crowd's surprised cry distracted him. He turned, his face stricken with astonishment as the young man who'd stared at Ariana stepped forward. There was no need for words—Ariana knew what transpired. The young man, with his artists' hands and kind eyes, was challenging the leader.

For an instant, the leader hesitated, and fear flickered in his eyes. Ariana wasn't sure why. His challenger might be near his height, but he was smaller in build and obviously younger. Her heart quailed. Her gentle defender didn't stand a chance against this brute.

Apparently, the leader's guards thought the same. They screamed and laughed, but clearly reveled in the battle to come. The leader threw back his head and roared. Though not civilized, the sound was terribly human, as if torn from the deepest core of the species. His primal roar echoed around the molten cavern. The others formed a semicircle around the two fighters. For the moment, Ariana and her group were forgotten. The other captives stood behind Ariana, but Lissa cast her an accusatory glance. "What have you done, Ariana?"

Ariana's mouth slid open. "What have *I* done?"

"Yes! You've riled them up. Why did you fight him?"

Ariana stared at Lissa in disbelief, but she gave no answer. The cavern echoed with shouts, chants, yelps. The sound of rudimentary drums began across the hall. Ariana watched spellbound as the brazen leader moved in a circle, facing his younger rival. No honor began the fight. The leader poised his stave, then swung it with deadly force at his unarmed opponent. But honor must have held some sway. Someone tossed the challenger a narrow stave. He caught it and whirled with surprising speed, catching the leader behind the knees.

They fought like animals, giving no quarter. The battle raged around the cavern. The younger man leapt from rock to rock. Despite the primitive weaponry, he fought with intelligence. He sought the higher ground, the better footing, and his intelligence proved a match for the leader's brawn. But in so harsh a world, Ariana saw no place where brawn, violence, and power wouldn't ultimately triumph.

The leader bounded after his rival, then drove his stave headlong into his enemy's gut. The younger man doubled over, then fell, and the leader swung the stave to crush his enemy's head. Ariana bit back a cry, but the young man rolled, dove, then bounded across the cavern. With a yelp, heralding certain victory, the leader leapt after him. Ariana shuddered—in a world such as this, no losing challenger would survive. They would kill him, like animals tearing at prey.

But the young man wasn't fleeing his enemy. He jumped up along an inner hill, bounding higher, nearer to its summit. A red glow framed the battleground, boiling from inside the hill's summit. The leader followed, shouting in fury, and the throng gathered at a distance behind. Spellbound, Ariana followed, too, leaving the other captives behind.

To her horror, she realized that the intelligence of her defender had at last failed him, and his knack for finding the better ground had failed, too. For his last defense, he had chosen the edge of a volcanic pit, filled with molten

17

lava. The leader laughed as he too recognized his advantage. Again, he threw back his head and howled, heralding a victory that seemed inevitable.

But the challenger smiled, his brow elevated as if welcoming his opponent onward. Ariana held her breath as the challenge was met. There, in the instant of fury, of battle, of a barbaric rage, she saw her defender's wisdom. The ledge they fought upon was narrow, and only an agile man could hold his own. The leader was strong, brutal and skilled, but he wasn't agile.

Each time he swung, the challenger avoided his blow, then struck his own. Each time, the leader's balance faltered. The challenger bounded down, then up again on the leader's other side, perilously close to the pit below. Molten flames curled at their feet, but the young warrior drew the battle closer still, until both men reached a pinnacle, an outcrop of hardened lava that hung out over the pit. The leader's heavy stave sliced hard across the smaller weapon, shattering it, leaving Ariana's defender with only a short, blunt end. The young warrior reached the outcrop's end, and the pit below sent flames upward, splintering the red glow that framed their battle. Ariana climbed higher, though there was nothing she could do to change the final outcome.

With a howl of rage, the leader charged, his stave pointed at his enemy's head. The challenger ducked, whirled, swung his own broken stave, and cracked the leader with a heavy blow to his back. The leader dropped his weapon, stumbled, then fell forward into the smoldering pit. His horrific scream was abruptly cut off as another flame leapt toward the cavern roof. One man stood alone upon the pinnacle. He bent to his knee, one arm limp at his side, blood streaming from his forehead.

Stunned silence filled the cavern. Ariana's heart thudded so loudly that the sound seemed to fill her ears. Then, slowly, the young warrior rose to his feet. He lifted his broken stave above his head, and from his throat came a howl of conquest more terrifying and barbaric than Ariana could have ever imagined. It echoed and filled the cavern. It shuddered through Ariana's heart and she trembled, then backed away, edging from the jagged cliffs, away from *him*. . . .

He saw her, and he smiled. Not the tender smile of the boy he had been, but the smile of a hunter who has cornered prey. Maybe the thrill of a new chase restored his agility. He bounded down the hillside, then caught Ariana by her arm. He pulled her back up the hill to the edge of the pinnacle, then lifted her arm above her head, just as the leader had done. Again, he shouted, and she knew he said "Mine!"

As one, the people of the cavern shouted, chanting, and the drums rolled again as they heralded his blood-soaked victory. She knew suddenly that he wasn't just claiming her, but the leadership of this dark cavern. He was now the barbarian lord of a dark, sunless realm.

His grip on her arm was tight, unyielding. She had prayed for his victory, for the victory of tenderness over raw force, of intelligence over brawn. In his victory, she had seen hope for more than just her survival, for something good when all else had faltered. She had seen a rare sensitivity in his dark, sparkling eyes. She looked at him now, and saw the molten fire reflected in his face, his eyes shining not with hope, but with red flames.

Hate filled her heart. She didn't care what he would do to her—she hated him. He had betrayed her hope, her last hope for herself, and for humanity. An unfamiliar rage swelled inside her. Her gentle upbringing, her loving parents, her beautiful world, faded until all she knew was fury.

The dead leader had dropped his stave. She saw it. Still held by the victor, she dropped from his grip, seized the fallen stave, then jerked away. But not far. She held her own and faced her enemy. From below, she heard laughter, screams of disbelief. Some came from her own people, some from her enemies. All she saw was him. *I will fight you.*

She would fight. She moved toward him. Let him kill

her, let him die. She would fight. He was weak, injured, bleeding heavily. She might not fail. And when he fell . . . When he fell, she would be queen of this barbarian cavern. No one would defy her. She recognized her madness and didn't care. She would fight. She would kill him. Her whole body shook, but she knew in her most deeply human core that she would win.

Her enemy didn't raise his broken stave to fight or defend himself. He just looked at her. Slowly, so as to be almost indiscernible, his expression changed. His head tilted to one side as he stared at her, and his dark eyes filled with wonder. With impenetrable grace, a smile formed on his lips, but not in mockery. In tenderness.

Ariana would fight. She did not lower her weapon. But he took one step closer to her, and still he didn't raise his stave. He lifted his hand and held it out to her.

For an interminable while, she stood frozen with fire burning behind her. She neither broke his gaze nor looked away. And then, beyond thought or fear or wariness, Ariana placed her hand in his.

Chapter Three

"Yield to me, and I will heal you." Ariana knelt beside the young barbarian warrior and gathered her courage. He eyed her steadily, but she sensed his reluctance. She hadn't inherited the mind-to-mind healing technique of her father's people, the Ellowan, but she had learned practical skills and certainly knew more than anyone in the cavern tribe.

A serious-faced boy scrambled up the ledge behind and stared down at her as she examined the leader. The boy held a strange assortment of mushrooms, crystals, and a hollowed-out rock-bowl of steaming water. Ariana seized the bowl of water, sniffed it, then nodded. "This will prove useful. The other stuff..." She paused. "It will probably poison him." The boy hesitated, but he seemed to sense her competence. He glanced at the leader, who looked between them, took a quick breath, then motioned the boy away. The boy eyed Ariana with misgiving, then departed as if never expecting to see his leader alive again.

Ariana frowned. "You will all learn to trust me." She reached beneath her jacket and her snug bodice, then tugged away the soft inner camisole she wore close to her skin. It was finely woven cloth, perfect for her purpose. She extracted it carefully from beneath her jacket, over one arm, her head, then the other arm, then dipped it in the bowl. The leader's brown eyes widened with shock, as if she'd peeled away her skin, but then he seemed to repress a smile of some sort.

She met his gaze evenly. "I am going to clean your wounds."

His brow arched, and Ariana hesitated, afraid he might resist this necessary treatment. He was obviously a strong-willed young man, as he had already proven in several ways since his triumphant battle. Despite his injuries, he had led her from the point of his victory to a craggy ledge, which appeared to be the cavern leader's "royal chamber." She guessed this because before lying down on the skins and carved rocks that indicated a bed, he had motioned to a boy, who went to gather another set of bedding. Though in obvious pain, the new leader had taken great pains to arrange his own bedding and to discard his former adversary's gear. The other boys made a great celebration of tossing the dead leader's blankets into the lava pit after him. Ariana guessed he hadn't been well-liked and that his death wouldn't be grieved despite its horror.

In contrast, the tribe seemed visibly relaxed with the victor, and though Ariana had feared another of the barbarians would try to supplant him in his weakened state, they had been instead almost doting upon him. Soon after the young man's victory, the Automon dumped crates of food down tubes such as those that had deposited Ariana and her group, but before anyone ate, several young women brought the food to the new leader.

Ariana had watched in amazement as he took the food, nodded in thanks, waited until the women left, and then collapsed, weak, beside her. He was a proud man, whatever his heritage, and the blood of a natural leader flowed in his veins. She couldn't assess her feelings for him, but she was drawn to him. As he lay beside her, his dark eyes focused on her alone, strange feelings stirred somewhere deep inside her.

Despite the dirt, the unkempt long hair, and even the beard, he was a handsome man. Even if she couldn't assess the pure structure of his face, he seemed both exotic and powerful. His beauty was different from the cool, remote perfection of her friend Hakon. This man was dangerous— and curiously sensual. His body, though still bearing signs of youth, was sculpted to perfection, hard and strong. His chest rippled with lean muscle, his shoulders broad, his dark skin smooth. She wanted to touch him. Ariana gulped, then reached to place her hand on his bare chest.

"By the stars, you're not going to *touch* him, are you?"

Ariana jumped and drew back, then turned to see Lissa standing behind her. Her eyes narrowed. "I am going to heal him, Lissa."

Lissa's glance flashed toward the barbarian, though he took no notice of her. "Don't we have more important things to consider, Ariana? Such as getting out of this awful place?"

Struggling for patience, Ariana drew a deep breath. "This man saved my life, and I will heal him before I do anything else. When I've rested and had time to study the Automon's movements, I will turn my mind toward escape. I don't like it here any better than you do, but I don't think these people mean us any harm. We might be able to help them."

"You're already taking on more than you can possibly handle." Lissa paused and sighed indulgently. "It's so like you." Her gaze whisked again to the barbarian leader. "If you feel it's necessary, leave his healing to me. You should be putting your leadership talents to better use. Of the two of us, I have more skill with people. You're so much like Hakon! You're too lofty, my dear, to relate to the likes of this poor creature." Lissa hesitated, then shrugged idly. "I will tend to him myself while you engineer our escape."

A peculiar chill edged through Ariana. She felt compelled to defend herself, to insist she had as much warmth as Lissa, or anyone. But she wasn't sure it was true. Maybe she was spoiled, maybe her life had been too easy. If another could tend him better than herself, perhaps she should yield. But the barbarian fire that had kindled inside her by the lava pit's edge remained strong. "I am capable of healing him."

Lissa rolled her eyes, discounting Ariana's skill and her decision. "Don't be silly, Ariana. You inherited none of your father's Ellowan healing talent. What can you do?"

Ariana didn't answer, but she found herself leaning toward the young man, protective, and Lissa laughed. "It looks like you've claimed him for yourself!" She laughed again, careless. "Have it your way—you've always been so strong-willed! But don't be too naïve, Ariana. We aren't safe here. You have to consider the other girls as well as yourself."

Ariana glanced at the floor below the ledges. The three other captives stood together, but they, too, seemed more relaxed since the battle. Already Cara, the most outgoing of the group, was trying to communicate with a cavern woman. The other seemed ill, which concerned Ariana, but for now, there was little she could do to help. Lissa's shy friend, Kaila, seemed unsure and confused amid the rough tribe, but she was just the same among the Academy students, so Ariana wasn't worried. Hakon had once said Kaila would have been confused even when in her mother's womb.

Lissa looked down at them, too, then shook her head sadly. "I don't know what will become of poor Kaila. She relies on me so. She's terrified."

Ariana eyed Kaila. "She looks a little confused, but she always looks that way to me. I think she just hangs back and observes before taking part. It's her nature."

"I know her so much better than you do. Kaila claims to be fine, but I know better. She's terrified. This will kill her, if you don't find a way to get us out of here."

Ariana's frown deepened. Lissa always felt she knew people better than they knew themselves. "Maybe you should go down and stay with her, then."

Lissa's gaze snapped to Ariana, but her smile remained in place. "I don't dare leave you alone with him. Stars know what he has in mind."

Ariana glanced at the leader. "Rest, I think, and healing. Leave us, Lissa. He is my concern now."

Lissa's smile faded. "Because he claimed you? As a mate, perhaps? I hope you don't take that too seriously, Ariana. After all, you must remember that the battle he fought made him lord of this cavern, something he obviously intended to achieve anyway. When the former leader picked you, he had no choice but to contend for you himself."

Ariana looked at Lissa in surprise. Had it been that way? Ariana felt sure it had transpired in the opposite fashion—he had wanted her, and so he fought when otherwise he was content to follow. "That's not what I remember."

Lissa squeezed Ariana's arm supportively. "It's natural that you'd want to make more of it. Believe me, no one is more romantic than I am. I just don't want to see you hurt."

Ariana's eyes narrowed. "What do you mean?"

"Only that this tribe operates on a different level from anything you know, Ariana. Who knows who he would have chosen if you hadn't put yourself forward when we first arrived?"

Put myself forward, indeed! And yet, she *had* stepped forward when they landed in the cavern, thus attracting the interest of the males. Ariana glanced down at the wounded man. He was looking at her as if he'd never seen anything like her in his life, as if she held all the wonder of the universe. Her fingers tingled and her breath caught.

Ariana held his gaze for a long moment, and her doubt eased while something new and far stronger took hold. Her nervousness faded, and her resolve grew. "Leave us, Lissa."

Lissa started to object. "You don't know what you're doing. . . ."

Something unfathomable had changed in Ariana. She felt it, though she didn't completely understand it. But even her voice gained a new depth when she turned back to Lissa. "I am not the girl you knew. What I become now comes from something much deeper than I have ever been forced to see in myself." Her gaze shifted back to the barbarian. "But *he* knows. I will heal him. What comes after is my concern."

Lissa's eyes widened in shock, but she must have recognized the power in Ariana's voice. "Be careful, Ariana. You have no idea what you're getting into." She paused as if struggling to find more evidence against this unexpected union of princess and barbarian. "I shudder to imagine what Hakon would think if he knew what you were doing."

Lissa said Hakon's name with emphasis—she had always held to the belief that Hakon and Ariana were lovers, and she had never accepted the depth of their friendship or understood the platonic love they shared. Her words had no impact on Ariana. Hakon would understand what she saw in this primitive young man far better than Lissa would. Yet something lurked beneath Lissa's scorn. It showed in her eyes as she tried not to glance at the warrior's strong body, in the quickness of her breath when he made even the slightest motion. It was almost akin to what Ariana herself was feeling. Witnessing its force in Lissa, Ariana understood now what she felt. *Desire.*

With obvious reluctance, Lissa left them alone and picked her way delicately down the ledge path. As Ariana watched her go, she felt suddenly nervous and didn't dare look back at him. His touch on her arm startled her, but when she turned to him, he smiled. *He knew.* But despite his masculine awareness, the sweet wonder in his eyes didn't fade. He murmured something, not language exactly, but the semblence of it, and then he fingered the crystal hanging around his neck.

Ariana took a quick breath. She placed her hand over her chest. "Ariana. I am called Ariana. Do you have a name?"

He had no idea what she said, but his brow furrowed as he tried to understand. She repeated herself, trying to trim her words to the most basic. *"Ariana."*

He placed his hand over hers and his smile deepened, almost as if he felt her rapid heartbeat. "Ariana." He spoke with surprising clarity, his voice strangely accented, but even in that one word, she detected quick thought and a keen mind at work. *"Ariana."*

Ariana smiled, too, and nodded. She gestured at him, but he seemed unsure what she wanted. He spoke a word, which sounded most like "oo-nah." She recalled that word from the fight, directed not at him, but to the other warrior, so it probably meant "leader."

"Good enough." She paused. "Ooh-nah doesn't sound quite right, not like a name really." She shrugged. "I'll think of a better name for you later. For now, it's time I healed you."

Again, he listened, baffled, but Ariana kept talking, more for her own benefit than his and because she always talked when nervous. "I'm sorry I didn't inherit my father's healing skills. He is the greatest Ellowan healer who ever lived. My brothers inherited some, but nothing like his. He is a wonderful man. He's a leader, too, like you."

As she spoke, she examined his injuries. He watched her and revealed no pain as she bent closer to study his wounds. Calming her nervousness, she fingered his muscles and gently tested his bones, then breathed a sigh of relief. "This doesn't look too bad. Bloody, but not so deep. You're going to have some ugly bruises, but nothing appears broken." She tore off the hem of her pilot jacket, then bound the gash on his upper arm. Her voice edged up a pitch as her fingers grazed his firm, smooth skin. "By the stars, you are strong! You're even stronger than the men at the Academy who pursued Body-Shaping—that's hoisting ridiculous weights and grunting a lot. . . ." Ariana paused and tried to mimic the sounds of the straining men. She puffed her cheeks, pretended to hoist a heavy weight over her head, and then issued a rendition of the subsequent grunts. His brow furrowed, and his eyes shifted to one side. Ariana cleared her throat. "And you have no idea what I'm saying, do you?"

His smile gentled, and he reached to touch her cheek. "Ariana." Her heart moved at the sound of his voice. Weary, his dark eyes drifted shut, but he motioned to her. To her surprise, it seemed he wanted her to lay beside him. Close. In his condition, he certainly posed no sexual threat. Not yet . . . And even if he did . . . was it truly a threat? Ariana hesitated, then lay down beside him. He adjusted his position closer, then rested his arm over her, protectively. His breathing slowed, and Ariana relaxed. As weariness also

27

claimed her, she knew in this dark cavern she was experiencing the least likely sensation imaginable . . . she felt *safe*.

Days passed, though Ariana wasn't sure how many. No light came from outside the cavern, and only Kaila's timing device still worked in the dark underground. Kaila kept track of the time religiously—but Ariana had given up paying attention to the girl's deadpan announcements. She liked Kaila—the girl was shy and earnest, but they didn't have much in common, and Kaila seemed to look upon Ariana as an impulsive oddity. Instead Kaila relied on Lissa not just for support, but perhaps as a guide to how she should behave herself.

Tragedy had befallen them quickly. The girl who had seemed ill had lost consciousness during the second night and died in her sleep. Though Lissa consoled Ariana that there was nothing she could have done, Ariana felt guilty. When she had checked the girl earlier in the day, she suspected internal injuries that only the brilliance of her father's healing could have cured. But still, Ariana felt she should have done something more.

The barbarian leader had recovered with remarkable speed. And just in time, because the Automon arrived with stunning exactness each morning to herd the men from the cavern. Strangely frightened when he left, Ariana had tried to follow the leader, but he motioned her back, and the Automon prevented her from leaving the cavern. She figured that the men were used as miners, just as she'd guessed upon her arrival. The Automon ignored the women, and Ariana quickly learned that their sole purpose was procreation. On the second day, two Automon arrived to scan the females, then selected two who were noticeably pregnant. The women cried and one tried to cling to her mate, but they seemed to expect this sudden parting.

Witnessing this brutal, emotionless act bothered Ariana deeply, but there was nothing she could do to prevent it. She understood now why her group had been captured. They were breeders, meant to keep the cavern tribe strong with new blood. Where the pregnant women were taken, or where they gave birth and raised young, she didn't know.

With the men away, the women gathered mushrooms and other edible roots, did their best to tidy their humble surroundings, and cleansed themselves in a lava-heated underground stream. Cara, the girl who had best adjusted from the beginning, had already joined them and had found ways of communicating, but though Ariana tried to learn from her, she found her own attachment to language too great to discard in favor of nonverbal signs and motions.

With her warrior away, Ariana wandered around the cavern, lost and confused. She climbed the ledge nearest the lava pool and sat alone. She felt restless and strange, and she felt lonely. He was gone. She had no name for him yet. Nothing seemed adequate, or perhaps the right name hadn't presented itself to her mind. Maybe she didn't know him well enough to name him. Ariana sighed and gazed at the cavern ceiling. The low red light filtered through the crystals—a strange beauty, both forbidding and warm.

Like him. When he was gone, Ariana felt afraid. The memory of her capture pressed heavily on her when she was alone. That's when she felt the acute pang of helplessness and the great distance from her family. She wrapped her arms tightly around her body and stared at the wide cavern entrance. Soon, he would return. With each day, she needed him more. The length of the Automon work day never altered, but today the hours until his return dragged especially long.

Below, Lissa checked with Kaila, probably about the time, and then she positioned herself near the large gate at the entrance. She seemed idle, but she adjusted her hair, and Ariana noticed that what remained of her Academy attire had gotten progressively shorter until it resembled a scant loincloth over her hips and thighs. Unlike the other captives, Lissa still paid attention to her appearance.

Ariana reached up and touched the soft stubble that had grown back on her scalp. Unexpectedly, her eyes flooded with tears, not for the sake of her looks, but because of a deep fear that tormented her when she was alone. Her shaved head reminded her of her helplessness, that she no longer possessed the identity she once wore with such confidence. She didn't know who she was anymore. She was vulnerable, and here in this dark world anything could happen to her. She couldn't stop it, couldn't protect herself, let alone the others.

She was crying, and she felt weak. She felt like a helpless girl, not the strong young pilot she had once been. Her determination to escape remained, but her confidence faltered, and suddenly she saw a life without her parents, without their eccentric friends, without Hakon. She would never again see her beautiful home world of Valenwood, or stand by the golden sea and hear the song of the amber whales while her father played his harp on the king's balcony. She would never again lie in her soft bed, or see her mother's bright eyes shining with joy when Ariana entered the room.

Tears dripped down her cheeks, and she muffled a sob. *I am alone.* She had been so loved, and that was her treasure. But now, with those things stripped away, the memory felt like a curse.

The metal gates ground open, and Ariana leaned forward in anticipation as the cavern men returned down the long, sloping hall from the malloreum mines. The young men mulled together, but as always, they seemed downcast after the hard day's work. They hated their labors, and some had even tried to rebel against their captors. But the Automon yielded no quarter. They were never cruel, nor did they injure the miners, but there was no room for disobedience, no chance for escape onto the harsh surface of the dark planet. Rebellion was futile. Ariana refused to believe the same of freedom.

Lissa positioned herself closer to the gates, though Ariana wasn't sure for which man she waited. The first boys came through the gate, and Lissa ignored them, though a few of the older ones took note of the girl's apparent interest. No one captured her attention, but still, she waited.

Ariana searched the miners, expectant, her heart's pace quick. He was the last to emerge, and her breath signaled her relief, and her expectation. He walked behind the rest, and as he entered the dark cavern, he looked like a king. He stopped at the entrance, and the gates clanged shut behind him. Lissa approached him, but he ignored her and lifted his head. From across the cavern, Ariana felt the moment when he saw her. She rose, tall upon the far edge, aware of the red lava glow behind her, and she felt like a queen.

She couldn't see his face clearly, but she felt his smile. He strode past Lissa, past the others of his tribe, his attention fixed on Ariana alone. He climbed the ledges and came to her. With his every step, her pulse quickened. Their gazes met and locked, and his smile turned knowing. They knew few common words, but words were unimportant now. They understood each other on a level deeper than language.

"I've missed you so." The quaver of her sorrow still lingered in Ariana's voice, and though he couldn't know what she said, he seemed to understand. He held out his arms and drew her against his chest, and she hugged him with a need she'd never known before.

He murmured something, which might have meant, "I'm here," then kissed her forehead gently.

Ariana breathed deeply, again safe, then pressed her lips against his neck. She had never kissed him before, but the act seemed natural and easy. His body tensed, and she drew back. His dark eyes gleamed with the red light behind her, and his breath quickened to match her own. A youthful eagerness—and perhaps hope—appeared on his face.

He nodded. "Ariana? Yes?"

She wasn't sure what he meant, but her pulse quickened. She shrugged, and he seemed to sense her confusion. He looked around, then pinned his gaze on a concealed area of the cavern. Taking her hand, he led her along the ledges toward the private space. Ariana hesitated. "Where are we going?"

His eyes seemed brighter now, lit with an inner fire. "Ariana. Yes." He sounded more definite and more eager.

She hesitated, but he squeezed her hand and she followed. He led her down a steep slope until she could no longer see the rest of the tribe. She hadn't explored this section of the cave, though she had noticed members of the tribe headed in this direction every so often. She'd never considered what they were doing.

He led her to the area's floor, which was laden with tangled skins and blankets. Ariana's brow puckered as she considered what this might mean. She glanced at her strong companion and stopped short. Casually, he'd drawn back his loincloth and revealed his erection. His intention was now clear beyond doubt.

Ariana stifled a yelp, hopped back, and yanked her hand free of his. He eyed her in confusion, then smiled helpfully, and nodded. Ariana's reluctant gaze fixed on his erection. She had lived among the Ellowan, the most sensual, erotic people in the galaxy. She'd walked daily along halls decorated with mosaics depicting the act of lovemaking in its every conceivable form. Her parents adored each other and made no secret of their passion. But somehow, she'd never imagined . . . *this*.

Her heart pounded. She had expected to take a lover, one day. Lissa had told her she should get an anti-conception implant, but there had never been a need. She had been waiting for a love like her parents had, like Hakon's parents had, and there had always been ample time for that to occur.

And if it occurred, it would be in a soft, romantic setting, with a man she knew well, intimately. Maybe she had expected it to be Hakon, no stranger in any way, a man with whom she was perfectly comfortable. She expected it to be easy.

That . . . portion of *him* was large. It stood as a male testimonial to desire, rigid with a primal force. Perhaps that part of him was beautiful. She could see that it was, like the rest of his body. Her gaze whisked to his face. He looked bemused, but he nodded again. "Ariana? Yes?"

She puffed a quick breath. "No. No, no. I don't think so. I'm not ready for this. We don't even speak the same language! I mean, you don't speak any language at all! Oh . . . Help!"

Without thinking, she turned and darted away, then scrambled up the ledge toward freedom. He caught her arm before she knew he had followed. She froze and squeezed her eyes shut. Gently, he turned her to face him but she refused to open her eyes. She felt his fingers touching her cheek, and his gentleness pierced her heart. Trembling, she opened her eyes. She was standing higher than he was because she had been climbing, and he looked up at her as if she was a goddess of unimaginable beauty and power.

He whispered her name. *"Ariana."* He took her hand and held it safe in his. She stared into his eyes and saw the compassion and need shining in them.

And then she knew. She knew why she felt so lonely without him, why she felt safe only when he was near. She opened her mouth to speak, but her words came as a whisper. "I love you."

He didn't understand, but he sensed her emotion. He smiled. "Ariana. *Yes.*"

He led her back down to the lovers' niche. Now she knew what it was, and she was not afraid. They knelt together on the rough bedding, gazes locked, and she placed her palms on his cheeks, then softly kissed his mouth. He seemed confused, but he liked the sensuality of her touch. He returned her seeking kiss awkwardly at first, and then with growing passion and understanding.

She ran her hands over his body and felt his warmth and his power. She boldly kissed his chest. He restrained his own desire and hesitated before drawing aside his loincloth again. Ariana bit her lip, then seized the rough cloth herself. She edged it aside, and this time, her pulse soared at the sight of him. The images on the mosiacs of Valenwood came alive inside her—the wild sensuality of her people flooded her veins. She grazed the tips of her fingers over his taut flesh, then wrapped them snugly around his length. He groaned, and desire consumed her.

A passion came alive within her, and she was no longer a princess. The barbarian king lowered her sweetly onto the lovers' bedding and gently gave her himself.

Chapter Four

"There are some strange marks here...." Ariana climbed higher along the ledge to investigate, but he didn't follow. She glanced back at him, and he smiled. Her heart fluttered at the sight. He lay on his back watching her, naked, warm in the afterglow of love. As always, his warm brown eyes glittered with a tenderness that hadn't wavered since she had given him her hand, and herself.

It had been many weeks since her capture—even Kaila had lost count of the days, but at least three months had passed. Cara had taken a mate also and had blended with the rest of the tribe, though Kaila seemed as disoriented as ever. Lissa's attitude toward the tribe confused Ariana—she seemed to encourage male attention, and yet reject it in favor of something as yet unattained. But Ariana gave little thought to anything beyond her new romance.

She still had no name for him, and she had been able to teach him only a few words. He knew her name, and spoke it with the sweetness of a child, but he understood very little. She had tried to learn of his world, but it seemed that he and most of the others had been born here—though she had gathered there was another place where women and smaller children dwelt in much the same circumstances, primitive and without history or hope.

He didn't view himself as a captive. What existed in this cavern was all he knew. He knew little of the Automon, but regarded them with fear and loathing. Each day, the Automon herded the cavern men to mine the precious malloreum fuel. The slaves had no idea why, or what it was, simply that it was done. They hated it, and the older they were, the more they rebelled.

She had been distracted, by love, by sex, and by her first romance. She was fascinated by her new lover, and all he did enchanted her. Not only as a man and a lover, but as a leader he astounded her. He was fair and kind, and to be near him was to feel safe. He was primitive, barbaric, but inside his heart there was a prince as great as any in the Intersystem.

The fear remained. When he left, it crept over her again, no matter how she busied herself with womanly duties. But with him the fear disappeared, and she had found the greatest joy of her young life in his arms. She hadn't thought beyond the cavern in a long while, or considered the future beyond this life on the Dark Sun world.

But something was growing in her now. Time seemed pressing, though she wasn't sure why. So while he lay peacefully, she was hunting for some chance of escape, some clue to their whereabouts. Several questions pressed on her. Why were there no older people? Twice now, the Automon had come and removed noticeably pregnant women. But none of the older boys were removed, and there were no signs of old men.

Ariana fingered the wall. "As I thought. . . . At one time, not too many years ago, lava flooded this whole cavern. It was swift, rising and falling in less than a day, I'd say. It has happened several times, ten at least." She paused, glancing back at him. "And it was done on purpose. . . . As if someone released a dam."

He smiled, not understanding her, then motioned for her to return. Her heart softened at his expression, and her pulse quickened. But she had to keep her senses clear—he had a way of distracting her. Ariana climbed down and sat before him. He sat up and reached to touch her cropped hair, fingering the short, tight curls. He made her feel beautiful, though she couldn't imagine how peculiar she must look now, hair no more than a fingertip long, face smudged with soot and ash, eyes burning from the pungent air. But in his eyes, she felt beautiful. Ariana drew a breath. "Old men . . . Where are your old men?" He smiled, but shook his head.

Ariana picked up a small, pointed rock and drew a baby, as she had when learning of his childhood. He nodded, understanding. She drew a bigger boy, then a man, indicating him. He looked proud and tapped his chest. She smiled, affection filling her heart. Then she drew an older man, with a bent back, a longer beard. He shook his head as if it had no meaning. "Aren't there older men? What happens when you get older?"

He didn't understand. "No, no . . ." He seemed sorry to have disappointed her, then tapped his chest again. "Ariana, yes?"

He wanted to hold her. She wanted him, too, but something still worried her. Ariana glanced back up at the cavern wall, the lines of a sudden lava flow still visible in the red ashen light. It had been deliberate—she felt sure of it. Her heart chilled. But why would the Automon slaughter the inhabitants of the cave? She glanced around, and the answer formed in her mind. Already, these young men formed a more cohesive group. The barbaric leader had been replaced by a man with more wisdom. Wouldn't this always be the progression? With wisdom would come the intelligence and unity to rebel.

With rebellion would come the end of the mining colony. From what she'd seen upon her arrival, there weren't that many Automon available, and they weren't fighters. A sustained rebellion might work—if the slaves ever formed a group capable of working together. Already, that was happening. The Automon would learn as much. The evidence Ariana had collected already indicated that this mining operation had long been in use. But not for long generations. Unless those generations were abruptly cut short . . .

Her mind began to wrap around the reality of the colony, and her heart sank. "Mining Colony Fifteen. . . ." She had assumed the numeric title meant there was more than one of these operations, running simultaneously—but now she knew it indicated something far grimmer. This was the fifteenth generation—and that coincided closely with the lava rings she found on the cavern wall.

Women were taken away to rear children, wild, unschooled, but able to work. They were kept separate. New women were brought in, blood kept fresh and strong. But temporary, until they grew to become a threat. Then they were killed—killed in the same way the Automon did everything, with cold, impersonal efficiency. Then they would be replaced by the next batch of youth. Here in the cavern of the Dark Sun, everyone was expendable.

Ariana looked into her lover's eyes. He wasn't expendable, and she wouldn't let him die. "Somehow, we have to escape. . . ."

He didn't understand, but looked at her with that sweet mixture of curiosity and love that she had seen in him from the beginning. Ariana touched his strong shoulder. She ran her finger over his chest, over the brand that marked him as a member of this colony, this generation. A generation doomed to extinction. "We have to get out of here."

"Ariana . . ." He touched her face, and her attention wavered. He murmured something, words she couldn't understand. But she saw pure love in his eyes. As she gazed at him, he pulled off his crystal pendant and held it in both his hands. Then he etched a quick drawing in the loose dirt between them. A woman, her hand outstretched, handing something to a child.

"Your mother? And you?"

He saw that she understood, and he nodded. Then he

drew another symbol, an ∞, surrounded by a circle. Ariana's brow furrowed as she tried to understand its meaning. Failing, she shook her head. He placed his hand over his heart, then gently over hers. His beautiful hands moved in the same shape, that of an ∞. Then he placed the necklace over Ariana's head.

Tears stung her eyes. Whatever the symbol meant, this crystal pendant was his treasure, and he was giving it to her. She placed her hand over it. "I will treasure it always, as I treasure you."

Metal grates clanged across the cavern, the sound of food tunnels being opened. As always, the cavern tribe erupted, fighting for position as the hidden Automon tossed cartons of dried meat, bread, and some form of vegetable root down among them. The leader sighed—apparently, he had other things on his mind besides food—but he rose, then held out his hand for Ariana.

Together, they left the ledges. The tribe parted as he walked among them. Ariana walked at his side, and realized with a strange thrill that she felt more like a queen here in this dark cave than she ever had as princess of Valenwood. Though the young men shoved and squabbled over the meat, none touched the fare until the leader had selected his portion. He took the largest, a dried and salted piece of meat on a stick, then bit into it with barbaric vigor.

He took his seat upon a natural lava outgrowth that resembled a dais as much as any king's throne and oversaw his people as they pillaged the Automon offering. Always, the strongest males chose food first, some greedily, some with restraint. The women waited—none challenged the stronger males, though Ariana had sometimes wished one would. She stood beside the leader watching, and realized she wasn't witnessing just the strange rituals of a primitive tribe, but the very core of humankind.

Here, power was all, and food, the stuff of survival, was the most coveted treasure. The strong shoved forward and took what was theirs. The weak waited. As she watched, the women moved forward, each in her own way. Some stood proud and silent until their chance came to select food. Some pushed each other and struggled. Lissa approached one of the older males, smiling, her expression both of fragility—and perhaps promise. The male assessed her, then gave her a portion of his meal.

Another woman cast a dark, forbidding glare at her mate, and he quickly gave her his bread, which she took as if accepting his penance. She then smiled, and the man blushed. Here in the cavern, food was power. Some took that power directly, for themselves—others chose more surreptitious methods of acquiring its force.

As he had done since their first meal together, the leader divided his portion and shared it with Ariana. He had learned that she preferred the bread and vegetable to the meat, and doled it out accordingly. Unlike the other males in the tribe, he never assumed to know what she wanted. In his way, he always asked and seemed to possess infinite curiosity about what she wanted and how she felt.

Though the bread was surprisingly good, considering that the Automon could have had no taste for themselves, Ariana's appetite waned. Something about the primal interaction of humankind troubled her. Was it always so, that power and all its mechanisms had such force it obliterated all else? Did the strong and the most manipulative truly determine the course of the future?

Ariana glanced at her lover. While the others squabbled over the last bits of food, he passed the meat stick to one of the smaller boys. Ariana recognized him—no more than fourteen, he spent his idle time carving drawings in the lava rock. The boy took the stick, seized his bite, and then shared it with a girl.

Moved, Ariana placed her hand on the leader's strong shoulder. He glanced up at her and smiled. No, there was something higher than the base drive for survival and power, and she had found it in him. He took her hand and kissed it gently. Life had given her the most precious gift, and she couldn't lose it now. Somehow, she would have to convince him to escape. She had to, or all that she had found would be lost.

"Lissa, we've found a way to escape."

Lissa set aside the bowl of water she had heated for washing and eyed Ariana doubtfully. " 'We'? Do you mean you've taught that barbarian to think as well as grunt pretty words?" She shook her head sadly, then touched Ariana's arm in a gesture of sympathy and understanding. "I'm so worried about you, Ariana."

"Why?"

Lissa hesitated as if she didn't want to answer but had to for Ariana's sake. "I know you so well. You give your heart completely, but you have to see that what he wants from you is just physical."

Ariana raised her chin. "He fought a battle for me, Lissa. I think I mean more to him than sex."

Lissa smiled, but the expression of sympathy deepened. "I hope you're right." Her tone gave every indication that she considered this unlikely, if not impossible. Lissa studied Ariana's face as if trying to read her thoughts, and she smiled. "Don't worry. I'm sure he cares for you." She spoke in obvious sympathy, as if offering consolation to a defeated child. "It's natural that he chose you. I had thought, devoid of your family and position, with your beautiful hair shorn . . ." She stopped and ran her fingers through her hair, then eyed Ariana's with misgivings. "I'm lucky my own is growing out straight—yours is just a mop of curls!"

Ariana's muscles tensed at the reminder of her shaved head and she touched her hair. Passing time had softened her cropped hair, and again, she felt it around her forehead and covering her ears in tight curls. Her lover fingered them often, amused by the contrast of her tight curls and his long straight hair, adorned with bone beads and leather ties, but her shaved head had been the mark of captivity, used by the Automon to differentiate new women from those born to the tribe. A mark of slavery, and more deeply, of her own vulnerability.

Lissa stopped and dipped a cloth into the bowl of water, then smoothed it over her cheeks. "You might wash, too, Ariana, lest your pretty face be lost beneath dirt!" She dabbed the damp cloth on Ariana's cheeks, smiling as if a small child had rubbed food all over its face. "I'm always afraid your lover will mistake me for you—we look so much alike."

Ariana eyed her doubtfully. Her skin was lighter and her hair darker than Lissa's and she was a head taller. But Lissa had often insisted on their similarities, even adopting a method of copying Ariana's Ellowan accent. Hakon had disapproved of this tendency, but it hadn't bothered Ariana— until now, with the suggestion her new lover might mistake *any* woman for herself.

Lissa studied Ariana's appearance. "I had thought you would end up with Hakon—the two of you have always been so close, but I guess the lure of sex outweighs real compatibility. For now."

"Hakon and I have never been more than friends." Ariana spoke through clenched teeth and felt an oncoming headache. "If you do not want to leave with us, I am sure I can send help once we return. That is my intention."

"If you ever get that far. Don't forget, Ariana, even if you do escape this cavern, you have no idea where we are."

"I know at least that we are near a Dark Sun, one capable of producing malloreum fuel. I know mining ships come and go, and they'll be run by only a few Automon. If I can secure one of them, I will navigate by the stars, and I will find my way home."

"And bring your barbarian back to Valenwood? Will you present him to your father at the Council or at a family gathering?"

"My father will honor the man who saved my life."

Lissa studied her face, thoughtful. "That may be . . . Arnoth of Valenwood was once something of a pagan himself. Then all will go as you wish, naturally. Why, he'll probably become king and follow in your father's footsteps!" She paused, and her eyes darkened. "You'll be the envy of girls everywhere—with a sex god who is also a king!" Lissa seemed to be teasing, but Ariana detected something else underlying her playful tone—jealousy.

With a keen pang, Ariana hoped that Lissa would stay behind. She had discovered a ruthless side to herself since her arrival in the cavern, but love had tempered its force and reminded her of her duty to others. Duty demanded that Lissa, as well as the other captives taken with Ariana, be included in their escape. Kaila and Cara had declined, preferring to wait rather than risk death by escaping. This left Ariana with Lissa only. But she wondered if pity and a sense of duty could stand in the way of happiness.

"If you would rather wait . . ."

"You can't be thinking of leaving me here alone in this awful place!" Lissa paused while Ariana endured an on-slaught of remorse. "I must go with you, of course. I can't imagine what you'd do without me. After all, we've been through so much together. Tell me your plan."

Chapter Five

"Ariana, no. No." The leader shook his head, then gestured back at the cavern where the others still slept. "No . . ."

She knew what he meant. They couldn't wait any longer for Lissa to join them. Lissa knew the time and place—if she had changed her mind at the last minute, so much the better. She would be a burden to their escape anyway. Once they returned to Valenwood, Ariana planned to send help for the others, but the fewer breaking away from the Automon now, the better.

Ariana seized her pack. It contained little—just dried meat, water, and the rocks she had fashioned into blunt knives. The leader carried his root stave and a pack of his own. He had placed in it a rock carved with strange symbols—an ∞ surrounded by a circle—symbols he seemed to feel important, though Ariana had no idea what they meant to him. He wore his bone choker and had decorated a braid in his hair with crystal beads. He had no idea to what fate she led him, but he would go with those small things he held dear, and he would face it as he faced everything, with courage and pride and innocence.

Her heart filled with love, Ariana took his hand. They hid behind a large rock as the Automon arrived to herd out the miners. Then they followed. As Ariana had expected, the Automon took no notice of them. The robotic guards had no reason to guard against people joining the miners—their duty was to be sure the slaves obeyed. Ariana and her lover followed the miners, heads down, then hid themselves behind an outcrop while the group passed onward toward the malloreum pits. Ariana had followed this path twice before to be sure it worked, and once again it did.

They crept up the Automon route and found it unguarded. The Automon had no reason to fear escape. Even if one of the miners had found his way out of the cavern—and from what she gathered from her lover, some had ventured out before—they would be met with only a barren waste, cold beyond long endurance, with no knowledge of the outside world to guide them. They had no hope at all of hijacking a spacecraft unaided. The Automon hadn't cared who they abducted, but their carelessness was their error—they had kidnapped one of the best young pilots in the galaxy.

Ariana had conceived this plan and worked it out in detail. She hadn't been able to convey its finer points to her lover, but he seemed to understand the general idea. He couldn't understand where they were escaping to, but he trusted her.

Ariana crept along the rock hall until it became a metallic runway. They passed door after door and still saw no one. It seemed almost too easy. The air cooled, but the burning scent was harsh, almost painful to breathe, especially after the warmth of the caverns below. Strange how that environment had become familiar, like a dark womb, and from it sprang this race of men, untamed, wild, and yet stronger than anything she'd ever encountered. There where it seemed most unlikely, she had found love and tenderness beyond measure.

They came to the open air, and Ariana stopped to peer out. The Automon's landing platform stretched out before them. As they looked out, a small ship landed. Ariana recognized the same model that had transported her own group. Perhaps the Automon had seized another group of women. Her heart clenched. The ship's door slid open, but only one Automon ascended the ramp to greet its arrival. Six had greeted her group, the number of the expected captives. She heard sounds of a scuffle, and her heart labored.

I must help them. . . . But her lover took her hand. "Ariana, no." He shook his head, and she knew he was right. This was their only chance for escape. If they succeeded, they would return for the others. If they failed, at least the others still stood a chance.

When the Automon left the new ship, Ariana saw their moment. They ran together. At her side, her lover's eyes glowed, not with wonder, but something deeper and more powerful. He was free. Breathless, Ariana gestured at the transport craft. The rear gate was still open. This ship would have no crew—and it would have no capacity for defense against her planned piracy.

Only a few Automon moved across the platform, engaged with other craft, loading fuel cylinders onto a huge black ship. Not too difficult to avoid. Ariana looked into her young lover's eyes. "There is a word in my father's language, *'damanai.'* It means 'my treasure.' " He looked at her, struggling to understand. She clasped her hand over her heart, and whispered again, "My treasure." Her meaning reached him, and he placed his hand over his own heart. Softly, he repeated her. *"Damanai."*

She touched his bearded cheek, and tears stung her eyes. Soon, they would be free, together. But sorrow clutched at her anyway. "My treasure."

They looked at each other for a silent minute, then turned together for their final run. Ariana seized a desperate breath, then ran toward the ship, her lover beside her. They bounded on board through the rear gate. Then she found the control panels. He waited while Ariana learned the nature of the guidance panel. It wasn't as difficult as she'd feared. Within seconds, she programmed it for automatic departure in the opposite direction of its usual track. That, she hoped, would take them far from Dark Sun Space. When freed of its confines, she would search out further navigation, by the stars if necessary, and find the way back to the Intersystem territory.

Her lover stirred beside her. His tension had increased rather than abated once they gained access to the ship. His warrior's instinct seemed raised, and Ariana's own nervousness grew. She punched in the last of her code, then turned. With the precise, even footfalls that haunted her dreams, she heard them coming. The Automon had boarded the ship.

In a nightmarish whirl, Ariana knew that the Automon had learned of her escape. How they knew, she couldn't guess, but they had come up across the outside platform. One tall black metallic figure boarded the vessel and came through the control room door before the others. With his stave, her lover drove the Automon back against the hull, and it teetered near the edge. Ariana raced to engage the ship's engine, while he held the next Automon at bay. They came on, relentless, one after another, but her lover drove them back each time.

She saw him as he turned back to her, their gazes locked across the empty hull, and she realized he understood more than she had known. If he stayed on board, they would both fail, and both be taken captive. He looked at her, smiled, then placed his hand over his heart, speaking without words. *My treasure*. Then he turned back to the oncoming Automon, bounded down the ship's ramp, and raced headlong against them.

The ship lifted as Ariana screamed in fear for him. She raced back to the guidance panel, wanting suddenly to land. How could she leave without him? But she had set the controls beyond her own ability to alter. Desperate, she ran back to the rear view port. The Automon surrounded her lover, and then moved in on him. He fought, but they battered at him, methodically, without rage or desire for vengeance.

She saw him crumple and fall, surrounded by his lifeless captors. Her vision faltered—he faced death alone, and she couldn't reach him. Her consciousness swirled in a haze of tears and sickness. She gripped the view port edge, horrified, in agony. Ariana swayed, tightly clutching the crystal pendant he had given her. As she watched, the Automon assessed her lover's still form. With the same methodical, emotionless precision that they did everything, they dragged his body into the caverns.

"She is near death, Sierra. I don't know how she survived this long." Arnoth of Valenwood gazed down into his wife's eyes and she saw his tears, immobilized by the shock of their only daughter's return. He shook his proud, beautiful head. "If Hakon hadn't found her . . ." His words trailed, but Sierra placed her hand on his arm.

"You can heal her, love. The king of the Ellowan is the greatest healer in the galaxy. You've brought many back from the veil of death." She swallowed hard. "You can heal Ariana now."

Arnoth turned his agonized gaze to their daughter as she lay pale and unmoving on her large, soft bed. "To heal her, I must have her assent, Sierra. She must desire life, or I cannot make the healing bond."

Sierra's throat clenched. "Of course, she wants life! Ariana is more filled with life than anyone." Tears puddled in her own eyes as she remembered her strong-willed child, flinging herself at life, impulsive almost from the moment of birth. It had been no surprise to learn that Ariana had led an expedition into the wild, lawless region of space, even without Hakon at her side. Sierra hadn't worried, but Arnoth had sensed her danger. Even before the reports came of her abduction, he had sent Intersystem scouting ships to look for her.

Weeks and months had passed without word, while all searching failed. Only two boys had returned alive from Ariana's ship—they reported an attack, and when they had woken, all the women onboard were gone. The only mem-

47

ory they had of their attacks were the sleek black ships that moved at a great speed, with far greater agility than anything devised in the Intersystem. Ships of the Dark Sun, the most dangerous and mysterious in the galaxy.

Somehow, Ariana had freed herself, stolen one of the ships, and made her way into space. Somehow, she had survived, and the ship was spotted in the Border Territory where neither the Intersystem nor any other world held sway. There, Hakon had found her, and in his arms, held her until they returned to Valenwood.

Hakon sat outside Ariana's room now, his head in his hands, grieving that he had been too late, that he should have gone with her. He was too young to know that nothing he could have done would have made any difference.

Sierra gazed at her daughter's pale face. She had been through so much—it was written on her face, her thin body, her hair, now hanging in short curls around her forehead. Very gently, Sierra stroked Ariana's hair. Tears dripped down her cheeks as she recalled patting Ariana's curls when she was a small child. A sob racked her chest, and Arnoth gathered Sierra into his arms, cradling her head against his wide shoulder.

"Arnoth, what happened to her? What did they do to her?"

He closed his eyes as if to blot the nightmare of their daughter's abduction. "I will heal her, Sierra." But his voice betrayed his fear. He drew himself together, then knelt by Ariana's bedside. He leaned over her, then placed his fingertips on her temples and forehead. Sierra watched as her husband entered the healing trance of the Ellowan, delving deeply into their daughter's mind, into her heart, and her soul.

For a timeless while, he labored, but when he drew back, drained, Sierra saw the defeat in his eyes. She couldn't speak at once, and neither could he. If Ariana denied her father, denied life, there was nothing anyone could do. She would die. Sierra couldn't ask, but her mouth moved, unwilling to hear his answer.

Arnoth shook his head. "She did not deny me, but neither did she acquiesce. She has been deeply wounded. I sense shock, loss, a terrible emptiness." His words seemed torn from within him. Sierra knew how much he hurt to feel his daughter's wounds. "The damage they did was grave." Something else troubled him, had turned his dark face to ashen gray. He took Sierra's arm. "Come, let us speak outside."

They stepped outside and Hakon rose from his seat, his own fair face pale with worry. "Is she . . . ?"

Arnoth bowed his head. "She has not been healed. Another matter has arisen. . . ." He hesitated as Hakon's bright eyes glittered, ready for any challenge. Sierra loved him as she would a son, and she took his hand while they waited for Arnoth's report.

He glanced between them as if uncertain how to say what he had learned, or perhaps if it should be said in front of Hakon. But Arnoth took Hakon's other hand. "You are her dearest friend, and you know my daughter as well as anyone. It is right that you should know, here, where her life hangs in the balance."

Sierra began to tremble. "Know what?"

Arnoth paused, then looked his wife in the eye. "Ariana is pregnant, Sierra. She bears a child."

All the blood drained from Sierra's face. Hakon's grip on her hand tightened compulsively. She knew what he feared, but could not allow the thought to form in her mind. She saw her fear reflected in Arnoth's eyes, too, but none of them could give it words. She saw her husband's vulnerability, and her heart quailed.

"Sierra, what do I do?"

Hakon drew a breath. "You can't tell her. Heal her first, and then tell her, when she is well enough."

Arnoth seemed uncertain. "She has not responded to my call, Hakon. As she is now, I am unable to reach her. She has not refused, but she cannot survive much longer in this condition."

Sierra fought against her fear. "What of the child?"

49

"The child lives. It is small yet, only a few months, but it appears strong and well."

She wasn't sure if she was relieved, and her own conflict raged. It would be easier if there were no child, if it slipped away, unknown and forgotten. She glanced at her daughter's closed door, then opened it to look in. Ariana lay unmoving, but Sierra remembered when it had been a crib rather than the wide, canopied bed, when she came through this door to find her gray-eyed daughter awake, bouncing, reaching for her mother's arms. *"Mamma, play!"* She remembered her own joy, opening that door to find her child, eager for life, and how very much her heart had expanded once a baby had come into her world.

"Tell her."

Both Arnoth and Hakon turned to her in surprise. Arnoth hesitated. "This news may destroy her, love."

Sierra nodded slowly. "She is near death now. Tell her of the child."

Arnoth didn't answer. Hakon caught a breath as if to object, but restrained himself. Arnoth squeezed Sierra's hand. "Wait here with Hakon."

She didn't argue, but when he went inside Ariana's room, the wait turned interminable, and each second passed like hours. She sat close beside Hakon. Neither spoke, but his presence comforted her. The force of life flowed strong in Hakon, his hope indomitable, his courage endless, his heart as wide as the sea. But even he seemed wounded by Ariana's shattered life.

An endless while passed, and the door opened. Arnoth appeared, his face grave and drawn from his ordeal. Sierra looked into his eyes and saw tears. He took her hand and she rose. Hakon rose beside her, unable to speak. Arnoth looked at both of them and his tears fell, but they were tears of joy.

"Ariana has reclaimed her life. She will live."

Chapter Six

She had won. For a long, perfect moment, Lissa of Lower Nirvahda stood alone on the platform, her attention fixed on the spot where Ariana's ship had disappeared. If Ariana were alive or dead, it didn't matter. In Lissa's mind, victory was already hers.

She saw it all unfolding, perfectly. Herself, in a moment soon to come, freeing the bold young cavern leader from the Automon. She envisioned how she would help him, guide him back to the cavern. Heal him. Comfort him. *Make love to him.* The pain of his loss of Ariana would only serve to enhance Lissa's importance to him. There was no one so vulnerable as a man who has just suffered a wound of the heart. And she would make use of that vulnerability to become his lover. From the moment she had first laid eyes on him, even as he stood behind the brutish leader, Lissa had wanted him. Why, she wasn't sure. Unlike the first leader, this man had exuded a greater power, a sexual power, a force that she recognized. She wanted it, and him.

He had chosen Ariana. She told herself that it was she,

51

Lissa, who had first captured his attention, diverted only when Ariana put herself in front of the rest. But the image of his face as he gave his hand to Ariana haunted Lissa, even as it fired her fury to have him herself. How often had she seen his eyes darken when Ariana walked by, and how often had jealousy stabbed into her when he would lead Ariana to the ledges? Sexual jealousy was the most powerful force Lissa knew, and from it, her desire sprang like an eternal phoenix.

But she had won at last. Her victory was all the sweeter because of Ariana's lofty heritage, a disparity between them that Lissa felt bitterly. Ariana had been born a princess, beautiful and beloved. She was intelligent and strong, her impulsiveness both charming and compelling to all who knew her. From the first time they met, Lissa had seen in Ariana everything she wanted for herself—the image of beauty and grace, and the power to get what she wanted. Ariana was always the victor, even when she hadn't realized there was a competition between them.

Hakon adored Ariana—and he had rejected all Lissa's attempts to engage his attention. Since the first time Lissa met them, it was obvious that everyone in the Intersystem elite expected Hakon to wed Ariana. It would have been the perfect satisfaction to capture his interest herself. She hadn't lusted for him—despite his good looks, he was too noble, too pure, like Ariana. But the sting of his rejection cut deep all the same—he had made her even more aware of the differences between herself and Ariana. It was in Ariana he confided, Ariana he understood. They belonged together. If Ariana did manage to survive, let her return to Hakon— they deserved each other.

This man was different. He was strong, he exuded the most intense sexuality Lissa had ever encountered. To think of him lying with Ariana—this was more than she could stand. Lissa understood desire. Unlike Ariana, she had engaged in sexual conquests, but never to her satisfaction. She had never encountered a man so able to inspire lust. It was right that she, not Ariana, should fall in love with the rugged leader.

Lissa's heart throbbed with expectation and the rush of success as she hurried back to where the barbarian king lay unconscious. The Automon moved slowly as always, without passion or fire, without love or hate, anger or desire—the emotions that drove Lissa constantly. It had been no difficult task to set them after Ariana—she directed them to the escape, then waited. While Ariana had been working on her escape plan, Lissa had been quietly studying the Automon. She had soon learned that the monsters weren't interested in killing—just in subjugation. They wouldn't kill their victim—just immobilize him, get him under control and return him to the colony. With the barbarian's safety assured, Lissa's own plan had formed . . . *perfectly*.

The Automon had now left their captive alone, and Lissa went to him. She found him waking, his breath rapid as he fought his bindings. She forced her own mood to alter from what it truly was, desire, to what was necessary to achieve her ends—compassion. But even as he strained against his ties, she saw his muscles bulge, his black hair against his dark skin, and bold lust flashed through her. Not yet, she told herself. *First, he must see my empathy.* . . .

"Don't struggle, I'll help you." Her voice was soft, perfect, but he started and his dark eyes widened in surprise when he saw her. Lissa knelt beside him, breathing rapidly. "I came as soon as I could, but Ariana had already gone." He wouldn't understand her words, but she couldn't be sure how much Ariana had taught him. He would certainly hear the caring in her tone.

She cut his ties, and he leapt up, looking wildly around for the Automon. Lissa grabbed his strong arm. The touch sent a shudder through her. She couldn't let him know, not yet, how much she wanted him, but he didn't seem to notice her touch at all. Instead, he moved to go back toward the platform. He meant to follow Ariana, somehow.

"You can't go back. She's gone." Lissa offered the words kindly, with sympathy. He looked at her, and she saw tears in his eyes. Tears revealed evidence of a passionate nature, and her pulse quickened. "Come, we must return to the cavern. Later, we can try escape. Together."

He didn't understand her, but apparently he, too, had come to this conclusion. He looked once more toward the platform, then turned his gaze to the dark sky. There, his gaze lingered on a single bright star. As Lissa waited, her own purposes fired with expectation and victory, he placed his hand over his chest, and whispered a word spoken in the Ellowan tongue: *"Damanai."*

Lissa didn't understand its meaning, but she recognized his emotion, and her lips tightened, though she forced a compassionate smile. "We must go."

He was injured, but still strong. Though she had imagined guiding him, supporting him, the barbarian king strode on ahead of her, paying little attention to her soft words of encouragement. He moved down along the cavern paths like a wild animal heading home after the hunt. She was hard-pressed to keep up with him.

Later, he would grieve. Later, she would comfort him, touch him. Even as she walked, desire flooded through her. She couldn't look away from his broad back, his narrow hips, barely clad in a leather cloth. She had stolen glimpses of his male form, and judged it well-proportioned, thick and long, befitting a barbarian leader. Already, she imagined him impaled within her, venting his lust, as she sated hers. Heat washed through her as she hurried behind him.

They came back to the cave, and even its heat seemed sensual. The barbarian king stopped, and she read the emotion on his face. He was envisioning Ariana, and facing that she was gone. He bowed his head, his wide shoulders slumped. Lissa came up behind him and placed her hand on his bare shoulder. The power of him radiated into her, so much that she almost felt dizzy. Her mind glimpsed a vision of Ariana in his strong embrace, and the fire of anger caught within her.

Gently, she stroked his back. "I know you miss her. But it never would have lasted between you. She is a princess.

She would have come to scorn you as soon as you left this place."

He gave her words no heed, and Lissa frowned. It was important that he learn language—what had Ariana been teaching him, if not to understand speech? Without words, how would Lissa gain access to his mind, his thoughts, his feelings? Hakon had once termed her "manipulative," and she had laughed as if he were joking. It was like him to insult her in front of others, but she had handled it well, as if he couldn't be serious, as if he was a dear friend, but so silly! Hakon was wrong. It wasn't manipulation, but intuitive communication that she so deftly employed. It had never yet failed her.

Ariana, she envied, and Ariana, she would defeat. But Hakon, Lissa hated outright. From the first, he had been bored by her, and even annoyed. He'd looked at her as if she'd crawled from a rock, as something beneath him, and far beneath Ariana. He hadn't trusted her, and often came between her and Ariana. But Hakon couldn't stop her now, any more than he could protect his precious Ariana.

If anyone brought the barbarian king back to Valenwood, it would be Lissa, and it would be Lissa at his side. How sweetly she would explain that she had befriended him, healed him, and how he had turned to her after Ariana's selfish desertion! Perhaps she would even hint at the erotic pleasures they shared, and admit, reluctantly, that she had loved him all along. She imagined explaining this to Ariana, sweetly, even sorrowfully. *Victory*.

Lissa slid her hand down his hard, muscular back, feeling its contours. Soon, she would be his woman. He was powerful, but he was lean, with the look of a man still growing—though already strong, he would become taller and even more masculine as he aged. Her throat tightened as eagerness swelled in her.

A group of older boys shouted from the far side of the cavern, the same wild braying she had endured when her own group first arrived. The barbarian king lifted his head to gauge the scene. The tunnel door slid open, but only one person emerged from its black depths. Lissa watched in surprise as a tall, thin girl scrambled to her feet. The red lava glow reflected on her pale blond hair—for reasons Lissa couldn't guess, this newcomer's head hadn't been shaved, though it appeared uneven, as if the Automon had tried, and failed, to complete the task.

The girl assumed a fighting posture, and the boys laughed. The barbarian king's head tilted to one side as if he assessed the situation. Then he walked forward, and made his way to the group's front. Threatened by the newcomer, Lissa followed, sticking close at his side. The sight of the girl relieved her doubts. Despite her height, she was young, no more than thirteen, too thin for real womanhood. Lissa chewed her lip—still, the girl was beautiful. She resembled the statuesque, pale-haired beauties of Thorwal but more delicate and refined; and strangely, the girl's ears were slightly pointed at the tips. She was young, but in this barbaric society, would age matter?

One boy reached for her, and the girl slapped him away. Another followed, laughing, a cruel sport of conquest. Tears streamed down the girl's golden-pale cheeks, but she kept fighting. Unlike Ariana's first attempt at defiance, this girl fought before they reached her, preventing anyone from laying a hand on her. A good tactic, but she wouldn't hold out for long. Lissa glanced around, wondering idly which man would finally force the girl's submission. But if the girl's fate bothered the leader, Lissa must also show concern. She waited to gauge his reaction.

The barbarian king watched for a moment, then strode forward. He placed himself in front of the girl, then turned to his followers. Lissa watched in growing apprehension as he threw back his head and bellowed the barbarian cry that meant one thing: *Mine!* He pounded his chest, and Lissa's mind raged in denial as he turned to claim his prize.

The girl was ready to fight. She wasn't impulsive like Ariana, and even now, terrified and childlike as she was, she assumed a strong, regal stance—as if nothing and no one could touch her. She was cold, like one of noble birth, but unlike Ariana, Lissa intuited that this one would fight to the death. As if he, too, recognized this quality, the barbarian king bowed. To Lissa's astonishment, he took a stave from one of his followers, then tossed it to the girl.

She caught it in surprise, but quickly positioned it as a weapon. He smiled, then took up his own weapon. Lissa's mouth dropped in disbelief as he moved cagily around the girl, holding up the stave as if inviting attack.

Attack, the girl did. She leapt at him swinging, and the sound of their clashing staves echoed in the cavern. Over and over, she pounded at her opponent, but though he answered her blows, he never struck back. Instead, he adjusted his weapon as if teaching the child to improve. He smiled, encouraging her, he nodded, issued strange grunts as if trying to speak. As minutes passed, the girl learned, and her skill increased. As they fought, Lissa saw the girl's fury fade, and her wide forehead puckered in concentration. She was a quick student. She dealt the leader a swift blow, surprising him, but he laughed.

The girl stopped. Everyone in the cavern fell silent, stunned and awed by what had transpired before them. Then suddenly, with the bright clarity of childhood, the girl laughed, too. The barbarian king lowered his stave and bowed. The girl's chin rose, and then she lowered her weapon. They clasped hands, and he turned to the others, shouting out some bold word of conquest. Lissa didn't understand what he said, but she knew what he meant, and she sank down upon a boulder in shock. Her plan had faltered. From now on, it would be this skinny, arrogant child at the barbarian king's side, and not herself.

Days went by. How many, she didn't know, but if possible, Lissa's misery was more acute than in the first hours of her captivity. The barbarian king hadn't taken a new lover. What he had done instead was an even greater barrier to Lissa's plans. He had taken an heir. Every free moment, he trained the child. He kept her with him, but as her protector. Already, he had learned many words of her language, and Lissa often saw them speaking together. Most often, it was he who carved symbols in the ground, and then the girl would explain. From a distance, Lissa gathered what she feared most. This upstart child was teaching him of the universe, of flight and space travel. From Lissa's little interaction with the girl, for he allowed no one else near her, she gathered that the child's world wasn't part of the Intersystem—but she might still know of Valenwood. In time, she might even be able to direct him to Ariana's home world.

Several times, Lissa had seen the two of them sneak out of the cavern, but each time, they returned. Each time, they seemed more excited, as if their plans progressed. Often, he seemed to be relaying these plans to trusted members of his tribe—but never to Lissa. Of her own party, only two remained, and of those, only one could she trust. Kaila was loyal to Lissa, and mercifully, had no notion of Lissa's own secret designs. The other had blended too fully with the tribe, and though not close to the leader, seemed unlikely to betray him.

Darkness cemented in Lissa's heart, and what had passed for love turned to hate. The barbarian's indifference to her cut deep, pitting her against a foe she was now even more determined to defeat—*Ariana*. As he gathered his people for a tribal council, a new power surged through Lissa. *This is not the end.*

She had no idea what the barbarian king was saying to his people, but she knew he was gathering them together, not for escape, but for rebellion. This rebellion would succeed, though it might leave many dead, because it was led by a man whose strength none could withstand. Somehow, he made his intentions known to his followers, and they agreed as Lissa knew they would. A loud chant rose from the tribe, and their barbarian leader answered them. One word rang clear in the mindless babble, and that word chilled Lissa's blood to ice. "Valenwood!"

Nothing else he said or did impacted her now. She knew what he would do, and she knew she had no power to stop him this time. The Automon, passionless, didn't stand a chance against him now that his course was set. But the fury inside Lissa refused surrender, because it had swollen past the point of return. Unbidden, she recalled Ariana's words from the transport craft: *"There must be some life, some mentality behind them. Someone created them. Someone, alive, must be directing them."*

Even as she smiled and cheered with the other members of the colony, Lissa knew where her future lay. With the one strong enough to create this hell.

Part Two

Border Territory

"And in the princess, a barbarian."

Chapter Seven

"I have business beyond the Border Territory, and I need a guide. That is all you need to know." Ariana pinned her gaze on the small, shady man seated across the table. He squirmed in discomfort as if she frightened him, but he was the best-suited person she'd found yet.

The man shrugged and looked uneasy. "What'dya want to go out there for, Miss? You want a guide, I can haul you anywhere you'd like. Payment, that's steep, but you say you're good for it." He eyed her closely. "Looks to be true, it does."

"I have shown you gold, and that is what I'm prepared to pay for your services. I am told that you have dealings beyond the Border Territory."

He glanced around over his shoulder, and back. "You landed here on an Intersystem ship, Miss. Ain't many of those landing here now, not when they're on the ups, anyway. Why ain't you using that for your travels?"

"An Intersystem vessel attracts attention. I need something less conspicuous." She paused, then adjusted her long, heavy hair back over her shoulder. Maybe she didn't look like a pirate, with hair that hung past her waist, but neither would she appear groomed and polished like most other Intersystem elites. Her long hair was more than a disguise— it was her badge of survival, a mark of an identity she had fought to restore. "And perhaps I'm not eager for the Intersystem authorities to know of my private dealings."

Her tactic worked well. The man grinned. "Same as is said by many visiting this outpost, Miss. Don't like too many questions, do we? Don't want the Intersystem sticking its fingers into our business, nor telling us what we can and can't do."

"I'm pleased we understand each other. Now . . . about my offer. . . ."

The man fidgeted, but he eyed the sack of gold she held up, obviously tempted. If nothing else, an outpost tavern frequented by pirates had no shortage of greedy men. "Where out there do you want me to take you? I got a right to know that, don't I, before agreeing?"

Ariana drew a tight breath. Here is where she had stumbled with the last four pilots she had asked. "There is a region in the Dark Sun space. . . ." Even before she finished, he sucked in a breath and leaned back, away from her.

"That's Automon territory, Miss. You don't want to go there. People as go there, don't get out."

"But ships do go there, and the Dark Sun fleet of pirates operates in that area. You have gone yourself, and not without reward."

"I ain't gone farther than their outskirts, and I'll tell ye, the profits weren't worth it. Them Dark Sun pirates—some say their lord has dealings with the Automon, but they're dangerous enough themselves. Why do you want to go there?"

"That is none of your concern. My dealings are private . . . but valuable."

He looked her up and down, then shook his head. "You don't stand a chance against those pirates, Miss. And to risk meeting up with the Automon . . ."

"I am capable of handling whatever threat arises."

The man laughed outright this time, then leaned back in his chair. "Is that a fact? Lady, you don't look strong enough to lift a fork, let alone take on the Automon!"

Ariana rose, twitched back her gray cape, and before the man blinked, aimed a laser pistol between his eyes. "I can do better than a fork. This pistol has enough power to level this tavern and leave a gaping hole in its place. As for what it would do to *you* . . ."

The man swallowed hard, then held up his hands. "No call for that, Miss. Guess you're a better fit here than you look to be." He eyed her more closely, and with considerably greater respect. "Don't rightly know what to expect on one of them Dark Sun worlds, but maybe you can handle it. Figuring there's good loot to be had, if nothing more."

"Loot there is indeed—if you can make it past the Automon torch guards. . . ." A low, deep voice spoke from behind Ariana. She startled and turned to face a tall man wearing a long, black coat. For a moment, she just stared and a flicker of apprehension darted through her. He was huge, a head taller than she, and she was tall for a woman. But it wasn't just his height that disturbed her. His long black hair hung loose over impressively wide shoulders, with two narrow braids pulling it back off his exotic face. She'd never seen a face like his—dark, intelligent, but also written with secrets, mysteries that tempted her and told her that this was a man best avoided.

He came straight out of a woman's darkest fantasies, and a sudden image flashed in her mind—a rogue pirate, skilled in the erotic arts. . . . Ariana gulped. With those dark, slanted eyes, and his full, deliberately sensual lips curving into a smile, he looked as if . . . as if he knew too much, and she didn't like it. "If you will excuse us, this is a private transaction."

She turned deliberately back to her prospective pilot, but his attention was diverted to the man who interrupted them. "What do you know about the Automon torch guards?"

"Too much," answered the dark man. "I have had dealings with their kind—you might say my 'business' takes me too close, too often." He seated himself at Ariana's table, then motioned to a waitress for a tankard of ale. She brought it hurriedly, as if any chance to be near this man was worth the trouble. He smiled up at the girl, teasing, and Ariana frowned. A rogue pirate, indeed.

"I do not recall inviting you to join us."

His brow arched. "You didn't. But our friend here might wish a bit more information before accepting your invitation."

"You don't even know what I offered!"

He nodded at the felt bag she clutched in her hands. She strangled its neck as if strangling him. "I know what you're asking is worth more than anything you've got in that bag."

"Is that so?" Angered, Ariana seated herself next to him, glaring. "What would you know?"

He took a draught of strong, dark ale, then leaned forward, bracing his powerful arms on the table. He fixed his piercing gaze on her pilot, ignoring Ariana. "I know the Automon. They patrol Dark Sun space, though you never see them coming. Tried it once, I did. Had them cornered, or so I thought." His voice grew lower, its tone flat as if he relived a dark, horrible memory. "Just one ship loaded with their malloreum fuel cylinders is enough to guarantee a whole crew's wealth for a lifetime. I considered it worth the risk." He paused, meaningfully. "I was wrong. They lured us in. Just two ships they had—I thought a band of hardened mercenaries who had disabled a Group Ten Intersystem ship could handle it." He relayed his tale with a dramatic, ominous tone, obviously deliberate. Ariana wasn't impressed, but her pilot gripped the arms of his chair with taut fingers.

"I take it you failed." Her tone was dry, tinged with sarcasm, but the pilot barely breathed.

The dark man glanced at her, and though his expression remained grave, she knew he enjoyed himself. "Worse than 'failed,' my lady. Not a quarter of the men I sent out returned alive. And the stories they tell . . . they're not pretty to hear. The Automon need tending for the ships—patch-work, you might say. And they don't care how they get it. When their ships need oiling, they grind it . . . from the flesh of living men."

Ariana grimaced. "That's ridiculous! Go away!"

The pilot wiped his sleeve over his lip and shook his head. "No, Miss. I've heard tales like this, and worse. The Automon, they'll put men into them grinders, use what they get for their giant gears. And there's no telling when they'll show up, or where. You'll be going along, ain't nothing on your panels, no sign of them. They ain't out for thievery. They're after human flesh for their grinders!"

The dark interloper nodded. " 'Grinders,' yes. And when they come upon you . . . No one, *no one* escapes."

Ariana's lips curled to one side and her eyes narrowed. "Obviously, someone escaped, or you wouldn't be here to torment us with this story."

He smiled. Her dislike intensified. "I'm here, yes. But I've seen those grinders in action." He closed his eyes as if the memory was too painful to endure. "One after the other, they drove us forward. Didn't matter how we screamed or fought or begged for mercy, they just kept on shoving us forward. One by one, into the grinders . . . feet first, head first, whichever part they could. . . ."

Ariana held up her hand. "Enough!" She cast a quick glance over his body. He was strong, muscular, lean, and hard. "You seem to be intact."

He grimaced, but his brown eyes twinkled as he returned her glance. "I got lucky, you might say. Hit a bit of a snag, they did, a warp in space. Jostled them enough for me to get the hell out of there, with what was left of my crew. The other ones. . . ." He stopped to shudder, and Ariana's pilot grew pale. "Well, let's just say there wasn't much left of them but . . . meat sauce."

Ariana resisted the impulse to strike him, but it wasn't easy. "This is disgusting, and I don't believe a word of it." She started to turn to her pilot, to offer reassurance. "Please don't listen to this extremely unreliable . . ." But the pilot was already leaving her table. He backed away, holding up his hands, and shaking his head.

"He's right, Miss. You ain't got enough in that bag to get me near a Dark Sun. Sorry." Ariana stood up to stop him, but he darted from the tavern, and she thumped back into her seat. Her opponent looked satisfied. She fingered her pistol and wondered if Border Territory law covered righteous murder.

"You were lying. I've never heard of Automon 'grinding' anyone."

He grinned. Her fists clenched. "No, but it was a good story, wasn't it? But I'm not the only one . . . 'exaggerating,' shall we say. You weren't telling the full truth either."

Her lips tightened. "That is none of your concern."

"It is if I'm to accept your offer."

"What offer? I haven't offered you anything, and I won't."

"Oh, I think you will. For one thing, you won't find any pilot here willing to take your gold, not after they've been reminded of the danger involved."

"Reminded . . . by you." She had fallen in with a rogue. The moment her prospective pilot had left, this dark villain had changed his manner. His speech altered and revealed greater intelligence than she suspected—and greater intelligence meant a greater capacity for mischief. Ariana forced a formal smile, suggesting superiority and disdain. "I believe I understand the situation. You intend to scare off all those people I query—and what? Take the job yourself?"

He leaned back, satisfied. "I *might*. If . . ."

" 'If' what?"

"Double your offer, give me an honest destination, and I might consider it."

She held up the felt bag. "This is all I have."

He laughed. "Is that so?" He moved so quickly that she didn't know what he was doing until he held up a second bag, nabbed from beneath her cape. "Yours, I presume?"

Ariana snatched the bag out of his hand. "Mine." He laughed again, and her gaze slipped to the side. She decided to ignore his skill, and her own small deceit. "Assuming I were willing to take you as my guide, why, pray tell, would I consider trusting you, a man obviously proficient at robbery, deceit, and stars know what other crimes?"

He took another long drink from his tankard, but his gaze stayed locked on hers. "Because I'm the only man who can deliver what you want."

She rolled her eyes. "I doubt that."

"Then consider this: No one else in ten regions pilots a Dark Sun craft."

Ariana gasped. "You have one of their ships?"

He smiled. "I do."

"How did you get it?"

He shook his head. "When you're ready to tell me your true destination, maybe I'll tell you a few of my secrets. For now, isn't it enough that I have one? There's not another pilot in the whole Border Territory with a ship that can outdistance the Automon fleet. Mine can, because to what I 'acquired' with my ship, I've added a few choice touches of my own. You might say you've stumbled on the perfect person for the job."

Ariana wasn't convinced. "If you're as brilliant as you say, which I doubt possible given your inflated estimation of yourself, what do you need with my bag . . . bags of gold?"

His grin widened. "Oh, I think the daughter of the Intersystem Prime Representative can come up with a lot more than two bags of gold."

Ariana blanched. "How do you know who I am?"

"Secrets, my lady, are to be earned, not given."

She swallowed and didn't answer. She had kept her identity a secret, lest it hamper her quest. She wasn't afraid of abduction. She was well-armed, and better skilled, but this roguish man was just the type to consider using her for such purposes. "I warn you, sir, that I am not to be trifled with. This is not my first task beyond the Intersystem, and I have earned my place on even the most dangerous missions."

"Indeed. . . ." He gazed upward as if searching his memory. "An expedition to Mardhead—a whole legion of blood-warriors routed, under your guidance. Another trek into the ice world of Lorren—thefts of precious malloreum fuel recovered—by you, and your well-known ingenuity. Your venture into Drakonian space is particularly renowned."

Ariana stared, aghast. "How do you know all this?"

He held out his hand as if to shake on an agreement they hadn't yet made. "I know a great deal, my lady. You want to know how? You will have to agree to my offer to find out. I am a busy man, and I have many other destinations that might prove more profitable to me than yours. Do we have a deal, or not?"

She hesitated. If nothing else, it might be dangerous to leave a rogue with this much information loose—and wise to learn how he knew some of the best-kept secrets of the Intersystem Council. She nodded, but she did not extend her hand. "Very well. I will inspect your ship, and if it is as you claim, I will take you as my guide, on the condition you ask no further questions until I am well satisfied that you are worthy of trust."

"I do not claim to be worthy of anything, my lady. But I will do the job you ask for, and you will return to Valenwood alive, no matter what dangers we face. That is my promise to you. What I ask in exchange is payment—in full, and a true tale of your destination."

Ariana hesitated. "As I told my previous querent, I am simply searching out new sources . . . inspecting territories to formalize relations with the Intersystem. . . ."

"What you told him was a lie. If you will tell me no more, there's no further reason for discussion." He got up to leave, but Ariana hopped up and caught his arm. She didn't like him, but she had run out of other options. If half the things he claimed were true, he might indeed be adequate for her mission.

"Very well. I will tell you this much. I wish to learn more of the Automon. We believe they have a connection to the rogue band of pirates known as the 'Dark Sun Fleet,' which has become increasingly aggressive throughout the Border Territory. They have intercepted every Intersystem vessel the Council has sent, and have virtually closed this region to our inspection. No one knows the location of their home world. No one knows whom they serve."

"Who says they serve anyone?"

"I know the Automon. They do not act or think for themselves, but they have a purpose. The Intersystem Council believes that purpose poses a grave threat to all worlds in this region. Especially if they happen to ally with the Dark Sun pirates."

"You're a spy." He studied her face for awhile, until she squirmed in discomfort beneath his penetrating gaze. "I cannot imagine that your father would send his daughter on so dangerous a journey."

Ariana's gaze shifted to the side. "It was not his choice, but he relented after much persuasion."

"Why?"

"Because I am the best suited for the task."

He studied her face for a long while. "There's more to your story than you're telling me, but we'll deal with that later. For now, Ariana of Valenwood, I accept your offer." He seized her hand and shook it, but Ariana didn't react. His touch was strong, warm, and almost electric in vibrancy. She glanced up quickly into his eyes, but he released her hand and turned away, then headed for the door. Ariana scurried after him.

"Wait! I do not know your name."

He stopped, and looked back over his shoulder as he held open the tavern door. "Do you not? Then call me Damen."

Chapter Eight

Ariana of Valenwood sputtered to herself as Damen led her along the back lanes of Outpost Gregor. She scurried along behind him, muttering and grumbling, but Damen resisted the urge to slow his pace, to talk with her, to look at her. For now, it was enough to have her near and to hear her voice. She was a beautiful woman—her delicacy and refined manner contrasted with her impulsive nature, and her self-confidence, which bordered on arrogance, served mainly to accentuate her vulnerability and restlessness.

He glanced back at her. She stomped along, her brow puckered, still muttering. Her long hair danced behind her, and her cape fluttered with her speed. He'd never seen hair so beautiful. Its dark waves reached past her waist, and too easily, he could imagine that sensual cloud falling against his skin as he held her.

She stopped suddenly and puffed an annoyed breath. "Where are you leading me? The Outpost landing platform is in the other direction."

He faced her and folded his arms over his chest. "You don't trust me."

She made a face. "No."

He nodded. "It was an impulsive decision to accept my offer."

Her eyes narrowed to slits. "I am regretting it more with each passing second."

"As is often the case with choices made in impulse." Her eyes fluttered shut as she fought for restraint. He waited, enjoying her mood. She opened her eyes, forced a formal, taut smile, then yanked her laser pistol from beneath her cape. "Unless you want to face the result of another 'impulsive choice,' I would show me your vessel. Now."

"The reputation you'll gain from shooting me will make it highly unlikely that you will ever secure another pilot."

Her jaw tightened, but she stuffed her pistol back into her cape. "It was a warning only. For now."

"An *impulsive* warning." Before she could draw her pistol again, Damen turned and strode onward. He heard her curse, but her quick footsteps behind soon followed.

He led her down narrow walkways, farther from the central outpost hub. Ariana furtively slipped a small instrument from her side-pack and employed it—a tracking device. No, she certainly wasn't ready to trust him. Yet neither did she seem frightened of him. She caught up with him, meeting his stride, and he glanced at her clenched hand as it concealed the device.

"You won't find that necessary—our destination is close."

She feigned a lack of surprise, then slipped it back into her pack. "If your vessel fails to intrigue me, I would prefer to find my way back without your assistance."

"As you will soon see, there will be no need."

They rounded a corner. A speeding hovercraft whipped around the corner toward them, scattering a cloud of debris in its wake. Damen grabbed Ariana's arm and pulled her out of its way. Maybe he had overreacted to the danger, but it had come so close.

She eyed him doubtfully. "What are you doing? Unhand me!"

He released her, with more reluctance than he'd intended. In fact, he hadn't intended to touch her at all. "It might have run you down."

She dusted herself off. "I can take care of myself."

"It was close."

Her brow arched. "As are you, but I can handle danger."

They started off again, but he stayed at her side. "You think me dangerous, do you?"

She offered a careless expression of disdain, but it seemed contrived. "You might be, I suppose."

"Yet you're willing to consider me as your guide."

She shrugged. "As you've accurately pointed out, I'm running short on options." She surveyed the landscape and sighed. "It's not exactly beautiful here, is it?"

"This particular outpost lacks charm, I agree, and cannot boast of the splendors offered by many others."

She glanced up at him. "Have you seen many worlds in the Border Territories?"

"I've traveled far, and seen many wonders."

"Why are you here? I doubt your only purpose was the chance of becoming my guide."

"A happy chance, my lady." This line of conversation might lead to dangerous territory. "And you—have you often traveled outside Intersystem space, aside from your renowned expeditions on behalf of the Council?"

"Not often, no. So little is known beyond these outposts. Once, when I was younger, I traveled to Lodder Vale. . . ."

"Ah! Lodder Vale, City of Pleasure—where pirates gorge their erotic appetites with women and strong drink. . . . Your tendency toward piracy started young, then?"

She frowned. "It was an adventure, and I was only an observer, not a participant. Much of what I saw appalled me."

"Much? But not all?" Her frown deepened, and he laughed. "Go on. What glories did you behold in the pirate city?"

"Fewer and less interesting than I'd hoped, but that is not what I remember of that time." She paused and sighed. "It did not end as we expected at all."

"What happened?"

"Never mind." Now it was her turn to divert the conversation. "I wished to see beautiful and exotic lands, that is all. Are there many such worlds beyond the Borders?"

She was changing the subject, away from her past. "There are, yes, but none more beautiful nor more exotic than your own Tiled City in Valenwood."

She stopped short. "You have seen the Tiled City?"

"Only once."

"What were you doing there?"

He smiled. "Seeking its treasure, you might say. I arrived during the Festival of the Singing Whales. Never have I seen such a spectacle."

She gasped, astonished. "The Amber Whales! You indeed arrived at the perfect moment. It is the greatest Ellowan holiday, celebrating the return of our people to their homeland, and the beginning of my father's reign."

"So I learned, though at the time, I didn't speak much of the Intersystem language."

She eyed him closely as they started off again. "The Festival of the Singing Whales occurs only once every eight years. The last was six years ago."

"Yes, it has been six years."

"I remember that day. . . ." Her voice trailed. "The children go down to the water, and the Amber Whales come close to the shore. The children throw flowers and join in the song, while the Ellowan King, my father, plays his harp from the highest balcony. I was with him—it was a beautiful day."

"Yes." He didn't look at her, but felt her penetrating gaze. "I saw you there."

"Is that how you know my name, and of my exploits?"

He hesitated. "I learned much of you that day, as it happens."

"Indeed? Such as what?"

"That you were beloved and happy, and much admired by your people. But if you'll remember, at that time, you were not renowned for any exploits other than survival."

75

"So . . . you know of that, too."

"I know you were abducted and held prisoner by the Automon, and that you escaped. Is there more to tell?"

Ariana frowned. "That is all you need to know."

"For now, my lady." He led her across the walkway, then to an older platform, rarely used in favor of the newer site. "There. . . . What do you think of her?"

Ariana stepped up beside him and gaped. The sleek black ship purred with subdued power, already set for takeoff. "It has been long since I've seen one this close—and never have I see a model of this variety. It looks built for speed rather than transport." She approached the hull. "Yet I see adequate defensive capabilities."

"More than adequate. Part of my design additions was to keep the illusion of a scout ship, while installing a higher attack level. Will you join me on board?" He didn't wait for her reply. He pressed the small monitor in his coat pocket, and the ramp lowered. He held out his arm, motioning Ariana forward, but she seemed suddenly reluctant, as if she sensed some danger ahead.

"Damen! The crew is restless, and already I have confined three to their quarters!" Fia's clear voice rang from the ship speaker and Damen smiled.

"You hear the voice of my First Officer."

Ariana looked up at the ship. "A woman?" As she spoke, Fia appeared on the ramp, hands on her hips, frowning. She caught sight of Ariana, and her expression changed. In her youth, her expressions ranged from mature contempt for those less capable, to bright-eyed curiosity when greeting something new.

She looked between Ariana and Damen. "Is this . . . ?"

He cut her off. "This is Ariana of Valenwood. She has engaged our vessel for her use, and is offering a fine payment for the service."

Fia's brow rose. "She's *hired* us?"

He cast her a quick look of warning, and she nodded. "Oh. Yes. Good." She waited on the top of the ramp, looking regal but still young, as he and Ariana approached.

"Ariana, this is Fia, my First Officer."

Fia stuck out her hand, pleased. Ariana seemed uncertain, but she shook Fia's extended hand. "I am pleased to meet you . . . Fia." She paused as if expecting some other name. And it was true—Fia herself seemed to demand a far longer name, complete with titles of ancestry. But Fia was the only name she knew.

"Welcome, Ariana, to *The Pirate's Treasure*. It will be nice to have another woman on board." She glanced at Damen. "Is she staying with . . . ?"

"Ariana will stay in the seventh cabin."

Fia hesitated. "The blue room?" She offered Ariana a polite smile. "I had the crew color each cabin differently, so we could tell them apart. The blue room is very nice."

Damen led Ariana on board, and Fia followed, still eyeing Ariana with interest and perhaps excitement. "I have promised to show Ariana around our vessel. Once she is satisfied of its quality, we may lift off."

"I shall instruct the crew as such!" Fia darted off, leaving Ariana standing in mute surprise.

"She doesn't look more than twenty, yet she seems so . . . efficient."

"She is twenty-three, but looks no more than sixteen to me."

Ariana hesitated, biting her lip. "Then she isn't . . . your . . ."

Damen grimaced. "Of course not! Though we're not related by blood, Fia is the closest thing to family I've got. She is, you could say, my heir."

He directed Ariana on a quick tour of the ship, and she seemed satisfied, even impressed by what she saw, though she attempted to look indifferent. He brought her to the rear galley, the most beautiful and best decorated area of his vessel, and they stood together looking out the view port. The distant yellow-red sun sank beneath the horizon, granting the only moment of true beauty to the bleak outpost. As it disappeared, the ringed planet of Ceribdas appeared farther in space.

"Well, my lady? What do you think now that you've seen my ship? Is she all I promised, or will you continue your hunt elsewhere?"

"It seems adequate." She glanced at him as if enduring guilt. "Most impressive, really." She turned to face him, her manner formal. "Very well, Damen. . . . Have you any other name, or is that it?"

"Only Damen."

"Very well, Damen, Captain of . . . what was it? *The Pirate's Treasure*, yes. I accept your offer of guidance through and beyond the Border Territories. We may commence at once." She held up the two felt bags, but he didn't take them.

"Before we go anywhere, you and I are going to have a talk."

"We've already talked too much. You've offered to be my guide. Having inspected your ship and found your claims justified, I agree."

"But *I* have agreed to nothing, my lady."

She looked alarmed, but also angry. "I am on board your ship. If you didn't agree, why did you bring me here at all?"

"Here, on my ship, I have you in my power. That seems reason enough."

He caught her hand before she could seize her pistol, then removed it from beneath her cape. "I won't hurt you, Ariana. But as I said in the tavern, you have not told me your true mission, and before I guide this ship, or you, anywhere, I will hear it."

He directed her to a large, padded bench and they sat together, though Ariana kept herself a safe distance away. "Well? Your story, Ariana. I'm waiting. I assume your persistent need for a guide is worth that much information, anyway."

"I've told you already! The Intersystem wishes to learn more of the Automon—Who do they serve, for example."

"A part truth, perhaps, but not the whole."

"It is enough!"

"Not for me."

She chewed her lip and looked uncomfortable. "What else do you want to know?"

"Well, for one thing, why you?"

"What do you mean?"

"You are the daughter of the Intersystem's most powerful leader. You are renowned of your own accord. There is no need to send you on a mission like this. Any other person with unscrupulous tendencies, dedicated to the Intersystem, could serve as well. Why you?"

She puffed a breath. "Because I've been there before, that's why. I am the only Intersystem pilot to have flown through Dark Sun Space. Though the ship I stole lost its navigation and left no records, my memory holds enough to guide me back."

"Ah . . ." He studied her awhile, but she didn't meet his eyes. "Which world do you seek?"

"A volcanic planet orbiting a Dark Sun. It held a colony. . . ."

"It holds a colony no longer—the last was destroyed ten years ago. What you seek is gone."

The blood drained from her face, and she bowed her head.

"Perhaps your task isn't as pressing as you thought."

She eyed him suspiciously. "How do you know of this? There are many Dark Suns, and the Automon keep many mining colonies."

"The Dark Sun you sought is the fifth, in a region known as north and east by Intersystem navigation."

"I have tried—the Intersystem has tried—for years to learn the whereabouts of that colony. That, if you must know, was the real purpose of my mission here. Since other Intersystem efforts have proved fruitless, I came myself with the intention of learning the whereabouts of the colony where I was held captive. For years, this has been my goal. To find all the Dark Sun colonies and to free the cavern people. As well, three of my original party remained behind when I escaped. It is my duty to find them, and to free them, too." She paused, her voice quavering. "It is my duty to . . . to all that I lost when I left that place."

"Your duty is a noble one, but too late."

She clenched her fist. "You can't know this. No one I've interviewed has been there. No one knew of its existence. How would you, one of the least trustworthy persons I've ever encountered, know anything of it?"

"I was born there."

Her eyes widened in shock, then narrowed into slits of suspicion. "That is impossible. I was there, and *you*, I am sure, were not."

"How do you know that?"

"Well, for one thing, because you're much taller than anyone I remember in the colony tribe. For another, you speak the Intersystem language, and several others. The colony had no developed language, and they certainly weren't inhabited by pilots—or pirates—such as yourself."

"The boys you remember were bearded, barely clothed, filthy. Do you truly believe you would recognize any of them now?"

"Yes!"

He held her gaze for a long while, then drew back his coat and his loose white shirt to bare his upper chest. Her mouth drifted open, her chin trembled. She reached with quavering fingers to touch the scar, then snatched her hand back with a suddenness that startled him. She glared, furious. "This could have been faked."

Damen laughed. "For what purpose? I have borne this brand since early childhood—the lines are blurred from my growth. How could I fake that?"

"You can't have been there. It's not possible." But he saw as she began to accept that it was. "You were there?"

"I was."

"How did you get out? Escape?"

"Rebellion." Even now, pride brought richness to the word. "The Automon had planned a darker fate for our tribe—for many generations, they had found it convenient to release a lava flow, annihilating those who had reached an age where rebellion became likely."

"That, I guessed. I tried to tell him. . . ." Her voice trailed and she released a small, shuddering sigh. "How did you stop them?"

"We fought. Many died, but the Automon were not expecting resistance, for we had not yet reached an age they deemed dangerous."

"Then it can't have been long after . . ."

"After you left? No, not long."

Her chin quivered as she fought tears, and he waited. "Then, if I had waited . . ." Her voice caught, and she stopped.

"If you had waited, Ariana, there would have been no reason for rebellion."

She looked up at him, confused, but he battled back his own emotion. "If you were there, then you must remember. . . ." She paused, almost as if afraid to hear what he would say. "There was a leader, a young man. He escaped with me, but they caught us, and he died." Her voice sank to a whisper and her face was plaintive.

He held her gaze evenly. "He did not die."

No reaction showed on her face. She seemed frozen, motionless. She drew no breath. Her words came like the sound of far-off rain. "I saw him fall, and the Automon took him away."

"He fell, but he did not die."

This time, he barely heard her when she spoke. "What . . . what happened to him?"

He heard his own heartbeat, felt his pulse, and it seemed almost that he heard hers, too. "Ariana. . . . You're looking at him."

She blinked. Her expression didn't change. Then, very slowly, the corner of her lip turned up, creasing until her cheek puffed. Her grey eyes formed slits and her head tilted to one side. If he hadn't taken her pistol before, she would have shot him. "You . . . you are a demon!"

"This is not exactly the reunion I'd hoped for."

She closed her eyes for a long while, her small face taut with anger. Then she cleared her throat. "There are few cruelties in the universe as dark as one who will attack where the heart is most dear. *You* are not . . . him."

"What proof would you have?"

"None. It's not possible."

"You have seen my brand, so you know I was there."

"I accept that, but that hardly means . . ."

"*Damanai.* . . ."

Her eyes snapped open, and they glittered with fury. "You are not him!"

"Then how would I know the name spoken by you?"

"I don't know. He might have told you."

"From one man with no language to another? No. . . ."

"You've learned language well enough!" She didn't let him answer. "You're tall. Huge!"

"I was taller than you then, too."

"Not this tall, and certainly not this . . . huge."

"Ariana, it has been ten years. I was a boy in the caverns. I have grown—I am a man."

"You're a liar, that's what you are!" She looked as though she might strike him, but Damen caught her fists and held them against his chest.

"I gave you a crystal shard—I put it around your neck. In the sand, I drew its history, and you understood. Do you think I tortured this information, too, from your lover's mind?"

She stood trembling, staring up at him. She knew. "It can't be. You can't be him."

"Much has changed since those far-off days. Yourself, not the least." Half reluctant, he touched her hair and remembered when tight curls had woven around his fingertips. He dropped his hand to his side and looked away.

He didn't look at her, but he felt her scrutiny as she studied his face. "Your eyes are different." She spoke more softly now, but hesitant, as if she still hadn't fully accepted that this man from her past had awoken and returned to her life. "I'm not sure how, but they are different."

"I have seen much. Perhaps that is the change."

"Yes, that is it. You don't look innocent anymore."

He allowed himself to see her, and he smiled. "Your own eyes have changed, my lady. I would say . . ." He reached to touch her cheek. "You no longer trust as you once did."

She edged away from his touch. "I have found little cause for trust."

"Life hardens, it tarnishes. Little is as it once was. I contemplated leaving this particular secret untold. But you would have guessed, sooner or later, and felt even more betrayed than you do now. It is best that you know here, so that you can lay your memories to rest, as I have laid mine in their proper place."

She stared at him, aghast. "What do you mean?"

"You hold to the memory of youth, untarnished, pure, and innocent. We were young—we are young no longer. Oh, no age shows on your little face, but all you have seen and endured, all that has wounded you and caused your heart dismay, I see that in your eyes. I want you to understand here, before we go any further together: I am not the man I was."

She swallowed hard, as if the bitter taste stung in her throat. "That much is certain." She bowed her head. "Why do you tell me this now?"

"So that you will face and accept what I now must do."

She heard something in his tone, apparently, because she glanced up with ripe suspicion. "What is that?"

He drew a long breath, and weariness engulfed him as he rose and aimed her pistol between her beautiful eyes. "Ariana of Valenwood, you are now captive of the Dark Sun Fleet, and at the mercy of its lord."

Chapter Nine

Damen stood outside the door of Ariana's cabin, but he didn't unlock the grid. What could he say to her, now? A soft, muffled noise reached his ears, and it struck him like a blow. He entered the code into the panel grid, and the door slid open. She shot up from her bedding, and blinked at the incoming light. With a quick dart of her wrist, she dried her cheeks, but her effort to conceal her tears was harder to bear than seeing them fall.

Damen said nothing as he went to her. She braced, but he seated himself beside her, still unable to speak.

"What do you want?" She sounded controlled, her voice even but still a little hoarse.

"I thought I should speak with you."

"You've spoken more than enough. If that's all you want, I would thank you to leave."

He didn't look at her. He couldn't. He just stared up at the low ceiling, lit with a dim glow mimicking nightfall. "You healed me, Ariana. You guarded me, you taught me. If not for you, I would have known nothing of other worlds, nothing at all of . . ." *Of love*, he thought, but he couldn't speak that word. "Of anything that mattered. You showed me freedom. And I have repaid you by treachery."

"Did you come to remind me of that? I know it well."

He allowed himself to see her, and all the pain written in her face seemed mirrored in his own. "I cannot explain fully, not yet, why this was necessary. But neither can I leave you alone to grieve."

"I would prefer that you did." Her words came thick and he knew she fought tears. He reached for her hand, but she pulled away, refusing his touch. "Why have you come? I did not desire it."

"I came to comfort you."

A brief snort said this was an ill-planned suggestion. "Forgive me for not welcoming your comfort!"

Emotion quavered in her voice. He remembered when he had lain beside her, listening to her talking, part to him, part to herself, and having no idea what she said. Sometimes, he had believed she was singing, because every sound she'd uttered had been like music to him. He hadn't realized, then, what could be communicated with words. His people had conveyed much, but with other senses, with facial expressions, with their bodies, with touch. Sometimes, words fell short.

Damen gathered her into his arms, and drew her close. Ariana squeaked and struggled, but he felt her body yield. Her breath came in short gasps, and every muscle clenched tight against him.

"Let me go!" She pushed her forehead against his chest, to shove herself back, but instead, he placed his hand on her head, then gently caressed her hair as he had done, long ago. She froze. For a moment, he heard nothing, felt no motion in her body. And then she cried. No longer small, muffled sobs, but deep and torn from her innermost core. She cried until he felt her tears soaking through his shirt, and he held her.

He needed words, to explain, so that she would understand. "This death is perhaps harder than the one we faced before." She stopped crying and looked up, shocked. He touched her cheek, but he fought back his own tears. "It is easier, sometimes, to face death than to witness change."

She looked so beautiful, so vulnerable and delicate, just as she had been when he first saw her. So alone. "You don't understand." Her voice came small, broken, but still sure as it faded to a whisper. "I loved you so. All this time, I thought you were with me. I thought, no matter how lonely I was or how much I missed you, that I had this, at least. That you had loved me." He wanted to stop her, but his throat tightened, and the look on her face penetrated too deep for him to respond. "I thought I would never love again, but it didn't matter, because I had loved once, and so perfectly. Now . . . You held a pistol to my head." She stopped and looked away.

Damen closed his eyes—he couldn't see her, not this way. "I wouldn't have hurt you."

He knew without looking that she didn't believe him. Maybe it was best that she didn't, but his chest ached as he endured confirmation of her pain.

She huffed, a small, ragged sound. "It's not just that."

He wanted to stop her, but he couldn't speak.

"You and I didn't meet by accident, Damen. I'm not that big a fool. You knew who I was, and where, and what I was doing here in the Border Territories."

"Yes."

"You have known for a long time."

"Yes."

"All this time . . ." He heard her pain, and could do nothing to staunch the wound as it flowed. "All this time, you have known where I was. But you presented yourself only when I became a threat to whatever scheme you have going here—Lord of the Dark Sun Fleet!"

"Yes." When it had become obvious that Ariana, and Ariana alone, would pose his greatest threat, he had known he would have to face her. He had foreseen the pain of their reunion, but could never have predicted the joy of looking into her eyes again, nor the strong pulse of his heart when she stood near him. "What you say is true, as far as it goes. . . ."

She pulled away from him. "I don't want to know. I don't want to hear you explain, or anything. All these years, I have been a fool, I have lived on a memory that was nothing but a lie."

Her words cut so deep that his stomach clenched. "That's not true. Ariana, there is so much more. . . . What happened, to both of us, when we parted . . ."

She frowned, her little face taut with emotion. "You don't know what happened to me."

"I know you survived and returned home to your father, to Valenwood."

"I survived—barely." She paused, her words tinged with bitterness. "The details of my return were never made public, and even now, only those closest to me know the full story."

He feared to hear her, to know what happened after he lost her. He had lived those first weeks and months by *knowing* she was safe, knowing it in his heart. "I knew you would find your way home, to Valenwood. Never once could I imagine that you might die."

She closed her eyes as memory enveloped her. "There were so many days that I wished for death. Not just days. Weeks passed—I do not know how many."

Without him. . . . "What happened?"

"I don't remember most of it. At first, I couldn't alter the ship's course, and then the instrumentation failed. I couldn't decipher much of the Automon system, and for a long while, I had no idea where I was in space. Then finally, I saw a star cluster I recognized, and I aimed for that. But I was sick, and there was no food but what I had in my pack. By the time my ship was sighted and recovered, I was barely alive. Hakon found me."

Hakon. . . . Where Damen had failed her, that man arrived to save her. "He was lucky."

"My father had sent out the whole scouting fleet in search, but, yes, it was luck that brought me to Hakon. He brought me back to Valenwood, but I remember little until my waking."

"It is said that your father is a great healer."

"He is, but I couldn't find my own will to live, and he needed that in order to save me. And then . . ." She stopped, and her pause indicated a disclosure she wasn't ready to make. How much would she keep to herself now that she knew him as lord of the Dark Sun Fleet? "And then I found a reason to live." She looked up at him, still with an element of disbelief on her face. "I thought you were dead—it never occurred to me that the Automon would let you live."

"I'm not sure they would have. The other woman of your group, she freed me, and we returned to the caverns. I suppose the Automon saw no harm in my escape, though I soon proved them wrong, but either way, they had no method of singling me out from the rest."

Ariana's brow furrowed. "Lissa saved you? What happened?"

"I had believed at the time that she had simply arrived too late to escape, but after our rebellion, when we took the Automon craft, she and another of your group set off alone, deserting the rest. The third female died during the first battle of the rebellion. I assumed the other two returned to their homeland, wanting no more to do with our primitive tribe."

"None of the others returned—I am sure of that." Ariana frowned. "I wonder where she went?"

"I have heard nothing of her or the other female since."

Ariana's eyes narrowed. "Sometimes I thought she wanted you for herself. I sensed it, but her words deceived me, and I trusted her. Eyes, I think, tell more than words, and hers were often fixed on you."

Damen tried to remember the woman's face, but little came to mind. "She had large eyes, dark, and smiled often without joy. She was smaller than you, but her bones were bigger, and when her hair grew, there were no curls."

Ariana swallowed. "With me gone . . ." She faltered. "I suppose you needed a mate of some sort."

88

"Part of the honor in becoming the cavern leader is to choose the best mate—as I chose you. In this way, the strongest blood is passed on, passed on to the next generation that we never even see, and handed to us from fathers we never knew. I remember my mother—she was taller than most, and the wisest of her tribe. It was she who carved the Beginning Symbols in crystal, and she who gave herself to the previous cavern king, my father. I know of him only through her, but she said he was a great fighter, yet kind, and she hoped I would be the same. By the time I freed the mothers, she had died, but they still remembered her with pride."

"Did she know of the Automon policy of destroying the colonies with lava?"

"I'm not sure, but I believe so. She would not tell me of it—what mother would pass this information on to her child, knowing no way it could be avoided? Before they took us, my generation of boys, she told me to live strong and well, and when I found my treasure, to hold it against my heart." He paused. "And I found you."

Tears welled in Ariana's eyes again. "You were so dear."

He hesitated. "Where is the crystal now? It is not around your neck."

Instantly, a veil covered her expression, too casual. "It is in a safe place."

"Not around your neck. You were wearing it when I saw you in Valenwood, but not now."

"It is needed more where it is." She stopped and cleared her throat. "What happened with Lissa?" She hesitated. "You didn't . . . She didn't . . . ?"

"Her manner toward me suggested lust, as I recall."

Ariana winced. "I do not want to hear this."

He laughed. "There is nothing to tell. My loss was too acute to be soothed with another woman's touch. As well, the ship that you took was the same that had brought Fia to the cavern. She was alone, younger than any women the Automon had thrown to us before. Perhaps her courage and

89

defiance reminded me of you, or maybe I just needed someone to protect, but I made her my heir, and from her, learned more of the universe than I had from you."

She frowned. "You didn't listen when I tried to teach you!"

"When you were near, I had other things on my mind." His gaze drifted to her open collar, then back to her lips. Color rose in her cheeks and she bit her lip hard. "At the time, I had no reason to care what lay beyond my dark world."

"So Fia taught you language? What world is she from?"

"I don't know, and neither does she. Not an Intersystem planet, though she had some knowledge of the Council's existence. She had heard of Valenwood, anyway. From what I've learned, Fia had lived like a treasured prisoner—even now, she has a taste for fine things. She had been raised by people she didn't know, treated well, but told nothing, until she was brutally seized and given to the Automon. To the Automon, she was just another breeder female, but I believe to those who had first captured her, she was some kind of threat."

"You've learned nothing more?"

"No. . . . At first, my only desire was to find you."

She gazed up at him in wonder, and a dawning of understanding. "You told me you came to Valenwood. . . . You weren't lying."

"No."

"You came for me?"

He closed his eyes. "For you."

"Then why didn't you . . . ?" She stopped, then just stared up at him.

"Four years taught me more than just language, Ariana. I learned of humankind—I learned I knew nothing. I had nothing, and I was no one, just a creature that crawled from a hole, and when I saw you there, the daughter of the king of kings, the greatest leader of men, I could not imagine any good I could bring to you."

"That is not all you saw when you came to Valenwood." Her lips twisted to one side, and she looked contemplative as she struggled to understand what had come between them. "I remember that day very well, for it changed my life. If you were able to see my necklace, you saw me much closer than across the bay on my father's balcony."

He felt uncomfortable, so he didn't answer.

Ariana peered at him, then nodded. "I am right. That day, Hakon asked me to marry him. I did not refuse."

He shrugged and tried to appear idle. "After I'd made my way through the crowd, I saw you walking away behind the White Palace with a light-haired man." He stopped, and a rueful smile formed on his lips. "I thought he meant to do you harm, so I followed."

Ariana smiled, too. "He meant no harm."

"I saw that."

"Then you saw our meeting, too?"

He didn't meet her eyes. "I did. I didn't understand your language then, but I knew what transpired. He was claiming you as his own."

Ariana frowned. "I wouldn't call it that, exactly."

Damen wasn't convinced. "A man knows, Ariana." He paused and sighed heavily. "I didn't stay to see more of your life. I believed you were safe with him, in the White Palace, and I vowed to release you from my heart." He paused. "Perhaps I never did. But it was plain to me that this man would give you what I never could. It seemed right that you should wed with him rather than a man like myself, a man without a real world to offer you."

Ariana drew a long breath. "It seemed right to everyone, I suppose. There was pressure on us to wed—my father especially desired it, and Hakon, I think, considered it his duty."

"He loves you, Ariana. I saw that much, even without knowing your language."

"There is a difference between loving, and being in love. As well, his reasons for asking . . ." She stopped and didn't continue.

"What reason did he have other than taking a beautiful woman to wife?"

She looked at her hands. "Pity, the desire to do good, to make right a wrong."

"That desire, my lady, has driven many men to darker fates than marriage. You didn't marry him. Why?"

"I might have, I suppose, and I thought it would be good for . . ." She caught herself, and again, he recognized a place where some secret lay. "For everyone."

"What stopped you?" Her life might have been better, and safer, if she had married the golden-haired prince, but he couldn't find much sorrow that no other man had claimed her as a wife.

"It was his father, Dane, who convinced us not to marry."

"His father was against your marriage?"

"He didn't say so, exactly. He just sat us down together and told us that if we married, we would have to kiss."

Damen hesitated. "That does seem reasonable." He paused. "What of it?"

"It seems almost comic now, but neither of us had considered that portion of marriage. Dane said we would kiss, and make love, then looked us straight on and asked us if we had kissed before. We both grimaced, and I remember we laughed."

"This is odd beyond measure. Why hadn't he kissed you? You are beautiful. He is passing in appearance for a man. . . ."

Her brow arched. "Have you kissed Fia?"

Damen recoiled. "Of course not! That would be . . ."

"Wrong—unthinkable?"

"Exactly."

"We felt the same, and we decided not to marry, though we remain the best of friends. He has been like a fa—" She bit her lip. "Like a *brother* to . . . me."

"Still, there are other men."

"The only man I have met since leaving that cavern who has stirred my blood toward passion . . . is you."

Damen gaped, but she smiled, then averted her gaze. "Me? You loathed me on sight!"

"You terrified me."

"You did not seem afraid. You seemed furious."

"Emotions mask each other, Damen. You were a temptation to me, in a dark sort of way." She looked as if this disclosure pained her, but Damen's mood shifted.

"There was always strong desire between us."

"Perhaps that is what Hakon and I lack."

"I saw love between you. I will admit that for a moment, my instincts reverted to something more primitive. I thought of killing him, there in that glade where he held my woman."

"I am glad you refrained. Hakon wouldn't be that easy to defeat."

Damen frowned. "I would have killed him in one blow."

"You have seen him, but you don't know him. You might find him more formidable than you imagine. And right now, he is captain of the fleet whose greatest foe is the Dark Sun lord."

"If we meet in battle, so much the better. But I didn't kill him then, because I saw that you loved him. Even as I raised my hand to attack, I knew I couldn't hurt the man who could give you what I could not."

Ariana stared, astonished. "So you just . . . left? Didn't you think I might be at least happy to see you, to know you were alive?"

"Oh, I knew you would. For a while, until you realized how little I belong in your world. I believed, too, that I had a purpose, and it was a dangerous one."

"What purpose? As a rogue commander of a stolen Automon vessel, and leader of a band of pirates? I suppose that's impressive, if not exactly noble." She paused, almost as if afraid to question him further. "Many on the Council believe the Dark Sun Fleet is in league with the Automon."

"Then they are mistaken. As yet, few Automon ships enter Border Territory, far fewer than rumor makes it. When they do, it is for the purposes of abducting females and other slaves for their malloreum mines, just as it was when they took you."

"Do you know who commands them?"

Damen hesitated. "As I told you before, I have no reason to believe anyone commands the Automon."

Ariana frowned. "You are no more willing to share your secrets than I am. Why, if you are not in league with them?" She leaned toward him, an eager light in her eyes. He knew what she wanted, and it was the one thing he couldn't give. "Wouldn't it profit us both to face this together? You might have done well enough on your own, but there has to be something more important than pirating malloreum fuel."

"The acquisition of that precious fuel has made me a force, my lady, and a wealthy man."

Her back straightened, and her eyes narrowed—she didn't like his words, but Damen couldn't soften them. "There has to be something more important than that! You didn't fight your way out of the Automon cavern just to seek wealth!"

Again, the answer came hard. "As I have seen since emerging from those dark caves, wealth and power go a long way toward crafting a man's fate in this universe."

"Do they, indeed? That is ridiculous! It is honor, and the pursuit of a greater good, which carves a person's fate!"

He glanced at her, long enough to see the distance widen between them. As it should be, as it had to be, if only he could keep himself from touching her. "And I suppose it is 'honor and the pursuit of good' that tiles your father's city in the majesty of pearl and silver? Or paves the street with white marble?"

"My father spent years uncounted living in a swamp, the leader of a band of rebels. You do not choose a good man for comparison, if you liken Arnoth of Valenwood to a greedy pirate."

"Perhaps his is a nobler heart than mine. Be that as it may, I doubt very much that the Dark Sun Fleet would profit from Intersystem interference."

"It isn't interference! We have helped many troubled worlds, without force. . . ."

"Oh? And what is this fleet your golden-haired friend commands? Not a travel service, I think."

"At least, we have not stooped to piracy!"

He liked her quick expressions, the flash of anger in her eyes. It reminded him of their first meeting, and of her first defiance. She had been ready to kill him then, too. And in her brave emotion, she enchanted him.

Damen touched her cheek. She puffed a furious breath, but she didn't move away. "It seems we stand on opposite sides in this matter, my lady."

"We do." She answered with heat, ready to fight. It was a dangerous and irresistible mixture.

He slid his touch from her cheek into her soft hair. She watched him in disbelief as he bent to kiss her. "But not, I think, in all."

Chapter Ten

Ariana held up her hand, but rather than push Damen away as she had meant to do, her palm spread against his chest and she felt the strong beat of his heart. He brushed his lips against her cheek, then near the edge of her lips. She didn't breathe. She felt his hands as he gripped her arms, she felt the warm, powerful energy of his body close against her. He whispered her name. Softer, she answered, "*Damanai*," and she turned her face to his.

His kiss was like memory, filled with the fire he had roused in her. Ariana wrapped her arms around his waist and kissed him back. Her breath came in short gasps and it seemed as if she searched for something, something that could be found in the tenderness of his embrace. Everything she treasured, she could find again in him.

His tongue slid over her lip, and she tasted him. He shuddered, and his arms tightened around her. Ariana reached for him and caught his long hair in her fingers, pulling him closer. She kissed him wildly, her eyes closed tight. She could almost feel the heat of the far-away cavern surrounding them, the dull, pulsing sound of molten lava beneath the crusty ground as he lowered her beneath him. His hair fell around her face and he pressed her gently back onto a soft bed—not a rock ledge, but a real bed.

Her senses reeled, the past and present mingling together in a wild, powerful struggle. She didn't know who she was, or where, just that she was with him. She felt his body hard against her, the male part of him engorged and ready for her, as she was ready for him. She murmured and slid her leg over his, encouraging him. Damen responded to her unspoken invitation with raw, primal desire. He moved against her, and kissed her neck, speaking to her in a language she didn't understand, but whose meaning she felt.

Over and over, he spoke her name, instilling the sound with the richness of some sacred invocation. He pulled back her jacket and then unlaced the snug vest beneath, baring her skin to his touch. He grazed his lips over her skin, and she shuddered with desire as he moved from her collarbone lower to her breast. He pulled back the cloth and her nipple tightened. He cupped her breast gently, then tasted, and Ariana bit back a cry of pleasure. *This cannot be. . . . I don't know you anymore. . . .* He teased her, then sucked, and her fingers clenched into his shirt. "I know you."

She would take him, they would make love, and then all that confused her so horribly this day would fade, and he would be hers once again. Ariana twisted in his arms, and he moved to kiss her mouth again. She tugged at his shirt and it slipped from his left shoulder, the shoulder that bore the cavern scar. "I know you now."

Her words seemed to catch him off guard, and he stopped. A deep, hoarse breath shuddered through him. He broke their kiss, then rested his forehead against hers. "It is to the past you yield, not to me."

She started to shake her head, but he sat up, away from her. Her breath came in ragged gasps, and she wanted to cry. She drew her legs up, clasped her arms tight around her knees, and tried to face him. "I do not understand you."

He glanced at her, but looked away quickly as if the sight

of her pained him. "But I understand you, Ariana. Too well. You cling to the memory of what we had, what we were once together. You think all that has happened since will fall away. It will not."

Tears welled in her eyes. "Is that so wrong?" She hadn't meant to speak in so small a voice, but the sound quavered, and she couldn't stop her vulnerability from revealing itself to him.

Damen looked at her again, this time without wavering. His expression changed from pity to something far more dangerous. "Make no mistake. You will give yourself to me, Ariana. But not this way. You and I will make love when you are ready to face what we are now, without the shadow of the past hanging over us."

"It is no shadow, but the only light!"

He smiled but his expression wasn't reassuring. "It is an illusion, the shadow of what was. What we are, that is something quite different. But no less powerful." He reached to touch her face again, teasing. She jerked away, but her skin tingled where his finger had traced its line. "You know that as well as I."

"You ask me to surrender to darkness, rather than to find the light I had with you. That, I will never do. You have changed—I see that well enough. If there is no trace of the man you were inside you now, there is nothing further for us to say to each other."

"You found the 'man I am' compelling enough back at that tavern."

She frowned, annoyed. "I found you irritating, smug, and over-forceful."

He gazed upward toward the ceiling as if searching his memory. "I think you said I had inflamed your passions."

Had she? She looked him straight in the eye without wavering. "I was exaggerating. I meant the passion of anger."

"Passion, all the same." He glanced at her chest, still rising and falling with swift breaths. "I would say that is beyond any doubt now."

Ariana gulped. "As you said, it was the past that . . . tempted me. Not yourself."

"Not exactly. You give yourself in the name of the past—but it is me that you desire." As if to prove his point further, he reached to her open vest and traced a line over her breast. Ariana smacked his hand away, but her own hands trembled too much to redo the laces of her vest. Damen tied them for her. She averted her eyes lest a new madness overcome her.

Damen fixed the laces in a neat bow, delaying its closure. "It is best, for both you and for me, to have this particular temptation covered. For now, at least."

She glared. "I think you kissed me to weaken me. As if I wasn't confused enough!"

Damen rose from the bed and stood looking down at her. A furtive glance told her that his own desire hadn't abated, and revealed itself in the fullness beneath his snug leggings. Ariana bit her lip and pretended not to notice, but Damen smiled. "Confusion, it seems, troubles us both. Perhaps another task might distract us." He paused. "If you can restrain yourself, that is."

"What 'other task?' "

"My ship is on course now for an event you might find interesting. If you would care to learn more of the Dark Sun Fleet, perhaps you would join me."

"Where are we going?"

"That, you will see when we get there." He held out his hand for her. With a cool, faraway shock, she remembered when he had done the same, with the red glow of the cavern fires behind him. Her eyes puddled with tears and her throat clenched. Damen withdrew his hand and went to her door. "Will you join me?"

Ariana adjusted her jacket and buttoned it high over her snug vest. She smoothed her hair back and took a quick breath to clear her senses. "I suppose that would be in order." She got up and went to the door, then peeked up at him. "As your prisoner, I assume?"

He hesitated. "Well, if you accept that role . . . I'll forgo acceptance of those two small bags of gold, at least."

Ariana's lip curled. "That's good of you! I hadn't intended to pay your commission, in light of your abduction."

"Still . . . It could be considered a bargain, given that I will show you all you wish to learn of the Dark Sun Fleet."

"And what of your promise to return me to Valenwood? Now that I know your identity, that must surely be a risk."

His expression grew more serious. "To that promise, I hold. You have no need to doubt my word in this."

"They will expect communication from me."

"And you shall give it." He withdrew her Intersystem transmission device, which she hadn't realized he'd taken, and gave it to her. "Contact them now. But do not attempt trickery, Ariana. I know the Intersystem codes as well as you do."

"For now, that won't be necessary." Ariana kept her expression clear, but her danger would have to be far graver before she alerted her family to this abduction. She knew how much they had suffered when she had been captured before. There was no need to alarm them now. She coded in a quick message, reassuring them that all proceeded perfectly. She told them she had hired an able guide, and would continue reports as she progressed.

Damen watched over her and seemed satisfied. "I see no attempt at subterfuge. That is wise."

Ariana punched in another quick message, and his brow furrowed. "What was that? Those words, I do not recognize."

Ariana closed the device. "It's nothing."

"*Urywen a storin*, I recognize. 'My love is with you.' But what are 'hyppos,' and why do you hope they arrive safely? This might indeed be a coded message."

She rolled her eyes, impatient. "Hyppos are large, fat water creatures—the world they inhabited has suffered a terrible drought. To preserve their species, my father has invited a number of them to Valenwood. Their ecosystem balances well with the Amber Whales, as they occupy the mouths of rivers and stir up a great deal of mud. Much of

Valenwood's animal population had been destroyed in the age before my father's reign and we have selectively added new creatures to replace those we lost. Hyppos are the newest."

"And this is important enough to relay to your father?"

"My . . . father . . . family . . . is very excited about the hyppos' arrival. Yes."

He shrugged. "It is said the Ellowan are a strange race, so perhaps this is possible."

"It is." Damen took the transmission device and stored it in his coat pocket. Ariana frowned. "They will respond to my message within a few hours, and expect me to confirm receipt."

"When that time comes, you will do so."

Ariana bit her lip. But *who* would respond to her message, and how much would Damen learn, before she was ready to tell him the full story of her life on Valenwood? "I would appreciate a certain amount of privacy when communicating with my family."

Damen glanced at her, perhaps suspicious of her nervous tone. "It's what you reveal to them that concerns me, not the other way around."

She exhaled muted relief. "Good. Because what my parents say to me is none of your business."

"Unless, of course, you're hiding something of importance?"

"I am not!"

"An Intersystem plot, perhaps?"

"If so, then they're not foolish enough to mention it on a transmitter."

He opened the door grid and Ariana brushed by him, then out into the hall. "You are my prisoner, Ariana, but I hope you will find your visit interesting. I will introduce you to my crew—that should entertain you, at least."

Ariana glanced up at him as he led her along the hall. "As your captive?"

"I think . . . as my guest."

"Then they don't know what you've done?" She paused.

"Fia did seem surprised when you mentioned I'd hired you."

He sighed. "Probably thought there was money in it. She'd prefer that to kidnapping you, no doubt."

Ariana didn't respond. She wondered what the young Fia would think of her, if she would be considered a threat or an enemy. She couldn't help a surge of envy that the young girl had known Damen so well, through all the years when Ariana had been without him.

The ship's halls curved, and with each turn, a new color decorated its inner hull. Doors were numbered with gold lettering, and near the end of the largest hall, Ariana spotted an arched passage. She stopped. "Where does that door lead?"

"It leads to my quarters." Damen smiled. "Perhaps you will visit me there later?"

"I will not." Already, she wondered what sorts of things he had stored as personal possessions, on what sort of bed he slept, what he kept for clothing and artifacts. "I couldn't care less about your quarters."

"Ah." He gestured to a larger doorway across the hall. "Then perhaps this will interest you more. You might find the dining hall welcoming, at least."

Ariana peeked in and saw one long table, with two shorter wings, all laid out with crystal and bright silver platters. She shook her head and sighed. "You live like princes."

"Kings, my lady. Kings."

"The price of malloreum fuel grows ever higher, I suppose."

He smiled. "It does."

Further down the hallway, Damen indicated another door. Here, the gold lettering was decorated with violet jewels, and in large letters of the Intersystem language was written, proudly, *FIA*, and beneath, a long series of titles starting with First Officer in charge of crew, deportment, scheduling. . . . Ariana stopped reading the list and glanced at Damen, who shrugged. "One queen."

"This is not the decoration left by the Automon. It's quite . . . homey."

"For much of our lives, this ship is our home."

He led her into an elevator, which whisked them first upward, then forward at a slightly uneven speed. Ariana gripped a rail to steady herself, but Damen took her arm in support. They looked at each other quickly, then away. *I want him.* She needed time alone, to think, to contemplate what had happened to her. Her greatest love had returned, but as a man who by rights was an enemy. And he had taken her captive. It couldn't be said that he was unkind—and his dark, smoldering gaze ignited something much more dangerous, and compelling, than fear. Ariana shook her head. "I'm confused."

"Apparently so."

She drew a long breath, then shot him a dark glance. He stood there, tall and strong, and so handsome. Ellowan men were beautiful, long-limbed, with fair, bright faces and black hair, but none she had ever seen exuded the exotic masculinity Damen possessed. Women revered Hakon almost as a god for his golden-haired good looks, but she had known him since they were small children, and it hadn't been possible to see him through anything but sisterly eyes. But this man . . . a man she had once loved—he was different. And he looked at her as if he knew her every thought, every desire.

Again, he seemed to read her thoughts. "You don't know what you want, Ariana. Not yet. Tonight, when you lie alone, you will think of it. You will think of me." His voice sank to a low, sensual depth and Ariana stood transfixed. She wanted to shake her head, to issue some bright, pert mockery, but no reaction came except a small, muted gasp. A slow smile grew on Damen's lips, and he leaned slightly toward her. "And when you think of me, know that I am thinking of you, too. Then you will come to me, and when you do, I will answer every tiny sigh you utter, every plea. . . ."

A high squeak burst from her throat and she hopped

back, bumping into the elevator door. She expected him to laugh, but he didn't. "I . . . I am your prisoner. I can hardly be expected to . . . visit you . . . at any point in time, for *anything*."

"I shall leave your door unlocked. For now, you can do no harm, nor do I think it in your best interest to try."

She shook her head. "You, my captor, are telling me you'll leave my prison unlocked in order that I might visit you in the night, for sultry purposes?"

He hesitated, then shrugged. "Yes."

"What makes you think I'll come to you?" Her brow furrowed. It would be easier if he came to her. She might resist, at first, and then he would be forced to seduce her. By coming to her, it would prove that the boy she remembered still existed somewhere in his heart.

His gaze traveled the length of her body and seemed to darken, his face turned sensual and his full lips curved as his dark eyes fixed again on hers. "You'll come."

"I won't." She swallowed. She watched in abject horror as he lifted his hand to his mouth, kissed the fingertips, then pressed them gently against her lips. Her whole body seemed to coil within and small tongues of fire lapped inside her.

She leaned back against the elevator door, but it swept open without warning, and she popped backwards, then stumbled onto the main deck of the ship. Her cheeks warmed as Damen's surprised crewmen turned toward her. Damen left the elevator tube and caught her arm, again. "A bumpy ride."

Ariana seized a quick breath, determined to deport herself with dignity, despite her confusion. She turned and saw Fia seated in a large central chair, complete with a panel and dials that indicated the captain's position. Fia eyed Damen, sighed, then rose with obvious reluctance. "I suppose you'll be wanting your seat, Damen?"

Damen smiled. "Thank you." Several crewmen issued

muted sighs of what sounded like relief. "Are we on schedule, Fia?"

Someone huffed, and Fia glared at a slender, dark-skinned young man who sat at a navigation panel. "Ahead of schedule, sir, and then some. She's been driving us like whorthogs to a trough!"

Fia's blue eyes turned frosty. "The captain directed his inquiry at his first officer, and not at the navigator, or any other of the lower-ranking officials. On a vessel such as this, ranking order must be followed."

The navigator rolled his eyes. "This ain't an Intersystem battle cruiser, Fee. We're a pirate ship, remember?"

She turned her head very subtly and pretended the navigator hadn't spoken, then cast a quick glance at Ariana. She looked . . . hopeful, and Ariana couldn't help but like the girl. Ariana smiled. "Intersystem battle cruisers do, indeed, have a very rigorous ranking order, and the higher ranks do command great respect." Actually, formality had long ago left the Intersystem fleet, and Hakon was most often addressed by his first name. But Fia didn't need to know that.

Fia nodded, pleased. "You see, Damen! Think how much more effective our missions would be if these people . . ." She sputtered, and Damen sighed.

"Feared you?"

"Yes!" She stopped and shook her head. "*Respected* me."

"They respect you now. They just don't bow."

"When I get my own ship . . ."

Damen seated himself in the captain's chair and gazed out the view port. "Then the galaxy had best beware. Until that time, however, I'd like your report."

Fia glanced out the view port, then indicated a red and golden planet in the distance. "Oh, that. The planet's there, upper right corner, seventh sector. I've blocked all Automon scanners, then sent in our usual signal. They think we're delivering."

"Very good."

Ariana moved to stand behind Damen's chair. "What is that planet? And what are we doing?"

Fia looked between them, surprised. "A Dark Sun, one of the newer colonies. We're going to break it up. Didn't Damen tell you?"

Chapter Eleven

Ariana turned to Damen, and her brow arched. "No, he didn't mention anything about rescuing colonies."

Fia looked pleased. "We've broken up many colonies, of course, but the Automon keep setting up new ones. Over the last few years, they've been quicker about it, and more brutal, so it's a hard job to keep up with them."

Ariana edged around Damen's seat to look at him. He kept his gaze on the view port, but he seemed uncomfortable. "You've been freeing other colonies? That hardly seems the duty of a pirate."

Fia beamed, cheerful. "Oh, we steal all their malloreum fuel, too, of course. We've gotten tons of it, you know. It's unbelievably valuable!" Her eyes gleamed at the thought of profit. "Just a cylinder or two, sold in secret to various Intersystem dealers, brings a vast amount. Think what we could do if we sold all we have, Damen!"

Damen cast a quick, dark look at his first officer, who fell immediately silent. "If you continue to inform the Intersystem's representative about our illicit dealings, we won't get the chance to profit from even one cylinder, will we?"

Fia eyed Ariana, innocent and surprised. "You won't tell, will you? You *are* one of us, really, and after all, we use it for a good cause."

Damen cleared his throat. "Thank you, Fia. But if you'd leave these explanations to me, from now on, I would appreciate it." He paused, meaningfully. "As a matter of *ranking order*, to which you, too, are subject."

Her face fell and she looked hurt, but too proud to argue. "Understood." She paused, but only for a moment. "Are you coming with us, Ariana?"

Ariana hesitated, then glanced at Damen. "I don't know. Am I?"

Damen looked between them. "I think it would be better for Ariana to remain here."

She frowned. "I want to go. You did promise that I'd see the Lord of the Dark Sun in action, after all."

"Invading a colony is not without danger, Ariana. You are weary—and we don't have time to brief you on our methods."

Fia clapped her hands. "She can accompany me on the ruse portion."

"No."

Ariana had no idea what "the ruse portion" meant, but she didn't like being discounted so quickly by Damen. "I will accompany Fia."

Fia smiled. "See? It will work better with two." She didn't wait for Damen's argument. "We can explain at dinner, which should commence shortly." She checked an arm band that held many dials, then poked at one. She held it close to her lips, speaking in a clear, raised voice. "Chef! Has the even meal been established and laid out in order?"

A weary sigh came across the small monitor. "Yes, mistress."

"Wine?"

"Yes."

"Very good." Fia clicked off her arm monitor and waved at the elevator door. "I assumed you'd want a special feast prepared, so I ordered Chef to locate some pleasant food-stuffs while we were on the outpost." She paused. "By the way, the navigator is being denied wine at dinner tonight because he was caught sampling it without my supervision."

The navigator made a face behind her back, but she turned sharply and administered a blistering glare upon him, and he shrank back. Pleased, Fia went to the elevator tube and entered, but she held the door open for a final command before it closed upon her. "I shall head down at once and see that everything is set up properly. You may follow shortly."

The door closed, and the crew issued a collective sigh of relief. The navigator leaned back in his seat and whistled. "Captain, there are times I think you've created a monster in that one."

Several voices chorused an echo, but Damen just smiled. "Sampled the wine, did you, Nob?"

The navigator grinned. "And damned fine vintage it was, too." He wiped his sleeve dramatically across his mouth, and the others laughed.

Ariana shook her head. "That young woman should be an Intersystem pilot. She doesn't belong with a bunch of pirates."

Nob leaned toward her. "The Intersystem ain't ready for that one, Miss. It's too . . . egalitarian for our Fee. She'd have the whole thing turned into the most tyrannical monarchy, with herself as despot. You don't know her."

"She seems very lovely and very bright."

Several men snorted, and a few laughed outright. Nob groaned. "And more than a few of us thought so, first time we met up with her. Oh, she's pretty, and no mistake. Old Graff over there even thought to make a play for her. . . ." A good-looking red-haired man near a computer panel clamped his hand over his eyes and groaned. "Remember that, Graff? Just one look from those cold blue eyes, and he got turned to ice. Think she had him locked in his quarters for two days before Damen realized what had happened to him."

Damen smiled. "She's a strong-willed child, and she knows her own mind."

Ariana gazed down at him, stunned by the strange interaction with his crew. He was proud of the girl, *like a father*. Ariana fought her own emotion and touched his shoulder. "She just hasn't met the right man yet."

Nob chortled to himself. "There ain't no man that can handle *that*, Miss. Hell, maybe one of them Automon!" He paused, then shook his head. "Naw . . . she'd freeze one of them, too."

The others laughed, and Damen rose from his seat. "If you gentlemen have your gauges set, then set the ship for standard Automon orbit, and join us for dinner."

Nob stretched and rose. "Good enough, sir. Like a chance to get to know your woman."

Ariana glanced at Damen, and to her surprise, color tinged his dark cheeks. "I understood I was your prisoner."

He cleared his throat. "For this even meal, you are my guest."

The others rose, too, leaving their posts with a casualness that astonished Ariana. "Aren't you afraid the Automon will spot you?"

"We expect them to. But for now, this ship will be considered as just another delivery vessel. We have nothing to fear—not yet, anyway."

"You seem awfully calm."

"Standard operating procedure, my lady."

"Ah."

Damen's crewmen gathered around the elevator door, and waited for her to enter first. She felt a breath of relief that she wouldn't be alone with Damen, and strangely at home amongst the odd assortment of pirates. Graff, the red-haired man who had apparently made the mistake of propositioning Fia, stood beside her as Damen engaged the elevator grid.

"You probably don't remember me, Miss, but I remember you."

She looked up at him—a young face, pleasant and intelligent. "I'm sorry. I don't recognize you."

"Figure I look different than I did."

Her throat tightened, though she wasn't sure why. "You were in the cavern, too?"

Graff edged back his shirt and revealed a brand like Damen's. "I weren't quite so old as you, but I remember the day you came to us. That day . . . changed everything." He paused and tapped his chest proudly. "It was me who tossed Damen his first stave, you know. Never liked the old leader—stupid brute, he was, though I think he was my brother or something like that."

Ariana stared. "Were many of you . . . there?"

"Oh, some, yes. Most now on this ship come from some of the other colonies. The first rebels, they're mostly captaining their own. . . ."

Damen again cleared his throat, a pertinent warning. "I hadn't realized my crewmen were so lax in their disclosures. I will thank you all to remember that Ariana is the daughter of the Intersystem Prime Representative, whose Council has outlawed our tradings in malloreum fuel, and from whom our secrets are best withheld."

Graff didn't seem convinced. "But she's one of us, Damen. She was your woman first."

Damen glanced at Ariana and his expression turned faintly sad. "She was a princess first, and it would be wise for all of us to remember that."

So. He had his secrets, too. It seemed fair, but Ariana determined to learn every one of them. "I have no intention of betraying you, but neither would I turn aside my father's wisdom. However, for now, you have no reason to distrust me." She paused. "How is it that so many of the cavern tribe speak the Intersystem language? You have done more than free colonies, it seems."

Nob pressed his way from the back of the crowded elevator forward to get her attention. He was shorter than Graff and Damen, and his cheerful face and engaging manner endeared him to Ariana. "The Dark Sun School, Miss, that's a thing to be proud of! I'd say it's even a contender with the best of the Intersystem academies. Proud thing, that. Trains pilots, scientists, everything! Why, we've even got a museum, or maybe it's an art gallery—Damen had us take whole slabs of colony walls down, those as had drawings and pictorials."

Ariana's mouth drifted open as she turned to Damen. "Where?"

"We've established a free colony. Its location, however, isn't something I'd like the Intersystem to learn just yet."

For now, she didn't care what the Intersystem wanted. "Will I see it?"

He smiled. "With luck, yes. It's our next destination."

The elevator door slid open and Nob popped out, then eagerly stood back for Ariana to exit. Damen led her down the hall, and his crewmen followed, chattering like boys at the Academy, some about the upcoming mission, and others about a game they'd been playing. Others made bets about Fia's next order, and who would be forced to clean up the dishes.

Ariana walked as if in a dream. The energy of Damen's ship flowed so free, uninhibited, and somehow . . . youthful. These men, they had seen so much, and yet they remained filled with joy. If Damen had changed, if he had lost the sweet innocence of youth, he had somehow preserved it in those around him, and allowed it to thrive in abundance.

They entered the dining hall and found Fia standing formally near the head of the table. The crewmen gathered and seated themselves idly, still chatting, but Fia banged a silver spoon against a crystal goblet. "The captain should be seated first!"

No one noticed, or at least, they pretended not to, but Ariana waited for her direction before taking a seat. Fia looked appreciative, then directed her to the left of the head chair, then she herself took the right. "I am the first officer, and from what I have studied, that position occupies the right. In the event of another officer, perhaps medical, that person takes the left, unless the captain or king has a consort, in which case, she, or he if the captain is female, takes the left."

Ariana hesitated, bewildered, but it was obvious that Fia as well as the crew considered her Damen's 'consort.' Perhaps they remembered when she had been at his side in the cavern better than he did himself.

Fia waited for Damen to seat himself, then sat down, too. She sat more stiffly than the others, more formally. Ariana wondered what race the girl was from, for she resembled no one of the Intersystem peoples. And yet there was something familiar about her. Legend spoke of a race of mystics, long-limbed and elegant, but wielding a power that Fia hadn't evidenced. They were proud and beautiful, wise, but from a world distant from the Intersystem, and none had been contacted for many ages.

Damen took a platter from the chef, and spooned out a nut and vegetable combination onto Ariana's plate, then placed bread beside it. A smile that seemed almost shy formed on his lips. "This is the sort of meal you enjoy, isn't it? If you would prefer something else, we can summon the chef."

"This is perfect." She paused. "Thank you." He served himself, and she said no more, but she remembered their lives in the cavern, long ago. In the ritual of feeding, many men had simply tossed food at their mates, but Damen had always watched carefully to see what she liked. He had never assumed to know her mind as if she had been a possession. It appeared that this grace, at least, had remained true.

It was obvious that he'd raised Fia to think for herself, anyway. The girl seemed supremely self-assured, and her personality was definite and strong.

"Fia, have you heard of a race called the Daeron?" Ariana's question surprised the others, and they fell into a relative hush.

Fia took a small sip of clear wine, but looked blank. "I don't believe so. Have they much loot?"

Ariana smiled. "I'm not sure. To my people, they are

113

mostly just legend. But you remind me of the tales I've heard."

"Really? In what way?"

"The Ellowan contacted the Daeron, ages ago, before the first destruction of Valenwood, and found a race that loved music, dance, and had immense power, for they responded to our call from the greatest depths of space. The images we have recorded, which they sent to us, were of a very tall, light-haired people, and it seemed to me that they glowed, slightly, as you do."

"Do I glow?"

"There is a light around you, yes."

Nob scoffed across the table. "We know that light, Miss. It's the light of tyranny!"

Fia pretended not to notice Nob's comment and she took another sip of wine. "I keep myself polished well—many at this table do not make adequate use of the ship's bathing facilities."

Ariana smiled. "I, at least, would appreciate them. And if they're anything like the rest of this ship, I expect they're lavish indeed." She paused while a stout, round man with pink cheeks began serving their meal. The crew began stuffing spoons into the various soups and sauces, but Fia waited to be served, a look of pained resignation on her young face. "Are there no other women in your crew?"

Fia leaned forward, pleased with Ariana's question. "There aren't many women yet, and none besides myself on the Flagship, but several are working their way up through the ranks and will soon take their places beside their male counterparts. I have great hope that their influence will civilize the males, who, as you can see, can be somewhat crude in manner."

Ariana glanced at Damen. "How many ships do you command, anyway?"

He kept his gaze fixed on his plate. "Enough. And not a number I wish to share with the Intersystem." Again, he eyed Fia darkly for divulging too much, and she shrank back in her seat. She hesitated a moment as if in penance, then sat forward again.

"You look exactly as Damen described you, Ariana. Except that you have hair. I had thought you might resemble the other Intersystem females, those who were still in the cavern when I first arrived."

Ariana remembered Lissa and the others—what had become of them? "The other women were not Ellowan. Lissa was from Lower Nirvahda, akin to my mother's people, but they aren't as tall."

"That one didn't like me, though she always smiled. Was she your friend?"

"I knew her from my days at the Academy. We were friends, though I often regretted confiding in her. It was my fault that we were abducted, though, and I felt responsible for her fate."

Fia looked thoughtful. "I don't remember her well, but I got the impression that nothing happened to her that she didn't design herself."

"That is what Hakon always said of her, too."

"Hakon? Isn't that the name of the golden-haired prince who tried to steal you from Damen?"

Damen cringed beside Ariana, and she cast a knowing glance his way. "He is my *friend*, and a very wise person."

"He sounds arrogant."

Across the table, Nob snorted loudly. "Then maybe he's your long-lost brother, Fee."

Again, Fia ignored the crewmen's teasing, but a pink tinge to her pale cheeks indicated that their words hit their mark. Ariana repressed a smile. "Hakon is very brave, and he is self-assured, as you are. He is much admired."

Fia brightened. "Perhaps that explains why Damen is so jealous of him."

Damen rose from his seat abruptly. "I think this concludes our meal. We have a job to do, in case you've all forgotten. Fia, to the tube, and Nob, get the casing."

Ariana had no idea what he was talking about, but she followed Fia eagerly. Damen left her at a lower passage, and seemed to be avoiding her eyes. "What will you be doing, Captain? Gathering malloreum for a steep price, or will I see you sooner?"

He smiled. "I'll start by offering up my greatest treasure. . . ."

Her eyes narrowed. "What treasure?"

His smile widened. "My dearest. . . . You."

Chapter Twelve

She shouldn't be afraid. After all, Fia lay calmly beside her, her legs and torso bound in the same Automon casing in which Ariana had once woken to find herself. She knew it was the slender Nob inside the black Automon disguise, but he moved with such an eerie likeness to the real Automon that she could too easily forget his humanity.

Fia continued giving orders as the ship lowered toward the planet's surface. "Have you sent the code for two instead of one? We don't want to confuse them, Nob!"

"Done it, Fee. But you'd better hush yourself lest they pick up your voice on auto-transmission."

Ariana felt nervous. "Are you sure this will work, Fee . . . Fia? What if they send more than two Automon for us? They have gas, you know."

"They won't use it—they think Nob is an Automon, re-member, and they don't like to gas prisoners more than once. Too many humans are susceptible to its fumes, and some succumb to death after its inhalation."

Ariana didn't respond. The grim memory rose in her

mind of a girl, dark-skinned like Nob, lying dead beside her, cast out into space. *Culled.* Ariana closed her eyes. "Perhaps I shouldn't have come."

"We'll be fine." Fia sounded relaxed, as if she'd done this many times, and had no fear. But the past returned unexpectedly to Ariana, and she remembered that first time she'd confronted her own vulnerability, her helpless terror. Still it was Fia beside her, not Lissa, and rather than fear, the air seemed tangible with self-confidence.

Nob casually engaged the hull monitor. "Group Twenty-nine speaking Language Four, engaged for distribution. Two captured, two living."

Nob had altered his voice to match the toneless Automon speech, but it was almost too real for Ariana. Her pulse quickened, and the old fear grew inside her.

A bell rang, startling her, and activity began all at once. Gears churned and echoed from her memory. Nob positioned himself by the open door, waiting silent and motionless. Ariana felt drawn back into the past, as if she was sliding into it, helpless to stop herself from crossing back into a nightmare. She struggled, but the casing Nob had bound around her held fast. Fia glanced at her and nodded her approval, as if Ariana were acting, but Ariana's panic refused to abate. Footsteps, too even for life, echoed up a long hallway. Those same footsteps still echoed in her nightmares, ten years later. Her heart throbbed in her breast.

The door whisked open and two Automon appeared. They turned, their creaking, jointed necks moving in unison as they seemed to greet the first Automon. Ariana closed her eyes. *It is Nob, only Nob. They won't hurt me this time.*

"Two females," reported Nob. "Both living. Distribution secured."

The real Automon positioned themselves beside Fia and Ariana, and Nob stepped back. Several smaller Automon entered, the same types she remembered from her first captivity. They removed her casing, then Fia's. Ariana started to rise, but Fia shot her a quick look of warning. Despite her fear, Ariana understood. She was supposed to be weakened by the poisoned gas—she couldn't leap to her feet unaided now without rousing their suspicion.

She hesitated, but an Automon grabbed her hair and pulled her up. It led her from Damen's ship, and she glanced frantically back to see the door close, with Nob left inside the ship. Another Automon dragged Fia along, but still the girl didn't seem frightened. *It is all part of the plan*. . . .

The heavy, pungent smell of lava and rock met her nostrils—and the distinct tinge of malloreum fuel tinged all the air. Two short Automon appeared, and Ariana stopped, not by her own will, but because her legs refused to move or bend. These square, multi-limbed Automon, she recognized. Too often, they had haunted her dreams. Too often, she had woken screaming, even on the warm, still nights in Valenwood, years after her abduction.

Why am I so afraid? Since that time when she had first been confronted by her own vulnerability, she had proven herself many times, on many missions more dangerous than this. Damen had reminded her of that fact. She had been brave—at times, fear hadn't made an impact on her when all around her had been terrified. She thought, then, that it had been because she had already known ultimate loss, and terror, and survived it. But here, on this replica of an Automon ship, reliving that first fear, she remembered what it felt like to be powerless, to have fear consume her.

Ariana began to tremble, but her guard shoved her forward, then bent her head forward. Her scream echoed her earlier cry, years ago. Tears blinded her like a sudden rainstorm, and she fought. Dimly, she was aware of Fia's surprise, but Ariana had lost touch with her mission, with where she was and who she was. All she remembered was this device that tore away her hair, her identity, *her self*. It was a primitive fear, one she never thought she would face again.

The short Automon began its clipping noise and Ariana fought harder, wilder than she had ever been, sobbing. She punched its hard shell and it rang with the force, but her fist made no dent. She punched again, harder, and still it bent her head forward. She heard Fia behind her, "Ariana! No, wait!"

But Ariana slammed her fist, now bleeding, into the short Automon. Footsteps echoed up the ramp, someone raced toward them. No Automon, it was a man. Ariana's captors moved, as always, slowly and methodically, turning without surprise to assess the new force. There was no time.

Damen bounded into the hall, followed by several other men. He leapt forward, whirled and kicked the shorter Automon aside. Ariana dropped to her knees, still sobbing. She saw him as she fought—he held a large weapon of some sort, but he didn't fire it. Instead, his body was the weapon, and his crewmen fought likewise. Someone tossed Fia a laser pistol, and she quickly disabled her captor. In short moments, the Automon guards were disrupted, then disengaged.

Ariana still knelt, trembling and shocked. She fought back her sobs, but her tears still flowed. Damen sank to his knees beside her and gathered her into his arms. He cradled her head against his shoulder and kissed her hair, then smoothed it from her face. "Ariana, my treasure. . . . Don't cry."

She looked up at him, her eyes wide with fear, with shock, but she couldn't speak. He took her wounded hand and bound it in a white cloth. Shock had driven away pain—she hadn't felt the sting of the cuts until now.

Damen kissed her forehead, and she saw tears in his own dark eyes. "I thought you knew what we had planned. I wouldn't let any harm come to you." He kissed her again, then closed his eyes. "I thought you knew. Didn't Fia tell you?"

Ariana shook her head, then swallowed, struggling to regain a semblance of her composure. "She said we would be fine, that you had everything under control. But when they came, Damen . . . It was just like when they first took me, and I was so afraid. When they cut off my hair, it was as if

I was nothing." She paused, and sudden, uncontrollable tremors still wracked her body. "I have never let it be cut again."

He smiled, but pity drenched his expression. "Never a strand, Ariana. Not a strand will be lost because of me, I swear to you."

She looked up at him, and she felt safe. "Twice now, you have brought light into my darkest moments." Her trembling stilled, and her senses returned. Ariana took a deep breath. "I'm all right. Thank you."

"There's no need. I should have warned you in more detail of our plans."

"Fia warned me, but she is so used to trusting you that she didn't think I needed detail. Perhaps she was right." She gathered herself together and stood up. "What now?"

"Now, I think, you should go back to the ship. Let us handle the rest."

Ariana smiled. "The worst, for me, is over. I will go on with you."

"Are you sure?"

She took a quick breath. "I don't know what came over me. I have endured much worse than this."

He smiled, too, gently, but concern still showed on his face. "I know. But perhaps the memory is what frightens you. There is no need to continue, Ariana."

Ariana dusted herself off, then pulled her hair back from her forehead. "I'm fine. What do we do now?"

She wondered for a moment what it would be like to stop now, to go somewhere alone with him, and to lose herself in his arms. To feel safe, *protected*, as she had only felt, truly, in this man's embrace. Interrupting her thoughts, Damen gave her a short, lightweight laser rifle. "I designed these to work against Automon shields. Our task is to disable the Automon one by one. If we tackle them this way, our task becomes much easier."

Ariana fingered the rifle. "What happened the first time you tried?"

They headed down the long metallic tunnel together, and

Damen lowered his voice. "Many died, but in the attempt, we learned a great deal. For one thing, only a limited number of us can confront them. Larger groups touch off their signaling device. So smaller numbers have a greater advantage. When the majority of the Automon are defeated, the others simply stop."

"How odd! Why is that?"

Damen hesitated. "I'm not sure, exactly." He spoke slowly, and she guessed he kept part of his suspicion to himself. "It is as if the greater power, or *consciousness*, that controls them doesn't react to small attacks, and then simply turns away when the larger groups falter. No single colony has much importance to . . . whatever that force is."

Ariana eyed him closely. "A person, a living entity, do you think?"

"I cannot say, not yet. But since childhood, I have *felt* something in connection with the Automon. They do not live, yet there is life behind them."

"I felt that, too, when I first woke on their ship."

Damen glanced at her. "Your race, the Ellowan, is perceptive, they say."

Ariana's brow furrowed. "There is something strange about the Automon. They terrified me at first, and they are relentless and efficient in attack. But not brutal or cruel, as are evil people who gain power from inflicting pain. There's something . . . sorrowful about them, not *in* them, you understand, but about them."

Damen nodded. "I have felt this, too."

"But if the being that controls them isn't cruel, why do this at all?"

"To that, I have no answer."

He slowed, and nodded ahead to an annex in the tunnel. "The others await us there, Graff and the rest. Fia is with them. Keep silent, and stay with me."

Ariana's own training and experience began to come back to her. As soon as they joined the others, she picked up her task and adjusted quickly to their silent signals. Damen said nothing, but she caught his admiring glances, and found she liked his approval. They came to a tube entrance that Ariana recognized as a feeding tube, then another where captive females were dumped upon the waiting males. She heard nothing but the familiar ache and groan of the molten lava, and quieter, more discordant, the metallic sounds of Automon machinery at work, processing the malloreum fuel the slaves had mined.

Damen nodded at a narrow alcove, which allowed in what minimal light the dark planet provided. Ariana glanced out and saw a black metallic building. He mouthed the word, "malloreum," and she guessed this was where they stored the precious malloreum cylinders. Fia glanced out the alcove, too, and her eyes narrowed with a greedy light.

Damen tapped his heir's shoulder as a reminder of their purpose, and she fixed her attention on the bridge ahead, though she looked a little wistful. They proceeded downward, until Damen held up his hand, and went on ahead. He came back smiling, then with his hand motion, signaled his crew's advance.

So much that they communicated left words behind, and useless. Expressions, gestures, they were second nature to these people of the cavern, however advanced they had become otherwise. It made them a formidable force. Ariana's time among them had left more than memory. She found she recognized much of his meaning, and that she followed instruction without being left too far behind.

They spotted the Automon guards standing motionless near an entrance to what Ariana guessed was the first malloreum reception area. Another group of Automon marched slowly across a narrow, unrailed bridge, each bearing carts of raw malloreum. Slowly, methodically, the fuel changed hands, and was set into tubes and placed in tankards near the malloreum station. With that done, the Automon for a brief while were on the bridge together, and at that moment, Damen gave his signal.

His crew moved with all the grace and stealth the Automon lacked. They positioned themselves at angles facing the bridge, hidden behind boulders and outcrops of hardened lava. As one, they fired, and Ariana fired, too. She hit her target and saw an Automon freeze, no less alive than it had been before, but immobile and impotent. Damen glanced at her and smiled, and her heart warmed.

The other Automon reacted, slowly, but without fear or the emotion of falling under unsuspected attack. They simply turned in the direction of the attack and commenced releasing streams of greenish gas. Here in the heavy air of the Dark Sun planet, its reach was cut short, and it came nowhere near Damen's crew. That completed, Damen signaled his crew to move closer, and again, they fired a barrage of immobilizing power.

It seemed easy, but Ariana realized this method had come about after much practice, and probably much loss. Over and over, Damen's crew fired, then moved closer. More and more Automon appeared, none hurried, none afraid, and all met with the same frozen fate.

When no more came, Damen emerged from the rocks, and they went down among their frozen enemies. Ariana went to one that she had shot and examined it. "How odd! They're hollow!"

Graff knelt beside her. "Strange thing, isn't it? We don't have a clue how they operate."

Ariana fingered the Automon's sensors. "These panels are receptors of some sort. They take in information, or energy, here, though I have no idea how." She rose and looked at Damen. "But what kind of energy?"

Damen didn't answer, but Graff shook his head. "Who knows? Whatever it is, it's strong enough to direct them all over the galaxy, or close to, anyway."

Ariana laid her palm on its black hull. "Once, these things terrified me so, just the sight of them. And yet, they seem so . . . helpless. There's something sorrowful about them."

Fia walked up and touched it, too. "I have felt this, too. We have taken a few for our museum—the children like them. Almost, you can feel sorry for the Automon."

Graff snorted. "They're pieces of machinery! What's to care about?"

Ariana sighed. "I don't know. But Fia is right, now that I see them this way. It's as if . . . as if they were made for some other task, and here they are, performing cruel, greedy, barbaric acts—all the things humans dislike doing themselves. And yet one feels that only a living thing, a thing with the capacity for both good and evil, could have set the Automon to such a task."

Damen touched Ariana's shoulder. "Once, I feared them, too, for it seemed they held life and death in their grasp, and valued neither. Now, they are nothing, just machines."

Ariana pressed her palm against the Automon's cold shell. "Not just machines, Damen. They were made to resemble humankind. Why?"

Damen didn't answer. He nodded toward a larger entrance, wrought with lava rock and metal together. "Come. Our next task awaits."

Together, Damen's group headed down along the long, winding tunnels, deeper into the volcanic hills of the Automon colony. As they maneuvered inward, Ariana saw differences between the colony where she had been held, and this newer one, but the Automon structure was the same. They ran past mining facilities, and then Damen and only a few members of his crew disabled the remaining Automon. So far, they had seen no humans, but by the tasks of the Automon, it appeared the day's work was complete.

Ariana glanced at Damen. "How did you time your attack this perfectly?"

"There's little need—the Automon are always the same in this regard. First, we will find and free the captive males below—the females, the mothers and children, we will find on a higher level above."

"But they won't know who you are, or what you're doing here. Isn't that dangerous?"

"It can be. But all living things desire freedom. When I have communicated this to them, I think you'll see little resistance."

Apparently, Damen had done this many times, but Ariana still felt nervous. Those young men fought first, and without language, would be hard pressed to understand who or what Damen was, let alone what he offered.

They came to the great Automon doors, much like those that had penned in Damen's first colony. Graff engaged several levers, and the doors ground open. Immediately, loud cries sounded from the cavern. Though she discerned no words, Ariana understood surprise. The Automon were nothing if not scheduled, so this opening must have caught the tribe off guard.

Ariana stood back as the doors grated open, but Damen took his place at the fore of his crew. He stood for a moment in the open threshold, with the light of smoldering red lava silhouetting his tall body. Ariana watched him as if taken by a dream. Never had she imagined to see him, never again to stand in this strange world. When she had loved him, he had been as a king. Now, he was something much more.

Still as if in a dream, Ariana watched as the events unfolded before her. The cavern leader approached. He was much younger than Damen had been, no more than sixteen, if that, but he was the oldest among those within. A group of smaller boys followed him, eyes wide as they approached Damen. All held weapons—the leader's was decorated with some sort of tassel. The crystals associated with malloreum fuel still hung on the cavern ceiling, but much higher than in the one she had known—out of reach. And so, the tribe within chose more accessible symbols to make themselves . . . *people*.

Only a few women joined the others—none appeared pregnant, or at least, not noticeably so. Ariana scanned the rock formation, then moved to tap Damen's shoulder. "They have not been here long. Look! There on the cavern wall, the last lava flow cannot have been more than a few months ago."

Damen nodded, but the young leader issued a strange cry, then moved forward again, staring as if wonder overcame him. Damen smiled, and again Ariana thought of him as a father. So strong, he was, but so gentle, and so kind.

He held out his hand, but the leader raised a stave. Behind Ariana, Fia puffed an impatient breath.

Damen didn't speak, but he communicated. With his hands, with his body, he urged the young tribe closer. His crew moved forward, then among them. The boys hopped back, some even sniffed at the newcomers, and then daringly touched the older men's arms. To Ariana's surprise, Nob hurried down the cavern hall behind them, dragging an Automon shell. With a wild cry, the cavern tribe burst into celebration. They recognized their lifelong enemies' defeat, and they recognized the victor.

"Sorry I'm late, sir." Nob paused for a breathless gasp. "First one I picked up broke apart on me, and the second one had oily joints. This one here, figured it's a good one."

Damen made a sweeping motion with his arm, indicating that all Automon lay likewise. Tears swarmed the cavern leader's eyes, and he sank to his knees before Damen. It was the worship of a god. Ariana held her breath, but Damen knelt, too, then placed his hand on the boy's shoulder. He placed his hand over his heart, then over the boy's. Ariana knew what he conveyed: *I was once as you are. We are equal.*

She exhaled a breath of relief that surprised her. He had been offered the power of a god, and had turned it aside. Whatever else Damen claimed to be, the prince she had first seen inside him remained deeper and truer than any pride.

Damen rose, and motioned to the tribe. Hesitant but eager, they followed, and he led them from the cavern. Ariana watched, mesmerized, as a few of the boys, and the young women, too, gathered their meager belongings. Food and clothes, such as those things were, they left behind. What mattered to them were their small artifacts, the carved stones, the molded lava, the beads and decorations they had made themselves.

A few stopped to look back at this, their dark, smoldering home, as if those few understood that wherever fate took them, this place had molded what they first were. And then they, too, followed Damen and his crew up along the hall.

By the time Damen had found the route to the maternal colony, many of the tribesmen had begun to understand his purpose. Some ran on ahead, directing the way, eager to see those women they could only have left behind a few short months ago.

Ariana was too overcome with emotion to speak, but as Graff and Nob opened the gateway to the mothers, Damen took her hand and squeezed it. Women poured from their confinement. Only a few held babies or small children. Because this tribe was new, breeding hadn't commenced seriously again. So it was mothers meeting sons only a short while parted that Ariana witnessed now.

Boys with slight beards hugged thin, bedraggled women, weeping. The mothers cried and held their children. As she watched, Ariana realized from their faces, *mother's* faces, that many had known of the lava fall, and many had believed they would never see their children again. Without realizing it, Ariana herself was crying and she held Damen's hand tight. She knew, had fate been different, had she never left the cavern, it might have been herself whose child had been forced from her arms and thrown into those pits, a slave.

She looked up into Damen's dark, beautiful face and saw tears glistening on his high cheekbones. Every time he freed a mother to return to her son, he must remember his own mother. Fia came up beside them. Though she said nothing, Ariana saw the girl's tears, tears she restrained because she was proud, and because perhaps her heart was so vast and so strong that emotion would always be there. Again, Ariana was reminded of the mystic Daeron, but Graff climbed up along a rock wall, and called back to them.

"Same cursed thing again, Captain. From here, these women could see the lava dam. They would know when it was released, though mercifully they would never see the results."

Damen sighed. "It has been so in every colony. Not a deliberate cruelty by the Automon, but a bitter sight for those of us who have lived here." He turned to the colony, then motioned to his men. "Come, we must go. In a short while, the Automon signals will have gone out, and more will come."

Ariana hesitated. "Shouldn't we wait, and fight them, too? Won't they just set up another colony?"

"So we feared ourselves, at first, but that is not the case. The Automon seem to consider their losses permanent. Now that the colony has been discovered and invaded by 'an enemy,' they will abandon it. There are more, but in time, we will rout them all out."

"What about all these people? Do you have room on your ship for everyone?"

"There is no need." Without explanation, Damen guided his group back to the landing platform, and the eager tribe followed him. Ariana watched as members of Damen's crew dispersed, then busied themselves loading malloreum fuel into Damen's vessel.

She sighed. "So now you pillage?"

Damen looked pleased. "It is the price we charge for our hardships."

The tribesmen helped, surprising Ariana, and soon the fuel cylinders filled Damen's hold. But members of his crew began investigating the other Automon ships, then chose three for conquest. Fia eyed Damen brightly. "Well? You promised!"

He issued a long, drawn out sigh, then murmured, "They have to grow up sometime." He paused, then sighed again. "Very well, you may have your pick of the ships, and take the crewmen of your choice to navigate."

Both Nob and Graff eased back, but Fia deliberately overlooked them. "You, there, with the small nose and little oval head. You seem a good navigator, and a good warrior. I name you my first officer." She paused as a young man behind Graff looked first right, then left, then at Fia in astonishment. She frowned. "Yes, you. What is your name?"

His eyes wandered to one side. "Reidworth, sir. . . . Miss! But I don't know nothing much about navigating."

"We have guides aboard. Study them!" Fia turned to her

next victim. "And you, whose name is Pottisense. You will accompany me, by virtue of the fact you don't talk too much, and know something of ship engineering. We shall devise a cook later. Perhaps among the new colony." She eyed a particularly pudgy female of the new colony, and motioned her near. Without words, Fia managed to convey both the importance of the job and the necessity for this woman to bear it. With her toddler child in tow, the woman followed Fia onto the Automon ship.

Damen watched her go, then sighed heavily. "She forgot to say good-bye."

A loudspeaker crackled in the heavy ashen air. "Damen! I have secured my vessel, which I hereby title *The Queen's Vengeance*. I shall take up the first position behind your flagship, and let the others follow where they may." A pause followed. "I thank you for entrusting me with this opportunity." A much longer pause followed, and her voice came small and somewhat embarrassed. "And I, of course, love you, my captain and father."

Nob chuckled, then slapped Damen's shoulder. "That's just about as misty as she gets, sir. Shall we board?"

Ariana gazed up at Damen. "It was very sweet."

He smiled, but the tenderness in his gaze pierced her heart. "She has never called me her father before."

Ariana had been looking for the boy she had known, but the man she had found instead proved even more intriguing. Soon, she would speak all her heart to him, and all that had gone so wrong when she had lost him would be regained. "You would be. . . ." Ariana swallowed to contain her own emotion. "You would be a very good father."

He eyed her doubtfully. "I know nothing of families, Ariana. Not really. I am the only parent Fia has known, so she considers me of that worth. I am not sure it is deserved."

Ariana smiled. "My Lord of the Dark Sun, you are capable of much greater things than you know."

Chapter Thirteen

Damen lay on his back in his quarters, staring at the low ceiling. His duties had kept him from Ariana since they had boarded his ship, but his thoughts had never strayed far from her. He wanted to be alone with her, to talk, to see how she was feeling. He wanted to know if the same light of desire he'd seen earlier still burned in her eyes. But the memory of her fear when he'd found her in the Automon grasp—that image haunted him as he lay alone.

He had wanted to take her somewhere safe and calm, and love her. He wanted that now. But he wasn't sure how to approach her when so much had passed between them. She responded whenever he touched her—that much was certain. But along with the desire in her eyes, he also saw fear, and doubt. She didn't trust him, and there was no reason she should. He didn't want her trust, not when the path that lay before him demanded uncertain twists.

But he wanted Ariana.

Someone knocked on his door, and Damen's heart leapt to his throat. He'd asked her to come, after all, but that she was taking him up on it . . . He gulped, then rose and went to the door. He glanced at himself in his mirror, straightened his hair, and tried to look casual. He paused, then unfastened a button on his shirt, then another. He cleared his expression, then engaged his door panel. As it slid open, his pulse quickened.

"Sorry to bother you, sir." Nob looked in and past Damen, unabashedly looking for Ariana's presence. He eyed Damen's open shirt doubtfully. Damen's heart sank and he edged Nob back from his doorway.

"What is it, Nob?"

Nob looked at once pleased, slightly alarmed, and chagrined. "It's our Fee and her new ship."

Damen sighed. Yet another duty to keep him from his contemplation of Ariana. "Is there a problem?"

"Looks like it, sir." Nob didn't bother to hide his grin now. "The thing is, minute we took off, her new ship, *The Queen's Vengeance* or whatever she calls it—Graff and me, we were saying it should have been called *The Tyrant's Missile. . . .*"

"Get on with it, Nob."

Nob nodded. "Anyway, first thing, Fee's ship headed backward, then off in the wrong direction."

Damen grimaced. Apparently Fia's new navigator hadn't found time to study his guides in the brief moments before takeoff. "What happened?"

"Well, she didn't contact us, so we wired over to her, figuring she could use some help."

Damen drew a patient breath. "And were you able to help her?"

"Nope. Said she could handle it."

"Did she . . . handle it?"

"Seems so, sir. Now she's got *The Dictator's Doom* on a straight course with ours. Just sent a curt message saying that her 'recruit is already immersed in his studies.' "

Damen visualized the scene—the boy wouldn't sleep for days, but he would probably become the finest, and most obedient, officer in the galaxy. "That sounds good. Fia can handle a ship." He paused. "Why are you troubling me with this news?"

"Figured you ought to hear it, sir."

"I have a monitor in my room, Nob."

"Didn't want to interrupt anything."

"I see." He did see, all right—he had the nosiest crew in the galaxy. "Is there anything else?"

"Thought you might want a report on your woman."

Damen hesitated. "What report?" Nob shrugged idly, and seemed likely to draw this out beyond Damen's endurance. "Now, Nob."

Nob winced. "Sorry, sir. Well, she's done a fine job, she has. Been below deck with the new colonists, helping to feed them and got them in better suits. Thought she did a fine job, too, down on the planet. Good addition to your crew, sir."

"I'm pleased you approve." He paused, not wanting to question Nob further, but still, wanting to know. "So she's busy below deck, then?"

"Not anymore, sir. Got them all situated, she did, she and Graff and some of the others. She said she was going to her quarters."

"Ah. She must be tired." She was probably already asleep. Damen restrained a sigh of regret.

"Don't think so, sir."

Damen's eyes narrowed to slits. "Why not?"

"Well, she went to her quarters for a little while, but then she came out again."

"Where did she go?" And just how closely was his crew watching Ariana, anyway?

"Oh, here and there. All over, really. Kind of wandered around, checked in on the bridge to ask if Fia was all right on her new ship then headed off down to the galley, then to the view port."

She might have been looking for him. And like a fool, he'd been waiting for her in his room. It was asking a lot to expect Ariana to come for him there. Yet to pursue her openly—he risked driving her away. Still . . . he often walked around his ship during the night-replica hours. Damen glanced past Nob into the hallway.

"Thinking to go for a walk, sir?"

Damen glared. "That is none of your concern."

Nob shrugged. "Because if you were, thought you ought to know, the lady went back to her quarters again. I saw her when I was coming down the hall."

Even if she had been coming to him, seeing Nob would have driven her off. Damen frowned. "Thank you, Nob. If there's nothing else . . ."

"Can't think of anything, sir." He paused. "Good job we did today, sir. Felt good to rescue such a young group. Not so much damage done as to the older ones, I'm thinking. Good to be working with you, Captain."

Damen's mood softened. "You did well today, too, Nob. Good night."

Nob left, cheerful. Damen waited in his doorway for a moment, gazed down the hall toward Ariana's room, then went back to his bed alone. If only he'd thought to walk the halls! But maybe it was too soon.

Someone knocked on his door again. Despite his almost certainty that it was Nob again, he couldn't help hoping Ariana had waited for his officer's departure, and now came herself. He jumped up, went to the door and engaged it, but saw Graff standing there, looking surprised as if he hadn't expected so quick a response.

"Sorry, sir."

"What is it?" He hadn't meant to be so abrupt, and unlike Nob, Graff wasn't the kind to pry. "Is there something wrong with my monitor, that my crew feels the need to bring their messages here?"

Graff looked bewildered, but he nodded. "Yes, sir, there is. Something wrong with your monitor, I mean. Nob had me tinker with the main panel so we could get a better routing to the other ship—Fia's new officer has been on the handle constantly trying to get help—and somehow, I disconnected yours. Mind if I fix it? Only take a minute."

Damen stood back, silent, and Graff hurried into his

quarters, ripped off the monitor panel and began tinkering. Maybe she had tried to raise him from her monitor, then given up. The whole ship conspired against him. Damen stood in his doorway, but he saw no sign of Ariana. Graff completed his task and held up his tools in victory. "All done, sir. Working fine now, she is."

"Thank you, Graff."

Graff came to the door, then hesitated. "Sorry to bother you, sir." He glanced around and looked a little disappointed. "Thought you'd have better company tonight." He sighed and shook his head, then headed off up the hall.

Damen frowned, felt the pangs of an imminent headache, then went back to his bed. He lay a long while, looking at the monitor, then at his door, then finally closed his eyes. Sleep crept over him, but another knock woke him with a jolt. Damen shot up in bed, his jaw set hard. He snapped his two buttons closed, then stormed to the door. He jabbed at the panel, shoved the door open against its natural speed, and growled, *"What?"*

Ariana hopped back, her eyes wide and her mouth parted in astonishment. Damen just stared. "Ariana. . . ."

"I didn't mean to bother you." Her voice came very small and somewhat tremulous. Damen reached for her, then backed away, then toward her again. He stopped and clamped his hand over his forehead.

"Ariana, I'm sorry. Come in."

She hesitated before entering. "It's not important."

He held up his hand and shook his head. "No, it's not you. . . . And it is important. It's just my crew. They've filed by here all night on various trumped-up reasons, and I thought . . ."

She looked confused, but she nodded. "If you're tired . . ."

"Not at all. I was just . . . working on the log." He tried not to blink, but her brow furrowed. She said nothing, but she reached up and fingered his hair. Damen gazed toward the ceiling as she fixed it—apparently, a portion stood out in the back.

A slow smile formed on her lips. "You were sleeping."

He smiled, too. "Not quite. I was lying down with a headache." If ever there was something a man didn't want to tell a woman, especially the woman he hoped had come to seduce him . . . Ariana looked at her feet, but he touched her shoulder, gently. "I hoped you would come, so much. This isn't the way I wanted to welcome you."

The vulnerability in her expression moved his heart. "I wasn't sure. I mean, I know you said so, but I have learned over the years that men say things, and don't really want those things they ask for."

He took her hand and held it. "When I say I want you here, know there is nothing in the universe I want more."

She looked around his room, shy, and suddenly, he felt shy, too. "I tried to sleep. . . ." Her voice trailed and she closed her eyes. "I couldn't."

He thought he knew what troubled her. "Your experience with the Automon today, that must be hard to shake."

Her brow arched and she smiled. "Actually, I hadn't thought of that again until you mentioned it." Her smile deepened and his heart skipped a beat. "It was my experience with you, in my room and in your elevator—those are the things that distract me, Damen, not the stuff of nightmares."

Better than he dreamed. . . . Damen swallowed hard and his whole body endured a wave of desire that threatened his already shaken state. "Are you sure?"

Her gaze lingered on his, her grey eyes darkening as she looked at him. "That I want you? Yes, I'm sure." Very gently, she reached to touch his face. "You have lived in my dreams for so many years. How could I lie in a bed alone, so near to where you are, and not come to you?"

Tenderness filled his heart and he touched her cheek. "If the tales of my crewmen are true, you paced the width and breadth of my ship before coming to this decision."

She bowed her head, then nodded. "I have debated much, not least what I feel for you."

"What do you feel?"

She peered up at him, thoughtful. "I'm not sure. You have lived in my dreams and in my memory for so long, but as something beautiful and pure, untarnished by the darker side of humanity."

Damen just stared. She had thought him beautiful, even though he'd been little more than an animal. When he'd seen her in a sunset glade with the most renowned prince of men, he had turned away like a shamed beast. And for a long while after that day, he had lived like one. "I cannot claim to be untarnished, my lady."

She sighed. "No, I can see that." Ariana moved slowly around his room as if seeking evidence of who he had become since she had lost him. She didn't pry, nor open drawers, nor even glance at his log console, but she seemed interested in what he had acquired over the years apart. She ran her hand over a carved wooden statue that depicted a raging beast, then stopped to examine a multihued crystal cluster of immense worth. She glanced over at him, her brow raised quizzically. "Loot, I presume?"

Damen smiled. "A pirate's treasure."

"Ah. . . ." She circled the room, and her gaze caught on his wide bed, then skipped over it as if embarrassed. She stopped and watched him thoughtfully, as if she'd absorbed a sense of his past from his berth. "You have seen much. More than I have, I think. It shows in your eyes, in the way you move, in everything. You know how appealing you are, how handsome, and how erotic."

He felt awkward, as if he stood before an angel, and the darkness of his own life loomed like a shadow between them. "Since I left you with another man on Valenwood, I cared little for love, nor where I fed my appetites. I have known many women who sought the same from me."

She didn't look away as he expected. She just looked a little sad. "I suppose, had things been different, I might have followed a similar path." This, he didn't like—to think of Ariana as some man's meaningless lover. He might be a beast, but she . . . she was something much more. She sighed again. "I had come to think that love hurt too much to ever seek again—and I have seen myself reflected in eyes of desire."

He had felt the same, so he couldn't fault her. And it was natural that men should covet her. Her beauty and spirit would inspire lust, but he didn't like the image, all the same. "Hakon?" Too much jealousy showed when he spoke that name, and Ariana's brow arched knowingly.

She placed her hand tentatively on the back of his shoulder, then massaged his muscle. Happiness swelled inside him at her touch, but he tried to remain casual. "I think I've told you this already—Hakon and I are too close to look at each other that way."

She believed this, obviously, but Damen wasn't fooled. That golden-haired, blue-eyed fiend wanted her. Given her attitude toward love, he'd been clever to make her consider him a friend. "If you say so. . . ."

"There are other men, and the Ellowan race is renowned for sensuality." Ariana paused. Her deft fingers worked their way to the back of his neck, and Damen closed his eyes. "Although Hakon's mother *is* primarily Ellowan herself. . . ." She was teasing him, the vixen, and he was falling for it.

Her soft, gentle hands worked from his neck to his shoulders, then along his spine. He loved her touch, so he tried to pretend her teasing didn't affect him. "Apparently, he's not sensual enough to have seduced you properly."

"I don't recall that he ever tried."

Perfect! He was decidedly jealous now. If this Hakon learned that he had a competitor for Ariana's affection, this state of affairs might change. "What prevented you from following the brazen path?"

Ariana's massage slowed, her hands warm on his skin. "I remember thinking I might lose myself in a man's embrace, and wondering what I might be if I turned to erotic pleasures. But then . . . I had other duties."

"Your family? They keep a close watch on you, then. Good!"

She eyed him quizzically, a small smile on her lips. "It

was important to me that I live well, to set a good example for my . . . people. But still, I wonder now what it would be like. . . ."

There was something about her mood that inflamed him. She might not have lived the "brazen path," but it was in her blood, all the same. He saw it in her bright eyes, he felt it in the warmth of her nearness. She had come to him, not for the past, but for a sample of those things he had experienced, as if through him, she might awaken to all she thought she had missed.

She had missed less than she thought. Erotic appetites were fed and forgotten, the women nameless soon after. And the heart was left emptier afterwards than it had ever been before. If anything, it showed how much he didn't have, and how lonely he was. But Ariana was looking at him as if he held some secret, and he didn't want to disappoint her, not when her mood aroused him this much.

Damen turned and took her hands. "Thank you, my lady. My suffering is much reduced." He smiled. "Gone, in fact."

"I'm pleased I could help."

He felt nervous, but there was nothing to do but ask. "We might find great delight together, you and I, my lady."

"Maybe that is possible. Before, I had the memory of you to hold. But you've taken that from me." He winced, but she patted his shoulder in a kindly gesture. "It's all right. I mean, I understand. You did care, I feel that. And you believed I was safe with another man."

"I believed that you loved him, and would soon marry him. I didn't learn until very recently that you hadn't."

"When?"

"About an hour before I interrupted your meeting at the tavern."

She clasped her hands together, surprised and, he knew, pleased. "How did you learn of my marital state?"

He hesitated. "Well, the ship that brought you . . . the pilot . . . He and I had words."

Her eyes widened in alarm. "What did you do to him?"

"Nothing . . . much. He wasn't entirely cooperative about

revealing matters pertaining to you. You command much devotion, no matter where you go. But I persuaded him, and in doing so, mentioned the foolishness of your husband in allowing you to undertake such a dangerous journey."

She huffed. "As if any husband of mine would have a say in what missions I accept!"

He folded his arms over his chest. "I might not be able to stop you, but by all the stars, you wouldn't be going without me."

Her expression altered from indignation to shy happiness, and she looked suddenly young. "That would be fair enough, I suppose. But I would not want my husband to leave without me, either."

"In such a situation, it would be best, I think, for a husband and wife to venture forth together, given that they'd know each other so well."

She seemed to like his response. "I agree." They hesitated, looked at each other, but she bit her lip as if fearing to say too much. "They would work well together . . . because they would *trust* each other so completely."

Here, he fell short.

His silence obviously disappointed her and she gazed at him wistfully. "So my pilot corrected you, and said I had no husband?"

"He said everyone expected you to wed this Hakon, and in time, you would, and that any man who dared harm you would answer to the proud and noble Hakon himself."

She didn't seem interested in her pilot's threat, but her brow furrowed in concern. "Did he tell you anything else? About my life, I mean?"

"No. At that point, I tossed him out the door."

She puffed a breath of relief. "So you haven't inquired into my personal situation deeper than that, before this venture?"

"I knew where you were, what missions occupied you. But to be honest, I didn't want to hear the details of your blissful life on Valenwood. I had seen you together with him. That was enough for my mind to bear."

"Good. . . ." She stopped herself, then smiled. "I would not want to know if you loved another, either." She paused. "Why haven't you taken a wife?"

"I considered it. I thought I might find a woman like myself, of ignoble birth, with whom I might settle down and find a measure of contentment. As you said of your own duties, I had Fia to consider. She knew nothing of my exploits—I had that much consideration, and she was often on our home world, schooling, which she took very seriously. But always, there was something missing in the women I chose. Their interest was physical, as I thought was mine, and no one ever occupied a place deep in my heart. I never met one I couldn't forget, or live without." *Except you.*

"I think it would hurt more if you had loved someone, more than just . . ." She paused, embarrassed. "*Experienced* them."

"Well put, my lady."

She looked at him closely, and it seemed to him that her grey eyes darkened as a shadow of desire crossed over her. "But those experiences . . . When I am near you, I feel what might be, if only my heart didn't ache this way. If only I didn't remember . . ."

The shadow seized him, too, and he placed his hands on her shoulders. "This I can teach you now, Ariana. What we might have together, that is beyond anything I have known. The ache, an ache we both feel, is a fire that burns hotter than endurance, and beyond the power of memory. It must be touched to be known."

She closed her eyes, and her whole face softened in her sensuality. "Then touch me, because I want to know."

He drew her closer, and let himself feel the warmth of her near before their bodies touched. "Then, my angel, you will know."

Chapter Fourteen

He had almost kissed her when Ariana's eyes opened suddenly. Damen restrained his impatience. "What?"

She gulped. "I think we should set certain . . . boundaries . . . parameters between us, first."

Damen frowned. "What 'boundaries'?"

"Well . . . it might be said that you are dangerous to me." *Not half as dangerous as you are to me.* "I will never let anything harm you."

"I do not speak of physical danger, but emotional."

"Hmmm. You may be right." In fact, it might be wiser for them to stay at opposite ends of the ship. When he first realized that he would see her again, because she was a threat to him and his plans, he had understood the threat. He had foreseen the heartache of their reunion—but not the joy of seeing her smile, of feeling her warmth as she stood facing him. "It might be wise to set up boundaries, after all." He paused. "Such as what?"

"Well, we agree that we share a common attraction."

"Yes."

She bit her lip. "At times, overwhelming."

"Yes."

"But we are both old enough to know that such emotional entanglements can yield pain, given who we are at this point in our lives."

"The price is high, without question. For both of us."

Her expression indicated solid agreement. "Besides that, we are engaged in conflicting missions, and will probably find ourselves at greater odds as this journey progresses."

"As we have already, that seems certain."

Her eyes narrowed. "For instance, I cannot allow your pilfering of malloreum fuel to go unreported, and the Intersystem will undoubtedly take steps to stop you."

"And *I* cannot allow the Intersystem to interfere with my profits."

A silence followed and then she peeked at him. "But I want you."

He swallowed. "I want you, too."

"But you must understand, I *must* return to Valenwood."

Whatever she felt for him, her heart was there, in that beautiful city of white tiles and glittering marble. He couldn't go with her, certainly, nor would he ever ask her to stay. "Until that time, I would have you, Ariana. It may be that nothing in your safe Intersystem world can compare with what I will give you here. There, you are a princess. But here . . ."

She smiled and her eyes flashed. "I am a barbarian. Still . . ." Her smile faded to seriousness. "You have taken me captive, after all. In a way, I am at your mercy."

It wasn't mercy he intended to show her tonight. "You came to me of your own accord."

"Yes, but you lured me here, using more subtle methods than force."

"Such as what?"

She huffed. "You know." She waved her hand absently at his body. "You look like . . . that. And the things you do . . ." Her voice trailed and a small shudder seized her. "The finger-kissing episode. . . . *You know.*"

143

Damen couldn't restrain a surge of pride, though the act hadn't been premeditated as she presumably imagined. "I would not say, my lady, that you can claim total innocence in this regard, either."

"What do you mean?"

"That you have done quite as much to lure me, if not more." He scanned her clothing and his gaze fixed on her bodice as it peeked out from beneath her brown jacket. He gestured at her soft, alluring cleavage. "That, for instance. . . . If it isn't an outfit designed to trigger a man's imagination, I don't know what is."

Her mouth widened in indignation. "This is standard Intersystem attire!" She paused, probably struggling with conscience. "I mean, for exploratory agents."

"You mean spies."

She didn't argue. "I thought it looked like something. . . ."

"Like something a pirate queen might wear? You were right. Whoever designed it gave ample consideration to highlighting your perfect little body in all the right places."

"I designed it myself!" As if realizing the impact of what she said, Ariana blushed, then shook her head. "I designed it purely for comfort."

"Which is why every bit, from your shoulders to your ankles, hugs every enticing curve? Generally, comfort is found in loose, flopping, baggy robes."

She grimaced, and Damen laughed. She eyed his body again. "I don't see any excess material covering your own firm backside! And your thighs . . . every hard muscle shows itself to utter perfection. . . ." She sounded a little breathless. Damen's pulse quickened.

"My lady, beneath this jacket . . ." He edged it aside, off her shoulder, baring her well-formed, sleeveless vest. "You wear a tiny bodice, *laced*, which can only make a man think of *unlacing* . . . and baring your skin one precious portion at a time. And the cloth you chose in your 'design of comfort,' leaves not one delectable bit of your own arousal hidden. . . . Did you know that?"

She glanced at herself in surprise, eyes widening when she, too, took note of her own pert nipples against the fabric. Ariana gasped, then snapped her jacket shut to cover herself. But in glancing downward, her vision caught on his well-evidenced desire, and her hands dropped limply at her sides. She looked . . . hungry.

Damen shifted his weight, but nothing could hide the effect she had on him. They looked at each other. For a long moment, the air hung heavy and taut between them. Then she exhaled a shuddering gasp, and Damen's breath caught, and they reached for each other.

He kissed her face and her mouth, and she kissed him. A fire burned between them. He grasped her by the waist and lifted her off her feet, and still she kissed his face with wild, passionate hunger and a need he couldn't begin to refuse. He held her up so that their heights nearly matched and she wrapped her arms around his neck. Her breath came swift and short, broken with urgent murmurs as she pressed her soft lips against his cheek, his forehead. She buried her face against his neck and he felt the tip of her tongue as she tasted his skin, then sucked. Damen carried her to his bed, blindly, and they sank together across its width.

He could have taken her then, as she wrapped her long legs around his, as her beautiful head tipped back in primal feminine invitation. Clothing separated them, a fragile barrier, but it kept him from entering her. The wild torment of his ache grew so strong and so hard that it felt like steel against her soft body. He wanted her, and she wanted him. . . . But he wanted more.

Damen fought the beast inside himself and drew back from her. She opened her eyes as if from a dream and looked up at him, breathless and stunned, and so vulnerable that he thought his own heart might break to see her. With his gaze locked with hers, he pulled off his white shirt and let it drop beside his bed. Ariana trembled as he unfastened his black trousers, then freed his erection to her view. He was harder than he'd ever been in his life, his body sensitized to a point where a whisper of her breath upon his flesh might drive him to madness.

Her small, delicate hand reached out, and she curled her fingers tight around his length. He closed his eyes tight and he groaned as her palm slid to his base, then back and over the tip. Ariana squirmed beneath him, maneuvering herself so that he straddled her. She lay on her back, looking up into his eyes, with her beautiful hand wrapped around his shaft as she poised it close to her lips. . . . The image was almost too erotic to endure. Before he knew what she was doing, she swept her tongue out and over the tip, then took him in her mouth. Every muscle in his body grew taut, so hard that he couldn't move. She took him feverishly, as if all thoughts had fled her, leaving only the primitive and erotic instincts of . . . *a barbarian.*

He cried out in hoarse pleasure, still trapped in his lowered trousers while she made love to him in the sweetest torment he'd ever known. Nothing mattered but the feel of her tongue and her lips, the warmth of her mouth, the fire of her passion. With her fingers wrapped tight around his base, she slid her mouth around and up, and then down, until he could endure no more. His muscles quivered, almost too taut for release, as the wildness in Ariana soared like a fire across dried fields. In the depths of his conscious thought, he recalled hearing legends of Ellowan females, the most erotic lovers in the universe. Though he had known her as a lover before, she had shown him nothing like this. Youth hadn't held half the power that this woman now revealed.

Her tongue swirled around his tip, and every portion of her seemed bent on this moment, on *him.* Her long hair spread out like a river around her, over his bed, and over the side in its length, but she arched upwards, taking him with the fury of a goddess who would see no denial, who would have all that she desired. His hips moved with her pressure and she claimed him as he fought each thrust. He had meant to have her . . . to show her no mercy. Instead, it was he who succumbed.

Damen clasped her face in his hands. For one instant, he slid deeper into her delicious mouth and she murmured a greedy moan of conquest as she responded. She shocked him, and she owned him, and he couldn't stop as she urged him closer. But he wanted more.

He entwined his fingers in her long, wavy hair and grasped her head, then freed himself from the heaven of her mouth. She exhaled a furious breath, like a warrior-queen whose army had suffered some vital setback. Her grey eyes burned in the dark light of his bedroom, her lips pink and parted, but he saw no relenting as they curved into a smile.

"You deny me, my barbarian lord." Her voice came low and throaty, and the sound alone threatened to defeat him. But Damen moved aside and tore off his tangled leggings, then flung them off his bed. His erection stood out from his body, hard and aching, moist from her tongue. A bead like dew formed at the tip, which she saw. Painstakingly slow, she trailed her finger over it, then pressed her fingers against her lips. She was a demon—the eroticism of the Ellowan females hadn't been exaggerated.

Damen caught her hands, then kissed her fingers. She struggled to free herself, for stars knew what further torment she might inflict, but he pressed her downwards, then pinned her wrists against the bed. "I deny you nothing, my lady. . . . Except victory."

It had become a battle between them, a battle fueled by years apart, years when their joined souls fought to return to this place, together. He held her wrists, then sank down, kissing her chin, her throat, and he let his lips linger over her pulse as it raced. She struggled, to join him, to conquer him again, but he moved lower, then sat up. Smiling, he straddled her body without weight, then edged aside her snug jacket. Ariana fought to sit up, then yanked it off with a fury that delighted him. But he stopped her before she could remove the vest.

"Not so fast, my angel. This garment of yours has incited my fantasy since I first beheld you in it. It comes off at my speed, and my way."

She caught her breath, then waited with a fiery eagerness as he caught the laces in his fingers. His vision moved from her eyes to his task as he unlaced the vest, bringing the swell of her bared breast visible to his sight. He trailed the freed strands of her lacing over her soft skin, knowing that every portion of her was sensitized to his touch now. He watched her face as he freed first one breast, then the other. Her head tipped back, her lips parted, grown full and sensual, still pink from her wild ministering to him. He dragged the strand over each taut nipple, hardened peaks that strained against the touch.

His thumb replaced the string as he teased each nipple, watching her. She leaned toward him with a low moan, her eyes closed. He closed his fingers around the tips and she whimpered with sultry pleasure. He bent and took one peak between his lips, then licked, and then sucked. She gasped and moaned, then cried out when he sucked harder. He felt her body burning with life, with the power of desire, and she quivered until he knew he'd brought her near the place where she had held him. But he wanted more.

Damen slid his hands down her arms, then caught her wrists again. A ragged cry burst from her, frustration evident as he again moved back from her. "There is a law of the universe, Ariana, that whatever you dole out to another, that will come back to you threefold what you gave. Do you know what you did to me?" Her eyes flashed open, her lips parted with astonishment, and he smiled. "Then know what you gave has yet one more phase to endure in response."

She seemed stunned, too shocked to resist as he lowered her back to the bed, then knelt beside her. He removed her own trousers, slowly lowering the soft fabric over each curve of her bottom, then her thighs, over her perfectly shaped calves, her slender ankles, her narrow feet—her little toes were curled tight in restraint. He ran his hands from her feet, up her legs, then positioned himself between her thighs.

She wasn't an innocent—she knew what he intended as he bent lower. Her fingers caught his hair and entwined, gripping him as he breathed against her woman's mound. He ran his fingers over the soft curls, the dew of her glistening upon them. Hunger swelled in him, a desire beyond anything he had imagined or come close to experiencing. He found her small feminine bud and circled it with a light touch. Her legs clenched, then bent tight on either side of his shoulders. Here was the core of her, the center of all he adored, and he adored her now.

He swept out his tongue and it flashed over the tiny peak. Ariana rewarded him with a harsh cry of feminine shock and forbidden pleasure, and he tasted her again. The sweetness of her, soft and warm and delectable, intoxicated him beyond thought, and he teased her until it became worship, and until her hips arched and writhed, until every breath she took became a cry for release. He slipped his finger inside her warmth and felt the swell of feminine invitation, the moisture that fired his own need to complete them.

She twisted and moaned, gripping his hair, and he felt the first twitches of her ecstasy. And he wanted more.

He rose above her like a great warrior. She opened herself to him, her eyes wide, her legs urging him closer. As if wind and rain and fire raged behind him, all the forces of nature at his back, he drove himself inside her, and she screamed with a primal cry of victory. He had heard such a sound before—in the tribal cries of the caverns, long ago, and from his own throat when he claimed his first victory, and his Ariana.

He thrust deep inside her and she rose to meet him. His own hoarse gasps echoed with hers like a common breath, and he sank inside her again, then withdrew. Her hips rose to meet him, to draw him in, harder and deeper, and she wrapped her legs around his waist. He held her fast while he drove within her. Her dark hair spread over his bed and rippled with each thrust. She squeezed him hard from within, with attuned feminine skill, hugging him there, pleasuring herself around his length. He watched, spellbound, as her movements escalated, as her desire took complete control of her. Her body moved with the wild pulses of ecstasy, and she murmured and whimpered, and writhed around him. With each twist, his own pulses tightened, until his groin felt like a drawn bow, until he could stand nothing more.

She moaned her release, and he poured his own into her. It took him in waves, stronger with each vibration, gripping all his body, and all his soul, and entwining everything with Ariana. The spasms of rapture lasted, and lasted, longer than anything he'd ever experienced, longer than he thought possible. Wrapped around him, Ariana soared on the same prolonged pinnacle, until all the energy between them was spent.

They collapsed together, breath ragged and intermingled. Neither spoke—no words could form in Damen's mind, anyway. He rolled her over so that she lay atop him. She gasped to catch her breath, her arms dangling at his sides, her legs limp on either side of his. Weak, he folded his arm over her back, holding her close as their heartbeats galloped and then slowed.

He kissed the side of her damp forehead and she turned to kiss his jaw. They had forbidden each other endearments and tenderness, but as overpowering as his lust for her had been, his need to kiss her and care for her was just as strong. Ariana whispered his name, sweetness in her voice. She slid off his body, then placed her palm over his chest. Her fingers trailed an idle line over his skin, as if every part of his body enchanted her.

Gently, she kissed his chest near the scar, and he sifted her long, tangled hair through his fingers. She curled her leg over his and he wrapped his arm around her. She snuggled close to him, and the warmth in Damen's heart threatened to surmount even his passion. Even if he had been able to resist the desire between them, he could never deny the love.

Chapter Fifteen

"That was more than anything we did in the caverns." Ariana propped herself up to look into Damen's face. He looked as shocked as she felt, and as sated.

Damen reached to touch her cheek, and he smiled. "I think, my lady, because *we* are more than we were in the caverns. Such innocence as we had then, we have no longer." He paused. "I cannot mourn the loss, when you have taken me to such a place as you have tonight."

"It's true. I never thought of such things then. But now . . ." She leaned a bit closer to him. "I can think of so many things to do to you."

He closed his eyes and groaned. "If you do more, it will kill me."

Ariana yawned. "Not just now. It is wearying, this passion, and I am not accustomed to it, not yet." She rested her cheek against his hard, warm chest and felt satisfied. "And I feel so weak."

"You feel weak! What you have done to me . . . I wonder if I will be fit to walk tomorrow, let alone command a ship!"

She peeked at his face. "Then this is unusual for you, too? I had thought, perhaps, this is your way."

He eyed her in amazement. "I have never experienced anything that comes close to what we did tonight, and no erotic dream I've ever had compares."

"Good!" She paused. "But these arts, they are not just known to the Ellowan."

"No. . . ." Damen's lips twisted to one side as he contemplated this. "I have had women who practiced 'art,' as you say, in every stretch of the imagination, actually." He seemed perplexed, but Ariana frowned.

"Indeed."

"Yes . . . women who wanted nothing more from me than what pleasure my body could give. . . ."

She squeaked and clamped her hand over his mouth. "Say no more!"

He nodded. "Such things are generally deemed the height of eroticism. Yet I felt nothing compared to what I feel with you."

"Such things were once common on Valenwood before its fall, and it is entirely likely that my own people invented them. Still . . . it is a repellant thought."

"To me, also, though I see no reason it should be. We vowed to share our erotic desire before this encounter. And yet . . . it is as if, with you, there is something more to be had, to be known."

Love. "There is something between us greater than desire."

"We're connected." His expression softened and he played with her hair, then smiled. "One heart, Ariana." Damen yawned, too, and his eyes closed. "One heart, like the Beginning Symbol."

"The Beginning Symbol? What is that?"

He didn't answer, but a gentle smile curved his lips. "The crystal."

To Ariana's surprise, he sank into sleep as she watched him. "The crystal you gave me?"

Damen murmured something that she couldn't understand, and his breaths deepened. They lay together, facing each other, their foreheads touching. Half asleep, Damen took her hand and held it against his chest. She listened for a while to the sound of his strong, even heartbeat, then drifted into sleep, and the words "one heart" filtered through her dreams.

"Damen! We have a signal from an unidentified vessel, and the codes they use are of the highest Automon level."

Fia's voice burst over the monitor, and both Ariana and Damen shot up in bed, eyes wide, panting. Damen shook his head, groaned miserably, and then engaged the monitor. "If you would please, in the future and henceforward, preface your messages with a signal of your own, rather than busting in here like a siren, I would much appreciate the effort."

A brief silence followed. "Are you still in bed?"

"I am."

Another silence. "But it's midmorning! I have had my crew at toil for several hours. Reidworth is engaged in his studies, and has already passed his first exam, administered by myself. And my new chef is proving herself more than adequate. I would recommend that she join my . . . your staff on the home world, as she shows great skill and talent. . . ."

"Fia . . . the signal you received."

"Oh, yes. The odd thing is, it's different from other signals. It's not a warning. I had both Graff and Nob go over it, and they concur."

"Well? What is it?"

"An invitation."

Ariana eyed Damen, but he looked as surprised as she was. "Since when do the Automon 'invite' anyone?"

Damen shrugged. "I have no idea."

But she suspected he knew more than he let on. Damen sighed, then touched her arm. "Duty calls, my lady. Though I can think of more pleasurable ways to wake than this."

She looked into his eyes and the memory of their night

together flooded across her senses. She drew a short breath, and he smiled. "I . . . well, yes. I suppose it's important that we remember our own respective duties."

He rose from the bed, naked, his strong body warm in the growing light. His male appendage was still engorged, or perhaps he had woken this way, and Ariana's fingers tingled. He glanced down at himself before drawing on his black leggings. "I have been in this state almost constantly in your presence. Never have thoughts of sex distracted me this way."

"I, too, find it hard to focus my attention elsewhere." Ariana glanced around the bed and found her unlaced vest. She remembered his touch, and the eroticism in his eyes when he'd stripped it away, and she shuddered. "It is important that I keep this . . . event . . . in its proper perspective."

She put on her vest, then laced it tight—if he liked the sight of her in this garment, there was no harm in enhancing the effect. She pulled on her snug jacket, but left it open for his view. He slowed dressing himself to watch her, so she stepped into her soft brown trousers with special care, and found the effect of bending slightly worked well to hold his interest. She glanced at him over her shoulder, then adjusted her hair, sensually over one shoulder. Her skill was evidenced by the growing size of his desire, a distinct bulge beneath his already snug leggings. As if in challenge to her own arts, he buttoned his white shirt slowly, giving her a lingering look at his wide, muscular chest.

By the time both had dressed fully, Ariana felt as if they'd stripped before each other. A dark tingling sped through her, centering on her sensitive core. "Duty, Captain, awaits."

They each breathed deeply to clear their senses, then headed together to his door. Damen reached to engage the panel, then stopped. He smiled, and she felt as if the years they had been apart were nothing. He kissed her mouth, then her cheek, and then he opened the door.

She followed him to the elevator, feeling spellbound,

giddy with her happiness and her proximity to her lover. They stepped in together, but Damen leaned back against the wall. "I am not prepared for this day, or its challenges."

"But, my Dark Sun Lord, you are well prepared for the night to come."

He smiled, and his brown eyes darkened. "You are dangerous to me in more ways than I feared, lady of Valenwood. I was a fool to think I had taken you captive. . . ."

Warmth and power surged inside her, and she touched his chest as she moved closer to him. "When it is you who are my prisoner."

She rose to kiss him, but the transport shaft halted, and the door opened. Ariana hopped away and heard Damen issue a deep breath, then another. They entered the bridge, and Ariana felt suddenly embarrassed. They had been unrestrained, and loud, in the night. If the crew had happened by Damen's door . . .

But the faces of his men seemed grave, and intent on their panels. Nob, however, turned cheerfully and inspected both Ariana and Damen with a clear, curious gaze. "Good night, after all, was it, sir?"

Damen cleared his throat. "That is none of your concern, Nob."

Ariana studied Nob's face. He was a small, alert man with a rather round face, bright, round eyes, and a tuft of curly, reddish-brown hair from which two somewhat large ears protruded. "He reminds me of someone . . . or something."

Damen glanced at her. "Nob? Don't tell me there's another person like him in this galaxy. I'm not sure I could bear it."

Ariana shook her head. "Not a person, exactly."

Damen eyed her doubtfully. "Then what?"

"A lingbat." She paused, seeing his confusion. "They are small, flightless winged rodents."

"Some resemblance, possibly. But other than 'small,' what do these creatures have in common with Nob?"

"Not all lingbats. I was thinking of one in particular. 'He

Who Flames with Courage,' who is known less formally as 'Batty.' "

"You name these beasts? Are they pets?"

Nob looked between them eagerly, and still cheerful, awaiting Ariana's further disclosure of the species.

"They name themselves, and no one—*no one* would dare term them 'pets,' I am sure."

"Another odd Ellowan mystery?"

"Not Ellowan, in this case. They are an ancient species, 'capable of any number of wonders,' or at least, that's what they say of themselves."

"*Say?* They talk?"

"They do, and often, too much. That, at least, seems to be a commonality between lingbats. But they are very different in character. One is like a grumpy old man, wise, always one step ahead of his humans. Another, who is found most often upon Hakon's shoulder, is a tiny, nervous militant, giving orders that echo whatever Hakon has suggested. The one who reminds me of Nob, however, has a way of asking the most personal questions in an innocent way, so that you can never get mad at him."

Damen stared at her. "I have never heard of such creatures."

"No, they are quite unique. It was Hakon's father, Dane, who taught them the art of speech, and he has never quite forgiven himself for doing so. But he loves them, and they love him. It is a strange thing to behold."

"Strange enough to hear."

Ariana smiled. "Perhaps you will meet them, one day."

His brow tightened and he turned away. "Unless their species spreads to the Border Territories, that seems unlikely."

Her smile faded, but she said no more as Damen went to the captain's station. Maybe she was allowing herself too much fantasy. Their night together had confused her. She wanted to tell him that they had already created together something more beautiful and more lasting than he knew. She closed her eyes and saw a vision of her child's small face—Damen's child, and hers. She wanted to tell him, but she was so unsure of what he was now. He was a wonderful lover, and a powerful man, but what remained of her good senses gave her enough cause to doubt him. She couldn't risk the most precious thing in her life because passion had swayed her judgment. *Later, I will tell him. Later, when I know I can trust him.*

Damen engaged his panel and studied the message Fia had sent over. A bell rang, and he pushed another button. Fia's face came up on the monitor, a transmission from her ship. "Have you read it yet, Damen?"

"I am going over it now."

"What do you think?"

He glanced up at her, but Ariana detected a restrained smile. "That I need a moment further to see what it conveys."

"Very well." Fia looked impatient, then squinted, probably trying to make out the faces of those behind Damen on her own screen. "Hallo, Ariana! Isn't this exciting? This is the first time they've contacted us directly!"

Damen pushed a button, which seemed to startle Fia. "Fia. . . ." His voice was a warning, and she scrunched her face in dismay.

"I will leave that disclosure to you, then."

"Thank you."

"Of course." She paused. "Are we going to meet them?"

"They suggest a conference between their leader and myself. It appears they have contact with a rogue trader, one with some offer, and they request that he, also, attend this meeting."

Ariana caught her breath. "So they do have a leader! And you knew it!"

He glanced at her. "I know nothing for certain, as I told you."

"Are you going to meet them?"

"Yes, but not on these terms."

Fia leaned forward so that her bright face filled the screen. "What terms shall I send back to them?"

Nob glanced at Graff and shuddered. "That's scary, that is—the face of a tyrant looming above all. . . ."

Graff uttered a breath of agreement. "Scarier than facing the Automon leader, at any rate."

Fia clearly overheard their words, but an imperious glint shone in her eyes and she managed to give the effect of looking over their heads, and above them. "I am ready for a return transmission, Damen. What do you want to send?"

"Tell them I will agree to this meeting, and agree to include this rogue leader, but that seven sectors must be cleared of vessels. We will meet on the planet Eisvelt, where few weapons, even those of the Automon torch guards, operate at peak efficiency. I believe that in this, the Automon leader is in earnest, and it is not a trap, but there's no need to take unnecessary risks. I will come with one ship, and a shuttle, and expect to see only one of theirs, and that of the rogue."

Ariana stared at him, fighting to understand what he planned. "What do they want with you?"

Damen didn't look at her. "The issue of malloreum, and the fact that my fleet has captured so much of it, are probably primary items on their agenda. But there may be other factors."

"Such as what?"

"That, I will learn when I meet with them."

He knew more than this—Ariana felt sure of it, and disquiet grew in her heart. She wanted to trust him, but the blindness of love was legendary on every world, and she was in grave danger of falling into it. "When *we* meet with them. I am going with you."

He jerked around in his seat. "You are not."

"Try to stop me."

"That shouldn't be too hard, given that you are my prisoner."

Fia's bright voice broke their agreement. "Oh! I forgot. The Automon message specifically requests Ariana's presence. It's at the end of their transmission."

Damen's eyes widened, and Ariana stood stunned. "How would they know I'm here?"

Fia answered. "I wondered that, too, but they referred to you as 'a woman known as Ariana, an Intersystem representative,' and included you in the invitation."

Damen scanned the message, then nodded. "She's right."

Ariana folded her arms over her chest and felt smug. "Then I guess I'm going. You don't want the honorable Automon leader to think you've done in a representative of the Intersystem!"

His lip curled. "If I didn't know it was impossible, I'd think you doctored this message."

Nob cackled happily at his navigator's station. "Don't think that's likely, sir! I'd say your woman's been up to keeping you distracted, but she ain't had much time to do dealings with the Automon in her spare time!"

The other crewmen exchanged knowing glances, and to Ariana's surprise, color tinged Damen's cheeks. "If you gentlemen would mind to your own affairs. . . ."

Nob nodded, his face knit and serious. "And we'll let you mind to yours. Right, sir!" He paused. "Seems you've got things well in hand *there*, sir."

Now Ariana herself blushed. Fia, however, picked up none of these subtleties at her end. "There's another thing, Damen."

He looked up at the view screen, relieved by her interruption, as was Ariana. "What?"

Fia hesitated, and looked uncomfortable, as if she endured conflicting loyalties. "I detected another transmission early this morning. I believe it came from Valenwood. I didn't decode it, but it should have been received in your vessel."

Damen glanced at Ariana, and she held her breath as he fished her transmitter from his coat pocket. He engaged it, scanned it quickly, and his brow furrowed. Ariana seized a quick breath. "Well? If you are finished prying into my personal transmissions—I am sure there is nothing secretive."

"No, it appears not. But strange."

"In what way?"

He passed her the transmitter. A quick glance told her the contents weren't enough to reveal her secrets, but they might indeed incite some suspicion. "What troubles you?"

"Hyppos again. The entire message is filled with details of them." He paused, and Ariana repressed a smile. "It appears these creatures eat a great deal and are supremely fat. And this fact pleases the message sender very much."

"As I told you, yes, they are fat."

"What I don't understand is why your family feels the need to send you this peculiar and unnecessary information in the midst of a dangerous mission. They must realize that your transmissions might be tracked."

"Nowhere in the message will it state my family's status, nor any of their names. I see no danger."

"Maybe not, but it is odd."

"If you don't mind, I would like to reply to my message."

"Go ahead, but I'll view what you send."

Ariana considered her words carefully, then entered her message. She conveyed her joy about the hyppos' arrival, and her eagerness to meet them firsthand, then said briefly that she was happy, and assured all recipients that she was well. She ended with a word of love, then allowed Damen to inspect the message.

He did so, and seemed to see no subterfuge in the contents. "Peculiar in subject matter, but not disturbing. You may send."

Ariana entered her code and sent the message, then snapped the transmitter shut. He still eyed her suspiciously. She cleared her throat. "So . . . when are we going to meet the Automon commander, Captain?"

"It will be a while yet. We will return to our Dark Sun world first, and deliver the colonists to their new home. As the Automon message indicates, their leader is still some distance away. Going home for a brief while should also give me time to prepare."

"Prepare what?"

"That, you will learn in due time, my lady." Damen motioned to Nob. "Homeward, navigator." Nob engaged the panel, and Ariana watched as Damen's flagship changed course. The stars shifted, straining into lines as the ship's speed increased. Through a side portal, Ariana saw Fia's vessel in perfect alignment, slightly behind. The third ship hung back the same distance behind Fia's.

Ariana came to stand behind Damen's chair. He looked up at her, and she saw a new light kindled in his dark eyes. A slow smile curved on his lips, and she felt more than ever that she didn't truly know him. The light burned, and he clasped his hand over hers, then spoke in a quiet voice.

"Ariana of Valenwood, we are going home."

Part Three

The Blue Moon

*"And into hope, love walks
blind. . . ."*

Chapter Sixteen

Three suns in close proximity lit the sky outside the flagship's view port. Ariana stood at the bow, gazing out in wonder at the sight. Damen rose and came to stand beside her. He placed his hand on her shoulder. "Three suns of Marzarbel. A good marking point for a hidden world."

"I know of these suns, but the pull of their gravity is deemed too strong for Intersystem vessels to navigate. I take it this force doesn't hamper the Dark Sun ships."

"At first, the going was treacherous. But what the Automon ships couldn't endure, our own technology bettered, and now the gravitational pull offers little hindrance to our travel, although we will be slowed somewhat."

As the ships maneuvered in an arc around the three suns, the bows indeed turned inward, and the tug sent Ariana to a nearby seat. But Damen seemed used to the disconcerting force and remained standing, his face aglow in the reflection of the fiery suns. The first, the smallest, burned with a blue-white fire, hottest and most distant of the three. The second burned red, but the third glowed with a magnificent light, the like of which Ariana had never seen in the galaxy. Gold and yellow intermingled with red and orange over immense patches of jet black, all swirling in clouds of fathomless gases. Fueled by its inner fire, it spun more rapidly than the others, and outside its sphere a pale golden aura filled the sky.

Ariana stared in wonder. "It is a Dark Sun, but greater than any I've seen."

Damen looked proud. "A fitting home for the Dark Sun People, wouldn't you say?"

As he spoke, the ship rounded the arc, then broke free from the pull. Ariana saw several planets in alignment, and she gasped aloud at their splendor.

"We have arrived home at a fitting hour, for this is the time when the seven planets are all visible to the traveler."

As in most solar systems, the seven planets took various shapes. Some were huge and gaseous, uninhabitable. Two were small and dark red, closer to the Dark Sun. Damen indicated the larger of the two, orbited by a small red moon. "There, we found one of the first Dark Sun colonies. It was less hospitable than the others, and apparently less profitable, for the Automon themselves abandoned it. But we found there a remnant of a forgotten colony, surviving like animals, the most primitive tribe of all."

Nob sighed heavily. "Yep, sir. It were a dark place. Ain't my happiest memory, childhood, and that's a fact."

Ariana turned to the navigator in surprise. "You were there, Nob? But you seem so . . . civilized."

Nob looked flattered, but he shrugged. "Well, Miss, you were mentioning them lingbats, and how they're up to talking now. Sounds like to me civilizing someone ain't so hard."

"Apparently not. But such reasoning goes against much of the teaching in our galaxy."

Nob shrugged again. "From what I've seen, Miss, a person just carries what he is inside, if you follow me. You can't take it from him, you can't break it. It just is, good or bad, or both. We've all got our paths laid out before us, and we've all got our choices to make along the way. So it don't really matter much whether you was born in a forgotten slave hold, or even in the Tiled City of Valenwood. You're on your path, all the same."

Ariana smiled. "Are you sure you're not a lingbat in disguise? You're beginning to talk like one, too."

"Like to meet one of the little fellows one day." Nob glanced at Damen. "Figure I will, when the captain gets around to it." Before Damen could comment, Nob turned back to his work and concentrated on landing procedure.

Ariana peered out the side portal, then the front again. There loomed a large planet of red and gold, encircled by several rings of the same colors. Many moons surrounded it, too numerous to count at a glance. Just beyond lay a midsized blue-green world. It looked the most habitable of the lot, larger than Valenwood, of a type similar to her mother's home world. "Is that your planet?"

Damen smiled. "You would think so, and indeed, it appears the most habitable of the seven, does it not?"

"It does. Other than the old colony planet, I see no other remotely able to support life."

"And that, my lady, is the beauty of the Dark Sun home world. . . ." He didn't explain further, but Nob's course veered from the blue-green planet, and turned inward toward the dark-ringed orb.

Ariana's brow furrowed. "Not there? I'm not a scientist, but I have studied enough of planetary formations to know that world is just fiery gas."

Damen smiled. "Look beyond, Ariana."

Ariana gazed in wonder as Nob directed the ship through an array of small moons, same little larger than asteroids. One by one, they passed them by, then came into orbit around a small blue moon. "Is that it? It appears to be mostly ocean."

"Mostly ocean, it is. Yet as you will see as we descend, there is more."

The ships lowered with the precision of all Automon vessels, yet guided by gentler hands toward a smoother landing than the Automon had managed. As they lowered through the atmosphere, Ariana saw mountains of white clouds, parted for shafts of golden sunlight, mingled with the red shafts of light from the ringed planet, and then caught with the more distant blue fire and warm red of the other two suns.

They descended through the clouds above a great blue ocean. Ariana saw no sign of land, and wondered if somehow Damen had devised a colony under the sea. She glanced at him, wondering if any feat was beyond the power of the Dark Sun Lord. But Damen pointed to the left horizon. "There!"

A great island of endless green rose like an emerald spike from the blue ocean. The ships slowed, and lowered still more. Below, the waves turned white as the star-flung vessels glided toward their home city. Though the speed had slowed measurably, they approached fast, and Nob slowed more, then circled the island, followed by Fia and the other ship.

From the sky, no city towers were visible, nor had the giant forest been felled or cleared in any obvious way. Ariana looked at Damen. "Where do your people live?"

"In paradise, my lady."

As he spoke, the three ships came to a virtual stop, then lowered just above the ocean's surface, maneuvering with a precision Ariana wouldn't have thought possible. Graff contacted a base below on a monitor, and within seconds, nine golden hovercraft sped out from the forest toward them. Ariana waited as the craft combined docking procedures, three to each ship. Then Damen held out his hand to her. "Will you come as my guest, lady of Valenwood?"

She smiled. "As your prisoner, shouldn't I be in shackles?"

"I don't think there's need for such devices, not when curiosity burns in your eyes as it does now. Come."

Ariana hesitated, but her heart was full, and she could think of no reason why any danger awaited her here, not now. She placed her hand in his, and he led her into the elevator, followed again by his crew. All seemed excited, but Damen himself was quiet. Nob chattered like a lingbat, telling Ariana of docking procedures and directing her along halls she already knew. "The bridge crew takes the first shuttle. The other two will take the colonists to where they'll be settled in and tended. Same on Fia's ship, and the other." He glanced eagerly at Damen. "Should be a good welcome, wouldn't you say, sir, what with you returning with your woman and all."

Ariana looked up at Damen. "They know of me, here?"

Damen looked uncomfortable, but Nob slapped his hands together. "In the city of Ariana-annai? I think you'll find yourself welcome, and no mistake!"

Ariana's eyes widened and distinct color flooded Damen's cheeks this time. They stopped outside the docking door, which grated as the seal was made outside. "I was young when we formed this world, and I had a slight tendency to christen places in your honor."

Nob whistled. "A *slight* tendency? The Temple of Ariana, Ariana Theater, the Ariana Academy of Higher Learning. . . . For my first few years here, I thought 'Ariana' was a word meaning 'anything.' " The others laughed, but Damen looked pained.

Ariana beamed, almost too happy to speak. "You named *everything* after me?"

He refused to meet her eyes and seemed to be studying the portal door with deliberate intensity. "All this was done in the first three years of our freedom, before I had found the way to Valenwood."

"I think I understand." She did, and the image pierced her heart. He must have been so proud. He was building a world not *of* her, but *for* her. And he had meant to bring her to it once they were reunited. Tears welled in her eyes. "And then you came to Valenwood. . . ." Her voice trailed and he answered her plaintive gaze.

"And then it was no longer necessary."

Nob seemed to miss the poignancy of their interaction. "Them first three years saw the invention of a world and a whole culture, Miss. Just wait till you see it! Ain't nothing in all the galaxy quite so fair, no matter what lies out there."

Damen sighed. "It is a tiny outpost in an endless sea, Nob. But not until I first beheld Valenwood did I realize how small it was."

Nob didn't appear convinced and he issued a brief snort. "Can't imagine that, sir. Oh, Valenwood might be pretty, with the desert sand dunes I've heard tell of, and the dark forest, and the golden ocean, and what with the white city, but I don't expect anything matches just the *air* of this place, sir. Wait till you feel it on your face, Miss! Like a soft touch, it is, and it seems to heal every part of you! Maybe it means most to those of us born in ashen air with the smell of fire everywhere, but I don't think there's another place where just breathing can take up your whole day!"

Ariana swallowed hard to contain emotion. She felt what this place meant to them, and to Damen most of all. "I am pleased you have brought me here."

As she spoke, the portal opened, and two excited young women greeted them. They clasped their hands together in what appeared to be a ritual greeting, then bowed slightly as Damen entered the vessel. They murmured a soft word, but the rush of air blurred it from Ariana's understanding. It sounded almost like *damanai*.

Ariana looked back at them in surprise, but Damen guided her on board the hovercraft, and Nob took over the guidance panel. With a precision outmatching anything in the Intersystem, the golden craft sped lightly toward the green jungle. As they drew near the shore, Ariana saw white beaches of glittering sand, and beyond, giant trees with huge leaves fanning in a soft breeze. Nob followed a barely visible trail past the beach and into the trees, and here Ariana began to see the true wonder of Damen's world.

Brightly colored birds flew up from the broad branches, startled into the sky by the craft. Strange furry creatures leapt from branch to branch, squawking and calling out in mysterious voices. As they penetrated deeper, Ariana saw that the forest didn't darken nor grow thicker, but instead,

opened in spaces to allow for human habitation, though as
yet she had seen no signs of dwellings. Nob jerked his craft
suddenly left onto a narrow trail, dislodging his passengers,
several of whom cursed. The other craft went on straight
ahead, but Nob rounded another sharp corner, then
stopped abruptly.

Damen growled a warning, but Nob didn't seem to notice. "Figured your woman ought to be seeing this, at least,
sir!"

"Now is not the time, Nob."

But it was too late. Ariana rose from her small seat and
grasped the edge of the front view port. Nob popped open
the view port panel and a soft, balmy breeze caressed Ariana's face and ruffled her long hair like a cloud around her.
She closed her eyes and its grace seemed to absorb into her,
filling her with its own peace, as if it had an emotion of its
own.

Nob tapped her shoulder, directing her attention to the
left of the hovercraft. A multicolumned structure loomed
before her, wrought of pure crystal, shining with the gold
and red light of the three suns, blazing with every light in
the galaxy. It seemed ancient, and yet, it was young. . . . It
had stood less than ten years. "How . . . how . . . ?" Her
voice trailed as wonder overcame her.

"We got all that crystal from the old caverns. Went back
a few times till it was up complete. What do you think,
Miss?"

Ariana just stared, then slowly looked back at Damen. "It
is the most beautiful thing I've ever seen. What is it? Not
a dwelling."

Damen seemed too uncomfortable to respond, but Nob
waved his arm excitedly. "Why, that's the Temple of Ariana, as I mentioned afore, Miss! Pretty, ain't it? Look there,
on the arch. . . ."

Ariana's eyes widened as the golden symbols flashed in a
shaft of sunlight. There she saw at the arch's summit a
carved ∞, encircled by a rim of gold. And beneath, on either
side, the dusting of golden stars, all which began in the ∞

shape, spreading out in a symbol of everlasting growth. She turned to Damen. "The Beginning Symbol. It is on the crystal you gave me. What does it mean?"

Nob looked between them, confused. "Why, it means 'beginning,' Miss."

"The beginning of what? Do you have priests who explain its meaning?"

"It ain't that complicated, Miss. It's the start of things."

This explanation conveyed nothing to Ariana, and Damen didn't seem likely to supply more. "What do the joined circles mean, Nob?"

Nob looked horrified, and a little superior. "Don't you know, Miss? 'Two joined by one.' "

She began to see why Damen lost patience with Nob. "One what?"

Nob shook his head, mystified by her confusion as he returned to the controls. "*One heart*, Miss. What else?"

Ariana sat back down, staring at Damen. She couldn't speak, but Damen shrugged. "It seemed obvious to me."

She sat back, still staring. "What you describe is almost exactly the foundation belief of the Ellowan."

Damen looked surprised. "Is it?"

"It is. From our most ancient beginnings, it was said that all existence was created in the birth of love, and that love itself created two individual beings, and in their love for each other, which surpassed all else, they gave birth to the universe. Some refer to them as a god and a goddess, or the original lovers. This birth of love followed course in our own history. The first Ellowan queen was the priestess of the Dark Wood, who once led her people into battle against the Prince of the Desert, from whom, incidentally, my father is descended." She paused. "Hakon's mother is the last of the Priestess line, and descends from the Dark Wood People."

Damen's brow angled doubtfully. "They met in *battle?*"

"So it is said. They met by the edge of the golden ocean, a neutral zone, to discuss terms of surrender—each expected the other to yield. But when they came face to face, they fell in love, though both resisted their desire. They yielded first to physical passion. . . ." Her voice trailed as she recalled her own passion with Damen, and his eyes darkened in recognition.

"And then?"

"After much conflict, renewed battle and vengeance, doubt and heartache, their love proved stronger and they wed, uniting their people, though their two races endured separately. It was at this time in our history that the priestesses realized the nature of existence, and formed the culture of intertwined lovers. From each pair, more souls are born, and so eternity is created evermore."

Nob sniffed, casual in the revelation that his beliefs were shared by other cultures. "That's it, pretty much. The golden-white circle represents the energy that bonds all things, of course."

Ariana kept her gaze pinned on Damen. "How is it that your people, who had nothing, no language, no hope, no freedom, have come up with the same theory of hope and eternity that founded the Ellowan race?"

He seemed mystified by the connection. "I have no idea, but though simplified from what you tell, this is what my mother conveyed to me also."

Ariana's brow furrowed as she considered the similarity. "Many races of many worlds share similar beliefs—but not this close. Some lean more to the side of the god, and some to the goddess. My father says those are imbalanced and will need to shift their ways before they can know peace." She glanced at the temple. "Maybe that is why it seems ancient, though it is still young and new. The belief that wrought it, that is ancient indeed."

She felt stronger, and more certain in her heart than she had since first encountering Damen on the outpost. She seated herself again and the warmth of her surety calmed all doubts. Other forces might exist, but love was strongest and deepest, and if this was true, then no force in the universe could take him from her now.

Damen motioned to Nob. "To the city, Nob. We are expected."

Nob whistled. "Yes, sir! Don't want Fia catching up with us and getting there first, or she'll have them all marshaled into some kind of parade." With a quick jet of speed, Nob caught up with the other hovercraft, then idly passed them. He rounded several tight corners effortlessly, and they came without warning to a city. If the crystal temple surprised her, the city of 'Ariana-annai' stunned Ariana even more.

Living trees were joined together, bound and laced with crystal of all hues and depth. Bridges and walkways were lined with shimmering gold and sparkling gems, and there, in the midst, were homes and buildings, wrought of living trees, shadowed by great palm leaves, and filtered with the light of the three suns. The structures formed a wide semicircle, framing a plaza of crystal and a silver-white metal. High fountains sprayed into the air in great arcs, and as the hovercraft lowered to the ground, the sound of birds singing intermingled with the tinkling of water.

Graff opened the hovercraft portal and lowered a ramp, smiling from ear to ear as Ariana looked out in amazement. Damen came to her side, and as he appeared, a flood of people poured from the buildings to greet him. Ariana watched spellbound as men and women, children and babies, people young and old, came forth to welcome Damen home.

A chant arose, in a chorus of differing voices, almost a song. It rang with the primal passion Ariana remembered from the cavern, but more musical, filled now with the endless hope of a people who had come from the grim darkness to see this bright world. The chant blended, and became as one voice, and the voice became a word she recognized: "Damanai."

They chorused this word, beloved of her people, and Ariana turned to Damen in wonder. "Why do they speak this word?"

His brow raised and he looked confused. "It is my name,

of course." He paused, doubtful. "You gave it to me yourself."

Ariana's mouth slid open. "*Damen* . . . Damanai!"

His eyes narrowed. "When we parted, you named me this. It has been shortened to sound like the more common names of the galaxy—perhaps 'Damanai' is too poetic for a pirate, but I am surprised you didn't realize."

"It is a name, my lord, you took for yourself. In the tongue of my people, it means 'my treasure,' and is gifted to those we love best, a term of endearment."

His eyes shifted to one side. "Then it wasn't my name?"

Her heart felt swollen with love and she touched his hand, then closed her fingers tight around his. "It is a perfect name, and it fits you."

His people called to him, joyous at his return. A change came over Damen's dark face, and again the golden sun glowed upon his face, sparkling in his eyes. He stood before them, then lifted Ariana's hand in the air between them. He held his head high and as she gazed up at him, she saw a king beyond the power of any she had known.

He looked out over his people, his proud face filled with the love of a king, and a leader of worlds. With one hand clasping Ariana's, lifted above her head, he placed the other in a fist over his heart. His voice came deep and strong—less primitive than his shout of conquest in the caverns years ago, but no less powerful. This time, the word he cried was a name: "Ariana!"

Chapter Seventeen

"It was important that I introduce you thus, for your arrival is a moment my people have long awaited."

Ariana sat opposite him across a round crystal table, staring. She had stared this way since they left the hovercraft, and hadn't taken her eyes off him even as they walked through the throng of his people and into his private dwelling.

She stared now, grey eyes luminous as they reflected the green and purple crystal light of his walls. He wished she would speak, to question him, condemn him, whatever occupied her mind, but she didn't. Damen cleared his throat.

"You may be wondering why I didn't tell them you had . . . well, as I thought then, married and settled happily on Valenwood." He paused. Her brow arched, very slightly, but she said nothing. "It may be hard for you to understand." Her brow may have arched still more, but he couldn't be sure. "You had become a symbol of hope to more than just myself, Ariana." He felt almost embarrassed speaking her name, now that she knew how many places and buildings it had graced. "To all my people, you were a memory of courage, of a bright hope that took us beyond our world. No other woman brought to any of the Dark Sun colonies inspired such change in its people. Even Fia, who has the spirit of a queen, had no real hope for herself, for she had lived in gilded bondage, a prisoner of some unknown design. But you . . . you shone with the light of your people, of who you really are, and that hope passed to us."

She folded her arms and leaned on the table, and she didn't say a word. She stared, her gaze piercing in its intensity. He felt she commanded him to go on, but she said nothing.

"Bringing you here, it was a gift to my people." He paused. "It is helpful, of course, that you are not happily settled on Valenwood with your golden-haired prince, but that is of no consequence." He averted his eyes from her, lest she see too much of his heart. "Though my own hope was gone, I couldn't let it be taken from my people. You were a symbol of that which we cherished. . . ."

She spoke at last, and her words astonished him. "I am the 'Beginning Symbol.' "

He smiled. "Part of it, yes."

She smiled, too, but her eyes glistened with tears. "You are the other part. And the part that joins in the center . . . one heart."

His voice sank to a whisper. "Yes."

She stared again, looking thoughtful. "Well, this part of the One Heart doesn't understand the other. You say you will return me to Valenwood, and it is true—I *must* return. But if you value me so, then why do you not open your heart to me?"

His brow rose. "Have you opened yours to me, lady?"

"No. Not yet. If I believed I could trust you . . . But there is the matter of the Automon, and this leader you say you don't know. My secrets are precious, and not easily given."

"The same is true of mine."

"I keep them, not for my own sake, but for others."

He met her gaze and saw the depth of her heart. "Then we do the same, for those I would protect must mean more than my own fate."

"We think the same, at least." She closed her beautiful eyes and leaned back in her seat. "For that, we have one heart to thank, I suppose. But in this way, it keeps us apart, because I do not feel sure of your plans, nor why you will not include my people in your blanket of protection."

"Ariana, don't you know? It is for your people, too, that I do this."

Her eyes snapped open. "Do what? I do not understand!"

"Maybe it's best that you do not."

Ariana thumped her small fist onto the crystal table. "I don't think so!" Fortunately, the glass remained intact and didn't splinter, but Damen placed his hand over hers.

"The workmen designed this for beauty, my lady, not to endure violence."

She squeezed her eyes shut, but he saw tears on her lashes. "Oh, why must things be so difficult? Why couldn't you have come to me when you saw me in Valenwood?"

Damen held her hand in his and waited until she met his eyes. "Would it have worked, Ariana, no matter how much I loved you, or how much you wanted me? I was nothing. . . ."

"It wasn't 'nothing' that created this world!"

"So I thought myself, at the time. But think—what would I have done among your people, had I stayed with you then? I had little language. . . ."

Tears swelled in her eyes. "If you had loved me . . ."

His throat tightened with emotion, but he smiled. "If I had loved you, I would have left. And I did."

She shook her head. "I don't understand."

"Don't you? You will, one day. I knew the Dark Sun worlds, Ariana. I knew the Automon, and I knew my people weren't safe, and that many more colonies existed beyond mine."

"I know this. It was your mission and your duty to find them and free them. But I could have helped you!"

He hesitated. "It is more complicated than you understand, and for now, it is best that I say no more."

She frowned, then stood up, removing her hand from his. "Very well. I see that much still lies between us. So be it!" Ariana went to his door and looked out. "But for now, I wish to see more of my city."

Damen stood up too, suspicious, though he wasn't sure what she might be planning. "Your city?"

She glanced back at him, pert. "It was named for me. Therefore, I feel a certain kinship and obligation to it."

"You're a spy to the core. You intend to worm your way amongst my people and learn from them what purposes I might have."

Her eyes widened in false innocence. "I have no idea what you're talking about." Her expression altered, and he recognized a formidable opponent. "But should I learn anything, by accident, of course . . ."

"I could keep you locked in my bedroom. . . ."

Ariana tilted her head to one side, and her brow arched. "In the city of Ariana-annai? I don't think *that* would be a popular decision at all!"

She was right, and so was he, and he hoped his people had the good sense to watch their disclosures in Ariana's presence. "Very well. . . . You are free to go where you will, for the time being, and as long as you refrain from mischief."

"Mischief?" Her innocent expression proved nothing, except that she wasn't cowed in the least. "I don't know what you mean." She pulled off her jacket and tossed it across the back of a chair. "It's warm here, and I shall find need for more suitable clothing. That will be my first task."

His people wore almost nothing. Fine for them, but to see Ariana thus garbed might prove . . . troublesome to his composure. "I can have garments designed to cover . . . clothe you."

"I shall handle that myself." Before he could argue, she hurried out the door, her head high. Damen stood watching her, but already she moved among his eager people, chatting with them, gesturing. Her long hair floated along behind her like a soft, dark cloud, and she motioned to a scantily clad woman, then to her own attire. The woman understood, and they headed off together. He was in trouble this time.

Damen tried to keep his mind on his preparations, but failed miserably. Throughout the morning, his crewmen reported on Ariana's various activities, and he couldn't keep his thoughts on anything else. Nob sat cheerfully at Damen's crystal table, fingering a goblet of iced wine. "The people love her, sir. Some remember her from your colony, and by all accounts, she remembers them." Some of the other crewmen nodded.

"Has she been asking questions?"

Nob eyed him doubtfully. "I suppose so, sir. But everyone's talking so much, it's hard to know who's asking what."

"Wonderful. By nightfall, that woman will know every detail of our fleet, our missions, and probably have a firm idea of what I've got planned."

"Don't want to tell her, sir?"

"And alert the entire Intersystem to our plans, Nob? I think not."

"Just don't send her back 'til it's over, that's my thinking. Don't see why you'd send her back, anyway."

"As Ariana has said herself, she must return to Valenwood."

"Why?"

Damen hesitated. "Her family, I suppose, her duties. . . ." Something was dear to her there, anyway.

Nob didn't seem disturbed. "Well, she'll take care of it, sir, and be back among us in no time."

Damen's brow furrowed. "I doubt that. . . ."

His door popped open and Ariana entered, carrying a

large basket that overflowed with draping garments. She smacked it on the table, happy, then glanced casually around at his crewmen. "Planning something, are you?" Damen rose, but she picked up the basket and looked around his greeting room. "I assume I am staying with you?"

She didn't sound embarrassed or shy, and he couldn't help his pleasure. "If that pleases you."

She cast him a teasing look and his blood quickened. "It pleased me well enough on your ship."

After the first night on board his ship, he had moved her belongings into his quarters. He remembered the days before they arrived at his home world as sensual haze. Long, sensual nights together. Days when his duties seemed idle, and he joined her below deck with the new colonists. Moments when their eyes met, and desire flamed, and they hurried together to his quarters to make love. . . . It had been bliss.

Nob coughed and the men exchanged knowing looks, but Damen swallowed. "We are engaged in an important discussion here. Is there something I can do for you, Ariana?"

"Point me toward your bedroom, so I might change into something more suitable to your climate, and I will leave you in peace." She paused. "For the time being."

He led her to a passageway. "Down there, to the left. You will find a large room that overlooks the sea. I think you will find it pleasant."

"Thank you." She scurried off with her basket, and Damen fought his desire to follow her. He would have liked to see her first encounter with his room, with the crystal doors opened wide to the white sand beach beyond. He closed his eyes and imagined her standing there, naked, as the sea breeze caressed her. He had taken an unknowing step down the passage before Graff called him back.

"Meeting adjourned, Captain?"

Damen turned back and cleared his throat. "No. I was just . . . We have much to go over, and this plan must be foolproof. You know what to do with our fleet—every one of us must be ready for the second phase."

Graff, sitting next to Nob, drummed his thick fingers on the tabletop. "It's not the second phase that worries me, Captain. Figure we've got that as ready as we'll ever be. We either succeed, or we don't. We know what to do. But what about this meeting with whomever the Automon have commanding them?"

"We already have some idea of their purposes, and can be assured . . ."

Ariana emerged from the passageway, her entrance silent. Only his constant glances in that direction assured that she had overheard nothing more. Damen started to rise, then flopped back in his chair. She'd picked the most glorious costume devised by his people—and the most revealing. The top was white, wide enough to cover her breasts, barely, decorated with small crystal beads that caught the light as she moved. Another swath of minimal fabric covered her hips, leaving her long and beautiful legs bared. She had replaced her soft leather shoes with open sandals that laced over her ankles. Ariana had beautiful feet. Even the sight of her toes reminded him of how they curled tight when he made love to her.

"Ariana. . . ."

Nob whistled, and the other crewmen rose to their feet. "You're a sight, and no mistake, Miss! You'd fit perfect in the temple."

Ariana nodded, though she averted her gaze from Damen. That was for the best, because he was gaping, and she couldn't fail to see her effect on him. "Exactly why I am wearing it, Nob."

Damen's eyes narrowed. "What do you mean?"

"I am off with a group of your people to inspect my temple."

"Are you, indeed?" She sounded so pert. He wanted to go with her. "For what purpose?"

She approached him, so close that he caught the warm, feminine scent of her, mingled deliciously with some flower petal that she must have pressed against her skin. She was bathed in eroticism, and a torment to his senses. "When you are ready to tell me your purposes, Lord of the Dark Sun, I may consider telling you mine."

A demon. . . . She was beautiful and infuriating, and his desire grew despite all he did to restrain himself. "As you wish, Ariana."

He sat upright, formally, and pretended not to notice the light of challenge in her eye. He glanced at her. "And after you inspect your temple?"

She gazed at the ceiling, thoughtful. "Then I am giving a brief talk at the Academy of Ariana."

"On what subject?"

"On my experiences in the cavern, and how I escaped." She went to the door and adjusted her skirt, directing his attention purposefully to her slender thighs. "I may see fit to tell them something of Valenwood, and perhaps an overview of the Intersystem itself."

"Propaganda. I see."

"Call it what you will." She opened the door and looked out. "I trust I will see you later?"

He detected a note of longing in her voice, and he smiled. "You will."

"When your duties are complete?"

"We will dine together at a feast in your honor, tonight."

She nodded. "That is well. I am to take luncheon at the temple."

"Your itinerary is laid out admirably, my lady."

"I trust your schemes are progressing nicely?"

"Perfectly. Thank you." The distance between them seemed to fade, and he forgot everyone in his room but Ariana. "Until later, Ariana."

She drew a quick breath. "Later."

He watched her go, then sighed heavily, forgetting to disguise his own longing.

"Sir?" Nob shattered his reverie, and he turned back to his crew.

"Yes, Nob. I know. . . ." He took his seat and forced his

mind back to the venture at hand. "About the Automon commander . . ."

"And with that, my maternal grandfather handed over the chair of Prime Representative to my father, marking the first time in Intersystem history that the seat has remained in the same family, albeit through marriage in this case."

Damen positioned himself at the back of the auditorium while his people sat in rapt attention to Ariana's lecture. Her voice floated out over them, musical and enticing. He felt sure she had convinced every one of his subjects that union with this glorious Intersystem would benefit them all, and keep them safe from whatever might threaten them. Fortunately, his people knew too much of the Automon, more than Ariana suspected, and understood why the Intersystem itself was in danger, but Ariana was certainly a convincing orator.

She caught sight of him across the crowded room and waved. He felt as if some gauntlet of battle had been thrown, and he had no choice but to pick it up. "Would the lady of Valenwood extend the Intersystem's reign across the Border Territory, and sweep up all lands within and beyond into its embrace?"

"The more worlds that unite, the more good can be done. But never in all the history of our galaxy has there been a union that so beautifully preserved the individuality of its members. Some fear such unions, lest they lose that which makes them unique. But for my people, and those many races joining us, it is just this uniqueness that makes us strong."

"And what of the worlds who don't desire to answer to the Intersystem Council?"

Ariana got down from her podium and made her way through the crowd toward Damen. Her hair swayed as she walked, and her bright eyes focused on him alone. "My father once thought as you did, and was most reluctant for Valenwood to join the Intersystem."

She came closer. Her bare midriff proved Ariana's life

hadn't been idle. She was fit and trim. Beautiful. "Well? Has the Lord of the Dark Sun no answer?"

He'd forgotten what she'd said. Damen swallowed as she drew near. "Yet your father accepted his post heading the Council. It appears his reluctance had little weight."

She came to stand before him. He wanted to pick her up and carry her away, back to his house and his bedroom, and lock the door. "His good sense had more, and when he saw how sensible . . ."

He could stand it no longer. Ignoring the surprised looks of his people, he caught her around the waist, lifted her off her feet, swung her into his arms, and carried her from the auditorium.

Chapter Eighteen

Chapter Eighteen

"What are you doing? Put me down!" Ariana sputtered furiously, but Damen marched purposefully across the Crystal Plaza, shoved his shoulder against his front door, and pushed it inward. "This is so embarrassing! My speech wasn't finished!"

He dropped her to her feet, his brown eyes blazing. "You'd spoken more than enough."

She closed her eyes, furious. "How dare you? Your people hold me in respect and honor! You can't just . . . pick me up and haul me off like some . . . some . . ."

"Barbarian warrior?"

She trembled with fury, but he loomed over her, tall and strong and so handsome she thought she might die from wanting him. "Yes, that exactly! You are a king now. Some decorum . . ."

"I am a leader with enough power to know when to silence my opponent."

"Opponent!" She cast her head back, then waved her fist at his chest. "Well, maybe so, but you refuse to listen. . . ."

"I refuse to yield."

"You are obstinate."

"No more than yourself, my lady."

She shook her fist. "You . . . you are so infuriating!"

"Again . . . no more than yourself."

Her breath came in gasps. Defiant, she turned from him and reached for the door handle. Damen caught her arm, and drew her back. She struggled, but the fire between them blazed. He caught her by the waist again and picked her up. Curse his size! She kicked, but made no impact. Damen carried her without effort across his greeting room, down the passage, and into his glorious bedroom. He slammed the door with his foot, then pressed her back against the wall, her feet still dangling.

She stared, her blood raging with a lust for battle. They looked at each other a moment, as lovers and enemies, and then he kissed her. Not a gentle kiss of sweet seduction, but of overpowering desire and of passion that allowed for no shy smiles or delicate surrender. Ariana wrapped her arms tight around his neck and kissed him back.

She ached for him, as she had ached all day—with each denial, each resistance he had given, she had wanted him more. He pressed against her and she felt the size of his passion, hard, close to her woman's core. His tongue slid into her mouth and she sucked furiously, wanting more than it seemed he could ever give.

She wrapped her legs around his waist and he groaned as her slight wrap elevated over her hips. His hands cupped her bottom, and he tore away the brief covering she'd so happily worn. Bared to him, she felt damp and hot, furious that she couldn't deny the effect he had on her body.

"Have you wanted me so much this day?" His voice came hoarse, ragged with lust. "You tease me, Ariana, but you've inflamed yourself just as much." To prove his claim, he dipped his fingers inward, curving around her bottom, and he played with the evidence of her desire. Angered and passionate, she squirmed, but he laughed, and found a greater temptation as he teased her with his touch.

Ariana bit her lip hard, then realized her error, so she bit his shoulder instead. Apparently, he felt no pain from her nip, because rather than stopping his exquisite torment, he freed his erection, then tormented her with that instead. She wanted to scream and to fight him, to gain power herself, and to hold *him* against a wall, where she would have him at her own command. He recognized the battle, and as she had taken control of their first encounter on his ship, he now claimed her.

She couldn't stop him. She would have died rather than stop him. He held her with one arm, and with his free hand, guided his shaft against her moist cleft, over and over until she writhed from desire. Then without asking or warning, he drove himself hard up inside her, lifting her higher off her feet with his force. Ariana moaned with the force of pleasure, or maybe she screamed—her senses spiraled out of control as he thrust inside her body, touching her so deeply that she knew what it meant to be *one*, to be truly joined, even in the passion of fury.

She squeezed her inner walls tight around him, feeling his fullness, the heat and the power. Her own ecstasy came without warning, a sudden spiral and splintering that took hold of her. She cried out his name, and he cried out hers, and she knew the same pinnacle claimed them both. He throbbed within her, and she around him, and then she just hung there, her arms limp around his neck.

Without speaking, Damen carried her to his bed. Stopping short, he set her to her feet, then flopped down on his back, his breath ragged. Ariana stood looking down at him, at the length of his beautiful, strong body, warm with the aftermath of his passion. His erection stood poised from his body, still engorged, and madness overcame her. Without a word, she straddled him, then gripped its length in her fist. He stared up at her, astonished, but she smiled. "I want more."

She was shocked to hear herself speak, especially this way, but Damen's dark eyes glowed as if she'd carried him to a world unknown. She sank down over his still-hard shaft and took him deep into the sensitive passage of her body. She braced herself on his chest and then made love to him, rising and falling as he thrust upward inside her. She had never dreamed such a thing, so relentless and so perfect as their already awakened bodies resumed their familiar rhythm. Her release came with a slow build, shattering in its intensity, longer of duration and more powerful because she had reached some new level of her desire. Damen gripped her hips in shaking hands as she rode the tumultuous waves of ecstasy, and then she watched as the same waves crashed through him.

When their rapture subsided, Ariana sank down into his arms and he held her, still deeply imbedded in her body. She felt the erratic twitches of rapture's descent and listened to the power of his heart as it throbbed against her ear. For a long while, they lay together this way, content. Ariana gazed out the open door and felt the sea breeze against her damp skin. Paradise, he had told her, and he was right. "Is the ocean warm here?"

Damen kissed her head and turned also to look out the window. "In some places, it is so hot that it boils, but that is far to the south, at the equator of this moon. But here, yes, it is warm, and my people often swim. You'll remember that water was a scarce commodity in our colony, as in most of the others where we were held. Here, it flows in rivers through this island, in waterfalls of great beauty, until it spills again into the sea."

"It is a beautiful land." She turned to look into his face. "You love it very much."

"We thought to settle on Torol, the planet you saw when we arrived. It is habitable, as you guessed, but not entirely welcoming."

"What's wrong with it? Are there people there?"

"No people, but many living things. Huge creatures, some like lizards such as lived in the mining caverns, only much larger. There are giant mammals, and even massive and ferocious insects."

"Predators?"

"When we landed, it seemed only predators, though there must be other creatures that they prey upon. But we didn't stay long enough to find out. Nob almost had his head removed by a monstrous lizard with teeth bigger than he was. Later probes did reveal great herds of less ferocious animals—the prey, I assume."

Ariana shuddered. "Best viewed from afar, then."

"Indeed. Torol isn't without its beauty, but I wouldn't want to go back for another visit, and the climate has extremes that would make life a hardship for humans."

"Maybe one day you can arrange shuttles, tours that would skim the surface and provide viewing for children! It might be exciting to see those animals, if it could be made safe. I know many children who would delight in such expeditions."

Damen smiled. "Indeed, many children here have also suggested such ventures, but as yet, we have been too occupied elsewhere to arrange it." He paused. "What is life like for the Ellowan young?"

Her heart moved in a quick pang, but a voice inside her head whispered, *Not yet.* "Happy, and with much to fuel their imaginations. The Ellowan are a loving people, and we adore children. All festivals include them, and there are countless games and events where they are central, especially the theater."

"I have found that many of my people here have a tendency toward artistic pursuits, though why that should be after life in the dark caverns, I'm not sure."

"Maybe only through art could they find beauty. Or maybe they inherited these tendencies from their ancestors. You must have ancestors, after all."

"I assume our blood is so mixed that no race would be discernable after all this time."

"Perhaps . . . but there are tests that would reveal the heritage, at least all that comes from known worlds. It might be interesting to see where Fia is from."

Damen fingered her hair and sifted it through his fingers. "It might. She, at least, is unlikely to come from mixed blood, though I'm not sure her race would be 'known.' She doesn't fit here quite as well as the others."

"When she returned from settling the colonists, I noticed that she keeps her own body well covered, though the rest of your people seem remarkably uninhibited."

Damen's brow furrowed. "I hope I made no mistake in her upbringing. But it seemed she was always like this, restrained and slightly . . . elevated."

Ariana kissed his shoulder. "I wouldn't worry. She is a strong person, and very dignified. She isn't like any of the races I have seen in the Intersystem—and I have seen most at the Council meetings, which I often attend."

"You mentioned a race, the Daeron. I have never heard of them. What made you think of Fia?"

"I know little of them myself, but what I have heard reminds me of her. They have slightly pointed ears, and reputedly a faint glow about them. They are somewhat stiff, even in movements, tall and straight, but light-limbed."

"That's true of Fia—she can walk over snow and soft ground, barely making an imprint. I've thought it odd, since she has good height. But it is as if her will keeps her from settling."

Ariana moved to look down into his face. "You and I, it seems, might also be termed willful."

A smile curved his lips, and she kissed him. "After what we've just done, there's no denying our will."

"There is such passion between us! The Ellowan speak of such things, but I had assumed bliss would be found that resembled what we had when we first met—sweet and tender."

"The love of the young, Ariana, that is what we knew. Pure and innocent, we gave our hearts without question. But isn't that the way of things? You told me of Ellowan legend—your priestess and her prince didn't find bliss so easily. Instead, they fought and they hurt, and denied each other, and undoubtedly, spent much time apart. Why should we expect it will go easier for us?"

Ariana yawned. "Well, I hope the worst is over, anyway."

She peeked at him. "Although I can't deny that I like the battle."

He looked proud and happy. "I think each time with you I have found some new height, and then we go higher. It is as if we, as beings, go to the far end of our Circles, and then pulled by that which bonds us, go back to the center."

"That's a very romantic way of putting it. The center, I presume, is the rapture we find between us."

"It feels . . . creative."

She thought of the beautiful child their passion had created. "I suppose it is."

They lay together for a long while, dozing, then talking softly. Ariana left the bed to watch as the Dark Sun set and the distant blue sun rose in the distance. The red-ringed planet cast a brilliant light over sunset, and Damen, though used to the view, rose to stand in the doorway beside her. "It is beautiful, is it not? Never do I tire of the sight."

Ariana took his hand. "I had thought sunsets on Valenwood were the most spectacular, but nothing I've ever seen compares to this."

"No amber whales, though. Their song was something that amazed me. But I suppose such creatures couldn't live in water so warm as this."

"No, probably not. The amber whales have a distinct affinity for the waters of Valenwood."

He glanced at her. "What of these 'hyppos'? It appears they adjust to new climes with greater ease. My land could use more living things. There are many birds, as you saw today, but few animals save tree jumpers and some rather benign yet colorful insects. The ocean has fish, but nothing as interesting as these hyppos appear to be."

"They might adjust admirably, yes. Hyppos . . . spanning the galaxy. You will have to bring a few lingbats, too, to supervise. I doubt either would seriously alter your ecosystem."

He gazed down at her and Ariana filled with hope. "Perhaps it might be possible, one day. . . ."

What future they had together lay beyond—but beyond what?

"When do we depart for this meeting with the Automon commander?"

"I await a message now. But I expect it to come soon."

Ariana's brow puckered. "That could change everything. But for good, or for ill?"

"That, I do not know." He smiled, but she sensed that he, too, realized that much lay before them, despite her wish to have overcome all hurdles. "But for this evening, will you walk with me before the feast commences? There is a sight yet I would like to show you."

Ariana squeezed his hand, then rose on tiptoes to kiss his cheek. "I would walk at your side, my beautiful Dark Sun Lord, even into the caverns of fire."

He stooped and kissed her brow. "There will never be a need. Now choose something fitting from that basket of temptation you carried in here today, and we will go out among my people."

Ariana bit her lip. "I am so embarrassed. I mean, no one can question what we've been doing here."

"As you've observed, my people are uninhibited, and will think nothing of it. The caverns gave us this, at least, that lovemaking is no spectacle, but commonplace and natural. For reasons that elude me, Fia has not adopted this attitude, and keeps to herself, above such interaction. But for the others, love is accepted and cherished."

"It is the same for the Ellowan. In this, at least, we have no conflict."

Ariana rummaged through her basket of garments, then selected a long, flowing gown of gossamer-light fabric. It shimmered like cream satin, but subtler, with a moonlight glitter interspersed in the seamless weave. She pulled it on and found long fitted sleeves that peaked over the back of her hand, and a low-cut bodice that swept into a looser, full skirt. It floated when she moved, and its color changed from white to ivory to silver in the light. She admired herself in

Damen's crystal-rimmed mirror, then turned to him, shy with pleasure.

He stared in satisfying appreciation and she pressed her lips together to keep from giggling foolishly. He dressed, too, and her own appreciation soared. He wore a shirt of a similar material, but it bared his wide, strong shoulders and cut narrow over his waist. He wore leggings of slate grey and tied on the light leather shoes that she had seen the Dark Sun men wearing in the Crystal Plaza. He combed his long, black hair and it spread over his shoulders and down his back. Then he tied a strung crystal into a narrow braid and examined his own reflection in the mirror.

"You are beautiful, my Dark Sun Lord. And I have not missed that you have a large mirror in both your bedroom and your quarters on the ship."

He turned to her and grinned. "Do you speak to my vanity, my lady? Dare I ask what mirrors grace your own home on Valenwood?"

"I live in my parents' palace, as it happens—it is large and meant for many families, actually. But yes, I do have a mirror—or two—in my area."

"Or three, or four. . . ." Damen laughed, then held out his hand. "Shall we go?"

She placed her hand in his, and together, they walked from his house.

Chapter Nineteen

Damen's people mulled around the Crystal Plaza, and all appeared dressed for a feast. Some called out happily when they saw him, and some waved to Ariana, recalling their pleasant luncheon at the temple. Ariana felt at home, as much as she ever had on Valenwood, and perhaps more, as if these people who had survived the Dark Sun colonies truly understood her.

Fia stood near the Ariana Museum looking stiff and formal, though she had added a red and yellow flower to her blond hair. Her ice-blue gown revealed less than those worn by other women—it was long and cut straight, with a high waist, but she looked beautiful and young, and Ariana wondered why no man had claimed her heart.

"Has Fia had no suitors at all?"

"None that I know of, though her nature is so private that I'm not sure she'd tell me if she had. But I doubt it. She's never encountered anyone who made her nervous, who shattered anything of her composure. She's never met anyone she admired or respected more than herself."

"She respects and admires you."

Damen smiled. "She does, yes, but as a father. In that way, I am still viewed as her servant."

"I suppose that is generally true with parents." Ariana bit her lip, and said no more, but it pleased her that Damen had experience in this area.

Fia waved to them. Her gestures were somewhat stiff, as if she held every muscle at attention—as if to bend might mean to break, and she would prevent that at all costs. As they approached her, Ariana's heart moved in sympathy. Though Damen had saved her and tended her, and given her life a purpose, Fia still looked alone. It seemed she'd never found anyone who thought quite as she did, or perhaps, who understood the passionate—and restrained— nature of her heart.

Ariana held out her hand and squeezed Fia's slender arm. Fia looked at her in surprise. It would take more than friendship, or even Damen's fatherly love, to make the girl feel truly safe and truly connected. Ariana wanted to tell her there were other people like her in the galaxy, that grace and dignity were more than just bred in a race, but began in the soul. But she knew Fia wouldn't really hear her—she had to learn this for herself.

Fia stepped up to the doorway and held out her arm for their entrance. "Allow me to welcome you to the Ariana Museum and Gallery, Ariana. I personally took charge of its inception, and saw that its contents revealed the history and skill of our people."

From the far side of the plaza, Nob chuckled. "Tried to stop us from putting up any of the 'fancier' pieces, though."

Damen leaned to Ariana. "He means artwork depicting erotic acts."

Fia's eyes narrowed. "They were foul. Our premier artist convinced me that art, however graphic, must be presented, and I agreed." She paused. "But those depictions are in a reserved hall, and the children are not allowed to view them."

Damen shrugged. "It seemed a fair compromise." He

lowered his voice, and his brown eyes twinkled. "Of course, that particular gallery has become the target of many children's raids—I think they've viewed it more than everyone else combined."

Fia pretended not to hear him, but her lips tightened. Damen turned to Ariana and held out his arm, which she took. "I thought you might like a brief tour before the feast commences. Fia will join us."

As they entered, Fia took over as guide, and a small group gathered and followed along behind. "Within, you will see artifacts from all the Dark Sun colonies—as well as artwork designed and commemorated by the Dark Sun People."

Fia proceeded to guide them through a great hall filled with different nooks and smaller rooms, each depicting the unique colonies of the survivors. In one room, Automon shells were set up, representing each of the Automon shapes Ariana had seen. She looked at them closely, then turned to Damen.

"I see an alteration in some of these Automon."

"In what way?"

"Some of them have a more natural shape, designed after the human body. Yet others, those known as 'torch guards,' especially, have clearly been altered by less dexterous designers."

Damen nodded. "So our own researchers have noted. In fact, all functions of violence, even the neutralizing gas the Automon use, appear to have been added on or devised much later than the original structure, and by a different set of engineers."

"Interesting. I wonder what it means, on a deeper level?" She paused, then glanced up at him, seeking his reaction. "That more than one race has controlled the Automon, perhaps?"

"Perhaps."

She studied the Automon shell again. "I still find it odd that they're hollow, with no inner mechanisms to speak of. Have you learned anything about the energy source that controls them?"

"Not much, no, except that it's extremely powerful." Damen looked uneasy, and Ariana knew she had hit nearer to the mark than he liked. He knew more than he said, but with the meeting with the Automon commander looming before them, it might not be long before she found out the truth.

Fia's tour concluded with a visit to the art gallery section of the museum. This exhibit, more than any other part of the museum, touched Ariana's heart. Some carvings had been plumbed from cavern walls. There was rock art depicting workers at a task beyond their comprehension, and then scenes of tribal life, the feedings, and the violence. Some showed leaders engaged in conflicts such as she had first witnessed between Damen and his rival. Large glass cases held crystal-art, formations that had been carved and shaped, some resembling beasts, but most in a free-form art of the imagination.

The final part of the exhibit held newer art, those works created after freedom was won. Here, there were paintings and wood sculptures wrought of surpassing skill and beauty. Many reflected in various ways the shape of the Beginning Symbol. In the most striking, the left side of the ∞ was painted a dark, brooding shade of blue, and the other with a brighter, softer shade that resembled morning light. Where the colors entwined was painted white, representing the love that connected two separate entities into eternity.

"These rival Valenwood's finest artwork, and we are famed for our mosaics. . . ." Her eye caught on a dark-hued painting and she stopped short, then moved to look at it more closely. "That's me!"

Damen stood beside her, quiet as she stared up at her portrait. For a long while, she couldn't speak. She had known his people honored her and remembered her, but almost like a goddess, a fairy creature who had shown them the light of hope and then disappeared. But this painting revealed no goddess. Instead, a young girl looked back at her, her eyes wide and vulnerable. Her hair was a mass of

Join the Love Spell Romance Book Club
and **GET 2 FREE* BOOKS NOW—**
An $11.98 value!
Mail the Free* Book Certificate
Today!

Yes! I want to subscribe to the Love Spell Romance Book Club.

Please send me my **2 FREE* BOOKS**. I have enclosed $2.00 for shipping/handling. Every other month I'll receive the four newest Love Spell Romance selections to preview for 10 days. If I decide to keep them, I will pay the Special Members Only discounted price of just $4.49 each, a total of $17.96, plus $2.00 shipping/handling ($23.55 US in Canada). This is a **SAVINGS OF $6.00** off the bookstore price. There is no minimum number of books I must buy and I may cancel the program at any time. In any case, the **2 FREE* BOOKS** are mine to keep.

*In Canada, add $5.00 shipping and handling per order for the first shipment. For all future shipments to Canada, the cost of membership is $23.55 US, which includes shipping and handling.
(All payments must be made in US dollars.)

NAME: _____
ADDRESS: _____
CITY: _____ STATE: _____
COUNTRY: _____ ZIP: _____
TELEPHONE: _____
E-MAIL: _____
SIGNATURE: _____

If under 18, Parent or Guardian must sign. Terms, prices, and conditions subject to change. Subscription subject to acceptance. Dorchester Publishing reserves the right to reject any order or cancel any subscription.

The Best in Love Spell Romance!
Get Two Books Totally FREE*!

An $11.98 Value! FREE!

PLEASE RUSH MY TWO FREE BOOKS TO ME RIGHT AWAY!

Enclose this card with $2.00 in an envelope and send to:

Love Spell Romance Book Club
20 Academy Street
Norwalk, CT 06850-4032

short curls, tumbling this way and that, unkempt. Her face was small, and distinctly dirty. The impression was of earnest fragility, not the inner power of an unstoppable goddess.

She gazed up at Damen, shaken. "Is that what I looked like?"

"It is a good likeness, yes."

Her voice sank and became small. "So vulnerable?"

He smiled, tenderness in his eyes. "There is strength beneath the vulnerability, but yes, that is how I remember you."

She looked back at the picture, and with a rush, remembered what she had been. The fear, the helplessness, the dark, all came back to her. Tears formed in her eyes, though she hid them with great effort lest she wound the others by her reaction. "I will never feel that way again." It was a vow, and she surprised herself by saying it out loud.

Damen placed his hand on her shoulder, gently. "It is this we revere in you, Ariana. It may seem that we hold you as a goddess, as something great and strong and beautiful. And you are great and strong and beautiful. But your courage would mean nothing if the heart within weren't so piercing and exquisite and delicate. That's what this portrait reveals."

Fia looked up at the portrait, her face serious. "It is a good picture. I come here sometimes, when I feel lonely or the memory of captivity is heavy on me. I look at your face, and remember what it is to be strong."

Ariana looked around, abashed by the wisdom born in the Dark Sun colonies—wisdom that understood her, even when she did not. All her life, even before her abduction, she had fought in some measure this vulnerability, the acute sensitivity that so often caused pain. Yet it was here, where she was most frail, that she had found love, and now found herself honored. She stared down at her feet and felt small. "I have tried so hard to be strong."

Damen moved closer to her. The warmth of his body comforted her and she leaned her head on his shoulder.

"Your sensitivity is your strength, Ariana. It is in your eyes when you look at me, just as it was then. You see things others do not, and you are vulnerable, yes, yet you hold to your own heart and your own self the way the others in your party did not. It was this that claimed my heart, and this my people recognize. It was this the artist remembered in you, and captured here, so perfectly."

Ariana looked around. "Who is the artist?"

A slender young man stood in the corner of the room, so quiet she hadn't noticed him until now. Ariana stared at him and saw the deep compassion in his wide eyes, and she knew him. "You carved the rock art in the caverns!" She remembered Damen passing a younger boy a stick of meat, and knew this was the same man. He was the only one she recognized on sight, because the feature she recalled was the gentle light in his eyes, and the understanding.

As she looked at him, her tears returned. Here was someone who had seen inside her heart and into her soul, and had known her. Tears glimmered in his own eyes, because he saw that she understood what he had captured of her, and that his talent had reached the deepest places of his subject. She went to face him and a single tear slid down her cheek. "Thank you."

He bowed, his gentle face written with emotion. "Thank *you*."

Damen took her hand and held it in his. "Now that you have walked through our past, let us go now to what is, and we will feast."

Ariana glanced once more at her portrait. No matter where she went, she would carry this young girl with her, the image of what she had been. She had grown from this being. As it hurt to look at her own face, and to see her own fragility, another feeling emerged, stronger. Love. And even rarer—love of herself. Damen was watching her, and she saw a new light in his eyes, too. She heard his unspoken vow: *I will protect you, always.*

Ariana laced her fingers with his, and she whispered so that only he could hear. "I will protect you, too."

When they emerged from the museum, Ariana was surprised to find a long table set up in the center of the Crystal Plaza, and around it, numerous others, all decorated with crystal and silver. All had plates piled high with food of every imaginable type. She stood on the museum stairs and gaped, then realized she was very hungry.

"You dine outdoors?"

Damen started down the stairs—apparently, he was hungry, too, and Ariana followed. "It may be that my people favor the out-of-doors more because of our lives spent in darkness, but whenever the weather is good, we take our evening meal beneath the setting sun and rising stars."

He led her to the head of the table, and again, she was seated at his left. Fia stood at his right side, formal, but the rest of his people chose random spots and seated themselves as they wished. Damen's crew dispersed and mulled with the others. Graff seemed especially attentive to a dark-skinned girl, and Nob chattered happily with a group of children. No one seemed nervous, nor concerned about whatever plan Damen had laid out before them, but Ariana couldn't quite forget their uncertain future.

Bowls and platters were passed around the table, and no matter how much each person served themselves, there always seemed to be more, an abundance of riches. Ariana forgot her worries and eyed a platter of fruit. "What are those round, pink things? They look . . . succulent."

Damen grinned, then seized two for her plate. "We call these eplar—they grow in abundance all over this isle, and I think you will find they surpass anything you've eaten before."

She sank her teeth into one, tasted a tangy squirt both sweet and tart, then closed her eyes in bliss. "Much . . . appreciated." She spoke thickly, around the fruit, then stuffed in another bite. She swallowed, nodding. "Much more healthy than what you were forced to eat in the caverns. The Automon fed you too much dried, salted meat. It's a wonder you don't have serious health problems."

"Some suffered breathing ailments for a time, but as Nob observed, the air here is clear and healing, and all have recovered. As for meat, there is little source of it here, save fish, which we have in vast quantities."

He placed a filet of a white fish onto her plate, and she tasted it suspiciously. Her eyes widened, and she devoured the rest. "This is actually better than the fish we harvest in Valenwood! Lighter, but it's the spices your chefs have employed that make it so special." She eyed the platter, and Damen served her another helping.

He ate, too, but he seemed to be watching her, and after Ariana seized a second small loaf of raw-grained bread, she detected a smile on his lips. His own plate was emptied, and his attention wavered to another round of platters brought from the kitchens across the plaza.

"If we continue to eat like this, we'll resemble hyppos ourselves!"

Damen glanced at her body. "Have a care, Ariana! I enjoyed carrying you today—I don't want to be crumpled to my knees next time I make the effort."

She considered denying herself for her figure's sake, then abandoned the idea in favor of an interesting shellfish in a spicy sauce. Damen shook his head and laughed.

"I suppose a little more weight won't hurt you. If I lift you often, I should build up muscle enough. . . ."

She swatted his shoulder, then smacked her lips. "Delicious! That was my favorite dish so far. What's next?"

"Rolling you across the Crystal Plaza and hoisting you into my bed?"

"Ha! A day spent with you requires a great deal of energy—in more ways than sex, I might add! I have been very busy today. This is simply replenishment."

He leaned over and kissed her cheek, and Ariana realized with a warm rush of happiness that she was *content*. She wasn't afraid of him anymore, and she wasn't afraid of losing him. He had relaxed in her presence, too—maybe hours of shared rapture did that, but she felt comfortable at his side, and he was clearly comfortable enough to tease her.

She paused in her eating to gaze around. "I am so happy." She spoke with wonder and Damen placed his hand over hers.

"I have never seen you quite as beautiful as you are tonight, even with your cheeks puffed with food."

She swallowed, then glanced at him reproachfully. "Thank you very much."

"You once mentioned that Fia glows. I hadn't noticed it, or maybe I'd gotten used to the effect, but you have a radiance of your own, my lady. It's a softer light, an aura of hope and joy that I've never seen in another. It suits your nature, just as Fia's reflects her own grace."

She gazed up at him. "I suppose we all have this light that comes from within, from what we truly are. You have it, too. It resembles my father's somewhat, but his is different. He carries with him the light of what was, and he brings it into today. But yours . . . yours is the light of the future, of what will be. Hakon's, as I think of it, strikes me as a bright power that lives in both."

He frowned at the mention of Hakon, but she suspected the two could become friends, if Damen could overcome his jealousy. "You might like him, you know."

"I doubt that."

"He is very earnest. I think he would like you."

"Ha! He would scorn me as an inferior."

"He would not. Hakon is very perceptive of people's characters, and he always gauged them by what he saw, not by what they wanted him to see. I was never quite sure why he felt as he did about certain people, but he was generally right. He loathed Lissa, though I never knew what it was that annoyed him so. She thought as you do, that he considered her inferior, but I don't think that was the case. He saw something in her that he didn't like, and unfortunately, Hakon isn't very good at hiding his feelings."

"I can't wait to meet him." Damen's dry, flat voice indicated he would rather perish fighting the lizards of Torol, and Ariana sighed.

"I guess you're not likely to meet him any time soon. But he might surprise you, all the same."

"He's a pampered child of nobility, risking nothing, and all comes easily to him. I know exactly what to expect."

"I would thank you to remember that *I* am a 'pampered child of nobility' myself. Do you find this fault in me?"

"No, but you're special. You've endured hardship and pain, and you were of a sensitive and imaginative nature to begin with."

Ariana rolled her eyes. "Perhaps we can continue this conversation after you've met Hakon for yourself."

"Again, I can't wait."

Ariana shook her head, then turned to view the newest offering. "Pastries!" She wiped her mouth, then leaned forward as the desserts were served. "I was afraid you had only healthy food!"

Damen laughed. "Humanity requires something more than that, my lady. I would not condemn myself nor my people to a meal without sweet stuff."

"Good!" Ariana seized a round, flaky pastry, then snatched another that was covered in a pleasant and gently fragrant icing. She sniffed it and closed her eyes as her mouth prepared itself for the delicacy. She ate it in one bite, then regretted not having grabbed two—Damen's people had taken all the others.

Damen's brow angled. "Generally, people eat those in more than one bite." He ate his own carefully, deliberately savoring its flavor while she watched.

The goblets were filled with a light-colored juice that tasted like eplar fruit. It was cool and fragrant, and quenched thirst better than anything Ariana had sampled in her previous journeys. She drained her glass, then looked around for the decanter, which Damen supplied. At last, the platters and bowls seemed empty, and she sighed. "Is that all there is?"

He sat back in his seat and laughed. "In general, this is all that's required." He broke apart the last pastry on his plate, then slipped half between her lips.

Ariana ran her tongue around it. It was sweet and light, and dissolved pleasantly in her mouth. Damen finished his half, and Ariana at last leaned back in her chair. "There! That was the perfect ending to my day. Thank you."

The light in his dark eyes glimmered, and a new tingle stirred in her blood. "It was good, my lady. But as for the 'perfecting ending,' I promise you, that is yet to come."

Chapter Twenty

The days that followed were the happiest in Damen's life. All he had dreamed when he first left the Dark Sun caverns behind now came true in his life. Ariana was with him, living in the city he had built for her, sharing the bedroom he had designed thinking of the day he would bring her home. None of his youthful dreams had come close to the bliss they shared—he couldn't have imagined the fire between them, nor the eroticism inherent to her nature.

Each day gave him new joy—they swam together in the warm, blue sea, then lay on the white sand naked. He would watch her as she emerged from beneath the water, her long hair slick against her back. Wet, she offered still another glimpse of desire, and often, they hurried to some private nook and made love. He took her for walks in the forest, and along rivers, and they sat by the streams and talked for hours. When he brought her to the island's most beautiful waterfall, she led him into its spray, and they kissed until he felt as though they'd become one. When the warm rain fell on the island, they stood outside as everyone else sought shelter indoors.

It was the greatest bliss of his life, and he knew too soon it would end.

He felt the day's alteration before it came. Damen woke early, unlike him, and stood in his greeting room while Ariana still slept. He closed his eyes and heard footfalls outside. A soft but constant rain fell, and he discerned the squish of a man's soggy boots. He sighed deeply and opened the door.

Nob popped back in surprise, his hand still extended as he reached for Damen's door. "Sir! You did take me aback, you did! What are you doing here?"

"Answering my door."

"But I hadn't rung yet!"

"The message, Nob."

Nob's face puckered in concern and alarm, and perhaps suspicion. "You know about that, too, sir?"

"I am not that foresighted, Nob. But I knew it was coming, and your presence here in the hour of dawn indicates I'm right." He stood back and allowed Nob to enter.

Nob shook droplets from his coat, then handed Damen a printout. Damen scanned it, then handed it back. "Destroy this, and gather the men."

"Ready the ship, sir? How many are we taking?"

"The agreement is only one in seven sectors. We'll take the flagship, and one of the black shuttles. I'd rather they didn't learn about the gold-hued ones."

"Understood, sir." Nob sped away, leaving Damen's front door swinging.

"Nob may understand, but I do not." Ariana's soft voice startled him, and he turned to see her in the passageway, her long hair in disarray around her shoulders, her body covered only in a light green wrap.

"Ariana. . . ."

She entered the room and her face was grave. "Are we leaving?"

He hesitated. "It might be wiser for you to remain here."

"I don't think so." *I cannot lose you now*, her eyes said. "I'm going with you. They requested my presence, after all, and

207

you can't risk arousing their suspicions if I'm not there."

"I suppose you're right." He gathered her into his arms and held her, resting his cheek on her head.

Ariana looked up at him, her delicate face plaintive, as if she guessed somehow what was at stake. "Another hurdle between us, after all?"

He tried to smile, but his heart felt heavy. "Whatever happens, please trust me, Ariana. I haven't given you much reason, despite what we've shared, but please know that I do what must be done. Things are more clear than they may seem."

"You are making me nervous. Are you sure of this plan of yours, whatever it is?"

He shrugged. "As sure as I can be. Nothing in the universe is certain, my lady. But this meeting, and all that comes after, has been well thought out. I promise you."

She reached up and touched his face. "I hope so." She looked at her feet, and he felt an imminent disclosure, one he had sensed she wanted to make many times since they'd come to his island. She looked up at him again, her expression set. "There is something I have to tell you, before we head into danger. About the past . . ."

Damen pressed his fingers to her lips. "Angel, there is no need."

"There is a need. Damen. . . ."

Damen's monitor sounded, and Fia's voice broke in. "Damen! The crew is assembled, and the ships prepared for takeoff. Four hovercraft await us outside. I have taken the liberty of storing on board your vessel some of Ariana's belongings, as well as your own necessities."

Damen smiled at Ariana but she bit her lip. "It seems we're ready. What did you want to tell me?"

She gulped, but then sighed. "Perhaps now is not the time."

"Then later. We will be going at top speed, so the time of travel will be short, but we will have some time alone."

"After the meeting—we will talk then. You have too much on your mind now."

He gazed at her, but said no more. *The past.* For all the time they'd spent together on his island, they had spoken little of the time in between their first encounter in the caverns and their meeting on the outpost. Often, however, he had felt something hidden between them, a matter as yet undivulged. He had waited for her to open her heart, but now, when she seemed ready to do so, he wasn't sure he was ready to hear her secrets.

If she had known other lovers . . . Though she had told him he was the first to stir passion, that didn't mean she hadn't lain with other men, and she had said the Ellowan were a decidedly sensual people. He could accept that—after all, he had known many women that way. But when the moment came, he couldn't let her speak.

Ariana returned to his bedroom and dressed in her old but appealing attire, then emerged looking much as she had when he first saw her in the outpost tavern. She carried a small sack of her belongings, and as she bound it together, he spotted the gossamer outfit she had worn to the temple luncheon. He knew why she brought it—for memory's sake, and because she liked it so much.

Damen's heart sank because he knew too well what this meant. When this mission concluded, Ariana intended to return to Valenwood. Because he loved her, he would do nothing to stop her. But the blissful, sweet days together were at an end.

Only a skeleton crew traveled to the ice world of Eisvelt—Damen and Ariana, and Fia, Nob, and Graff, as well as a small engineering team below. They had passed the seven-sector mark and saw no sign of encroaching vessels, so proceeded onward, silent as they approached the lone planet of a distant, blue-white sun. From above, it looked completely white—and forbidding.

Nob gestured at the view port, though nothing could yet be seen besides the planet. "Scanners indicate a ship landed on the far side of the planet, sir. There's another nearby, looks like a one-manned craft."

"That will be the rogue trader's vessel, no doubt. The best of them travel alone, but those I have seen were formidable vessels—much faster than larger ships."

Ariana came up beside Damen and cocked her head to one side. "The best of them? I thought you were the best of them!"

"As a matter of fact, I've spent my share of time in a one-manned craft, and made a name for myself in the Border Territory."

Nob nodded, proud. "Them were the early years, sir. When you weren't quite so serious. Sure got a lot of loot, though!"

Ariana eyed him doubtfully. "I think it is best I hear no more of this particular tale!"

Damen grinned. "For the best."

Fia looked between them, frowning. "I want to go with you to the planet's surface. It might be dangerous."

Damen smiled at her, then touched her arm. "No, Fia. I need you here. No matter what happens down there, you must return to the home world." He paused. "If we don't return, you know what to do."

For the first time in her life, Damen saw Fia's uncertainty. "But what if I am unable . . . ?"

He bent and kissed her forehead. "When the time comes, you will do what must be done, and you will face whatever happens with the same courage you've faced everything in your life. I have faith in you."

His words strengthened her and Fia raised her chin. "I will not disappoint you."

"You never have."

Fia restrained any evidence of emotion, then took the captain's station. But Ariana was gazing up at Damen, and to his surprise, he saw tears in her eyes. She smiled, then rose suddenly on tiptoes and kissed his cheek. "You are a very good father."

Nob slowed the ship so that it moved in unison with the planet's orbit. "We're almost in position, sir. Everything's ready. Graff and I will man the bridge, and we've got another engineer below. Your shuttle is ready."

Damen looked at Ariana. She stood peering out the view port at the ice world, then shivered as if its cold had already reached her. She wore a white snow-coat, puffed to preserve warmth, over her jacket and vest. Her long hair hung loose. He pictured it swirling in the wind, blinding her, and he smiled, then passed her a white cap. "You might need this."

She eyed the cap doubtfully. "I will look very silly."

"But you'll be warm."

She glanced at his head. "You're not wearing a hat."

He hesitated. "I don't see a need."

She huffed and looked knowing, but didn't pursue the matter further. They both put on warm gloves, then descended to the shuttle bay together. Damen secured the hatch, and they entered the small shuttle. He took the controls while Ariana peered out at the looming planet. A frown grew ever tighter on her lips.

"I have a bad feeling about this. Are you sure they won't just shoot us on sight?"

"If I considered that possible, I wouldn't bring you with me."

She fell silent, but her dark expression didn't alter. "Still, there's something wrong down there. Some . . . *malice*. I feel it."

Damen glanced at her. "So among their other gifts, the Ellowan are foresighted, are they?"

She shook her head. "The ability runs strong in my father's people, though I haven't experienced it often myself. But I'm sure of it, Damen. The person—or whatever it is down there—is not to be trusted."

"You haven't been a pirate long enough, my lady. None of my deals or negotiations are ever based on trust."

"Even with me?"

"Even with you."

Ariana sighed. "No. I've made that mistake a few times myself. It is better to doubt."

They fell silent, together, but even as his mind steeled himself for the matter at hand, Ariana's words lingered in

Stobie Piel

his mind. Would he not place his life in her hands? He would. And now he asked her to place her life in his. As they lowered to the frozen surface of Eisvelt, the vow he made to protect her at all costs cemented in his heart.

He landed the shuttle, and Ariana leaned forward, squinting against the bright sunlight reflecting on mountains of pure snow. "I wish I'd brought reflector lenses."

It was a charming image to think of her with a black screen wrapped around her little face. "I believe I have some in the snow-kit Graff provided us."

Ariana's face twisted to one side. "No. I must present a dignified appearance."

He reached into the bag and fished for the lenses, then handed a pair to her. She hesitated before putting them on. "Only if you wear them, too."

Now he hesitated, sure they might indeed look foolish. He didn't care what the Automon commander thought of his appearance, but Ariana's opinion mattered. Ariana leveled a dark look his way, then rose to her feet in a commanding stance before him. "If you were any more vain . . . the sun is bright on the snow. Wear them!"

Damen laughed, then fetched the other pair from the bag. They faced each other, then placed the screens on their faces at the same time. Both smiled in unison at the other's appearance. Ariana moved to open the hatch, but Damen caught her arm and drew her back. He gazed at her for a while, then touched her cheek with his gloved hand.

"I love you, you know."

Her voice came small, quavery with emotion. "I love you, too. I always have."

They said no more, for there was no need, not now. Damen opened the hatch, and an icy wind stung their faces. Ariana shivered. "I hope it's not far!"

He pulled out a transmitter and a director, then pointed them in what he hoped was the right direction. Though the sky was blue and clear, snow swirled in the air, cast up from the ground in a white haze. They struggled to see, but beneath the low covering of new snow, the footing was hard-packed. Damen's monitor kept icing up, and he breathed on it, then wiped it with his glove to clear it. "We're on the right heading. It shouldn't be far now."

Ariana shaded her eyes from both sun and snow, then pointed. "I see something ahead. A ship, I think! It doesn't look like an Automon ship, though. It's way too small, even for one of their shuttles."

"It's the rogue trader's ship. He's landed a bit closer to the meeting place than promised, but given the poor visibility, I suppose that's no wonder. Come, let us veer somewhat right, and keep a good distance from his vessel."

They did so, and after a while further, another ship came into view. Like all Automon vessels, it was black, and though obviously a shuttle, it was larger than most.

Ariana stopped as if her own will prevented her from drawing closer. Damen hesitated. "We're almost there—if nothing else, their shuttle will provide some shelter."

She turned to him, aghast. "We're not going on board that thing, are we?"

"No, but we will meet near its hatch."

She nodded, but she looked tense. He hoped it was just the cold, because to see Ariana afraid pierced his heart too deeply. They approached the ship's portal, and the hatch opened. A wide plank lowered, then crunched softly into the snow. Ariana shivered beside him as they waited and he felt sure her teeth were chattering. Damen moved closer beside her, but it might be unwise to allow this Automon commander to know how dear the Ellowan woman was to him.

They watched, almost spellbound, as a row of Automon came forth. Not torch guards or battlers, but Damen guessed they still contained a supply of neutralizing gas. In this swirling wind, distributing it to a target would be nearly impossible. Their purpose wasn't to attack, though they might prove some defense if the Automon commander himself came under fire. Their purpose was clearly to impress, and perhaps intimidate. *Control.* This mattered above all else to the one who directed the Automon.

Ten Automon came forward and lined the walkway, five on each side. Damen waited, but Ariana's words echoed in his mind. *Malice*. He began to sense it, too, but though he had expected a formidable foe, there was something more personal in this energy, as if directed at him. The snow swirled around his feet, then up and around the plank. The Automon paid no heed, but beyond, the hatch portal was black. A single light focused down from the entrance, illuminating nothing of the vessel within.

Ariana tore off her reflector lens, then stuffed it in her side pack. Damen did the same, and they waited as another figure appeared. Taller than the Automon, a robed human appeared. Beside Damen, Ariana sucked in a quick breath. "I knew it! It had to be a human."

The human stood in the hatch, and at a signal, the Automon turned to face their leader. Slowly, the leader emerged from his vessel, and passed through his servants toward Damen. Damen looked up, waiting. All the pain and suffering of his people flashed before his eyes as the snow swirled around the leader's boots. With all his will in rebellion, Damen lowered his head and bowed.

Chapter Twenty-one

The Automon leader came to the foot of the plank, then stopped. His over-robe swirled in the wind. He pulled back his hood, revealing brown hair flecked with grey and a close-cropped beard. Despite his robes, he appeared fairly ordinary—though Damen had felt sure the Automon leader was human, he had expected a representative of a more exotic race.

The snow curled around the leader's legs, but he ignored the chill as he faced Damen and Ariana. His mouth formed what Damen guessed to be a perpetual smirk. The man gripped a black console in one hand, perhaps a device that imparted messages to the Automon.

The leader looked back, and another figure appeared in the black portal. Taller by almost a head than the Automon commander, this being defied human shape. It was wider, much more heavily robed, and walked with an awkward, thumping gait. As it drew up beside the leader, it issued a high, squeaking sound that startled both the leader and Ariana, whose eyes narrowed suspiciously. The strange being clamped its large, mittened hand—or paw—over its chest and the squeaking silenced abruptly.

Damen glanced at Ariana. "The rogue trader, I presume."

Her brow furrowed. "Maybe."

The Automon leader held up his hand, palm outward—a sign of peace and welcome, but it seemed like a false gesture, and one copied from the Dark Sun colonies. "I am Commander Camron Mallik, Governor of the Automon Empire. Welcome! I apologize for the weather, but Eisvelt has few pleasantries to offer."

Damen touched Ariana's arm, and together, they approached the commander. Though the leader had thrown back his hood, oblivious to the cold and swirling snow, the rogue trader remained fully covered, his face concealed beneath an odd, screenlike mask.

Damen held his head high in a posture of arrogance. Now more than ever, the guise of a pirate leader would be vital. " 'Governor?' Are you not the true ruler of the Automon Empire?"

Mallik offered a condescending smirk. "Surely, you cannot image that the Supreme Ruler, the High King himself, would deign to treat with the captain of even such a formidable fleet as yours?"

Damen's eyes narrowed. "King? From what system does his reign originate?"

"One vaster than your imagination would allow, I fear. Vaster by far than the paltry union known as the Intersystem."

Ariana huffed beside Damen. "And one by us unknown, apparently. Or do you fear to say its name, *Governor?*"

"Fear?" The commander gazed upward as if confused. "No, I do not fear, but its translation into the Intersystem language is ponderous. For your sake, I will simply say the title. I serve the High King of the Gyandorath System, many star leagues across the galaxy, ruler of a powerful race, and wielder of greater power than anything the Intersystem worlds have known."

"So it was these 'high beings' that sent out Automon to

terrorize other systems?" Ariana's grey eyes narrowed in anger, so Damen moved in front of her.

Damen assessed the commander with a casual and condescending frown. "I came here to treat with the true leader of the Automon, and no lackey."

He expected anger from the commander, but instead, Mallik returned Damen's challenging gaze evenly. "Though subservient to the High King, I assure you, Captain, I have complete authority to negotiate terms. The Automon fleet is at my disposal, and through the High King's power, they answer to me."

Damen frowned. He clearly had to succor Mallik before reaching the king. "Very well. The Automon Commander has requested the Dark Sun Lord's presence in conference. I have come. What might you offer that I could consider of interest?"

Commander Mallik laughed, still smug. "Well said, my *lord!* You get right to the point. I like that in a rival—or an ally?" He turned his attention to Ariana. "This must be the Intersystem representative." The man's eyes scanned Ariana, and his smirk intensified. It might not be malice, but this attitude was certainly grating. "Such beauty—perhaps it was Intersystem wisdom to send an enchantress to throw the Dark Sun Lord off his guard."

Damen grit his teeth and forced a casual air. "Allow me to present Ariana, whose presence you also requested. I would be interested to learn how you heard she was with me."

The commander waved his hand absently at the robed figure beside him. "The Keiroit here told me that you 'guarded' her on board your ship—and wisely suggested that she accompany you."

Damen opened his mouth to reply, but Ariana cut him off. "A *Keiroit?*"

Damen eyed her doubtfully, and saw her surprised expression. "You know of this race?"

She shifted her weight, confused. "I do. They are strange

217

creatures of the swamplands of Keir, a planet near Valenwood."

Damen glanced at the figure, sure he had found the source of a villainous plot. "Then his presence here seems unlikely to be coincidence."

"Indeed. . . ." She moved forward, ignoring the Automon commander, and fixed her attention on the other. "You're a Keiroit?"

The creature uttered an odd mumble, then bowed. "I am." Its voice was deep, but somehow reminiscent of the croaks uttered by the small amphibians that populated the lakes and ponds of Damen's island.

Mallik laughed again. "It may surprise you, Ariana, to learn that many of the Intersystem worlds send out 'rogue traders.' "

She cast a disdainful look at the commander, then backed away to Damen. She tossed her head. "It doesn't surprise me in the least. The Keiroits are well known fiends, disloyal and treacherous, and unable to hold any alliance for long. The Ellowan have long mistrusted them."

He wasn't sure why, but Ariana's tone didn't ring completely true to Damen's ears. It almost seemed as if she was protecting this creature, though he couldn't imagine what would inspire her to defend a traitor.

Mallik directed a mock look of condemnation and shame toward the Keiroit. "The lady thinks little of your kind, Keiroit. But some might say that to fall from grace in the Intersystem is a point in your favor."

The Keiroit muttered unintelligibly, then seemed to nod. "As I told you myself, Commander."

Damen looked between them. "What has this creature offered you? Tell me, that I might better it."

Ariana glanced at him sharply, but he kept his gaze pinned on the commander. Mallik seemed pleased with Damen's blunt manner, and stepped off the plank so that they stood face to face. Even in the swirling wind, Damen detected a faint odor of stale breath, the scent of a man who spends little time in open air, and whose diet is limited to food much-processed and flavorless. Apparently, Ariana noticed it, too, because she grimaced.

"The Keiroit has made . . . interesting propositions. But I will say first and foremost, it is the power of the Dark Sun Fleet that interests me most. What the Keiroit can deliver from the Intersystem has value, but the might you have accumulated—and the wealth, might serve me even more."

The Keiroit stepped—or hopped—down beside the commander, and seemed angry. "What can this villain offer the Automon Empire that I can't pilfer from my Intersystem sources? I've shown you proof of my wares, human, though in a small portion to what else I have at my disposal. What can he give you that I can't better?"

Keeping his gaze fixed on Damen, Mallik barely noticed the Keiroit. "Why, the power of the Dark Sun People, my good Keiroit. They have stolen what is rightfully mine, but even in doing so, they have proven their skill. If such a force could be brought under control, managed, directed, what more might we do?"

Damen recognized a truth inside the lie. Mallik wanted his people as slaves, probably for battle, where they would be considered more expendable than the Automon. But Mallik's desire for order was real, and probably innate to his character. Yet like many before him, he had taken it outside himself, and insisted on controlling others to inflate his own importance. Serving the High King, when he had no power of his own, must have given Mallik the impetus to seize that power in some other way.

Damen held Mallik's gaze. "What more, indeed?" He felt Ariana's shocked gaze as she began to understand what he was offering, and what the Automon commander wanted. But he couldn't look at her, not now.

Mallik glanced idly at the Keiroit. "Don't fret, Keiroit. I have use for your offer, too. Here, where the snow falls and all is concealed, let us three clasp hands and seal the agreement."

Damen couldn't look at Ariana, but he felt her. This moment was long planned and he couldn't be distracted now.

He held out his gloved hand in a fist, and the commander laughed, then nodded to the Keiroit. The creature placed its large paw—or fin—upon Damen's, and Mallik set his own black-gloved hand upon theirs. It was the agreement of kings and of pirates alike, but as it concluded, Ariana backed away. Damen allowed himself to see her. Tears glistened on her cheeks and froze there in the cold wind and she shook her head in disbelief.

"What are you doing? You can't enter an alliance with him!"

Trust me. But this time, she didn't hear his unspoken words. She moved away from him and his heart ached. "No. . . ." She turned to Mallik, a light of fury in her bright eyes. Damen feared that she might act rashly, and he caught her arm to draw her back. "Why did you want me here? The Intersystem offers you nothing." She paused to cast an accusatory glance the Keiroit's way. "Nothing that isn't stolen, and we have the might to resist you."

Mallik's patronizing smirk returned in force, and Damen's heart chilled. "Do you, indeed? I wonder. . . . Aligned with the Dark Sun Fleet, can even the prime worlds of the Intersystem Council long resist, should we decide to visit?"

Ariana's mouth dropped, then snapped shut and her small hand formed a fist. "You're damned right, we can resist! We will blow you out of the sky!"

Mallik held up his hand and laughed. "I do not say this is my intention—only that it might be wise for the Intersystem leader to consider my power. He's your father, isn't he?" At this the commander stopped, grinning, but the Keiroit looked at him quickly. *Surprised.* The Keiroit might have told the commander of Ariana's presence—but he hadn't revealed her true heritage. Of that, Damen felt strangely certain.

Ariana trembled beside him, refusing to meet his eyes. He knew her—she held hope that his actions were a trick, and she fought to trust him. But she didn't dare look at him lest she see something that betray that trust again. "So you expect me to return to my people and tell them it's in their best interest to treat with you? If so, you've miscalculated my response."

That smirk had become so irritating that Damen was hard pressed not to strike the man. Mallik reached out and patted Ariana's head as if she was a child. He dislodged her cap, no doubt purposefully, and it slid forward over her eyes. She jammed it back in place as he spoke. "What a charming creature you are! I'm almost sorry to have to give you up."

Damen's fist clenched. "Give her up? This woman is my prisoner, Commander. It is I who decide her fate."

Mallik remained nonchalant. "No longer, I'm afraid."

Ariana backed away. "What do you mean?"

"Simply that I've promised you to this Keiroit—by way of a payment for his services, and evidence of my good will. Seems he feels he can get quite a hefty ransom for you."

This, Damen hadn't foreseen. "This does not sit well with me, Commander. It may threaten our agreement, for I also have a stake in ransom."

Ariana froze, but Damen placed himself before her. All he had struggled to gain seemed meaningless if he lost her. His plan could falter—but he would not give her up. "The woman is mine."

"You have a big heart, Damen of the Dark Sun!" Another voice spoke from within the ship, and Damen looked up in amazement. A woman appeared, then stepped out from the darkness behind her. Unlike the others, she wore little covering. Instead, her attire was feminine, a blue gown with an open neckline, and her legs were bare. She paused as if her appearance at this juncture had been long rehearsed, even to the extent of positioning herself in the portal's only light. Ariana gasped in recognition, and though the Keiroit had been aboard the vessel, even if briefly, he seemed almost as shocked as Ariana.

Heedless of the Automon commander, Ariana marched up to the plank, her eyes wide with shock. "Lissa! It can't be!"

Damen moved closer to Ariana. "Is this the woman of your group from the cavern?"

Lissa smiled, and then he recognized her. It was a wide smile, used for effect instead of as evidence of real happiness. "Damen! That is what you're called now, isn't it? Damen? Oh, yes—we have heard of your exploits." She maneuvered slowly down the plank, careful not to slip on the ice and snow in her light slippers. "You are renowned throughout the galaxy. Who would have thought? But you were always so resourceful, and so strong."

Lissa made a wide berth around the Keiroit, then moved toward Damen and Ariana, but stopped beside the commander. Her gaze remained fixed on Damen. For an instant, the look in her eyes reminded him of Ariana when she caught sight of pastries. "You don't remember me." A contrived pout made him think of tavern wenches who had hoped he wanted more from them than ale. "I'm hurt. But I suppose I look so much different than I did back in the cavern." She paused as if awaiting a compliment. Damen remained silent.

She glanced at Ariana, and her smile turned kind, even sympathetic, as if she greeted an old, dear friend—one whom illness had ravaged, perhaps. "You are still pretty, I see." Her eyes narrowed as she inspected Ariana's face. "I see no wrinkles, nor any marked evidence of your hardships. Age doesn't show even the slightest bit on your face. It must be our Nirvahdi blood that keeps us looking younger than our years."

The Keiroit grunted its disdain. "If ever a trivial matter upstaged the great . . ."

Lissa looked at the Keiroit sharply, then smiled, but her expression was more uncertain this time. "Am I correct in guessing that you're the rogue trader Camron mentioned? I'm sorry I wasn't able to meet you when you first came aboard. I was getting ready for Damen's arrival." She reached out and touched the Keiroit's vast sleeve in a friendly gesture, but the creature recoiled as if she might harbor disease. "You must forgive us. Ariana and I are the dearest friends, and I love her like a sister. We were captured together. . . ."

The Keiroit's head tilted to one side, decidedly scornful now. "Her misfortune was double, then." Lissa's eyes narrowed, and her face looked suddenly hard. The Keiroit garbled, then croaked, one of the oddest sounds Damen had ever heard. "This reunion doesn't interest me, Commander. I am in a hurry."

Lissa went to Ariana, her eyes glistening as if she had been reunited with a long-lost sister. She touched Ariana's arm as if in comfort, then hugged her with a tearful sniff, but Ariana didn't respond. "You must be so shocked to see me. But I was just as shocked to hear of your presence on Damen's ship. His prisoner? That must have been so awful for you! I prayed it wasn't so, that Camron had misunderstood the message we received from this trader." She stopped and sighed, her face giving every appearance of genuine concern. "It appears that things haven't unfolded quite as you hoped back in the caverns. I was so afraid they wouldn't. I tried to warn you, but you have always been so impulsive and just fling yourself into things without preparing or being sure of the outcome."

Ariana hesitated, and Damen realized that though Lissa's brain might indeed be trivial, she had skill of another kind. She chose her words well, and like any well-honed weaponry, they hit their mark too often.

Ariana's lips twisted to one side. "What madness brings you here, Lissa? I cannot believe you would join with the one responsible for our abduction."

Lissa cast her gaze downward as if deeply grieved over some misunderstanding between them. "The High King of Gyandorath is a great ruler, blessed with powers we in the Intersystem can't understand, and Camron serves him faithfully. But truly, if we must blame anyone for our abduction, I'm afraid it must be the King. He is high above the likes of us and perhaps is somewhat indifferent to our fate."

"He sounds wonderful."

"The High King has many emissaries. We can't expect

him to know exactly what methods the Automon employ on each and every one. I know that Camron has only the best intentions for our galaxy."

Ariana's brow arched. "The whole galaxy, or just the parts belonging to someone else?"

Mallik frowned, but Lissa remained sympathetic, as if she understood that Ariana's sarcasm came only from hurt. "If you would allow yourself to know him, with an open mind, perhaps you would see him as I do. He has the most ordered mind, and his sense of structure could benefit so many! You know how the Intersystem Council runs things—countless races, all with their own little problems and demands. Your father is brilliant, of course, and much renowned, but really, you must admit that he is lax in the area of control."

Ariana frowned. "You mean, he doesn't interfere with others, nor dictate his will upon them. That, Lissa, is precisely why he was chosen as leader!"

Damen glanced at her, and he understood even more why even the pirates of the Border Territories spoke Arnoth's name with admiration.

Lissa stroked Ariana's arm in a sympathetic gesture. Damen fought an urge to slap her hand away. "Of course, you love your father. You're so much like him! I don't mean to suggest he's done a poor job—just that he might benefit from Camron's sterner methods."

"Like employing torch guards against undefended cities, or raising slaves to mine malloreum until they're bodies are broken—or until the Automon release a lava flood over their heads?"

"Those awful tales have been much exaggerated, I'm afraid. It was nothing as bad as rumor makes it."

Damen revealed nothing, but his anger soared. How often was this same lie told to cover countless atrocities throughout the galaxy, to diminish the suffering of humankind and their brethren, so that the others could march forward, in the same blind quest for power?

"As one born in a Dark Sun colony, I disagree." He stopped himself—this was no time to reveal his vengeance against those who had made his people slaves. "But it matters little to me now." His voice had a strange effect on Lissa. A distinct tremor seized her, and she seemed almost unnerved to meet his eyes.

"Of course, I have nothing but sympathy for the Dark Sun miners." He noted that she didn't refer to them as slaves, and he saw a careful mind at work beneath the veneer of emotion. And yet, he saw as clearly that it was emotion that drove her, that fired all she desired, and all she did. But what she wanted, Damen didn't know.

Lissa turned to Ariana, as if the sight of Damen had shattered her composure in some unfathomable way. "You should have seen him, Ariana! He was magnificent—leading a rebellion against the Automon, proving himself capable of any feat!"

Damen eyed her with misgivings. "As I recollect, you departed from my group as soon as you were able."

She cast her gaze upward and bit her lip as if tormented by an old grief, one that tore at her heart even now. "It must have seemed that way, I know. But Kaila and I were trapped aboard a barely functional ship. We tried, desperately, to contact you, but it had been auto-programmed by the Automon, and we were simply trapped, destined to follow its course. I was so lucky it was programmed for Camron's space station!"

Mallik looked smug. "I am the lucky one, to have the most beautiful woman in the galaxy delivered to my command center."

Mallik placed his arm over Lissa's shoulder. Though she didn't push him away, her lips tightened as if his touch pained her. "Lissa has become a great service to me."

The Keiroit croaked again, a sound of obvious scorn. "I'll bet."

Lissa shot a dark look at the rogue, but replaced it with a quick smile. "Camron has been wonderful to me, and he is incredibly powerful, of course. I couldn't ask for more." As she spoke, she managed to free herself from the commander's obviously unwanted touch. She bent to brush snow off her delicate shoes, then moved subtly away from his side.

Ariana looked around in disgust. "Where is Kaila? Has she also joined with our enemy? I remember that she was gullible, but not that big a fool."

Only a slight flicker in Lissa's dark eyes betrayed her anger with Ariana. "Kaila has passed, Ariana. She was always of ill health. With the journey and all our hardships . . . it was just too much for her."

"Passed?" Ariana huffed. "You mean she died. How convenient!"

Lissa winced as if Ariana's accusation wounded her. "I know how much pain you're suffering, Ariana, and that is why you are being so cold now." Again, she touched Ariana, and this time, Ariana's whole body stiffened. "You can't imagine how much I grieved to lose Kaila—she was devoted to me. For days, I did nothing but weep. You know how sensitive and emotional I am."

Mallik grinned, partly fond, and partly condescending. "I can attest to that, my dear."

She cast him a quick, playful glance, then turned back to Ariana. "I can't stand to see you suffering so terribly, Ariana. It hurts me as much as it hurts you."

Ariana's brow angled. "What makes you think I'm suffering?"

Lissa glanced at Damen. For an instant, he caught a hungry look in her eye, but it vanished, replaced with a look of feminine sympathy. "You can't fool me, Ariana. I've always been able to read your emotions—I know what you're thinking."

To Damen's surprise, Ariana laughed. "If that were true, you'd be running for your life and hiding in the back of that black ship!"

He repressed a smile. Clearly, Lissa didn't know the violence Ariana of Valenwood could inflict.

But Lissa didn't seem concerned. "You try to hide your pain, but it must have been such a shock to learn this man you thought you loved has turned into such a formidable opponent to your father's realm. It must have hurt deeply to learn of his prowess with women, especially. You must have heard of his legendary skill with women? Even far away on Camron's space station, I heard the rumors!"

Damen considered strangling Lissa then and there but Ariana shrugged, idly. "I pretty much knew of that first-hand, Lissa."

"Did you?" Lissa looked concerned, and even more sympathetic. "You haven't given yourself to him again, have you? Ariana! I can't bear to think of you hurt that way."

"I wouldn't say it *hurt*."

Defiant angel. But Lissa's eyes darkened, and beneath the smile she wore, Damen detected something much more dangerous—*malice*.

"It must be terrible to have believed you had Damen's heart, and then been forced to learn how little you mean to him, to realize you never really knew him at all." Ariana clenched her small hands into fists, and this time, Damen made no move to stop her.

But Lissa took no note of Ariana's budding fury. "Partly, it must be considered the fault of your raising. You have always been adorable, but you were just the tiniest bit spoiled." She spoke as if teasing, but the malice flickered ever stronger in her eyes. "And now, to find you're not important in . . ."

The Keiroit stepped abruptly forward and smacked Mallik roughly on the shoulder. "What is this, Commander? I don't need to hear any more of this inane babble. I came in good faith. I want the woman. Give her to me, and I will leave you to your dealings."

Damen's throat clenched. "That, Keiroit, is not an option. Find yourself another hostage."

The Keiroit faced him. It wasn't malice—it was anger, and a much more powerful will than Damen had guessed. "*You* find yourself another victim, pirate! She comes with me." The rogue withdrew a strange, short rifle from beneath his cape.

Mallik backed away in surprise and alarm. "What is the

meaning of this, Keiroit? You assured me you carried no weapons."

The Keiroit almost shrugged, though it was an odd, lumpy effect, and seemed to dislodge one of his shoulders. Something squeaked again beneath his robe, and one of his lumps seemed to move upward like a scurrying insect. Mallik didn't seem to notice anything strange in this—presumably the physique of Keiroits could take any number of shapes, but Lissa's eyes narrowed in suspicion. The Keiroit waved his short rifle idly, and in doing so, replaced the odd, crawling lump to his shoulder. "I lied. Thing is, Commander, we rogues don't trust no one. See? I came for the woman, and I mean to have her. She's worth a lot to me."

Fear gripped Damen's heart. "She's worth more to me."

Ariana studied the Keiroit for a moment, and the slightest of smiles curved her lips before she cleared her expression. She faced Damen, unafraid and strangely calm. "I will go with the Keiroit."

Blood drained from his face, but he shook his head. "No."

"Oh, make no mistake. Things aren't finished between us, my lord, and we will meet again. You can count on that."

"No!" He reached to grab her, but she went to the Keiroit and he took her arm.

Lissa looked between them, her suspicion intensified, though Damen wasn't sure why. "There is something wrong here."

The Keiroit glanced at her. "Only that you've delayed me from an important rendezvous. Come, woman."

The creature seized Ariana's arm roughly, then started away, but Damen leapt after him. Ariana looked back, and shook her head. Her eyes beseeched him for an understanding he couldn't begin to give. "You asked me to trust you. Then trust me. We *will* meet again." Her voice lowered, and her eyes shifted toward the Keiroit. To Damen's surprise, she even smiled. "And soon."

He had no idea what she meant, but the Keiroit dragged her away. Damen hesitated. *Do I trust you enough to let you go?*

Lissa spoke quickly to Mallik, and he signaled the Automon. "Stop, Keiroit! Wait!"

The snow swirled, and the cold wind brought the sound of a shrill squeak from the Keiroit's body. This time, Lissa herself shouted. "I know that accursed squeal! Stop him!"

Mallik eyed her doubtfully. "The Keiroit has what he came for. Let him go."

She whirled around, furious. "You fool! That is no Keiroit. He has tricked us! Don't let him reach his ship!"

Damen turned, but the Keiroit had broken into a surprisingly agile run, and Ariana ran beside him. The Keiroit bounded up a snow bank toward its ship. Lissa waved her fists and screamed. "Don't let them get away! Camron, summon the torch guards!"

Mallik hesitated, but apparently Lissa's word had more weight than Damen had at first imagined. He engaged the small black console to summon the Automon. Four torch guards appeared—the top half of an Automon built onto a hovering platform—and these were capable of greater speed than any of the known land shuttles. Damen's heart held its beat as four swarmed from the black portal into the swirling wind.

Lissa shouted at the torch guards. "Hurry! Don't let him get away!"

The torch guards ignored her plea, and adjusted methodically, then sighted their target. Ariana looked back as she ran, desperate, and she shouted something into the wind. The Keiroit whirled, then tossed his cumbersome robe aside to take better aim. Damen stared in astonishment as the harsh wind blew the disguise away, revealing a young man as he dropped to one knee and fired at the approaching guards. The sun glinted on a swirling mane of golden hair, and Damen knew him. *Hakon.*

A small brown animal clung desperately to Hakon's shoulder, no doubt the source of the 'accursed squeal' that Lissa had recognized.

The leading craft exploded into fragments, but the remaining torch guards sped forward. Hakon could never withstand them alone. A piercing, feminine scream burst from Lissa, but then she clutched at Mallik's arm. "Don't let them hurt Ariana!" Her panic seemed genuine, but from this heart of malice, even an emotion that mimicked love could be deadly.

Mallik spoke into his transmitter, his voice still controlled and even as he directed the torch guards. "Do not harm the female. But stop the man."

Lissa shouted into the wind. "Kill him!" The hatred in her voice chilled Damen to his very core.

He looked once at Ariana, and then at Hakon. Young and brave, the golden-haired prince fired again, and again shattered one of the oncoming guards. The fate of the Dark Sun People hung in the balance—perhaps the only hope for the Intersystem, as well. They weren't after Ariana. And it was Hakon's own interference that disrupted Damen's plan. If he fell, Mallik would return her to Damen. . . .

Damen leapt down from the platform, then raced after the Automon, but Mallik shouted after him. "Captain, stop! This is not your fight."

He called back over his shoulder, and it was the last chance he had at holding two variant strands of a single plan together. "If the torch guards can't handle that traitor, I can. I'll bring the woman back myself."

Chapter Twenty-two

"By all the stars, sir! Run!"

"I am running, Pip!"

Ariana glanced at Hakon as they ran. The lingbat bent forward like a rider in the wind, its pointy ears streaming back, and its wings clamped tight over its stomach. Pip cranked his small head around and squealed wildly. "Duck, sir! Now!"

Both Hakon and Ariana dropped to the ground, barely avoiding a blast from the nearest torch guard craft.

Hakon turned and felled another Automon, then leapt to his feet. "Now's our chance. Run!"

The Automon fired a ray of burning plasma, but the driving wind and snow foiled its normally pinpoint-accurate targeting. Ariana looked back as she ran.

"It doesn't matter. We've almost reached my ship."

The next blast exploded in the snow beside them as they ran, blinding Ariana with a spray of snow. Ariana stumbled as she ran, but Hakon grabbed her hand and pulled her along beside him.

Stobie Piel

She could barely see through the debris of plasma blasts and snow, but she kept running. Hakon's ship lay ahead, but just as they neared, a torch guard circled around, cutting them off. Hakon fired again, again hitting his mark, but one still remained. Over the snow, Ariana saw Damen running toward them with his black hair loose and flying behind him.

Ariana's heart leapt to her throat. "Damen! No!"

Hakon yanked her forward. "Stars take him, Ariana! We've got to get out of here!"

He spun to shoot again, but the torch guard fired. The blast missed Hakon by a breath, but the blast shattered his rifle and knocked him back into the snow. Ariana caught his hand and pulled him to his feet. They scrambled backwards, but it was too late. The remaining torch guard cut left in front of Damen, paying him no heed as it fixed on its target: Hakon.

Hakon stopped—there was no way they could reach his ship before the thing fired. His face set hard, and he shoved Ariana aside, then tossed Pip through the air. The lingbat landed on her chest, then scrambled up, squeaking violently. "Sir!"

"Get to the ship, both of you. It's Type Four. You can pilot it, Ariana. Go!"

"I won't leave you!"

He turned to her, determined. "It's me they're after. Go!"

Ariana stumbled toward him, blinded by tears that frosted over her eyes. "No! Hakon, no!"

Pip shivered and quaked on her shoulder. "We can't leave him, Miss." The small, plaintive voice pierced Ariana's heart.

"We won't, Pip."

The torch guard slowed, then took aim. Damen bounded up behind the hovering Automon. Ariana's breath stopped, her heart held its beat. He leapt astride the guard's platform, dislodging it, and the shot went wild. He jumped down, but the Automon reassessed its target, then aimed again at Hakon. But Damen took aim, too, selecting his

232

target with care. He knew the Automon so well—he would know exactly where to shoot at close range. Damen stood in the thing's shadow. If it exploded . . .

He fired, and the blast sent snow and black splinters flying into the whirling wind. Ariana heard herself scream, and she ran blind in the direction the craft had been. The cloud cleared in a gust of wind, and she saw him. She stopped. Her legs went stiff, and for a moment, she couldn't move. Damen lay sprawled in the snow, still, his chest blasted open by the exploding fragments. She swayed where she stood, dizzy and sick, but Hakon grabbed her arm.

"Come, Ariana. We must leave this place before the Automon commander can take off."

She yanked free from his grasp, then stumbled crying to Damen's side and sank down beside him. Grief overwhelmed her and she crumpled forward, sobbing. Hakon tried to pull her away, but she wouldn't move. "No, no." A convulsion seized Damen's body—but he was still alive.

Hope surged back into Ariana. "Help me!"

Hakon gestured at the Automon shuttle, blurred from their vision by the cloud of snow stirred up from the battle. "Ariana, it's too late."

"He's alive! It's not too late."

"This pirate tried to ransom you. Why would you want to save him?"

Ariana shoved herself up. "He saved you, Hakon, and sacrificed himself in the doing." Her throat tightened as a sob welled inside her. "My father can save him."

Hakon looked down at Damen, mystified by Ariana's loyalty to her captor. "What does he mean to you?"

She looked her friend deep in the eye. *"Everything."*

Hakon nodded, then bent and lifted Damen. Ariana grabbed his legs and they carried him together to the ship. Hakon fumbled for his controller, and the hatch of his small vessel opened. They hoisted Damen into the portal, and then Hakon laid him upon a low padded bench. "Watch over him. I have to get us out of here."

He closed the hatch, blocking out the driving snow, then

took his place at the controls. Ariana placed her hand on Damen's forehead, and the lingbat hopped from her shoulder to perch on the footboard of the bench. It squeaked and trembled, but seemed too upset to speak. The ship lifted with a jolt, knocking Ariana to the side, but she steadied herself and kept Damen from moving. Tears streamed down her cheeks, but she looked to Hakon.

"Can we outrun them, Hakon?"

He shrugged, and she wasn't comforted. "If we get enough of a head start, maybe. This ship is faster than it looks."

"But it's an Intersystem vessel." Ariana gulped. "And theirs is powered by malloreum fuel."

Hakon glanced at her and smiled. "So, my friend, is this."

Ariana gaped. "Truly? How?"

"The Intersystem hasn't been idle—and my Keiroit disguise wasn't wholly in error. Plenty of so-called 'rogue traders' work for us. We have two of these prototypes—one wasn't ready when I left, but it will be soon."

"But can we get enough malloreum to fuel them?"

"We have enough for two—and that's the problem, of course. We can't acquire enough malloreum to fuel more vessels." As he spoke, he engaged the reserve power source and the craft blasted upward and broke free from the ice world's atmosphere. He studied the sector screen. "If I jet out of here fast now, then keep an even speed, we'll stay ahead of them. They won't follow us through the Border Territory."

Damen groaned and Ariana leaned close to him. His voice came hoarse and ragged, tortured with pain. "Fia. . . . I must signal her. . . ." He grimaced in agony and Ariana kissed his forehead, then turned desperately to Hakon.

"We have to do something. He can't last like this."

Hakon set his course, then came to kneel by Damen's bed. He checked the wound—a gaping, bloody hole peppered with fragments from the torch guard's explosion. With innate skill he cleaned the wound and dressed it, but his expression remained grave. "I've bandaged it as best as I know how, but it doesn't look good."

Ariana bit her lip hard, fighting to retain her senses. "If only our Ellowan blood was stronger!"

He glanced at her. "You are half, and I am slightly less." He paused. "Had your father and my mother remained wed—but the heart doesn't go where it's most convenient, does it?"

She looked into his eyes, and saw the depth of his feeling. "No. I suppose it doesn't."

Hakon sighed, but his face was kind. "Sometimes I think . . . a shame. But the mysteries of love elude me." He covered Damen in a soft blanket, then studied his rival's stricken face. "An unusual face, exotic. I wonder what strange races went into his making?"

Ariana's eyes puddled with tears. "What he has made of himself surpasses them all."

Damen's head turned as pain gripped him, and he mumbled in his sleep. Again, he called for Fia, but then his dark skin paled and he stilled. Ariana fought tears, but Hakon tested his pulse. "He is weak, and soon will be beyond aid."

No. "My father can heal anything short of death. If we get him there in time."

Hakon's brow furrowed as he considered this. "If I go at top speed, we could reach Valenwood, perhaps, in time. But to do that, I can't use the necessary fuel to jet free of the planet's gravity. If I don't use the jet, the Automon commander will catch up to us."

"Isn't there another way?"

Hakon hesitated. "Well, we could fight."

"With what?"

Hakon gestured at the rear of his ship. "This ship has a few surprises. It's armed with the new torpedo our fleet has drummed up. Highest level of secrecy, mind you. I 'borrowed' two for this mission, but for now they're a scarce commodity."

"Can we defeat them?"

"No. But we can knock them back enough to delay them.

It might work." He paused. "But it's not a sure thing, Ariana. If we miss . . ."

"We won't miss."

Hakon smiled as he guessed her meaning. "No?"

"No. Because I will be manning the weapons panel."

The lingbat squeaked in alarm. "Sir! That doesn't sound at all good! Blasting in space and all!"

Hakon patted the bat's small round head gently. "Don't worry, Pip. We've been through tighter scrapes than this."

"Have we, sir?"

"Many times."

This dubious reassurance settled the lingbat's shaken nerves, but Ariana turned back to Damen. He murmured Fia's name, then gripped Ariana's hand tight. "Tell her . . . second phase."

Ariana squeezed his hand, and he sank deeper into the unconscious. "I will tell her. Rest now."

Hakon glanced at him. "What does he say?"

"He's calling for his first officer, Fia. We must send her a message."

"I have no idea how to contact his ship."

"Wait. . . ." Ariana fumbled around in Damen's jacket, then fished out his transmitter. "Here. See if you can raise her on this." She held Damen's hand, then wiped his damp brow. *Please hold on. Don't give up now.*

Hakon poked randomly at the transmitter, then startled when it engaged. Fia's voice crackled over the small monitor. "Damen! Where are you? Why haven't you signaled? Are you all right?"

Hakon frowned. "Quiet, woman! I'm trying to relay a message here!"

Ariana cringed, then closed her eyes tight as she imagined Fia's indignant reaction. No one, ever, had called the regal Fia "woman." The monitor displayed only static for a long moment, and then a cold, even voice replied. "Who are you that speaks in this manner to the captain of *The Queen's Vengeance*, and high-ranking official of the Dark Sun Fleet, as well as advisor to its prime colony and home world?"

Hakon's brow angled doubtfully and he glanced at Ariana. "Who is this woman?"

"She's Damen's first officer, Fia. The Automon dumped her into the Dark Sun colony where I was held captive, and Damen adopted her as his heir."

Apparently Fia heard her, because a gasp of relief came across the monitor. "Ariana! Is that you? Where is Damen?" She paused. "And I am not a first officer any more, actually, since I took command of my own ship. Where is Damen?"

"He's here, Fia, but he's badly injured. We are taking him to Valenwood, but he wants you to . . ." She faltered. What was she setting in motion if she passed on Damen's command? And what ill would befall them all if she didn't? *Trust.* "He said something about the 'second phase.' Do you know what that means?"

"I do." Fia's voice came quavery. Even across the distance of space between them, Ariana heard the girl's fear. "What about Damen?"

But it was Hakon who responded. "He'll be fine, Fia. Ariana's father is the greatest healer in the galaxy. But we have to get him there first, so we can't waste time explaining to you."

A pause followed, and then Fia's voice came through the monitor. "Who *are* you?"

Lest Hakon damage their relationship any further, Ariana leaned toward the transmitter. "This is Hakon, my friend. I mentioned him to you once."

"Yes, I remember. The arrogant one. Very well. I will proceed with our mission." She paused again, and her voice became small, almost lost in the static of space. "Please, don't let anything happen to my father. He's all I have."

Ariana fought her tears and forced a reassuring tone. "I will protect him, Fia. I won't let him die."

"I'm glad he is with you, Ariana. Until we meet again, farewell!"

The transmission ceased, and Hakon set the monitor aside, then scratched his ear. "*I'm* arrogant?"

The lingbat had listened intently, and seemed pleased.

"Very regal, wasn't she, sir, that female on the monitor? Tripped into it, you did, by getting her rank wrong."

Hakon glared at the lingbat. "I didn't 'trip' into anything, Pip. The rank of a fleet of pirates matters little."

Ariana smiled. "You don't know Fia."

"And after hearing her haughty voice on the speaker, I don't want to."

"You might change your mind when you see her. She's very beautiful."

Hakon snorted, then returned to the pilot's chair. "No woman is beautiful enough for me to endure *that* attitude!" His expression altered to concern. "They're on us, Ariana. I've sighted the Automon commander's ship, and it's closing in."

Ariana guessed his intention, and she seated herself next to Hakon, then took over the weapons control panel. "I've already targeted the ship."

"We've only got two torpedoes, and it will take both to do enough damage to slow them off our course. We can't miss."

Ariana drew a breath. "I won't."

Hakon smiled. "Then fire when ready, Captain!"

She engaged the weapon panel with quick fingers, then launched a small torpedo at the Automon ship. She held her breath, then engaged the second and fired it.

The torpedo hit its mark, and the Automon ship lolled to one side with the impact. Ariana cried out and shook her fist. "Good! I hope it hits Lissa right between the eyes."

Hakon laughed. "It should wipe that stupid smile off her face, anyway."

"And the smirk off the commander's! What an annoying man!"

"The desire to control others, my dear, is the root of all evil—I am sure of it. Mallik's whole existence is devoted to the concept of order. His order."

"Do you think there's really a 'High King' as he claimed?"

"I doubt it, but who knows? The realm of Gyandorath is

genuine, though little is known, and most of that is legend. The mystics of Daeron live in that region."

Ariana gasped. "Do they? I feel almost certain that Fia is kin to them somehow."

"I never heard they were bossy—just powerful."

"She's powerful, too."

"What would a Daeron female be doing in an Automon mining colony?"

"I don't know. But if Commander Mallik is from that region, others might have come, too."

"Still . . . it doesn't seem likely." Hakon adjusted his course, then sat back, satisfied. "There! That should do it. We've set them back—good shot back there, Ariana!"

"Thank you. Are we set for Valenwood?"

"We are, and at the top speed this ship can handle."

Ariana returned to Damen's side. He was pale and still, and his breathing was erratic, but his heart still beat strong in his wounded chest. She smoothed his long hair back from his forehead, then glanced back at Hakon. "How does Lissa fit in to the commander's order?"

"A bedmate, I assume—but there aren't many she can't manipulate to get her way. I told you that years ago. She manipulated you into feeling sorry for her, and half the Academy professors into befriending her, pitying her, or bedding her."

"You never liked her. It seems you were right."

Hakon stretched his arms behind his back. "Do you know why?"

"I assumed you have good intuition."

"Maybe, but with her it was an easy read. During our first year in the Academy, she had her attention pinned on me."

"I remember."

"I learned a lot about her then—a lot I didn't like."

"Such as what?"

"Oh, at first, I believed she was just an overly doting friend. But there were times when I'd see her looking at you, when she thought no one noticed, and I saw something dark in her eyes. . . . It was jealousy, damanai. Plain and simple jealousy. I began to notice more, too. She'd flatter you, sing your praises, but every time she'd add just a sliver of criticism, always to undermine your confidence, and in an attempt to undermine what others thought of you. Stupid things—she'd teasingly make fun of your messy hair, even when she called it adorable."

Ariana touched her hair. "It's not messy."

Hakon assessed her with a critical eye. "No, in fact it's beautiful, and I'm not a man to notice hair. But I've noticed people like Lissa use this tactic very effectively. They don't hit you where you're weak. They go after you where you're strong, where you're the most confident."

"Why?"

Hakon leaned forward. "Think of it, Ariana. An enemy doesn't rely on his weak points, but on the strong, where he's most powerful. But if you can undermine his strengths . . . you've got him."

"Are you saying she thought of me as her enemy?"

"Exactly. She envied you until it became a sickness. She's too small to see beneath the surface, too stupid to envy your true qualities, those of courage and imagination. No, she envied your beauty and heritage, and the power she presumed those things gave."

"You paint a dark picture of her, Hakon."

"No darker than I saw today."

Ariana sighed. "I suppose she wants power to exert her influence across the galaxy. Isn't that what all such people want?"

Hakon glanced at her doubtfully. "You give her too much credit—she's not that imaginative. She thought you were in love with me, and she was damned sure I loved you. And she couldn't stand it. From what I saw today, nothing has changed."

"What do you mean?"

"I saw what she wanted from the moment she walked out on that platform. She wants that pirate, Ariana, and that's all she wants."

She knew—she had known all along, but hearing it spoken outright chilled her heart. "Damen? But why?"

"My guess? Because she thinks he's good in the sack."

Ariana grimaced. "I cannot believe she would go to these lengths for that!"

"No? I'll admit, she's carried lust for your man a lot farther than I would have guessed. But she fancies herself in love. I could see it in her eyes."

Ariana's jaw tightened in anger. "She does not love him!"

"People like that always put a pretty face on their demons. But you're right—she doesn't really love anyone, especially you, no matter how many times she calls you her sister."

"I'm not stupid, Hakon. I knew that much."

He looked doubtful. "You trusted her in our days at the Academy."

"I did, it's true. But I never felt that I liked her as much as she seemed to like me."

"Because she hated you, hated you for being all she is not, for being *real*."

Real. Like the girl in the cavern artist's portrait, vulnerable and uncertain, but *real*. That was what Damen loved, and what no one, least of all Lissa, could ever destroy. Strange that something so vulnerable could be so indestructible. Ariana smiled. "She hates you more—you're the one she tried to kill."

"Only because she needs you alive, or stealing your man would lose its meaning."

Ariana considered Lissa's motives. "But if she wanted Damen so much, why did she leave them when they escaped from the mining colony?"

"My guess is that he didn't show interest in her. So she went out seeking power—power to have the influence she wanted, and to get herself noticed. And by the stars, did she find it!"

"In Commander Mallik? I suppose so. But he's not particularly . . . erotic."

"And his breath stinks. Did you notice that charming attribute?"

"I'm afraid so."

They looked at each other for a moment and smiled in unison. "I'm glad you're here, Hakon. I've missed you."

"I've missed you, too, damanai."

Sometimes, friendship was easier than passion. Ariana turned back to Damen. She thought of their time together on his warm, beautiful world. *Paradise.* There, she thought, she had found both friendship and passion. She held his hand and her fingers entwined with his. Occasionally, she felt a small squeeze, as if even in the depths of his injury, he reassured her.

Hakon watched her a moment, and his voice came soft and low. "He's the one, isn't he?"

She looked at him and nodded. "He is."

"Does he know?"

"Not yet. I haven't found the right way to tell him."

"I'd say the right time is coming. Once we reach Valenwood, you won't have much choice."

She nodded. "I know."

Hakon placed his hand on her shoulder. "I hope he's worth you, Ariana. But if he holds your heart, I'll do all that I can to help him."

She folded her hand over his. "I know you will. I know how it looked today when he met with the commander. But he's planning something, and I trust him."

"I hope your trust is founded. Because if this man really is the Lord of the Dark Sun Fleet, and he aligns with Mallik, we're in more trouble than we can handle."

Ariana glanced at him. "Do you think there'll be war?"

"Some on the Council think not. It's inconceivable to them that anyone would challenge us. But my father says we've become so advanced that we don't remember when worlds plotted for power—not when so many of our races have seen the futility in such quests. And my uncle, Seneca, has long warned of this danger. But from what I witnessed today, the danger is closer than even he feared."

Ariana clasped her head in her hands. "What are we going to do?"

"Head back to Valenwood and tell the Council what they're planning. But don't underestimate the Automon commander. They might not be able to overrun the Intersystem Fleet, but they can do serious damage before we could stop them."

"We can't let them get that far."

"No. My guess is that we'll send our fleet out into the Border Territory, try to stop them there, or hit them before they're aligned. And then we'll see what side your man is on, once and for all."

Part Four

Valenwood

In the mirror, a secret. . . .

Chapter Twenty-three

Damen lay unconscious on Ariana's pink-canopied bed. His black hair fell in disarray over her soft pillow, and though her mattress was large and wide, his feet reached the footboard. She stood beside him while Arnoth finished his examination. Arnoth shook his head. "He is far gone into the light, Ariana. It amazes me that he held on this long."

Ariana gripped her father's arm. "He isn't dead, Papa. You can heal him."

"Possibly." Arnoth didn't look hopeful, and Ariana's heart clenched. They had brought him to Valenwood at top speed, and she had been sure, once Damen was in her father's care, nothing could go wrong.

"What do you mean, 'possibly'? He's not dead, so he can be healed."

Arnoth laid his hand gently on Ariana's shoulder. "It is in this level where he now lies that a soul is most often reluctant to respond to healing. Life ebbs from him, but on the other side, the light calls, and once in its embrace, few are willing to give up its peace."

Stobie Piel

"Damen doesn't want peace!"

Arnoth shot her a quick glance and Ariana bit her lip. "I mean, he's not finished here. He wants life. I know it. Please try."

"I will try, but you must be prepared, my dear child, to accept whatever choice he makes."

She nodded, but she wasn't prepared for anything but his return to life. Arnoth placed his long fingers on Damen's temple, and Ariana waited as he entered the healing trance. She held her breath, and her heart throbbed as Arnoth's eyes closed and he sank deeper. Just then he shot upright, his dark eyes flashing with surprise.

Ariana held her hand over her heart to calm herself. "What happened, Papa?" Her voice sank to a whisper, and she trembled. "Were you able to make the connection and ask if he desired life?"

Arnoth frowned at Damen as if eyeing a new, and perhaps treacherous, species for the first time. "Yes."

Ariana bit her lip, barely able to ask. "And . . . did he . . . desire life?"

Arnoth turned to her, his noble face both proud and indignant. "He demanded it!"

Relief burst through Ariana and she smiled. "Then aren't you going to heal him?"

"I suppose so." Arnoth paused. "He is a man of strong will, and dangerous, this Lord of the Dark Sun you brought to me."

Ariana pinned her father with a meaningful gaze. "He is much more than that, and you know it."

"I suppose so."

"Then heal him!" She had never spoken to her father this way. Arnoth looked at her in surprise, as if uncertain how to handle a disobedience he hadn't faced before.

"Very well." He entered the trance again, and formed the healing bond. Ariana seated herself in a chair close to the bed and waited. The Ellowan healing trance could take a while, almost like the surgery of less advanced or gifted races, and she settled in, struggling for patience. Arnoth had

248

to reach Damen on the deepest levels, to guide his spirit through mending, to bring his power to each cell. When healing a being of another race, the labor could be even more time consuming.

Arnoth sat back, stunned, and Ariana tried to rise from her chair, but fear held her bound. "What's the matter, Papa? Why did you stop?"

Arnoth glanced at her, amazement written on his face. "I didn't." He paused as if wonder overcame him. "I'm finished. He is healed."

Ariana gaped. "So soon? But it was only a short while. Wasn't he as badly damaged as you thought?"

Arnoth's gaze shifted to one side. "Actually, he was worse off than I had believed. I have never encountered anyone like him. Not only did he accept my healing, but in places, took over!"

Ariana repressed a smile—her father wouldn't like his skills superceded. "That does sound like him, somewhat."

"A powerful man." Arnoth eyed her suspiciously. "Have a care with him, Ariana. Even in this deep state of connection, there are places he hides."

Ariana didn't answer as she considered what this might mean. Damen was planning something, something all his people knew about, and about which none would speak, even when she had pried with her subtlest tactics. Whatever it was Damen concealed, his people believed in him, because they loved him.

"This man, he is a strong leader. It does not surprise me that he has raised so formidable a fleet. I can guess why the Automon commander chose to treat with him rather than to assail his forces."

Ariana shook her head. "I don't believe it. It was a ruse, so that Damen could set the rest of his plan in motion."

"What plan?" When Ariana didn't answer, Arnoth nodded. "I see. He didn't tell you. Though he holds your heart, he has not shared his own fully with you."

Ariana gazed down at Damen. She couldn't refute her

father's words. He was right. "That may be, but I know him, Papa, and I trust him."

"Do you, indeed?" Arnoth eyed her intently for a while. "Remember, daughter—trust placed in the wrong hands can too easily be made a weapon. It can be used against you."

Ariana thought of Lissa, whom she had also once trusted. "I know."

Arnoth placed his hand on her shoulder. "I will leave you with him now, but there is also a guard posted outside your door."

"A guard? Damen doesn't need a guard."

"You said yourself he has a 'second phase' to this plan. And until he's willing to tell us what that involves, I don't want him escaping our custody."

"I want to show him our city!"

"That, I will allow, so long as he is unarmed and the shuttle ports securely guarded."

"You think he will try to steal a shuttle?" She wanted to argue on Damen's behalf, but if Arnoth insisted on holding him prisoner until he revealed his secrets, it didn't seem entirely unlikely. "When he wakes, I will talk to him. Maybe I can convince him to divulge the nature of his plan, at least."

"Do you know why he resists? What harm does he think we direct his way?"

Ariana's brow furrowed. "I'm not sure, exactly. I have spoken to him of this before, and he hasn't yielded. He is independent, and perhaps he prefers to handle things on his own. After all, no one rescued the Dark Sun People—they rescued themselves, and then went on to free other colonies. They don't trust our help, not when it failed them at their greatest need."

"Had we known of their existence, we would have freed them."

"But we didn't, Papa, and so, they have created their culture with a marked resistance to dependence on others. I don't think Damen will yield his secrets easily."

Arnoth frowned, then went to the door. "He'd better, or those secret plans will have to go forward without him."

Ariana lay close beside Damen, her hand over his heart. He hadn't awakened, but his breath came even and deep, and his pulse felt strong to her touch. For now, it was enough to be with him, though the questions her father had raised needed answering. Maybe it was time that Damen come forward with an explanation. After all, he had asked her to trust him. It was time he trusted her, too.

He stirred, then woke groggily, his eyelids heavy as he blinked. "Where . . . ?" He struggled from sleep as if fighting his way from beneath a heavy blanket. His eyes focused on her pink satin canopy and a look of utter bewilderment formed on his face. "Where am I?"

Ariana moved to look down at him. "You're in my bedroom."

His eyes shifted and a cracked smile formed on his lips. "I should have known."

Happiness filled her, erasing all doubts from her mind, and she kissed his cheek, then hugged him. "You are safe now. My father healed you."

"Your father? Then we are in Valenwood." He didn't sound pleased, and his brow knit. "What about the others? Fia and the rest?"

"I sent them a message as soon as we could. Fia has gone on to the 'second phase,' whatever that is." She eyed him carefully, but he seemed relieved and didn't answer. "I told her that we were bringing you here, and assured her you would be healed."

"I remember nothing of the journey. How long have I been in this state?"

When she told him, his eyes widened. "That's impossible! No Intersystem vessel could make that journey so fast."

"It could if it's powered with malloreum fuel."

Damen frowned. "So he's a thief in more ways than one, is he?"

"You're a fine one to label another thief!"

"Fair enough, I suppose, but having been born in a malloreum mine, I can't help feeling I have a right to it." He paused. "How did you escape Mallik's pursuit? I assume he went after you."

"He did, but we fired two torpedoes, and delayed them enough to escape. Hakon didn't think they'd follow us though the Border Territory, and they didn't."

Damen struggled to sit up. "I have to get back."

"Oh, no, you don't!" She stopped, and decided to leave the matter of Arnoth's order for now. "You need rest. Fia is handling things perfectly."

He lay back. "Yes. There is time yet." He looked around her room, and then smiled. "I knew it!"

She looked to see what caught his attention. "What?"

"Mirrors. Look at that!" He pointed to a full-length oval mirror near the corner of her room, then gestured at a small round one nearer the bed—it was suspended on a movable bracket and could be tilted to catch various lights.

"They're decoration!" He eyed her doubtfully, and Ariana hopped out of bed to defend her pride, then adjusted the mirror this way and that, catching the light of the newly risen sun. It glinted on the walls, bringing the desert marble to glittering life. "See!"

"And does it catch the light of your lovely face as well?"

She started to nod, then caught herself. She sat back on the bed beside him, and he held out his arm to her. "I see you are much recovered."

"I feel a little strange. Dizzy, and my nerves seem curiously active."

"That is the way of the healing trance. If you rest for a while, you will find by evening that you can walk."

Damen grinned. "It's not walking that interests me."

Ariana blushed, then lay back beside him, and he gathered her into his arms. He kissed her and her whole body warmed. "That, too."

"Just now, however, it's food that occupies my thoughts."

Ariana's eyes widened eagerly, and he laughed. "We think alike, you and I."

"Well, that's a terrifying thought!" Hakon burst into the room shoving a food cart in front of him. "Did I hear a request for food? Pip and I have rummaged through the palace pantry, and come up with more than enough for both of you." As he spoke, he seized a plump nectar fruit and bit into it.

Hakon placed the cart beside Ariana's bed, then seated himself beside Damen. He looked him over analytically, then nodded. "Looking better than you were, I see." He eyed Ariana as she lay beside Damen, then angled his brow. "Much better."

Ariana pulled herself together and sat up, then adjusted her vest. "Hallo, Hakon."

"Ariana. . . ."

Damen just stared. He looked slightly annoyed, but more perplexed by Hakon's cheerful presence in Ariana's bedroom. "What are you doing here?"

Hakon took another bite of nectar fruit and spoke thickly, while chewing. "Checking on you, of course. I almost got turned into a bloody splatter of gel by those cursed torch guards because of you, and then wasted a whole load of malloreum trying to get you back. Figured you're in my debt."

Damen sat up, glaring. "*I* am in your debt? You disrupted my entire mission, and almost got us all killed. If anyone owes anyone, it's you!"

Hakon glanced at Ariana. "Temperamental, isn't he?" He passed Damen a piece of fruit, which Damen accepted reluctantly. He tried it, and looked pleased, then ate the rest. Ariana seized one for herself before the two men could devour everything.

As they ate together, Arnoth appeared in the doorway. Hakon's father, Dane, joined him, and they stood watching for a moment before either spoke. Dane jabbed Arnoth in the ribs and nodded. "Familiar sight, isn't it? Reminds me of . . . us."

Arnoth frowned. "Your son, indeed, resembles you, except that his manner is more dignified and restrained. But as for myself and that pirate . . ."

Dane laughed, then entered the bedroom, nonchalant as he took a piece of fruit, then sampled the bread rolls. "So, up and about, are you? I understand you heal quickly, young man."

Damen glanced at Ariana, then back at Dane. He seemed hesitant, as if the strangeness of his Intersystem hosts hadn't been exaggerated. Ariana motioned to Dane. "Damen, this is Dane Calydon, the Intersystem Sage. . . ."

Dane cut her off pleasantly. "That means Wise Councilor, in case you didn't know."

"Wise, indeed! If ever a man stole a title . . . !" A small, high, but grumpy voice came from the area of Ariana's door, but she had to sit up to see the speaker.

Damen stared in amazement as the lingbat, Carob, hopped into his room, then bounced up onto the food cart. Before speaking again, Carob shoved his head in a wine goblet and drank. Ariana cleared her throat. "This is Carob, one of the lingbats I told you about."

Carob yanked his round head from the goblet, wine dripping from his cheeks. "Not only *one* of the lingbats, young female, but the founding lingbat, if that's saying enough."

Dane seized Carob and set him abruptly on his shoulder. "It's saying a lot too much. If anyone can be considered the founder of your noble race, it's me. I taught you to talk, after all."

Another series of high squeaks interrupted their argument, and Pip bounded into the room, breathless. "Sir! You left me behind!"

Hakon frowned. "Left you, indeed! I couldn't pry you out of the pantry!"

Pip looked hurt, then scrambled up Hakon's leg to his shoulder, where he puffed a breath that expanded his small, round chest like a balloon. "Sorry, sir. I was gathering more delectables for the prisoner."

Hakon eyed the bat doubtfully. "Gathering? What, in your round stomach?"

Damen turned to Ariana, and his voice came low with forced restraint. *"Prisoner?"*

Ariana bit her lip. "Well, I wouldn't say that, exactly."

Arnoth folded his arms over his chest. "I would. This door is guarded, young man, and you are not to leave until I am assured of your intentions."

This didn't please Damen, and Ariana cringed. "Is it the policy of the Intersystem Elite to hold a man captive for minding the affairs of his own people? Or perhaps the borders of this fine union go beyond that which is welcome, and ignore those who wish no part in it?"

Arnoth's eyes darkened with anger. "It is our policy to defend ourselves, and to prevent rogues and pirates from cutting a swathe of mayhem through space!"

Dane exhaled a growling breath. "Now is not the time for this discussion. Perhaps later, when the young fellow has rested—and your own temper has cooled."

Arnoth's frown deepened. "Very well. But this matter is not settled, and it will be raised again until I am satisfied with the results."

Damen appeared equally unyielding. "If you expect me to divulge my business to you, you'll be waiting a long, long time, for it will never happen."

This wasn't the meeting Ariana had hoped for. She cleared her throat and forced an awkward smile. "Damen, this is my father, Arnoth, King of Valenwood."

Damen wasn't impressed. "As I gathered by the imperious tone."

Arnoth's eyes narrowed, but Hakon poked at Damen's shoulder as if testing for ripeness, and probably to divert the conversation from spiraling any further downward. "Don't expect he'll be going anywhere for a while. He's still too weak."

Arnoth didn't look convinced. "His response to healing was unusual. He might be more fit than others in this state."

Carob hopped from Dane's shoulder to Damen's side, then leaned toward him as if the creature's eyesight had failed over the years. Damen leaned away suspiciously.

"What's the matter with you, young pirate?"

Damen hesitated as if unsure how to respond. "I have never seen a rodent speak before."

Carob radiated pride. "Only a lucky few have! But mind yourself, pirate! We are an ancient species, capable of any number of wonders. You could learn a lot from us."

Dane grabbed the lingbat again and stuck him near the wine goblet. "Aren't you thirsty again?" Carob's attention turned to the wine, but Dane reached to prod Damen, too. "There's a reason for his rapid healing." He looked around at the others, blue eyes twinkling. "And I think it will knock some of you off your feet."

Ariana leaned past Damen, eager. "What reason?"

Dane seated himself on the nearby chair and looked comfortable. "Did a few tests on him—just a hair sample is all it requires—while Arnoth here was busy bringing him back to life."

Arnoth frowned, impatient as always with Dane. "What did you learn that could be of even the remotest interest?"

"Got a whole profile of this young man's heritage. I think it may interest you especially, my good King."

Arnoth rolled his eyes. "Why?"

"Because the Lord of the Dark Sun Fleet is more than half Ellowan."

Ariana's mouth dropped, and Arnoth gaped at Dane, astonished. "That can't be."

Dane shrugged. "No doubt about it. He's Ellowan. Surprised me, too, as I'd figured he'd be mixed more."

Dane's revelation excited Ariana and she clapped her hands. "We're kindred!" She leaned over and kissed Damen, who seemed doubtful and intensely suspicious. "What's the other part of him?"

Dane hesitated and seemed uncomfortable. "Tyrikan."

Arnoth eyed him darkly. "That much, I could have guessed on my own."

Damen looked between them. "Who, or what, are Tyrikans?"

Ariana hesitated. "Well, they're an *interesting* race, from a small world beyond the Border Territories. They're aren't exactly part of the Intersystem, though we do protect them at times."

Carob huffed. "Interesting? That's a nice way to put it! The Tyrikans are the most violent, primitive humans in the galaxy! They fight everything and everyone—they live for battle."

Ariana frowned at the bat. "They are very powerful, Carob." She glanced at Damen. "And huge, though they grow late into adulthood. I guess that explains your size."

Arnoth shifted his weight and seemed uncomfortable about welcoming his long-lost kin. "Clearly, the Tyrikan blood outweighs Ellowan, despite its lesser proportion. But I don't see how any Ellowan could have ended up on a mining colony."

Dane tapped his chin thoughtfully. "I suppose they were taken when the Tseir invaded Valenwood, an age ago. They probably had dealings with the Automon, and sold off some of your people as slaves."

Arnoth sighed. "That is a grim thought, but not unlikely. There was no accounting of the dead, for most of our race was annihilated at that time."

Damen's brow furrowed. "Who are the Tseir?"

Dane shook his head, sad. "A mistake, more than anything else. They were a race of clones. . . ."

Hakon cut him off. "Not clones really, father. A clone is a separate being begun from the cells of another. It's more accurate to call the Tseir 'replicas,' because rather than creating an entirely new person, which a clone is, these were simply extended from the original, over and over, until the diluted beings were so weak that they couldn't live. And clones are born to a natural mother, whereas the Tseir were reproduced at whatever stage the original was at."

Dane leveled a dark look at his son. "As I was saying, the *replicas* invaded Valenwood, and several other worlds, before we stopped them. After their defeat, we set them up on their own planet, but because of the manner of their creation, they weren't long-lived, and all have perished in the ensuing years. It taught us, if nothing else, that efforts to improve any race will fall to ruin, and often tragedy. But humanity learns by doing, and to that fate, we are bound."

Carob looked small and smug. "Fortunately, lingbats are smarter and don't cause all this trouble. But now that we know that the Ellowan race itself spawned this pirate, now what?"

Damen remained doubtful. "If I am indeed, as you claim, of the Ellowan race, then why do I have none of its healing powers?"

Arnoth studied him reluctantly. "Though natural to our people, this skill must be taught to be developed enough for use on other humans. It's probably not strong enough in you. . . ." He eyed Ariana. "But in your children, it might again become powerful."

Ariana watched for Damen's reaction to Arnoth's comment, but rather than the fond smile she'd hoped for, he turned away, almost as if the thought of a family pained him. Her heart fell, and she looked down to hide her disappointment. Dane rose from his chair and patted her shoulder. She looked up at him, and saw in his blue eyes kindness and understanding. He was, like his son, a wise man, but with an added depth of compassion that only the years bring.

Dane motioned to Arnoth, then tapped his son's shoulder. "Our dark Ellowan-Tyrikan appears weary. Let us leave them for awhile."

Arnoth kissed Ariana's forehead and seemed more protective than usual, and Hakon also appeared somewhat reluctant to leave. Dane rolled his eyes, then went to the door and held it open. "If you gentlemen are ready . . ."

Pip hopped from Hakon's shoulder to the food cart and seized a quick bite of the bread. "Figured I'd stay awhile, sir, if you don't mind."

Hakon nabbed the little fellow and held him firmly around the stomach. "I brought this food for Ariana and her pirate. There isn't enough here for an army of lingbats, too."

Pip cranked his small head to look at Hakon. "Just the two of us, sir, myself and my grandsire. Hardly an army."

Hakon's lip curled to one side. "Two is all it takes."

Carob took the hint and jumped down from the cart, then bounded across the floor toward Dane. He scrambled up Dane's leg and positioned himself on Dane's shoulder. "The boy finds us formidable, lad. And he's right!"

Dane cast a forlorn look at Damen. "So you don't have these creatures on your Dark Sun worlds, eh?"

Damen hesitated. "No."

Dane sighed again. "Might not be so bad, after all."

Arnoth seemed reluctant to leave, but Dane waved at the door, a pertinent look on his face. "He needs rest." This didn't work, so Dane marched to Arnoth and took his arm firmly, then directed him to the door. "And those two need to be alone. They have *much* to discuss."

Arnoth administered a final glare upon Damen, then nodded. "I suppose so. Ariana, the Council will need a further briefing of your mission. Not all the representatives have arrived yet, though Seneca is on his way from Dakota, and the Zimdardri and Tellurite ambassadors are also enroute. Those are the highest-ranking officials, and wisest, and they will require a detailed account. Be ready."

"I am prepared, Papa."

The three men left, but still Ariana glanced around the room, trying to seem casual, before turning to Damen. As she feared, his face was set in an unyielding expression, and his lips were drawn tight with displeasure.

"You might have been more gracious, Damen. They are willing to listen to you."

"They might have been more gracious to me! I am not here to win their favor." He looked at her angrily. "And you! You are my captor as much as any of them!"

Ariana angled her brow. "Is that so? And how, exactly, would this be any different from what you did to me?"

"I had every intention of returning you to this place. You, on the other hand, in accord with your father's dictatorial schemes, have plotted to keep me here indefinitely. You

259

could destroy everything I've worked ten years to create!"

Damen's accusation stung, and tears welled in Ariana's eyes. "He just wants to know what you're doing, Damen. Has it occurred to you that he might help you?" Her own anger grew. "Unless, of course, your methods and designs really do threaten our peace?"

It was probably a mistake to confront him now. His expression hardened. "My lady expects trust from her captive, but gives none in return."

Ariana swung her legs off the bed and marched to the door. "Trust! You have nerve, my Dark Lord!" She issued the term deliberately, then raised her chin. "I trusted you while you dallied with the enemy, and while you formed an allegiance with the most deceitful and evil person I've ever beheld. You had no trouble bowing before the man who enslaved all your people, yet you speak to my father, one of the greatest leaders the galaxy has ever known, with the disrespect of a common knave!"

Damen's brown eyes glittered with anger, and perhaps unshed tears. With insurmountable will, he rose from the bed and stood to face her. Weakened as he was, the effort must have been unimaginable, but he didn't sway nor waver, and his dark gaze penetrated her with his power. "I am a common knave, Ariana, and a barbarian leader of a tribe of barbarians. Had you forgotten this?"

Her chin quivered, but she returned his gaze evenly. "How could I forget when you allow yourself to be no more?" She gestured around her room, then at the door. "You're held prisoner by more than my father's guards. You hold yourself enslaved, and all who would love you fall under that same yoke."

Her tears threatened to spill, so she went to the door. "When you have recovered from your stubbornness and pride, I will, perhaps, return. Until then, you can rest on your own!"

"And when you have seen past the blindness and tyranny of your sheltered upbringing and freed yourself from your dictatorial father, I may, perhaps, welcome you. Until then, we have nothing to say to each other."

Stubborn man! Ariana yanked the door open, startling the guard, then stormed away without looking back. She fled down the corridor, then dove into an empty room where she sank back against the wall and cried.

Chapter Twenty-four

Even in dreams, she tormented him. Ariana . . . no, it was an army of Arianas, sailing across a golden ocean borne, every one of the little fiends on lavender wings through a pink gossamer mist. She, and the rest of her troop of Arianas, swooped down over him, tempting him and infuriating him, but they darted upward and away when he tried to catch one. Slowly, he sank downward into a turbulent sea, and the turbulent sea darkened from gold to a dark indigo blue.

Damen fought upwards through the sea, but soft, mocking voices whispered that it was Arnoth of Valenwood who held him there, captive. The voices softened and became smaller, kinder. This voice would free him from Arnoth.

They say you are Ellowan, and that your daughter will be a great healer. I wonder if that's true?

Damen tried to answer. *I am not Ellowan. I am a pirate. . . .*

A pirate Ellowan, the voice responded, and it sounded pleased, as though a happy child had spoken.

Damen rose upward through sleep until he knew he was dreaming. As he struggled to consciousness he had the peculiar sensation that someone was watching him. From beneath the heavy blanket of sleep, he opened his eyes and looked directly into the wide green gaze of an Ellowan child.

Damen gasped and bolted upright in bed, and the child jumped back, then approached him again like a wild animal. She bit her lip in what was somehow a familiar expression. She was a slight, lithe child with long, black hair and darker skin than seemed usual for the Ellowan race. He couldn't guess her age. She was small and delicate, but she was younger than Fia had been when he made her his heir. She held her small hands clasped in front of her, both wary and curious.

Damen hesitated, then tried to gentle his expression. "Hallo, little person." He paused again as her brow knit, possibly unsure if she liked the term 'little person.' "

She spoke warily, her voice small and tentative. "Hallo, large dark person."

Damen restrained a smile. "What brings you here? You're not, I trust, my new guard?" And how odd the guard let an innocent sprite of a child in a dangerous prisoner's room! Clearly, Arnoth was lax in the protection of his people's children. Such a grave mistake wouldn't happen on the Dark Sun world.

"No, I'm not a guard." She paused, and looked proud. "I snuck by him."

"Did you?" He huffed. "Can't be much of a guard." If this child could sneak by the guard, Damen should have no trouble escaping his confines—when he was good and ready to do so.

"He's a good guard. I'm just a better sneak."

He decided he liked the child. "Well done, then." He held out his hand. "I am called Damen. What is your name?"

She took his hand and shook firmly. "I am called Elena, but I prefer Ellie, because it sounds more friendly, and less

263

confusing because Hakon's sister is also named Elena."

"Ah. Well . . ." He eyed her, hesitating. "Why are you here?"

"I wanted to look at you."

Damen's eyes wavered to one side. "Indeed?" He waited for more to be forthcoming, but Elena . . . Ellie . . . seemed to relax in his presence.

"This is a good time to wake, because it is sunset." She went to his window and fiddled with it, then motioned fiercely to him. "This window is stuck, and I can't open it. Can you help me, please?"

Damen got off the bed, slowly, but strength was returning to his limbs. Apparently, it had only been a few hours, because the sun had been high in the sky when Ariana had stomped out of his room and abandoned him alone in her fiendishly feminine bedroom. He examined the large window, found the hinge, and then swung it open. A soft breeze touched his face, less humid than the gentle wind of his planet, less fragrant with foliage and flowers, but clear, as if it had originated on some high mountain.

His window looked out over the ocean, as if this whole south face of the palace itself extended over the sea. Before him, the water gleamed like beaten gold. To the left stretched a long, curved beach, and the sunset glimmered on the white tiled homes of the city, smaller and less grand than the palace, but still beautiful, as if the city had been wrought by a single hand. To the right, the shore cut more dramatically southward, and there, a blue-green river opened into the ocean. Great trees with pale grey boles and wide, drooping branches hung over the river on either side, and far to the right beyond, he discerned the pale golden sheen of the great desert.

"They are singing. Can you hear their voices?"

Maybe this child was mystic, too. She might disappear on that wind, and he wondered if he was still dreaming. "I hear nothing."

"Listen more carefully!" Elena leaned out the window,

her face rapt with concentration, an eager light in her green eyes. "There! Do you hear them now?"

Damen listened. Far out across the sea, he heard an exquisite sound, low and rolling, mournful with sorrow, so poignant that it could only come from one heart calling to another. "I have heard this song only once in my life, but I will never forget its beauty. The song of the amber whales."

Elena eyed him doubtfully, then shook her head. "Not that!" Her brow furrowed in displeasure. "Listen more carefully! The *other* song!"

Damen listened again. A strange, deep grunt interrupted the song of the whales. "All I hear besides the whales is an 'umph' noise, like a fat amphibian has croaked. . . . Or burped."

Elena's face lit like a star. "That's it! That's them." Her expression softened to a wistful expression of love. "They are very, very *fat*."

Damen stared, and then he smiled. "Let me guess. This would be the song of the hyppo."

She beamed, and he knew his guess had made them friends. "You know about hyppos?"

"I know they are exceedingly fat, and of great interest to the Ellowan."

She nodded excitedly, then pointed out the window. "If you look there, to the mouth of the river where it empties into the sea, you can see them."

Damen shaded his eyes against the sun. "I see a round grey object with two holes."

"Yes! That's the hyppo's snout. But if you look more closely, there are others nearby. The fattest is the father, and they have a new baby that I have not been allowed to see up close, because the females are very protective mothers, as is my own, and can be fierce. The best time to see them is when they're eating, because you can get up close to them and they don't notice, because they're so intent on food."

Damen smiled. "I know someone like that myself." His

heart had softened toward Ariana, however stubborn she was. This child had gentled his spirit. Perhaps Ariana was ready to talk to him, and maybe he was ready to talk to her, too. He touched the child's head, and she looked up at him, happy.

"Maybe later you can take me to see the hyppos. I have to go with an adult, you see, and the others here are getting tired of taking me."

If Arnoth of Valenwood ever released his shackles. . . . "If permitted, I would like that very much." He gazed down at the little girl. "Tell me, what is it that you admire about these creatures?"

She sighed. "They're *fat*." She spoke lovingly, but then a small frown twitched at her lips. "That brat, Vender, teases me because I like fat creatures. Then he said the hyppos like him better than me." She paused, looking proud. "So I struck him. He said I had a weak punch, but then he ran away."

Damen hesitated. "Who is Vender?"

She shrugged, too idle for disinterest. "He is the son of the Desert Prince, although the prince is simply the leader of the desert city, and not really a prince. As I told Vender after I hit him."

Damen considered this, and remained confused. "Ah."

"Vender's father is mostly a biologist—he is one of the Old Ones, from the time the king lived in exile on Keir. Vender's father supervised the hyppos' arrival on Valenwood, and that is why Vender thinks he knows more about them. But in ancient times, the prince of the desert was supposed to marry the priestess of the wood, the eldest daughter of the Ellowan King, and when the old king died, he would become king."

"For such an advanced race as the Ellowan, it seems odd that the kingship should always pass to a male."

"Not really. The Priestess has equal power, but we don't have a priestess now. Things haven't followed the ancient way very well for the past generations."

"No? Why not?"

The door opened, and Damen glanced back to see who entered. Ariana came in, looking nervous, and he knew without asking that she had endured the same pain from their argument, and now faced the same softening heart. Elena turned, too, and looked happy. "Hallo, Mamma."

Damen's breath caught and a shock rang through his body. His heart beat with a static, rapid pulse. *Mamma*. He looked down at the child, then at Ariana, then slowly back at Elena again. A bright face, small and delicate, the promise of great beauty, and even greater charm. He couldn't guess her age. . . .

Ariana gulped, then drew a quick breath. "Elena! What are you doing in here?"

"I was telling the Ellowan-pirate about the hyppos. They are singing."

Ariana's brow furrowed doubtfully. "Are they? All I hear is an odd 'arff, arff' noise."

Damen smiled. "I had thought it more of an 'umph' sound."

She smiled, too, but he thought she was trembling. Elena frowned and shook her head. "That is their song."

Damen eyed her. "What are they singing of? Love, do you think?"

"Food, I think."

Damen nodded. "That seems most likely."

Elena went to her mother, and Ariana embraced her. What had the child said? "Very protective mothers, as is my own. . . ." Ariana would be a good mother, and devoted to her child. Elena hugged her mother, then waved at Damen. "I like you very much, Ellowan-pirate. Tomorrow, you can take me to visit the hyppos, around feeding time, and we can see them eat." She peeked up at her mother, guileless. "Can he go with us, Mamma?"

Ariana glanced quickly at Damen. "Perhaps. We will leave that to tomorrow."

Elena's mouth crooked to one side, an expression he had seen on Ariana's face many times. "You mean, if Grandpapa takes away his guard." Her eyes narrowed. "I will have a

267

talk with Grandpapa, I think." She marched to the door—even her gait resembled Ariana's when she was determined. Ariana went to open it for her, but Elena caught her hand. "Let me, Mamma. I want to sneak by the guard again."

She opened the door a crack, then slipped away, unseen and unnoticed by the guard. Ariana shook her head. "So much for our guards. I guess it's obvious that the Ellowan haven't had to deal with many prisoners."

Damen couldn't speak. He sank back on the edge of the bed and stared at nothing. She came around the bed and stood beside him, silent and waiting. At last, he looked up at her. "Your daughter . . . ?"

She nodded and her eyes never wavered from his. "Yes."

The past . . . Was this the secret she had kept, and tried to tell him? The secret he hadn't been ready to hear . . . ? He took two breaths. "Who . . . who is her father?"

A slow smile curved Ariana's beautiful mouth, though her soft grey eyes filled with tears. She stepped back from his bedside and adjusted the round extending mirror, then tilted it toward him. A single teardrop fell to her cheek. "Damen . . . you're looking at him."

His chest constricted and a shimmery veil covered his eyes, and he was crying, though no sob sounded, just tears running down his face. She cried, too, silent, and then she came to him. She sank down before him and placed her hands on his knees, looking up at him, her face more beautiful and sad than he had ever seen her. "I wanted to tell you, so many times. But . . ."

He cupped her head in his hands and bent to press his lips on her forehead. "But you didn't trust me."

She bowed her head, and she nodded. "I'm sorry. You have said I'm impulsive, and it's true. But I was afraid to tell you, for so many reasons."

"She is the reason you had to return to Valenwood."

"Yes. It was Elena who sent the messages about the hyppos."

Damen smiled and his heart felt swollen in his chest.

"That much, I guessed already." He paused. "Does she know?"

"No, not yet. She knows her father was Lord of the Dark Sun colony, and how we were parted. I thought you were dead, so that is what she believes now. I told her all about our time in the cavern. She is the only person who knows everything."

"You didn't tell her the . . . shocking parts, did you?"

"I told her I loved you very much, and you were the greatest man in all the galaxy, and that her life began in love between us."

"Good. Then you didn't get into anything too graphic."

"You sound like Fia."

"My daughter . . ."

"And now you have two."

Damen gazed upward, amazed. "I have taken a father's role, though in truth, I can be only a few years older than Fia myself."

Ariana got up and sat beside him. "I have always feared you were somewhat younger than I."

He glanced at her, and he smiled. "Most likely." He stopped, but wonder kept rolling over him like an endless wave. "The crystal . . . You told me you put it somewhere safe, where it was needed. You gave it to our daughter."

Ariana nodded. "It hangs in her room, over her bed. She is still young, and has a tendency to lose things, so she only wears it on special occasions, for festivals, and for the celebration of her birthday."

Damen fell silent. His daughter . . . *We will have many children. A boy, more girls . . . And they will play with hyppos, and swim in the warm sea. . . . It can't be hard to transport a hyppo or two to the Dark Sun planet. . . .* Hope gave way to a sudden weariness, and Damen bowed his head as the sweet image faded and cold reality returned. "You can't tell her."

Ariana looked surprised and hurt, but she spoke softly. "She has a right to know . . . to know *you*, Damen."

Pain throbbed in his heart, bitter and hard, almost im-

269

possible to endure. "Not now, not yet. Please, Ariana. Not until . . ."

"Until what?"

"Until what comes . . . has come."

She sighed. "I hoped you had softened in this, and might tell me, at last, what you have planned."

He closed his eyes, and hot tears threatened again. "I can't. Ariana, you don't understand. I can't. There is so much at stake." He paused and looked into her beautiful eyes. "If I reveal all to your father as he demands, don't you see? All would be lost. He would not permit what I must do, or worse, would seek to join me. But if I fail . . . if I fail, Ariana, then not only the Dark Sun People, but your own world, this beautiful palace high above your mystic sea . . . it will all fall to ruin. I cannot let that happen."

"I want to believe you—I do, so much. But it is hard, because I don't understand. Why must you face this alone?"

"The archer must get close enough to the dragon, Ariana, to fell it from the sky." Her eyes narrowed as she pondered what his words might mean, but he sighed. "There. I have said too much, even now. Please, ask me no more of this."

"It may be enough for me, but not for my father. Even if you persuade Dane, who seems your most likely ally at this point, it is my father whose judgment prevails at the Council. Most often, he has been right. He won't let you go if you tell him nothing of your intentions."

"That, I cannot do, so I will find another way to elude him."

"You mean, to escape."

He didn't answer, but he wouldn't lie, not now. "I will do what I must."

She took his hand suddenly. "If you go, then take me with you."

Damen lifted her hand and kissed it, then held it against his cheek. "I can't do that, Ariana."

"Then I will follow you."

"I would not put your life at risk this way. It has always been my intention to return you to Valenwood before the true danger arises. I have done so, though not by my own method."

Her chin quivered. "But I want to be with you."

"No. At least, promise me this. Stay here with our child, where your father can protect you."

"Damen, I want my future with you."

"If fate allows, and our paths hold true, then all we desire will come at last. But I cannot promise the end of a road I have not yet traveled."

Ariana drew a quavery breath and seemed to steel herself. "Then there's only one thing left to do."

Weariness threatened to overcome him, partly from his healing injury, but more, from the knowledge of what he must soon face, and all he could lose. "What's that?"

Ariana eased him back into her soft bed. Damen hesitated, then surrendered, and lay back. She kissed his forehead, then smoothed his hair gently. He wished he felt stronger, faster, and could take her into his arms, but instead, he yawned. "Go to sleep, so that you will be recovered for tomorrow."

He could barely keep his eyes open. "What awaits us tomorrow?"

"Well, my father has summoned a Council meeting, but that's not what I was thinking of."

"Then what?

Her brow angled. "Hyppos, of course. What else?"

Chapter Twenty-five

"The Council meets at sunset, when the other ambassadors have arrived." Arnoth stood at the center point of a long green marble table. He offered no greeting when Damen entered the room, nor did he seemed pleased to have consented to allow Damen freedom. "You have until then to decide your fate."

Damen held the king's gaze evenly. "My decision has not changed with the passing of one night, nor will it. I owe you no allegiance, nor do you have substantial evidence that my people pose any threat to you."

"You abducted my daughter!"

Damen glanced at Ariana, who looked uncomfortable and didn't meet his eyes. *Had to tell him that, didn't you?* "And *you* sent her into dangerous territory where far worse fates could befall her!"

Arnoth's eyes narrowed to slits. "I can think of none darker than falling into your clutches."

Dane Calydon entered the room, looking cheerful. He took a seat opposite Arnoth, then poured a decanter of pink juice into a goblet. "This is approximately the same conversation I remember you having with your own wife's father, Arnoth, my friend. Shortly before you argued against Intersystem interference with Valenwood."

Arnoth's lips pressed into a straight line, but he hesitated as if certain similarities came back to him, too. He muttered something unintelligible, but then his face softened into a gentle smile. The change was astounding, and Damen turned to see what could have altered his mood this much. A tall, beautiful woman stood in the dining hall entrance, holding Elena's hand. *My daughter*. His own mood softened at the sight of the child, and she smiled at him as if they shared some special secret.

Ariana seemed relieved by their presence. "Damen, this is my mother, Sierra. . . ."

Elena pointed at Damen, excited. "That is the Ellowan-pirate, Damen, Grandmamma. He wishes to visit the hyppos. Can we go now?"

Ariana's mother smiled. Her face resembled Ariana's, but without the poignant air of loneliness that Ariana carried. Her gaze reflected wisdom, and less suspicion than he saw in Arnoth. "After breakfast, Ellie. The Ellowan-pirate was only recently healed. He must eat to recover his strength."

This appeased Elena. "Like the hyppos do."

Dane laughed. "And do often, from what I'm told. I would like to see these creatures myself. After breakfast, I will gather the lingbats, and my son, wherever he is, and we will go with you down to the river mouth." Dane paused. "Where is he, anyway? I expected to find him at breakfast."

Arnoth seated himself. "Hakon has gone to revitalize his ship." He cast a quick, challenging glance Damen's way. "Another shipment of malloreum fuel has arrived, and Hakon is supervising its distribution."

Damen frowned. "The Intersystem fuels its fleet by theft. And you call me a pirate!"

Ariana rolled her eyes, seized his hand, and directed him to a seat at the far end of the table from Arnoth. Sierra seated herself at her husband's side, but she smiled at Damen, and he decided he liked her, despite her imperious husband. Elena left Sierra and came to Damen. She peered at him shyly, and he noticed that her hands were again clasped tight in front of her small body. "Can I sit with you?"

His throat tightened with emotion, but Damen smiled gently. "I would be very happy if you did." He pulled out the chair next to him, and she seated herself. Her age must be ten years, but her feet still dangled from the high Ellowan chair, and her toes didn't quite reach the floor. She crossed her legs at the ankles, folded her hands in her lap, and tried very hard to look polite. To be near her was to endure a flood of images, of each day since her birth, each year of her growth, and an even more painful picture of the future they might have. . . . *If only* . . .

Breakfast wasn't distributed by the army of servants Damen had expected from Arnoth's royal household, but by strange, hovering trays. The others seemed accustomed to these devices, so Damen tried to restrain his wonder. If he assessed how the others handled them, he could show a casual disinterest. Unfortunately, the floating platter containing the swirled roll he wanted sped by him twice because he didn't grab it in time, and in fixing his attention on that platter, he missed several others as they passed by. He frowned, sure Arnoth had somehow programmed the trays to avoid him. Ariana, naturally, was too intent on her own breakfast to notice his discomfort.

Elena eyed Damen, then pinned her determined gaze on the tray. She watched intently as it approached again, stood up in her chair, and then grabbed it as it attempted to pass. "Got you!" She held it steady before Damen. "Would you like one of these, Ellowan-pirate? They are very tasty. It is lucky Hakon isn't here because usually he tries to eat them all, and I must often attack him in order to get one for myself." She paused and sighed, proud. "Of course, I always win, and get several of his, too."

Elena served Damen two spiral rolls, then took two for

herself, though her plate was already loaded with various foods. Ariana glanced at her child and beamed with pride. "What else would you like, Ellowan-pirate? Grandpapa says we must have fruit, and there is a mixture of nuts and grains that he makes me eat, but if you mix it with the fruit, it's not so boring."

"What else is there?"

"Fish salted with sea-grains, which is very good, and Grandpapa promises it will make me both strong and large. I am taller then Vender by several tree knots."

"Tree knots?"

"Yes." Elena took a large bit of her roll and spoke thickly as she chewed. "If you stand against one of the Bending Trees which grow down near the river mouth, you can be measured, and mark the height on the bark." She stopped chewing and assessed Damen's height. "I think you are even taller than Dane, and Vender had to climb up into the tree to reach the top of his head." She cast a dark look Dane's way. "And I had to stay by Dane's feet because he kept standing on tiptoes to cheat!"

Dane grinned. "I knew your grandpapa would do the same, because it irks him that I am taller."

Damen glanced at Arnoth. He couldn't imagine teasing Ariana's regal, humorless father, but somehow, Dane managed. A slight smile twitched on Arnoth's mouth, though he didn't respond to Dane's challenge. How those two ever became friends eluded Damen, but Sierra laughed. "That is why he won't let you measure him!"

Hakon entered the dining hall, two lingbats perched on his shoulder. Elena waved, and he took the seat on the other side of her, then motioned at the spiral rolls. "I see you've beaten me this time, little one. I will have to get up earlier next time."

Elena nodded, pleased, and stuffed the last bite into her mouth, then licked her fingers with deliberate glee. Damen hadn't started on his, so she covered his plate with her small hands and glared fiercely at Hakon. "These are already taken."

The older lingbat, Carob, snorted loudly and derisively. "Don't worry about him! He got up in plenty of time to raid the kitchen, and devoured several of those delectables before any of you saw them!"

Hakon winced and Elena shook her head. "I should have known."

Dane eyed the lingbats. "It doesn't appear that either of you are diving onto the platters in your usual fashion, so I can only assume that you, too, made full use of the kitchen."

Carob puffed, though Pip looked somewhat shamed and cranked his little head here and there, looking at nothing. "Sorry, sir."

Carob's puckered face tightened even more. "Sorry, indeed! As a matter of fact, boy, we're out of crunch bugs. You'll have to gather some today, or expect to lose more of your larder to meet our requirements."

Damen glanced at Dane, but Dane held up his hand and shook his head. "Don't ask. As for the matter of crunch bugs, you are too recently healed to be faced with such a revolting subject matter." He gestured at Carob. "As a matter of fact, we're going down to the river to inspect the hyppos—they were under the water when I first arrived, the time of my measurement, so I didn't get a good look at them. You rodents can gather all the crunchy, chewy, crispy bugs you want there."

Catching Damen's grimace, Carob radiated pleasure. "Couldn't have described them better myself."

Ariana glanced at Arnoth, who had set aside his meal. "Are you coming, Papa?"

He hesitated, and Damen suspected he was trying to come up with an excuse to stay behind, probably to avoid Damen's presence. He wasn't sure if the others knew he was Elena's father or not. But having fathered Arnoth's grandchild probably wouldn't endear Damen to the proud king, and would most likely solidify his dislike.

"I am awaiting the arrival of the three ambassadors. It is best I remain here."

Hakon drained a goblet, then dried his mouth on a blue

cloth. "Seneca has signaled his approach into Ellowan space, and should arrive within the hour, and the Tellurite should be close behind. The Zimdardri representative and her mate arrived when I was in the hanger. They went directly to the guest quarters to enter their meditation."

Hakon sounded serious and respectful of the ambassador's habits, but Dane groaned. "When the five head Council Chairs were chosen, I went into meditation myself—to pray that Zimdardri female wouldn't be selected! Apparently, I don't have the knack for it."

Hakon looked confused. His earnest, serious manner reminded Damen of someone, but he wasn't sure of whom. "But, Father, meditation isn't for enforcing your will upon others, but to clear and open your mind and heart to the energy of wisdom."

Dane rolled his eyes and sighed. "You stay away from the Zimdardri, son—you're already too serious. They're a bad influence."

"It is wise to study the ways of other races. I know of your people and Mother's, but though the Ellowan are wise, there is much else to learn."

Dane huffed, then cast a bright glance toward Damen. "You notice he doesn't call my people, the Thorwalians, wise. Not so long ago, they could have rivaled your own honorable ancestors, the Tyrikan race, in bloodthirsty mayhem."

Hakon angled his brow. "Which is why I don't mention them."

Damen felt awkward and out of place seated among Ariana's loving family, but Dane seemed easier for conversation. "Why do you dislike the Zimdardri ambassador?"

Dane shook his head. "I don't dislike her, exactly. When you hear them talk, you'll understand."

Elena looked up from her barely touched bowl of grain and nuts. Apparently, the fruit wasn't enough to make it appealing. "I think they're pretty. They're blue, you know, and have strange, large feet. But they're also skinny, and they talk to children in a strange way. Once, the female cornered me and Vender and asked us how we 'directed our light,' and then she tried to make us sit still and think of a white cloud. Vender pretended he was going to throw up, and I said we had to get him to my grandpapa quick."

Damen patted her hair and his heart filled with love. "Well done."

Dane nodded a vigorous agreement. "Think I may try that myself next time she corners me."

Hakon grimaced as if he could too easily visualize the scene. "Father, that would not be appropriate."

Arnoth rose from the table. "Since when has that stopped him? The rest of you go along to the river. I will greet the ambassadors and brief them on our situation."

Arnoth left, and Elena hopped down from her chair, then took Damen's hand. Her hand felt small and warm in his. *My child.* She glanced to see that her grandfather had left, then lowered her voice. "It is perhaps for the best that Grandpapa stays away from the hyppos. He sees how fat they are, and begins talking about their diet—he thinks they eat too much, though I have told him that the fattest hyppos are the best."

Dane clapped his hands together, then marched to the exit. "I can't wait to see these creatures!" He went back to the table, seized Damen's uneaten spiral roll, and stuffed it in his pocket. "Let's see what the hyppos think of these, shall we?"

With Elena's small hand clasped in his, Damen followed the others from Arnoth's white palace, then on to a narrow, tiled lane that wound down a steep slope toward the shore below. Ariana walked just in front of him because the pathway was too narrow for more than an adult and a child to walk abreast. Dane went on ahead with the grumpy lingbat perched on his shoulder. The two seemed to be having an argument. Sierra followed behind Dane, and occasionally added to their conversation, seemingly taking Carob's side in the discussion. Hakon walked behind Damen with his own lingbat, Pip, who seemed both eager and curious.

Elena tugged at Damen's hand. "What do you think of the lingbats, Ellowan-pirate?"

"I'm not sure. They seem so different from each other." He raised his voice to reach Ariana. "Though neither particularly reminds me of my navigator, Nob."

Ariana glanced back. "You haven't met that one—that's Pip's father and Carob's son. He lives with his mate in the swamps of Keir among the Keiroits."

Damen glanced back at Hakon. "So such creatures actually exist?"

Hakon nodded. "They are large amphibious humanoids, strong warriors if necessary, though they are generally peaceful. Arnoth and my mother lived among them for many ages. I chose them for my disguise because when they leave the swamp, they must don a complete cover for environmental control purposes. My mother was disguised thus when she first met my father."

"I assume it wasn't love at first sight, then."

"I think not, though my father found her interesting, all the same."

Elena skipped beside Damen. "I like the Keiroits, though if you see them without their wrapping, it's a little scary. They have one bulgy eye, and one smaller one, and they burp often, which Vender imitates to annoy me."

A normal little boy, this Vender. . . . They reached a plateau where the tiled path widened onto a lookout, and there, Dane stopped and waited for the others to catch up. He gestured back toward the palace, and Damen turned. Arnoth's home glittered in the morning sun. The Tiled City itself stretched north. Eastward, levels of homes were built into the eastern cliffs, and beyond, the dark green of the great forest stretched endlessly northward. As it had the first time, the sight filled him with awe. "I have seen the Tiled City once before, and thought it magnificent."

Dane nodded. "It's quite a view, isn't it? What impresses me most is how Arnoth managed to create something straight out of Valenwood's history, as if he's brought all the grace and beauty of the past into the future." He paused and his gaze met Damen's. There was more thought and depth in Dane Calydon's eyes than Damen at first had guessed from his light manner. "That is what Arnoth does best—bring the glory of the ancient times forward, and retain them in his memory when all others would forget. That is why you annoy him, Damen, and why he annoys you in turn. You carry with you the future, with a certain disregard for the past."

Damen frowned. "The circumstances of my birth allowed for no glorious past. It is the future that interests me. The past is written and unchanging. The future will be molded by our deeds, and is ours to direct."

Dane seemed to like his answer, but Damen felt oddly like a child who has said something that amused a tribal elder. "Has it occurred to you that you're both right? You might benefit from understanding each other. Ironic, isn't it, that you and the king of Valenwood share a common history?"

"Despite your test, I think my Tyrikan heritage is more true."

"Undoubtedly. The Tyrikans are the strongest warriors in the galaxy. How I would love to be among them, to witness one of their great tournaments!"

Elena hopped from foot to foot. "I would like that, too! Mama, can we go to a Tyrikan tournament?"

Ariana chewed her lip. "They are rather too violent for us, Ellie."

Elena sighed, but Dane shrugged. "Used to be, that's certain. At one point, the strongest warriors gathered in combat—and the final battle for the championship was fought to the death."

Ariana cringed. "That's it! We are *not* attending a Tyrikan tournament."

Dane patted her shoulder. "They abandoned that practice for the obvious reason that each such battle ended with the loss of one of their two most powerful warriors. Now, their rules are stricter, and death results in forfeit. Because of this development, however, their fighting skills were vastly refined and no one in the universe, I'd imagine, can match them in physical combat, though some bold fighters have entered the Tyrikan competition, so far with little success. All the same, I would dearly love to test my own strength against their warriors."

Carob snorted derisively. "In a flat minute, you'd be a pile of mush beneath a warrior's boot."

Dane frowned into indignation. "Thank you, rodent, for your unflinching loyalty."

"Just trying to keep you from getting killed, boy. And not for the first time!"

Damen found he liked the idea of Tyrikan tournaments. "I, too, would find this test of strength and manhood appealing."

Ariana groaned and rolled her eyes. "You are more than half Ellowan, remember? You'd end up as a pile of mush, too!" She grabbed his other hand and pulled him forward. "Come! The hyppos await."

They left the outlook and continued downward toward the river below. The path widened, and Hakon walked ahead with his father, but he seemed quiet and contemplative. "I'm not sure what use these 'tests of manhood' really are, Father. It seems to me that the more refined physical arts have greater value, such as the mind-body technique Seneca practices. I have learned a great deal from that."

Dane shrugged. "I studied Seneca's technique for a while, but it takes enormous focus. It's a little boring, isn't it? The Tyrikans summon tremendous energy from within themselves, too, but there's no 'balance on one foot until the sun sets and then rises again.' I endured that tedium for about five minutes, then made a quick exit."

Hakon looked serious. "I found that particular lesson most enriching."

Dane groaned. "Probably stayed on one foot all night."

Hakon hesitated. "Yes."

Dane stared at his son as if a new species emerged before his eyes. "Where did you come from?" Hakon started to answer, but Dane held up his hand. "No. Don't say it. From your mother's womb, I know."

Hakon smiled, then elbowed his father. "I was going to say 'from an impatient father,' but your answer is also true."

Damen watched them, mystified. What had his own father been like? Had the blood of the violent Tyrikans flowed through his veins, or had it been tempered with the mystic grace of the Ellowan? He glanced down at Elena. What had he missed in that primitive cavern that could never be replaced? How could he expect to be her father when he had no model or guide?

Elena squeezed Damen's hand and gazed up at him thoughtfully. "I am pleased you could come with me to see the hyppos, Ellowan-pirate."

"I'm pleased I was allowed free. For that, I think I have you to thank."

"Carob the lingbat often says that his species is capable of any number of wonders." Her green eyes twinkled. "I am, too."

Chapter Twenty-six

"Curses! I don't see a thing. They're all under the water again." Dane shaded his eyes against the morning sun and squinted at the murky river. "I have bad luck with hyppos. Perhaps another day."

Elena's small face fell in disappointment, and she plunked down to sit on the riverbank, crossing her arms over her knees. Damen sat beside her, and folded his arms over his knees, too. "I will wait with you until they appear."

She brightened and looked more hopeful. Carob bounded off Dane's shoulder, but his attention diverted from the river. "Come, lad! There's feasting to be had here, and no mistake! There, upriver a bit, I see a rotting log swarming with gnats."

Pip hesitated and remained on Hakon's shoulder. "Don't much care for gnats, grandsire. No flavor."

Carob waved his wings violently. "Not the gnats, boy! But where there are gnats, there are bound to be fat crunch bugs. Those are worth a chew, mark my words."

Pip brightened, then scrambled off his human perch.

"Coming, Grandsire. Coming!" They bounded away together, and Dane came to stand beside Elena.

"If nothing else, you'll be seeing two fat lingbats by noon."

Elena sighed. "Not as fat as hyppos."

A high, clear voice called from across the water, and a small boy with wavy reddish brown hair appeared from amongst the green alders. He waved excitedly. Elena gave no response, but she tensed. Damen smiled. "Vender, I presume?"

She affected a disinterested expression, then glanced at her nemesis as he waded down to the river's edge. "That's him. He always shows up whenever I'm here, to pester me." So her rival's interest equaled Elena's. Damen waved at the little boy.

Dane called over to him. "Greetings, young prince!" Elena rolled her eyes at the title, but she didn't correct Dane. "It seems we're out of luck today. No hyppos in sight."

The boy splashed into the water. "Just wait! I know how to bring them out!"

Ariana headed down to the river. "Don't get too close, Vender. Hyppos are reputedly quite fierce."

The boy shrugged. "They know *me*, because I'm their friend. *Others* ought to stay back, though."

Elena clenched her teeth, then shoved herself up. "They like me just as much as you! More!"

"Oh, really? But you don't know how to get them up out of the water, do you?"

Elena didn't answer, so Damen assumed the boy had a point. While they waited, Vender yanked several large pink fruits from a nearby tree, then tossed them into the water. The pink fruit floated slowly downstream, but just as Damen decided the hyppos weren't hungry, a ripple appeared on the quiet surface. Elena's body drew tight and she held her breath. She stared at the water as if a god might emerge, and quivered with expectation.

A brownish-gray snout appeared and sniffed at the fruit.

Damen's own excitement mounted, and Ariana positioned herself by the shore, her hands clasped in front of her body in a posture closely resembling Elena's. The hyppo lurched suddenly up from the water, devoured the largest fruit in one gulp, and then surfaced to float on the water. Dane whooped, his face lit like a child's, and he turned to the others.

"Did you see that? What an amazing creature!"

Hakon eyed his father doubtfully, then glanced at Sierra. She stood close, smiling, her face warm and beautiful in the morning sun. "When I first saw them, I reacted in the same way. But I thought Elena would fly with happiness at the sight."

Hakon shrugged. "She has brought me here several times, but I do not see that they actually do much of anything. They just hang there in the water and occasionally . . ."

The hyppo issued the low grunt Damen had heard from his window, and Hakon nodded. "And occasionally, they grunt."

Elena just stared, enchanted. "Aren't they wonderful? So *fat*."

Damen eyed the creature. "Fat" was an understatement. The animal was enormous, with a large round snout, a simple head with small eyes and tiny ears, and the appearance of a great, sagging chin that extended into a body of vast proportions. At the end of the hyppo's body, a small, pointed tail protruded, an oddly delicate ending to the otherwise massive body. No wonder Arnoth considered putting the creatures on a diet!

Ariana seemed almost as excited as Elena. "I've never seen anything like them! I've seen them in pictures, but no image does this creature justice. Look! He's so serene, so peaceful. Not a restless bone in his body." She sounded almost envious, as if these were qualities that had eluded her, but Dane laughed.

"Not a bone at all, I should say, by the look of him."

Elena glanced between them. "It's not a 'he,' Mamma. That is the baby, and she is a girl."

Damen gaped, stunned. "That's the *baby?*"

As if to prove Elena's point, two other vast creatures emerged from the muddy river. They were at least triple the first hyppo's size. Vender ran up and down along the shore, but the hyppos paid no attention, though they eyed Dane and Ariana with a slight sense of suspicion.

They really do know him. Apparently, Elena noticed this, too. "They like him." She sounded a little disappointed, but also admiring. "It is because Vender dares to go into the water to feed them." Her lip quivered and she bowed her head. "I am not brave enough to go so close."

Damen got up and took her hand. "I have an idea." He picked her up and set her on his shoulders. "With two of us, we might approach them safely. What do you think?"

She gazed down at him with gratitude, but she didn't speak. Instead she nodded, her eyes wide with joy. He walked slowly to the river's edge, past Dane and Ariana, until he stood knee deep in the water. The largest hyppo surveyed him thoughtfully, then returned to eating. The female nudged a fruit toward her young, and the baby ate it greedily.

Vender called across the river. "They're running out. If I don't get them more, they'll return to feeding under the water, and we will see only their snouts." The tree had given up all the fruit off its lower branches, and Vender had to climb into the branches to retrieve more. He cast a few into the water, then went higher for more.

Dane's expression shifted to concern and he joined Damen in the water. "Be careful there, Vender! Those higher branches are weak."

"I go this high all the time."

Ariana came up behind them. "He's too high."

Elena's fingers gripped Damen's hair. "Make him come down. Vender! Get down from there! The hyppos are full!"

Vender's high laugh came from the leaves. "That shows how much you know! Hyppos are never full, Ellie!"

"You are such a brat! Get down from there right now!"

He ignored her order, and Damen tensed as a branch swayed dangerously low. "There's a big fruit just above me. If I can just . . ." The branch cracked and broke, and the boy screamed. The hyppos startled and disappeared beneath the surface.

Dane whirled to Hakon. "Go! Get Arnoth—he may need healing!"

Hakon raced away toward the palace and Damen set Elena to the ground, then dove into the river. His heart pounded in fear as he swam through the cold water, but he came to the far side, then bounded up the wet bank to where Vender had fallen. The boy lay crumpled at the base of the tree.

Damen knelt beside the child. Tears streamed down the boy's little face. "My ankle . . ."

Damen checked Vender's leg. "Your ankle is broken, I think."

"Who are you?"

"I am Elena's . . . friend."

Vender's chin quivered, but he fought his tears. "Did she see me fall? Did she laugh?"

Damen lifted the child into his arms. "She is crying because you are her best friend."

"Did she say that?"

"I can tell."

Vender closed his eyes, but he held tight to Damen's neck. "I knew that, but I didn't think she did."

Damen waded into the water. "The king is coming to heal you, but I will carry you back across the river. Can you hold to my back while I swim?"

Vender nodded, and Damen lowered into the water, then gently eased Vender onto his back. The hyppos had emerged farther downstream and watched motionless as Damen swam back to the near shore. He carried Vender from the river and laid him gently on the soft grass, cradling the boy's head on his lap. Elena sank down beside him, her small face wet with tears. "Why did you do that, Vender?

The hyppos can wait for more fruit to grow. You didn't have to climb that high."

He peered up at her. "But I wanted to show you I could."

Elena's head tilted to one side, and a strange light kindled in her eyes. She leaned closer to her small rival, then reached to touch his forehead. Her eyelids drooped as if weariness assailed her, and her fingers moved on Vender's brow and temple. Damen watched in amazement as her eyes drifted shut. Her lips moved, but no sound came, and she bent lower still over his body. She whispered something softly that Damen didn't understand. He glanced up at Ariana. "What does she say?"

"She is speaking in the ancient Ellowan tongue." Ariana paused, astounded. "She says, 'Yield to me, and I will heal you.' "

Tears welled in Damen's eyes. A deep and resonant warmth seemed to rise from Elena's body and surround her, then pass from her into Vender. Ariana knelt beside Damen. "She has entered the healing trance of the Ellowan!"

Sierra and Dane stood beside them, gazing at the children in wonder. Sierra spoke softly, amazed. "Arnoth has sensed that Elena has healing gifts. But he didn't think her Ellowan blood was strong enough for such power."

Her Ellowan blood—which came from Damen's own heart. As Elena bonded on some unfathomable level with Vender, Hakon returned with Arnoth in a white hovercraft. Arnoth leapt out before the vehicle stopped, then ran to where Vender lay. A strange, very tall blue humanoid female followed after Hakon. Arnoth sank to his knees beside Elena, and tears came to his eyes as he realized what she was doing.

Elena drew back, then sank against Arnoth, weakened from her trance. Arnoth held her as Vender opened his eyes. "My ankle doesn't hurt now, but it tingles." He looked at Elena, then struggled to sit up. Surprised, Damen helped him, but the boy crossed his legs and looked comfortable. "It is good you can do this, Ellie. If one of the hyppos becomes sick, you can fix them."

Elena sat straight. "That's true. I can." She paused. "Can you walk now?"

"Sure." Vender rubbed his ankle. "But I don't think I can run or climb." He braced himself on Damen's shoulder and stood up, tried his ankle, then motioned to Elena. Damen stood and watched as the two children walked to the water together, then sat side-by-side watching the hyppos.

Ariana glanced at her father. "I thought you said the Ellowan healing technique had to be taught?"

Arnoth rose to his feet, but he seemed uncertain. "*I* was taught."

The blue-skinned female came to stand beside him. "For once, you do not look far enough into the past, Arnoth. Such a gift as the Ellowan possess did not come from a scientific study. It can only have come from the heart, when one being saw another it loved in pain. Because the Ellowan physiology is graced with remarkable empathy, it allowed a soul of great love to reach into another and lend its energy toward healing."

Arnoth considered this, then looked to Elena and Vender. "I had feared no great healer would come again. Most of the surviving Ellowan have married off-worlders, and to the betterment of Valenwood. But these traits can only be inherited." He stopped, and his piercing gaze fell suddenly on Damen. A look of doubt crossed his face, and then he turned away. "I must return to the city to greet the arriving ambassadors." He paused, then glanced at Damen again. "The Council meets in one hour. You will be present."

Damen frowned. "Do I have a choice?"

Arnoth didn't respond at once. "You have a choice. Be sure it's the right one."

Sierra sighed, then took her husband's hand. "I'd best come with you. The Tellurite ambassador can be very demanding."

Hakon held open the hovercraft shell for them to enter. "I'm going, too. Seneca should be arriving soon, and I want his wife's advice on a procedure I'm attempting. Are you coming, Father?"

Dane waved, but didn't seem eager to leave. "I'll walk up with the others. The lingbats haven't returned, and I wouldn't want to miss their tales of conquest."

Damen eyed Dane with misgivings. "Conquest?"

Dane grinned. "Just wait. If you thought the hyppos were fascinating, you'll love the descriptions of the various insect specimens that those two fiends have devoured."

Ariana shuddered. "Perhaps we should leave, after all."

The Zimdardri female motioned elegantly to Hakon. "I, also, will remain here a while. The air is clear, enriched by organic growth and decay and regrowth. It cleanses my spirit with its purity."

Dane took a step toward the hovercraft, but Hakon lowered the shell and it departed. Dane drew a long breath, then addressed the Zimdardri female. "Ambassador, how fortunate you could come at such short notice!" He didn't sound as if he felt it was *his* fortune, but the ambassador ignored him, turning her attention to where Elena and Vender sat tossing leaves into the river for the hyppos.

"It is I who consider myself fortunate. Rarely have I witnessed such a spiritually compelling moment as I have here."

Dane glanced casually around as if hoping the ambassador would say no more, but Ariana peered at her with interest. "Do you mean when Elena healed Vender?"

The Zimdardri nodded. "The connection between those two is very strong, and it is pure because it is young."

Damen eyed the blue Zimdardri ambassador, unsure after Dane's earlier comments if he wanted to query her further. But if she had insights into Elena's gifts, he wanted to hear them. "Young? Do you mean because they are children?"

The Zimdardri's long, narrow face softened into a sublime smile. "I speak of a soul's age, and not the body that harbors it. Their spirits are newly born into human form, though they have lived other lives, in more primitive forms. Perhaps that is why the hyppo fascinates them so—it may be familiar to their cores."

Dane cocked his brow and issued a pertinent look that

said, *I warned you.* He eased away from the conversation before the ambassador could continue, then joined Elena and Vender. He tossed the roll he'd taken from breakfast directly into the mouth of the baby hyppo, who issued its strange grunt in gratitude. Elena and Vender both cheered.

Seeing Damen's confusion, the Zimdardri moved closer and looked deeply into his eyes, searching. "You are not young. I see in you a great span of lives, from the power and confidence of your earliest beginnings, through the discord and rebellion of the middle ages, and now, into the dawn of wisdom and understanding."

Damen hesitated, doubtful about posing further questions. "How does this pertain to my . . . to Ariana's daughter?"

"It is Elena's purity of heart and the simplicity of her soul that allows the Ellowan healing power to flow so easily. This also explains why Vender accepted healing so completely. The soul's journey spirals on unique paths, and so I will not predict what twists may befall them in lifetimes to come. With the inevitable pain and rage of the middle ages comes separation—separation from our mates and from ourselves, that which we truly *are.*"

Ariana sighed. "That isn't entirely encouraging, Ambassador. It seems a shame for a spirit to spiral at all."

The Zimdardri's strange turquoise eyes grew luminous. "Then imagine the power of a love that has endured pain, tarnished seemingly beyond recall. When the light of love . . ."

"The appetite of a hyppo rivals a lingbat's!" Dane rejoined them, but he seemed dismayed to find the ambassador still talking.

The ambassador gazed at the river in a wise, knowledgeable fashion. "The hyppo is pure. . . ."

Dane coughed, then eased away. "If you'll excuse me, I think I hear Arnoth calling." He bowed quickly, then hurried off. The two lingbats burst out of the shrubs upstream and sped after him.

Stobie Piel

Pip squeaked and bounced ahead of Carob. "Sir! Wait! Stop!"

Being older, Carob puffed along behind his grandson, but his command remained forceful. "Now!"

Dane stopped, sighed miserably, then bowed his head in utter defeat. The lingbats hurtled themselves to his shoulders, and Carob caught his wing tip, deliberately, in Dane's shaggy blond hair, then yanked. "Thinking to lose us, were you, boy? You can't expect an honored bat of my years to pick my way up that hill!" He yanked again. Dane didn't respond, but he looked pained. He cast a sorrowful look toward Damen, but his blue eyes twinkled.

"Thought the walk might wear off some of the bugs you rodents have ingested. I'm the one stuck carrying your rotund forms all over creation."

Pip chattered something about protocol, and Carob commenced a lecture that Damen felt sure would last for the duration of the walk. Shoulders slumped miserably, Dane headed off, but within a few paces, his gait had quickened.

The Zimdardri ambassador placed her long, blue palms together like a shaman commencing a sacred ritual. "Lingbats, of course, are living Guides, ancient beyond measure, vast in wisdom."

Ariana shrugged. "That's what they're always telling us."

Dane bounded up the slope toward the Tiled City with the two lingbats clinging to his hair, flightless wings flailing as they squeaked commands.

Ariana watched him go, and she smiled. "Dane has more joy than anyone I've ever known. Is he also a very new soul?"

The Zimdardri looked impossibly serene, and Damen had to fight the desire to dart after Dane. "Ah! I see why you would think so. But it is not the case. He is ancient, even older than myself and my mate."

Damen eyed her doubtfully. "But he is nothing like you."

"You mean he lives life to its fullest, rarely sits still, and would rather face an army of marauding crunch bugs than join the Zimdardri in mediation?"

Damen smiled. "That is approximately what I was thinking, yes."

"Each soul has its own character, and each joined pair is unique, both as individuals and together. Though we expand our understanding through experience and time, the core of a being remains true. Dane will always prefer action to introspection, just as Arnoth will remain forever regal in nature. Wisdom has never meant dilution of character."

"A shame. The king, it seems to me, could use some 'dilution.'"

Ariana poked him, then turned back to the Zimdardri. "What you say, Ambassador, reminds me of the Beginning Symbol of the Dark Sun People, two joined by one heart."

"This same image is displayed by many cultures in different fashions. For the Tellurite, for instance, it is two snakes devouring each other's tail in an eternal circle." The ambassador paused. "It is like the Tellurite to put a certain violence into the image."

Ariana glanced at Damen. "You haven't met the Tellurite ambassador yet. Though dauntless and brave, the Tellurite have quick tempers. You must take care not to anger him."

"Given your father's unyielding attitude and the sway he holds with others, I see no way to avoid it."

Ariana called to the children, and Elena came running across the grass, her face bright and eager. "Can Vender stay a while to play? We are planning a show for the hyppos."

Vender looked hopeful. "I'm all better now."

Ariana hesitated. "I suppose that will be all right. I'll send a message to your father, and Hakon can take you home later in the hovercraft."

Damen picked up Vender, then set the boy on his back. "It is time we returned. You have a show to rehearse, and I have a Council to defy."

The Council meeting did not go well, but no worse than Damen had expected. Arnoth demanded that he reveal his plans for the Dark Sun Fleet, and Damen refused. Damen's defiance had, indeed, angered the small Tellurite ambassador, who had issued several threats that Damen ignored. Seneca, the ambassador from Dakota, seemed the most thoughtful, and had suggested, rightly, that the Intersystem's authority didn't cover the actions beyond its space. None of them seemed to believe in the existence of the High King that Mallik claimed to serve, but perhaps that was for the best. When the vote came, Dane and Seneca argued for Damen's return to the Dark Sun world, but the Tellurite and Zimdardri ambassadors voted with Arnoth, to hold him in the palace until they learned the Automon commander's purposes firsthand.

Hakon and Ariana had sat in on the meeting, and the lingbats, too—silent for once. Hakon told of their encounter with Mallik, but though he was surprisingly restrained in detailing Damen's apparent allegiance, Arnoth demanded more of an explanation than Damen would give.

All during the meeting, Damen had been aware of Ariana's disappointment. After the grueling meeting had adjourned, she went to put Elena to bed without speaking to him. Given the most recent turn of events, he doubted she would return. His heart ached, because he knew this night would be their last together.

Damen sighed and went to gaze out the wide window. The sun had set, but a large nearby planet had risen and brightened the night sky with a warm glow. The ancient and beautiful amber whales sang, and closer, lower to his ear, came the strange, deep rumble of the hyppos. Celebrating their latest meal, no doubt.

"Do you know how the lost world of Valenwood came to be restored?"

Damen startled at the quiet voice, and turned to see Arnoth standing in the doorway. That proud face, the ancient, dark eyes . . . everything about Arnoth of Valenwood spoke of nobility and wisdom. But he was blind to the future that Damen saw all too clearly.

"By the valor of the Ellowan, I assume."

Arnoth entered the room and stood beside Damen, his

dark eyes glowing as he gazed at the sea. "Then you assume in error, for that was not the case. An age ago, five hundred and more years as the Intersystem measures time, Valenwood was indeed a perfect world. In that time, our high priestess, for whom I named my daughter, found herself shipwrecked on the ice world of Thorwal."

"Thorwal . . . isn't that Dane's home world?"

"It is, though it has changed much from those far-off times, and is now the home of a somewhat dour and methodical people. Dane is an exception. But at the time of which I speak, the Thorwalians were nothing but barbarian warriors, primitive and violent, engaged in bitter feuds and bloody conflicts amongst themselves."

"Dane says they were much like my Tyrikan ancestors."

"Not that bad, but violent, all the same. Yet the priestess Ariana fell in love with a barbarian chieftain, and brought him back to Valenwood as her mate. Hakon became our greatest king."

Damen's eyes narrowed. "He was called Hakon, too?"

"He was. Dane named his son for our great king." Arnoth's regal gaze searched Damen's face. "As you guess, it was my fond hope that my daughter and Dane's son would find the love their predecessors shared, and thus restore the ancient line of the Ellowan. We had hopes previously for my eldest son and his daughter, but she wed a Thorwalian and lives happily with him, while my son chose a Nirvahdi woman who shares my wife's cheerful nature." Arnoth sighed. "Things do not often go as we design, and that is perhaps for the best. But because King Hakon had replaced my own father, who was the priestess Ariana's betrothed . . ."

Damen cut him off. "*Your* father? But you say this time was five hundred years in the past!"

"As indeed it was. Like Dane's wife, I was born in that far-off age. We prolonged our lives using a ritual unique to the Ellowan, where there is life without death, and in this way, we defied our conquerors, and lived to see the restoration of Valenwood. But not before Dane stole my second mate and wed her himself, and not before I succumbed to the charms of a Nirvadhi female. . . ." A smile curved his lips and Arnoth's proud expression softened. "But none of it could have been if not for King Hakon. He and Ariana survived the barrage that destroyed most of our population—Dane's wife and I were off world at the time, and so, escaped death, nor did we know for countless years that any of our people survived. But King Hakon gathered what remained of our people, hid them in caverns—and there they survived until we defeated our enemy and freed them."

Arnoth fell silent as Damen pondered Valenwood's history. "Why do you tell me this?"

"Like her ancestor, Ariana has chosen you, the barbarian over the prince. Before you go, I wanted you to know that Valenwood remembers how great a barbarian can be."

Damen rose and faced Ariana's father. At last, they understood each other. Arnoth had forbidden him to leave Valenwood, all the while knowing Damen couldn't be stopped. "Take care of Ariana. She will seek to follow me, but you cannot allow it."

"If I can stop her, I will, but like you, she can be determined." Arnoth went to the door, but then he turned back. "Do not throw your life away needlessly, Damen. My daughter needs you." He paused, and his proud face gentled with a smile. *"And yours."*

Chapter Twenty-seven

Ariana stood outside the door of her bedroom. *Why do you have to be so stubborn?* And yet, she couldn't help admiring Damen as he defied the most powerful leaders in the galaxy. He was so strong, and so sure he could place his trust in no one but himself. She had kissed Elena goodnight, then sat on her daughter's bed listening to the child chat happily about Damen—how brave a man he was to rescue Vender, and how kindly he had treated her. She didn't seem interested in her own act of heroism by healing Vender, but Damen had risen almost to the glorified level of hyppos in Elena's estimation.

Ariana opened the door. The guard sat across the hall and seemed groggy. She entered and found Damen gazing out at the darkening night. He turned and saw her, then drew the window shut. "It is colder here than on my world, but the air is clear."

"It is the winter season on Valenwood, but it is never as warm as your planet." Ariana went to stand beside him. She hesitated, then placed her hand on his shoulder. "You were very brave today."

He eyed her doubtfully. "For swimming through hyppos? I assure you, I have faced greater dangers. Though if they were very, very hungry, I might make a wider berth around them."

She smiled. "Rescuing Vender was a good act, but that's not what I was thinking of."

"No? Then what, standing up to your father, or enduring the lofty allusions of the Zimdardri female?"

"You faced something much more difficult, I think. Our daughter. It would have been easier for you to keep your distance from her, but you didn't."

Damen sighed. "It might have been easier, but impossible. She is so much like you, so dear and so delicate, yet strong, as she proved when she healed her friend."

"So often during her life, she has reminded me of you." Ariana paused. "It means so much to me to see you with her. She fell asleep with the words 'Ellowan-pirate' on her lips."

They sat together on the edge of her bed and Damen gazed into her face. He seemed sorrowful. "All this time. . . . You were pregnant. . . . In all the years since I lost you, it never occurred to me that you might bear my child."

"It was a surprise to me, also, though perhaps it shouldn't have been. Lissa told me when we were at the Academy that she had an implant, a small device placed beneath her skin that prevented conception. She said I should get one, too, but I didn't like the idea."

Damen touched her hair, then tucked a strand behind her ear. "I have a similar implant myself, in my shoulder. I hadn't thought to tell you—when my attention is focused on you, I forget such practical matters. After I first left you in Valenwood, I knew I couldn't bring a child into life, not with my heart so disconnected as it felt then. Those born in the Dark Sun colonies know how precious life is—I wanted to be sure I created no misery by siring a child whose mother I couldn't love."

"I suppose that is noble of you. . . ." Ariana chewed the inside of her lip. "Do you mean you can't have any more children?" She hadn't thought of conception, either, but she wasn't sure how she felt about his disclosure.

Damen cupped her face in his hands, his lips close to her forehead. "It can be easily removed, when the time is right."

Ariana hesitated. "If the time is right . . . would you want more babies?"

The glow in his eyes answered her before his words were spoken. "*Yes*. Each one is new, each one a different room opening in the heart. Together, we have the capacity to open many such rooms."

Ariana gripped his forearms and her heart beat with firm purpose. "I want that so much, Damen. I want a life with you, and with our daughter. Can you imagine how wonderful Fia will be with Elena? Fia likes to lead, and Elena will delight in following her. I can visualize it so perfectly, to the smallest detail. I know what I want, but I'm so afraid it will remain forever beyond my reach."

"I told you once that I can't promise where our journey will lead, but this I would have you know. Whatever I do, however it may seem to you, it is with this dream in my heart, that you and I will be together." He paused. "So you have never considered such a device as Lissa suggested?"

Ariana angled her brow. "You are fishing to see if I've had other lovers. Haven't I told you that before? You're the only one. Though I'm not sure it seems equal considering that you rampaged through the galaxy."

"I wasn't that bad."

"Lissa heard rumors."

Damen frowned. "Not the most reliable source of gossip, I think." He paused to huff. "If that woman advised you to have an implant placed in your skin, it is wise you refused. It would probably have killed you."

"I was afraid that you would believe her. She can be convincing."

Damen eyed her doubtfully. "Love wears many faces, my lady, but none of them have eyes glittering with malice as hers do when looking at you."

"Hakon says that Lissa seeks power thinking not of great causes, but simply to gain influence over the trivial things she wants." Ariana fell silent. Damen was that "trivial thing" Lissa desired—she felt sure of it. She even felt sure of Lissa's goals and methods. They weren't complex, but if successful, they might be devastating. She had aligned herself with the powerful Mallik with one purpose in mind. With this new power and influence, she would lure Damen to her side, first as Mallik's subordinate ally, and then with intent to usurp Mallik, putting Damen in his place—and with Lissa at his side.

Damen touched Ariana's cheek. "I know what she wants, Ariana. And she will never have it."

Ariana's lips parted in surprise. "You know?"

He smiled. "I have no desire to supplant Mallik, but I promise you, if I did, it would be you at my side, and not Lissa."

Ariana smiled, too. "You're too aware of your appeal."

"She looked at me the way you look at pastries, or the way the lingbats fix their round eyes on crunch bugs."

"Oh, thank you very much for *that* comparison!" She paused. "Although I suppose you do have a point. There is a similarity." She paused again. "Do I look at you that way, too?"

Damen's mood shifted. "Not exactly. Oh, I've seen lust in your eyes, when you can't wait to touch me. But she sees only what she thinks I can do for her, and how it would look to others, especially you, if she had me for herself. I see much more in your face when you look at me. You adore me."

"You are so confident!"

Damen's brown eyes darkened. "Ah, but it's the light in your eyes that makes me so sure, my lady. It pleases me, I think, to turn that light to fire." He rose from the bed and with deliberate hesitation and care, slowly stripped away his clothing. Ariana held her breath as each piece dropped to the floor. He bared his chest and smiled, then dropped his shirt. Damen unfastened his leggings, so slowly that she ached, but even when he bent to lower them, his gaze remained fixed on her. Ariana bit her lip and tried to steady her nerves, but nearly screamed when he stopped short of removing the narrow wrap beneath his leggings.

She wanted to jump off the bed and remove it for him, but he held her transfixed. He eased aside the wrap so that his strong hand grazed over his erection, and the sight made her weak. Slowly, he tantalized her with the touch, so acute that she felt the heat of him, the size, and the hardness as if gripped in her own palm. And those dark eyes never wavered. He just watched her as she squirmed, her breath uneven and shallow, her pulse racing. He tossed aside the wrapping and stood naked before her. Then he walked around her bed and lay down by her pillows, propped up on one elbow as he watched her.

It was a game, a challenge. In challenge, her nerves steadied like a warrior's, and she rose from the bed, looking down at him. She kept her gaze locked with his, then unwrapped her dress from around her body. As slowly as he had moved when tormenting her, she moved slower, so that every breath had meaning. She dragged the satin cloth over her skin, so that each portion of her came bared to his sight, and as it slid over her breast, he caught his breath and his eyes burned with desire.

He lay there, so beautiful, his dark skin warm in her low lamplight. His strong legs, his wide chest . . . he was expecting her to collapse with need, to fall into his arms. She fought the impulse to succumb, though her knees felt shaky and weak and her heart pounded with need. Ariana offered a challenging glint, then lay opposite him, so that her feet curled near her pillows, and she peered up at him, teasing.

"Will I go to you, or will you come to me, my lord?"

A slow, sensual smile formed on his lips. "You tease me, my lady, so I will give you neither, and better than both." Before she realized what he intended, he leaned up, then eased her onto her back. He didn't right himself as she expected, but instead placed his strong hands between her legs, parted her thighs, then bent to kiss her most sensitive core.

Ariana gasped and tried to sit up. She felt the tip of his tongue against her and had to clench her hands tight with restraint. He had won too easily, and she was surrendering with a madness for rapture. As he adjusted his position for better access to her vulnerable desire, his erection brushed near her cheek. Power soared back through her, and she gripped his length in one hand, then slid her tongue over its tip. Damen groaned with both surprise and delight, but his own delicious ministrations intensified. He sucked and teased her small peak with his tongue, while drawing his finger along her woman's cleft. He dipped inward, and she took his shaft full in her mouth.

He reciprocated her passion and made love to her with his mouth, and all the while, she received him and urged him, and their bodies entwined. She gripped his thigh to steady herself, to take him deeper, to blend with him, and he held her hips so that she couldn't move nor writhe, though currents of fire swept through her. Wildness possessed her, beyond anything she had known or imagined. Everything but Damen disappeared, everything but their joined bodies, everything but giving all that she had, and taking all he would give. Her body spiraled, her nerves caught fire, and they moved like two pulses of water, like waves against each other. When the spiral burst, it came simultaneously between them, and she took him inside her, savoring his taste and the feel of him, as he carried her through her ecstasy.

Drained as she was, the wildness remained, the desire to feel everything, to know him, and to have him inside her. More even than their first encounter in his bedroom, once was not enough. This teasing they'd shared, the rapture they'd witnessed in each other, called out for more. Ariana rose trembling from the bed, responding to the fire that burned inside her. She cast a seductive glance at him, turned aside, and then wrapped her hands around her bedpost.

He knew what she wanted, and he was ready, despite his first release. He left the bed, positioned himself behind her, and gripped her shoulder with one hand, then slid her hair forward with the other. She ached with a need that seemed impossible to fill, but he bent her forward, and she felt his thick shaft sliding over her bottom, then between her thighs. Her teeth cut into her lip as she fought for restraint, and he teased her until each breath was a shuddering plea. She wanted his hard thrust, the ache relieved, but instead he entered her slowly, so slowly that she felt every inch of him as he slipped deeper inside her. He withdrew and entered her again, and she closed her inner walls tight around him. He moaned, then thrust harder. She clutched the bedpost to keep herself steady, pressing back against him as he drove harder and faster, until she heard his ragged breaths. The power of his thrust lifted her to her toes, but he clasped her hips tight, and she took more, and felt more, and wanted more than she had ever dreamed possible.

And then he slowed, and took her again, denying them both the final ecstasy, until no strength was left in her legs, until every muscle in her body quivered. Damen's release came with hers, and he bent forward to kiss her. She felt his lips on her shoulder, on her neck, and he gripped her long hair in his fingers while ecstasy rippled through him. Her own pinnacle burst and finally subsided, and as it faded, her knees gave way beneath her.

Damen caught her and picked her up, then placed her gently on the bed. He adjusted the pillows, then lay down beside her. They stared at each other, almost a little scared. Their breath came in shallow gasps, and Ariana's heart raced as if she'd run all the way up the path from the river.

Damen touched her cheek, but his own hands were shaking. "I told you I love you. But I think you should know. . . . I lust for you, too."

A soft, lazy smile formed on Ariana's lips, and she kissed his fingertips. "Our lust comes out of love." She paused and yawned. "I think it's better that way."

Damen kissed her forehead, then gathered her into his arms. She fought sleep just to feel his closeness, but the sound of his heartbeat lulled her ever deeper into its warm embrace. There must be a million things they could do, a million ways to explore each other, to arouse new feelings, satisfy new desire. . . . In a perfect life, they would follow their own individual paths, they would share the raising of children, the creation of a home, but this passion, this would always be theirs together. As Ariana drifted toward sleep, she silently vowed that's just what she would have.

Morning came cooler on Valenwood than she'd expected. Ariana woke to its chill, then remembered it was winter on her world. She had been dreaming of Damen's balmy, warm planet—they had been floating on the ocean waves, and together, realized they could fly by simply feeling themselves upward. She opened her eyes and glanced out her window. Early yet. She rolled over thinking to wake Damen. . . . And he was gone.

He could have gone anywhere. For a walk, to fetch her breakfast, to her washroom.

He had stolen a malloreum-powered spacecraft, and left Valenwood. She knew, beyond logic. She knew that he had been saying good-bye. She knew he had meant to leave her behind.

Someone rapped on her door. The guard, or perhaps Arnoth. Dizzy, she leapt up from the bed and wrapped her white gown around her body, tying it at the waist as she went to the door. She seized a short breath, then opened it. It was Hakon with Pip on his shoulder.

Hakon eased by her, closed the door behind them and met her eyes. "He's gone."

She nodded, fighting tears. "I know. I woke to find him gone. He's taken your ship."

"Ariana. . . . That's not all he's taken."

Her brow furrowed. "What do you mean?" Hakon looked pale, even frightened, and Ariana's heart skipped a beat. "What do you mean?"

"I think. . . . Ariana, I think Elena went with him."

A tiny relief relaxed her fear. "That's impossible. Damen wouldn't take Elena—he loves her. He wouldn't put me in danger, and he certainly wouldn't risk anything happening to our daughter."

Hakon gripped her arm, tight. "He wouldn't take her . . . if he knew she was there."

Fear returned, then doubled. "If he knew . . . ?"

Pip squeaked and hopped on Hakon's shoulder. "My grandsire is missing, too!"

"Carob?" Ariana shook her head. "Do you think they went together?"

Hakon shrugged. "It's possible, but I doubt it. I don't think Carob would risk Elena's safety that way. He's probably just stuck in a food bin somewhere, but we don't have time to look for him now."

Pip hopped from foot to foot. "I think he went with her, sir. He mentioned last night that it was funny for Elena to be so tired and then ask to go to bed early."

Ariana's mind raced. Elena had pleaded an unusual weariness, barely able to keep her eyes open when Ariana kissed her goodnight. Or so it seemed. "She was faking. But how would she know what he was doing, or what ship he'd take?"

"There was only one, Ariana. Mine. The other wasn't fully functional because I'd taken out the fuel core."

Ariana rubbed her forehead, fighting to understand. "Why? What for?"

"With the help of my aunt and my father, I finally came up with a way to minimize the malloreum burn. I tripled its value, Ariana. We could make the journey from Eisvelt to Valenwood three times for the fuel we used."

"What about the ship Damen took?"

"I fixed that one first. But they're both ready now."

Ariana pulled her pack from her marble bureau, and stuffed in her necessities. She hurried to her dressing room and put on her old spy clothes. Hakon didn't wait for an explanation. Together, they slipped quietly from the palace, retrieved Hakon's hovercraft, and then raced to the spaceport. None of the technicians questioned his presence—at his orders, they had waited to report the theft of his ship. Hakon hesitated before entering the remodeled craft. "Should we tell our fathers, or at least, mine?"

Ariana glanced back toward the palace. "They will know."

"We could leave Pip."

The lingbat squeaked indignantly. "You can't leave me, sir! I belong with you!"

Hakon sighed, but he was smiling. "I guess you're right, Pip. I couldn't do without you, and I've got a feeling that whatever's out there is going to take every one of us to defeat."

They climbed into the vessel and Hakon engaged the engine. Though powered with more force and more speed, the reduced intake of malloreum had the effect of quieting the takeoff. They sped from the port and out into the blue morning sky, no more than ten minutes since Ariana had woken. She stared out at the horizon, straining to see, knowing Damen was far ahead.

"Can we catch up to him?"

Hakon shrugged, hesitating. "I'm not sure. It depends on how quickly he divines the operation of my vessel. It's not standard, but then, neither is your pirate."

Ariana held her hand over her heart as the vessel burst free of Valenwood's calm atmosphere, out into the shock of black space. "Do you think he will realize she's there? Elena can be very deft."

Pip cranked his head around to look at her. "My grandsire says she's sneaky, and she got that blood from you, Miss. Said you used to sneak in and out of places all the time."

Ariana tried to smile, but tears dripped down her cheeks. "I don't understand why she would do this. Or how she knew he was leaving. I know she liked him, but to run away. . . ."

Hakon detected the ship far ahead, then plotted his course after it. He turned to Ariana, his face kind though worry furrowed his smooth brow. "If she stowed herself away on his ship, there can only be one reason."

Ariana met his gaze, and her heart lodged in her throat. *"She knows."*

Part Five

The King of the Dark Sun

Treasure restored. . . .

Chapter Twenty-eight

The light of Valenwood had long ago faded from Damen's sight, and he had already passed into the Border Territory. The Intersystem ship was fast and surprisingly quiet, although an odd and uneven rumbling noise sounded from somewhere in the ship's hull. Since the vessel progressed evenly, he doubted the sound portended anything serious.

Damen stood looking out the view port of Hakon's vessel, trying to keep his mind fixed on his duty. His hope lay behind him now—ahead lay danger and an uncertain fate. At least, he would know that Ariana was safe, and their daughter happy and loved in Arnoth's household. He even trusted Hakon with their care, but still, it hurt to leave.

"Where are we going?" A small voice spoke behind him. Damen whirled and gasped, and Elena hopped back in alarm. He held his hand over his heart and stared.

"Elena! What are you doing here?"

Apparently, he'd frightened her because her lip quivered, though she didn't cry. She clasped her small hands in front of her body and bowed her head as if to gain courage. She peeked up at him. "I'm going with you."

Stobie Piel

She had inherited Ariana's spirit and his independence, that was certain. Deeply moved, Damen knelt before her. "I am leaving because I must, little one. But you belong with your mother. She will be terribly worried to find you gone."

"I am old enough for adventures now. Mamma will be proud of me. She is very brave, you know. I have heard people in my grandpapa's palace speak of her deeds. I am brave, too."

Damen touched Elena's small cheek. "I'm sure she is proud. But she will still be scared." He paused. "Why have you done this, Elena?"

"I wanted to go with you. I knew you would leave because at dinner last night, you looked at Mamma and at me, and even the lingbats, as if you might never see us again. If you meant to leave, you would have to take Hakon's ship, because it is fastest."

"Good thinking." This wasn't easy. Emotion clouded his reason. It might have been more effective if he could speak harshly to her, but he looked into her little face and his heart couldn't summon even the semblance of anger. "Why?"

Very gently, Elena reached to touch his face. "Because you are my father."

Damen's mouth slid open, but his heart labored and tears welled in his eyes. "How did you know?"

Elena smiled. "Mamma told me that my father died, but I knew she never stopped looking for him. When she brought you to Valenwood, I knew she had found him. I used to dream that you were still alive and one day would come and take us to your planet, which would be beautiful and warm and have great herds of hyppos!"

Damen smiled, too, but he struggled also against tears. "If I could, I would bring you both to such a world, and if they weren't there already, I'd fill the oceans with hyppos."

Her brow furrowed. "Hyppos don't live in oceans, Father." She paused, as if feeling the term on her tongue.

"*Papa* ... They prefer rivers and mud. Does your planet have mud?"

He hesitated. "It has rivers. I suppose with enough hyppos, there would be mud, too." He clamped his hand over his brow, then shook his head. "I am not going home, Elena. I have a duty. A dangerous one."

Elena bowed her head. She was too young to fully understand what danger lay ahead. She peered up at him, her face knit and thoughtful. "You are just what I dreamed my father would be. You are large and kind, and you held my hand just as fathers do. But maybe I am not what you hoped a daughter would be."

Damen's heart clenched. He held out his arms and drew his child against his chest, and he hugged her for all the years she had lived without him. The tears broke from his eyes and he cried silently, but she leaned against him contentedly. Damen contained his emotion, did his best to shrug his shoulder against his tears, and then drew back to look into her earnest face. "I have never felt more joy than when I learned that you were my daughter."

Elena relaxed instantly, then puffed a breath of relief. "Good! Vender said he thought you liked me, but I wanted to be sure."

"Vender knows about this, too?"

"I told him. He says I look like you, because my skin is dark like yours and because I'm taller than he is. He said I would make a good pirate."

Damen sat back on the floor and stared at her, but Elena went to the view port and stood on tiptoes looking out. "So where are we going?"

Damen pushed himself to his feet and went to stand beside her. He placed his hands on her shoulders and looked her straight in the eye. Fatherhood also meant stern decisions. "*I* have a duty to perform. *You*, on the other hand, are going back to your mother."

Elena's eyes narrowed. "If you go back, Grandpapa will lock you in a room again, and he will put many guards around all the ships."

"Good point, again. But unless I miss my guess, I won't have to go back."

Her eyes narrowed still more. "What do you mean?"

He went to the captain's panel, checked the readings, and then nodded. "As I suspected, we are being followed. Your mother, and probably Hakon, too, have come after us. I will slow my speed until they catch up, then dock alongside their vehicle, and they will return you to where you belong."

Elena folded her arms over her chest and looked stubborn, but she didn't seem certain how to avoid her mother's retrieval. Ariana might not want to leave, either, but with their daughter to protect, she wouldn't have a choice. Damen gestured at the pilot's chair. "Until they arrive, make yourself comfortable."

Elena hopped into the chair, her legs crossed at the ankles, feet swinging. "If you're a pirate, does that mean we're going to raid other ships?" She sounded eager, and Damen winced.

"My reputation at piracy was much exaggerated." She looked disappointed. "Although I did manage to make off with some pretty good loot, every so often."

Elena perked at this. "I will be a good pirate, too. I have practiced sneaking into places, as you have seen, and I like loot."

"We have a lot in common." Damen patted her head, then checked the panels. "Your mother's ship is close enough now for contact." He fiddled with Hakon's transmitter, then opened a connection to the other vessel. "Ariana?"

The monitor cracked, and then he heard her desperate voice. "Damen? Is Elena with you?"

"She's here. She surprised me, but she's safe. If you, and Hakon, I presume, will join me, we can dock and I'll send her over to you."

"We will do that. . . ."

Hakon interrupted her. "Hallo, Damen. Hope you're enjoying my ship! Don't overload the malloreum into the fuel jets. I have it dispatched at a low rate, and you could blow the whole system."

Damen frowned. Hakon could be surprisingly dictatorial. "I had ascertained that on my own."

"And about docking . . ." Hakon paused. "Don't think that's going to work."

"Why not? Ships dock in space all the time."

"Well, these aren't standard vessels, and there's no way to make a tight portal between them. The Intersystem only made these two prototypes, and we didn't get around to the docking apparatus."

Damen rolled his eyes. "Wonderful. Now what?"

"Where are you going?"

"I have no intention of telling you that." Damen chewed his lip. "In fact, I'm not completely sure myself, not until I contact my fleet. The arrangements for this mission were laid in advance, and thanks to you, I've been delayed."

Hakon huffed. "Thanks to me, you're alive."

The lingbat's high voice came broken over the monitor. "He's got a point there, sir!"

Damen found the lingbat's voice curiously comforting. "Hallo to you, too, Pip."

"Is my grandsire with you, sir?"

Damen looked around, confused. Elena shrugged. "He means Carob."

"I don't see him. . . ." The strange, rumbling noise came to his ears again—more organic than a ship's usual sounds. Damen looked at Elena, and she hopped down from the chair, then went to a small, square shelf. She tugged it open, and there lay the old lingbat . . . asleep.

Damen groaned. "Is there anyone else stowed away on this ship? Arnoth? Dane? Perhaps the sleeping guard?"

Carob opened one eye. "Took you long enough to find me, pirate. I might have been stuck in here for days!" The bat righted itself, stretched its wings, and then hurtled itself to Elena's shoulder. "So, made it aboard, did you? Figured you would."

"Carob!" Hakon's voice burst across the monitor. "What

are you doing there? My father will be worried out of his mind!"

Carob gazed at Damen as if enduring the prattle of a child. "Your father was the one who advised I accept this mission, boy!"

"*What?*" Damen spoke, with Hakon echoing him through space. "He advised you to stow away on my ship?"

Hakon cut in again. "My ship!"

Carob peered out the view port as Ariana's vessel came into view. "He couldn't stow away himself, though I think he was tempted. But he said it was your mission, the three of you, and he had a fair idea the young sprite would make her way aboard, too. Knew you'd benefit from my advice, so here I am." Carob tapped at Elena's head. "Over there, young sprite, you'll find my pack, a bag of crunch bugs that my human supplied when he stuffed me in that drawer. Fetch it, will you?"

Damen just stared, but Hakon sputtered over the monitor. "Let me get this straight. My father brought you aboard, hid you, and supplied you with *crunch bugs*?"

Carob looked proud. "Stayed up half the night fetching them for me, too. Gotten good at it over the years, he has."

Damen sank back into the pilot's chair and bowed his head. "What was he thinking?"

Elena found the bag of bugs and gave one to Carob, though she tilted her head away when he ate. Carob cranked his head toward Damen. "He was thinking you'll be needing all the help you can get."

Ariana's voice came over the monitor. "What do we do now?"

Carob chirped and seemed excited. "I'd say that question's already been answered. Look!"

Damen looked out the view port, stunned as a huge array of ships dotted a central point, then fanned out in approach. Over the monitor, he heard both Ariana and Hakon gasp, and Pip squealed wildly.

"We're under attack, sir! It's Automon ships!"

Elena froze, but Damen looked to her and smiled. "You

have no cause for alarm, any of you." He paused, and pride at the vastness of the assembly filled his heart. "Behold the Dark Sun Fleet!"

"Damen! What is that extra vessel, and what took you so long to be healed?" Fia's dictatorial and commanding voice pierced the monitor, even at long range, but Damen's heart warmed to hear her.

"My healing took a little longer than I expected, and my exit from Valenwood wasn't exactly approved."

Elena tapped Damen's elbow. "Who is that girl?"

Fia overheard Elena's question. "Who is that small person speaking, Damen?"

He glanced at Elena, then spoke into the monitor. "The answer, to both of you, is . . . your sister."

Elena clapped her hands with glee, but in the background from Fia's ship, Damen heard several men groaning, and the distinct sound of Nob saying, "Not another one!"

Fia returned to the monitor. "We're not close enough yet to establish visual contact. As soon as you arrive in our midst, I will see my sister." She paused. "What is your name, little person?"

Elena put her mouth close to the monitor and spoke very distinctly. "I am Elena. What is your name, please?"

Fia must have liked the polite tone. "I am called Fia, but I have many other titles."

"Are you pretty, Fia?"

Fia hesitated, then answered in a bewildered voice, "I don't know."

Damen smiled. "She is very beautiful. She's tall, and her hair is light like Hakon's, and her ears are very slightly pointed."

Elena tugged at her ears. "I wish my ears were pointed."

Fia's crew must have overheard the conversation, because someone shouted, "She's a tyrant and she's running us ragged over here!"

Damen adjusted the monitor lower. "We will join you

shortly. Do you have the sector of the Automon Commander's space station?"

"He sent it to us a short while ago, which is why we've amassed here, as planned." Fia paused. "Why did you bring my sister, Damen? She sounds of a small age, and it seems unwise to place her in danger. Although, of course, Mallik suspects nothing. I wired to him that you had escaped the Intersystem, and my first officer, Reidworth, advised me to add that you'd killed several Intersystem guards in the process."

"Very good! And good thinking on Reidworth's part." Damen paused. "I take it he's working out, after all?"

"Brilliantly, as I knew he would. He has passed all his exams, and has shown a good head for strategy, in particular. He is piloting my vessel, *The Queen's Vengeance*, since I am in command of the flagship."

"Send me the coordinates of the space station."

Fia hesitated. "What about the other ship that's behind you?"

Hakon's voice burst over the monitor. "We're coming with you!"

Ariana spoke more softly. "The space station . . . I think I understand."

Damen drew a long breath, then spoke into the monitor. "I can't explain to either of you, but if you're determined to come along, then you have to follow orders, and you have to trust me."

Pip squeaked excitedly. "Are we going to attack them, sir? Those ships of yours look like they could wipe out the whole Automon fleet!"

"We're not going to attack them, Pip." He paused. At last, everything would depend on Ariana's faith in him, but if fate sent them forward together, it was time to trust her with the truth. "We're going to join them."

Hakon sighed over the monitor. "My father would be so proud."

Ariana cut in over Hakon. "How are you going to explain two Intersystem ships, Damen? One makes sense, given that you stole it on your 'rampage' through my planet, but not two."

Fia answered before Damen could comment. "Ariana has a good point, Damen. Perhaps we could abandon one of the ships on a nearby planet. There's a planet suitable for habitation on our onward route."

"You are not abandoning my ship anywhere!" Hakon spoke loudly so that Fia would hear him, but Fia sighed.

"Why did you bring *him?*"

Damen smiled. "He came uninvited, but perhaps he will be useful."

"I doubt it."

Before either could reply, Damen took the monitor. "We will do as Fia suggests. We'll land the two Intersystem ships. Ariana and Hakon, and Pip, will join me, and then we will regroup with the fleet. When we reach the station, I will contact Mallik."

Ariana's voice crackled over the monitor, sounding higher than normal and nervous. "And what then?"

"Then you will see the results of a plan well laid, my lady, and learn whether or not your trust in me is well founded."

Chapter Twenty-nine

"My fleet is at your service, Commander. As promised, I have delivered the entire might of the Dark Sun People, and await your orders."

Damen closed his end of the monitor and Ariana held her breath for Mallik's reply. Before reaching the space station's parameters, they had abandoned the Intersystem vessel on an arid, hot planet, then traveled beyond the territory neither Hakon nor Ariana knew. Elena held Ariana's hand, but she seemed unafraid and excited about the adventure to come. Carob perched on her shoulder, his head tilted as if trying to hear better.

Before them, the Automon space station loomed almost as large as a planet. Just its front quarter filled the view port—a far more massive construction than even Damen had foreseen. Like the Automon themselves, the station was black, constructed from a central core at its narrowest point. From that point, it fanned outwards with many levels and hangar decks below, and a domed top where Mallik's transmission had originated. Near the top level of the dome,

Ariana saw a wide deck with lookouts, and from the magnifying focus of the ship's view port, she could discern a single human shape standing by the window. She knew who it was—Lissa, waiting like a spider for the fly she had coveted to fall into her web. *Damen.*

Ariana pointed at the image, and Damen nodded. "All goes as she plans, it seems."

Ariana drew a shuddering breath. "I hope not."

Mallik signaled a reply to Damen's message. Damen reopened the line. "An impressive showing, Captain. Your fleet is as good as your word."

"Before I commit my force to your direction, Commander, I would see evidence of that which I have earned by my loyalty and good word."

"Of course. My signal will direct a small ship toward entry. The great ships of your fleet are too large, but a shuttle may land with ease."

Damen hesitated. "I am currently onboard the Intersystem ship I relieved from Valenwood. It's small enough to land in your hangars, but I request that one shuttle of my flagship be admitted also, so that I can present my first officer to you."

"A good suggestion, Captain. The signal will direct two ships into the primary hangar. My Automon guards will meet you, and direct you to my command deck." Mallik paused. He sounded as smug as Ariana remembered him, and too confident, as if all his plans and machinations had taken their rightful shape. "Captain, I await you."

The transmission closed, and Damen breathed deeply. Ariana peered up at him. "He certainly doesn't sound suspicious. Now what?"

"We do as he says."

Ariana glanced at Elena. "But what about. . . . If we land this ship, he can't know she exists, Damen. And what about myself and Hakon? Won't it ruin everything if they find we're aboard, too? You could say you took us prisoner, I suppose, but that won't explain Elena, and anyway, I doubt they'd believe you."

Stobie Piel

Damen held up his hand. "Just wait. Neither Mallik nor Lissa will have any idea you're here, nor Fia either. As for Elena . . ." He stopped to ponder her fate while Elena held herself very still, hands clasped tight before her. Damen smiled. "I don't dare to leave her behind, but I think I have just the solution."

Ariana rolled her eyes. "If you wouldn't mind telling me, for a change."

"No time." Damen signaled to Fia's ship and coded a message, but he seemed surprised by the message she returned. He shrugged. "It seems Fia has already thought of Elena's disguise, and made the necessary arrangements." He seemed satisfied, but he didn't explain further.

Large hangar doors opened slowly, and a signal indicated it was safe to dock. From Fia's flagship, a shuttle emerged and lowered toward the hangar. Damen seated himself in the Intersystem vessel's cockpit, then engaged it for landing.

Hakon paced around the deck while Pip paced back and forth in the view port window. Carob seemed to be squinting as he leaned forward on Elena's shoulder. The ship lowered slowly and the space station seemed to open like a giant throat as they entered its grasp. They landed softly beside Fia's shuttle, and the hangar closed around them. Ariana closed her eyes, but Hakon stopped to look out the view port. "I feel like we've been swallowed."

Pip squeaked, then dove from the view port to Hakon's shoulder. Elena stood perfectly still, just as Ariana did when she was terrified. Damen turned and noticed Elena's expression. He knelt before her and he smiled as Ariana took her daughter's hand.

"I won't let anything bad happen to you, little one. I can't explain everything we're going to do in this place, but it's a good thing. No matter what I say, or what it looks like I'm doing, know that I'm just pretending."

"I . . . I didn't like that man's voice."

Damen shook his head. "No, it's a very grating voice, and though I seemed to be nice to him, I don't like him, either.

He's a very bad man, and we are going to make sure that he can't harm anyone ever again."

Ariana bit her lip, but his gentle tone quieted her fears. "I knew you would."

He glanced up at her. "Now, about your disguises . . ." He didn't explain, but he motioned for Ariana and Hakon to keep low and out of sight. Ariana took Elena aside, and they hid themselves behind the cockpit wall. Damen went to the portal and opened it. A tall black Automon entered the ship, followed closely by Nob. It moved in perfect order, stiff and without emotion. Elena trembled beside Ariana and they gripped each other's hands tight.

Nob stepped aside, and the Automon engaged a small panel on its chest. Within moments, two more Automon appeared, pulling one of the quicker, shorter models Ariana had seen on the Automon transport ships. They entered the Intersystem vessel, and Damen closed the door behind them.

Damen jumped back, but Nob tossed the first Automon a short pistol. Together, they fired in quick succession, disabling the three others. Damen caught one of the tall models before it crumpled. "Well done! Now, the rest of you . . ." He gestured to Ariana and Hakon. "We have no time to lose. Get these on."

Hakon emerged from hiding and stared. "Get what *on?*"

The duplicitous Automon turned in his direction, still stiff, but no longer devoid of emotion. It pulled off its head, which was a mask, and glared. "Get these shells on, of course!"

Hakon's mouth dropped as Fia emerged from her disguise. His blue eyes widened as if he'd never seen anything like her. For the faintest second, a smile formed on his lips, but then he frowned. "Let me guess. Fia, First Officer and Tyrant Queen."

Fia's eyes narrowed to slits and her lips angled in a frown of equal measure. "Hakon." Her voice came low and even, but Ariana detected the slightest wavering, as if Hakon, too, surprised the girl in some way.

Stobie Piel

Damen waved his hand impatiently. "Fia, Hakon. Hakon, Fia. And this is Nob. All of you, this is my daughter, Elena, and two proud lingbats, Pip and Carob."

Fia directed her gaze away from Hakon, but her face softened when she saw Elena. "I am pleased to meet you, small sister."

Elena gazed up at Fia in wonder. "You are very pretty! I like your ears."

Fia looked pleased and a little embarrassed. "Thank you. You look like your mother and like Damen."

"He is your papa, too?"

"Well, he didn't create me, but he raised me, and so he is my father in a different way."

Damen watched their first meeting with a strange expression, and for the briefest instance, Ariana thought she saw tears in his eyes. But he cleared his expression and stepped between them. "If the introductions are satisfactory to all, we have a job to do." He didn't wait for comments or questions. "Ariana and Hakon, get into the two tall shells." He turned to Elena. "And you, little one, will have the most comfortable disguise."

Elena's fear had dissipated, perhaps because the Automon were so easily disabled, or maybe from her own excitement at the thought of disguise. Fia pulled the shorter Automon to Elena. "I rigged this while we were still en route. It should fit you perfectly, because I accurately assessed your size and shape from your voice. These little Automon are common, and no one will notice your presence." Fia looked proud, and Elena beamed.

Damen worked the small Automon shell carefully over Elena's body. Before he placed on the top, Carob squirmed closer to her neck and was safely encased beside her. Damen adjusted the headpiece so that she could see, removing the sensors and replacing them with a panel provided by Nob.

Nob helped Hakon with his disguise, fitting Pip near the Automon's chest panel where the bat, too, could see out, and Damen assisted Ariana. Because she was smaller, she couldn't see as well, but Nob tinkered with the shell until her view was adequate. Nob stood back and checked their appearance. "Looks good, sir!" He paused, then glanced at Fia, who replaced her headpiece. "So. . . . I'm the first officer now, right?"

Fia muttered from inside her shell. "For now."

Hakon elbowed Fia, almost knocking her over. "Looks like you've been demoted."

Damen positioned himself by the door. "Fia knows what to do, so the rest of you are going to have to follow her. First, you will come along as my escort to Mallik's command deck. Then, if all goes as planned, we will make our way to the core."

Ariana tried to slow her breaths because the inner lining of the shell felt moist. "What's the core?"

Damen's dark eyes glinted. "The core of everything, I hope. The heart of the Automon empire, and the source of its power. Its *consciousness*, Ariana, which you and I both have felt."

"But isn't it Mallik who controls them?"

Damen moved closer to her. "Is it, Ariana? Is that what you felt?"

She hesitated, then shook her head. "No. What I felt was . . . sorrow. Mallik is smug and controlling, but he doesn't have that strange poignancy." She gazed at Damen in wonder. "Do you know where it comes from?"

"No. But I know where it will be found. *The core.*"

A chill swept through her as Damen went to engage the portal door. He glanced at them one last time. "You taller Automon must walk stiffly." He paused and cast a quick glance at Hakon. "That shouldn't be any trouble for you, but Ariana will have to concentrate." He turned to Elena who had moved up beside him, eager to begin the adventure. "As for you, little one, your model of Automon is much more active, but remember that Automon don't speak or run."

"Mamma says they spoke sometimes."

Damen paused. "Well, they do, but they don't sound like a little girl."

"I won't talk."

"Stay close to your mother, and you'll be safe." He glanced at Hakon. "You lingbats, also, must refrain from speech or squeaking. It was Pip's squawk that Lissa recognized on Eisvelt."

A long series of apologies emanated from Hakon's chest, but Carob issued a derisive snort from within Elena's headpiece. She giggled as if it tickled, then silenced herself. "Lingbats require no instruction, human! We know what we're doing at all times!"

"Do we, Grandsire?"

"That's why we're here, lad."

"Oh. Yes."

Damen nodded, accepting Carob's assurance more easily than Ariana would have done herself. He engaged the door and it slid open. Ariana marched out behind Fia, with Elena close beside her. Hakon followed, and a quick glance told her he had indeed adopted the Automon gait and stance to perfection. Nob went ahead with Damen, holding himself with surprising dignity as befit a first officer.

Strangely, Ariana's fear eased as they entered the station. As they moved down into the hanger and across the deck, she saw other Automon, but none paid any attention to the new arrivals, and went about their business with their usual, methodical precision. Fia moved up beside Damen, hesitated only briefly, then found her way to a transport shaft. They entered together, no one speaking lest their voices be detected. She entered a code into a side panel, and the transport lifted them upward.

The transport came to a halt, and Damen's expression altered. Gone was the gentle father, the kind leader. Instead, here stood a pirate who had conquered the galaxy. The doors slid open and he stepped out without hesitation. Nob followed, and Fia led the others from the transport. The shaft opened into a wide deck with a vast clear panel looking out to the stars. The room was decorated in black and grey, with no adornments or artifacts of beauty.

From the far end of the wide hall, Mallik greeted them.

"Welcome to Hel, the space station and command center of the Automon Empire."

Ariana choked back a gasp. Had he meant to name his contrived planet replica for the dark underworld, the Doom of Humankind, a legend that resonated through the galaxy?

Mallik stood by a large black console. Screens of varying sizes revealed vast ordered plans, the depictions of colonies and guides for future creations. Here, Mallik's mind must find its true release. It occurred to Ariana that in a stronger man, a man more sure of himself, those qualities might have served him well, and served others, too. He could order the structure on worlds suffering hunger or drought, plan cities for comfort on crowded planets, or even design systems for the processing of information that would serve everyone.

Instead, he turned his logical brain to the control of others. As Ariana watched him approach Damen, she felt as if she finally understood. He wasn't so different from Lissa, despite their vastly different attributes. He wanted importance and control because he cultivated nothing of his real self within. Instead, he sought it from others, outside himself, but in facing a man for whom everything had grown from the powerful core inside, Mallik would soon find his own limitations.

Mallik crossed the deck, then stopped, preferring that Damen come to him. Every move was designed for control, for advantage. Damen went forward with Nob at his side. Mallik cast a disparaging glance at Nob. "Your first officer?"

Damen nodded. "Nob . . . barad. . . ." He must have felt the need to extend Nob's name. Ariana smiled beneath her disguise. "Nob-barad has served me through many missions. Given that it was he who led the raid upon Garthgoron, I thought he deserved the rank."

What raid? But apparently Mallik recognized this victory. "Indeed? You routed an entire caravan of malloreum from an envoy of rogue traders. They didn't succumb easily, I understand, but you deposed of them admirably. They were, I believe, intent on taking over a small but populated planet in Border Territory."

"They didn't get that far, and the malloreum resigned itself to much worthier hands." Damen paused, smug. "Ours."

So . . . the Dark Sun Fleet weren't pirates, whatever loot they'd been awarded in victory. Damen had saved a planet from marauders, and Ariana suspected, not for the first time. But apparently his explanation for the battle satisfied Mallik.

Damen glanced around the hall as if mildly interested, but not remarkably impressed. "A strange name, you've given the command station, Commander. 'Hel.' "

Mallik looked confused. "In the language of my world, 'hel' means 'order.' Has it another meaning for you?"

Damen smiled. "Not really. I'm sure it's eminently suitable."

Lissa entered the hall from a far door, then presented herself as if a goddess had emerged. She wore a long, black gown that exaggerated the size of her breasts, and had the effect of baring her legs when she moved. Beside Ariana, Hakon emitted an almost inaudible groan of irritation.

"Damen! You've arrived, I see, in splendor beyond anything Camron or I had envisioned."

Damen glanced at her without interest, then turned his attention back to Mallik. "I promised the might of my fleet would exceed your expectations. If you are not disappointed, then may I assume we have an agreement?"

Lissa waited, but Mallik offered no hesitation. "As you requested, I hereby appoint you captain of my fleet, and second in command to my own division."

They shook hands, but Damen glanced around. "I assume you require no confirmation from the 'High King' you mentioned on Eisvelt?"

Mallik's eyes narrowed, but he forced something resembling a smile. "The King has given me power and leave to offer such assignments and positions to those I see fit. I assure you, his will operates through me without question."

"Ah. Then our alliance is forged in good will, and to the betterment, no doubt, of us both."

Lissa came slowly forward, lingering as if hoping to draw Damen's attention from Mallik. She positioned herself near the console, a good distance away from her lover. "You will lead our allied fleet to greatness, Damen."

Damen smiled like a rogue and nodded toward Mallik. "I assume that our first target, as we have agreed, is still Valenwood?"

Ariana stiffened, but beside her, Elena remained calm, and even Hakon gave no sign of reaction. *He had agreed to invade her home world?*

Mallik braced his arms over his chest as if trying to seem more regal than he was. "The best plan is to hit where the Prime Representative lives—that will shake them up enough to bring them under control. We'll negotiate with them, surely. Once they've been faced with our combined might, I'm sure the Intersystem Council will find itself with a new leader."

He didn't need to say whom he intended to replace Arnoth—Mallik himself desired that seat. Damen gazed around the room, idly. "From what I saw, the Intersystem leaders could use some disruption."

Lissa studied him closely. "Then you are not concerned for Ariana's fate?"

He issued a scoffing, scornful gaze. "She turned me over to her father. I saw where her true allegiance lay. Because of her betrayal, my desire for vengeance burns particularly hot."

His declaration pleased Lissa. "I love Ariana dearly, but when she ran off with Hakon, knowing full well it was him—I'm sure they had her rescue long-planned—I knew she had lost you for good."

Damen thumped his fist into his other hand. "Then imagine my humiliation when that golden-haired devil dragged me before her father's council! No, I want a woman who yields to me, not one who defies me at every turn."

Mallik laughed. "I couldn't have said it better myself. Though for such a beauty, it might be worth making her a captive and training her to take a . . . more receptive position."

Damen engaged in a laugh of equal male supremacy. "I'll remember your suggestion, Commander. Bending that female to my will has a certain appeal."

Just try! Ariana caught herself. Damen's performance was a little too good.

Lissa cut Mallik off, probably disliking the suggestion of Ariana as even Damen's unwilling mistress. "Ariana isn't important to Damen anymore, Camron. We can offer him so much more." She paused, and her lips twitched with a frown. "Now that Damen's fleet is here, don't you think you should begin the alignment of the lower-level Automon? We have no time to waste if our plans are to go forward."

Mallik eyed her as if taken off guard. "I had thought to direct the captain and his first officer to their quarters, but perhaps you are right. I have worked out the schematics on my console, but it may require my presence below."

Lissa fixed her hungry gaze on Damen. It was all Ariana could do to stay put. "I will attend to Damen and his officer personally."

Mallik hesitated, but then left without further debate. Lissa glanced at the four Automon. "What are they doing here?"

Damen didn't hesitate. "Those were the Automon who directed me to this command center. The first which greeted us programmed them to attend us, and I will say, I appreciate having them work for me rather than as enslavers." He smiled, a teasing glint in his eyes. Ariana frowned. "You wouldn't deny me this, mistress, that I at last take some pleasure in finding them subservient to my will?"

He was a demon. Lissa came closer to him as if he'd invited her to his bed. "I would deny you nothing, Damen."

She's certainly not wasting any time. Beside Ariana, Hakon allowed for a small sigh, which echoed Ariana's reaction.

Damen didn't back away, and indeed, seemed to lean closer. Ariana's blood fired with anger. "A promising alliance then, mistress. Although I was under the impression that your alliance was with Commander Mallik?"

Lissa turned her head aside as if grieved. "I owe him so much, Damen. He has been so good to me. And yet . . ."

Ariana frowned. *Here it comes.*

"And yet? Doesn't he treat you as you deserve?"

Lissa caught a quick breath. "He became more forceful, perhaps lest respectful of me, as time wore on between us. I don't think, truly, that he's capable of the feeling and the passion that a woman like myself needs. He is a brilliant man, of course, and his power is boundless. No one else would have thought to devise a way to harness . . ."

"To harness, mistress?"

Lissa pressed her lips together as if she'd wandered into dangerous territory. "To harness such power, I mean."

Damen nodded, then folded his strong arms over his broad chest, assuming a posture that mimicked the commander's. He was the virile image of masculinity and Lissa seemed to bend toward him like a planet drawn to a sun. "He has harnessed the power of the Automon. I understand. An impressive feat, indeed. Yet the power to control them, he says, comes from this High King."

"But it is Camron who bears the burden." No, Lissa wasn't yet falling for Damen's attempt to reveal more of this mysterious king. She moved closer to Damen, then placed her hand on his arm. Ariana stiffened. "I am so glad you're here, Damen. For personal reasons as well as for the benefit of Camron's plans."

"Indeed?"

She looked up at him, her lips parted. "You cannot imagine how much I admired you in that Dark Sun cave, so long ago. You were such a strong leader, you had such magnetism that anyone, especially a woman, would follow you. I have committed myself to Camron, it's true, but I was the one who convinced him to ally with you, for the benefit of you both."

"I had no idea you were so instrumental in this arrangement. I am grateful." He paused and bowed, and Ariana's fury reached a new pinnacle. He may not have had any idea, but Ariana had known full well.

"Together, there's nothing we. . . ." Lissa stopped herself with a quick breath. "You, myself and Camron, of course . . . nothing we can't do. Valenwood, the seat of Arnoth, your enemy, is just the first step. With the power of the Intersystem in your hands. . . ."

Damen's brow arched. "In my hands? Surely you mean in the hands of Commander Mallik, and in service to the High King?"

Lissa's dark eyes gleamed. Ariana saw it in her face. *Victory.* "Such issues of rank, of who serves who, matter little. You have the power, Damen. With my help, you can secure it for yourself, and soon it will be Mallik who serves you!"

"An ambitious plan." Damen paused as if considering, and liking, her suggestion. "Yet not without its merits."

"Then you agree?" Lissa closed her eyes, then tipped her head back. "It must be done carefully, of course. Over time." She gazed at him with the open hunger of a predator closing on prey. "We will be so good together, Damen. I knew it from the first moment I saw you. Now that you're free of Ariana, I can admit my feelings for you. She came between us, but only I can see the man you can be, if you take all the power that is offered to you." Lissa's voice quavered with lust.

As Ariana watched in horror, Damen reached for her as if to draw her into his embrace. Lissa yielded to him, but he caught her, spun her around, then clamped his hand over her mouth. She sank back against him, then struggled as if belatedly realizing that his intentions weren't what she hoped. "Nob! Now!"

Nob hurried across the deck, then aimed a small gas canister at Lissa's face. Damen turned aside as it caught Lissa head-on. She crumpled and Nob dragged her across the floor to where the others waited. "What do we do with her now? Can't leave her, I'd say."

Damen hesitated. "We have to take her with us." He

went to the transport door and motioned for Fia to engage it.

Ariana stared. "Where are we going?"

"We've only got one chance, Ariana. We are going to find the core."

Chapter Thirty

The space station Hel was vast beyond anything Ariana had comprehended, far more detailed and elaborate than any the Intersystem used. More than a station, it seemed like a mimicry of an organic planet, with the Automon mimicking living creatures. As they followed the disguised Fia down seemingly endless halls, another presence made itself known—a presence Ariana had felt before. *Sorrow.* As they walked, it became more and more acute. Hakon moved beside her, carrying the unconscious Lissa in a large sack. He, too, seemed to feel the mournful presence. "It reminds me of the amber whales."

Ariana drew a tight breath. "But without the promise of joy their song possesses."

Damen had overheard Hakon's comment, though it was spoken low. "I thought of them also."

Ariana sighed. "My father says they sing of what was lost when so much life was destroyed on Valenwood, but also with the hope of what will be born again."

Damen's face set in a grave expression. "This voice has no hope."

332

His quiet words chilled Ariana's heart. She felt the hope-lessness too. Apparently, Elena felt it as well, because she moved close to Damen and said nothing at all.

Lissa stirred in the sack, and Hakon hissed at Damen. "She's coming around. What do we do with her?"

Damen glanced around. None of the Hel Automon paid them any heed, continuing about their business—although Ariana thought they moved more quickly here on the space station than they had in the Automon colonies, maybe be-cause they were closer to the source of their power. Damen nodded toward an alcove, and they stopped. Hakon set Lissa to her feet, yanked off the sack, tore a shred from it, then stuffed it in her mouth and gagged her. She came to, bleary-eyed and stunned, and then she tried to scream.

Hakon beamed. "I wouldn't, if I were you." He loomed over her. She must have recognized his voice, because de-spite her situation, hatred gleamed in Lissa's eyes. "If you try anything, I will slit your throat." Ariana winced and tried to signal to Hakon for silence, but he didn't notice beneath her disguise. "Believe me, Lissa, there's nothing I'd like bet-ter than to see your head lolling. . . ."

Ariana hopped forward, then remembered to stiffen her legs. "Hakon! Could we please remember that there is a small . . . *Automon* present?"

Hakon glanced at Elena and his shoulders scrunched. "Sorry." He turned his attention back to Lissa. "Just wanted her to know."

Lissa stared at Ariana. Her voice must also have been recognizable beneath the disguise. She eyed Fia's Automon as if wondering who else accompanied them, but paid no attention to Elena's model. Damen ignored Lissa. "Keep her in line, Hakon. I doubt we'll encounter Mallik, and she doesn't have a signaling device to control the Automon, but just in case, be sure you get her aside if we see him. I'll go a little ahead with Fia—you keep her to the rear."

Hakon grimaced. "Can't we just knock her out and stuff her somewhere?"

"We can't risk anyone finding her." Damen hesitated,

and his dark eyes flickered. "She might be useful, when we reach the core."

Lissa's eyes widened with more fear and alarm than when Hakon had threatened to kill her. She shook her head wildly, but Damen motioned them onward. Fia took the lead, and they continued down long, narrow passages lined only in black and grey metal. The Automon boots clattered and echoed on the metallic surface. As they moved inward, slender tubes became visible on the ceilings, and seemed to shimmer with power. Nob glanced at Damen. "What do you make of them pipes, sir? A power line, do you think?"

"They transfer something. . . . Power, certainly. But from what source?"

As they drew ever closer to the station's center, the mournful presence washed over Ariana so that she felt almost dizzy from its weight. Damen's party fell silent, but Lissa grew tense and watchful, her breath ragged around the gag. They saw no other Automon, and a strange heat filled the lower corridors. Fia stopped suddenly and swayed, but Damen caught her. "Are you all right? What's wrong?"

She shook her head. "I don't know. . . . It hurts. . . ."

He placed his hand on her shell. "I feel it, too."

Fia steadied herself and walked ahead. They turned, then came to a wider hall. A black squared entrance glowed with an odd pale light. It spread as if escaping some restriction. From that entrance, thousands of sliver-wide tubes ran. A low, deep hum surrounded the entrance, dulling and dimming all other sounds. Hakon dragged Lissa up beside Fia. "By all the stars, what is that?"

Damen took a deep breath. "The core."

Ariana stood beside him, her Automon glove on Elena's squared shoulder. "It's not a power cell. There's no smell of malloreum at all, not in this whole station, now that I think of it. I feel no tingle of radiation." Her heart quailed unexpectedly. "What's in there?"

Damen glanced at her, and she saw the same sick apprehension in his eyes. "There's only one way to find out."

Lissa struggled against Hakon, so wildly that he had to

use force to restrain her despite the vast disparity in their sizes. She shook her head, her dark eyes wild with terror. Damen hesitated, then went to her. "Remove her gag."

Hakon resisted. "She'll squawk and bring the whole station down upon us!"

Lissa shook her head. Ariana looked into her foe's eyes, then nodded. "It's safe, Hakon. Take off the gag."

Reluctantly, Hakon ripped the gag from Lissa's mouth, none too gently, and held it ready should she defy him. "Well? Speak!"

Lissa took several gasps, then turned her plaintive gaze not to Damen, but to Ariana. "You can't go in there, Ariana. Damen is right. That room harbors the core of the space station's power. But it's deadly! You mustn't enter, not for anything!"

Ariana hesitated. "I sense no radiation, nor even a fire."

Lissa reached to grasp Ariana's covered arm. "Its power is far greater than radiation! Please, don't go in, for your own sake!"

Ariana glanced at Damen. "Maybe she's right."

Damen fixed a hard, dark gaze upon Lissa. A slow smile crossed his face. "So for our own sakes, you warn us? Such a horrible power! Do we not all feel its force? You tremble before it."

Lissa met his gaze. Faced with his indifference and what should have been obvious defiance, it seemed clear to Ariana that Lissa hadn't given up her desire nor her expectation of victory. "You can easily defeat Mallik, Damen. You can take his place and harness this incredible power for yourself! Come, quickly, and I can show you. . . ."

"Defeat him? Replace him? You mistake me, mistress." Damen turned to the others. "From this room, all the Automon of this galaxy are controlled. From this room, Mallik seizes incredible power, and yes, it is strong enough to conquer the Intersystem. Do we dare to enter it? Lissa claims it is deadly, and in this, I believe her. But I will enter, because the fate of my life is bound to this doom that lies within."

Hakon dragged Lissa forward. "I will go with you, and this miserable wench, too. Let her see firsthand how deadly it is!"

Ariana went to Damen. She fumbled with her Automon helmet, then pulled it off. He smiled at the sight of her face. "Where you go, I go also. My life also has been bound with this doom we both perceive, and I would face it full-willing."

Hakon ripped off his helmet, too. Lissa sneered at the sight of his bright, beautiful face, but he offered a mocking smile in return. "Get better looking every time you see me, don't I?"

Pip squirmed free and popped out to sit on the Automon shoulder pad. "That's what you're always saying, sir."

Elena struggled out of her disguise and bounced free. Carob was entangled in her hair, but he removed himself carefully, then perched on her shoulder. Lissa stared at her, shocked, but the malice in her eyes intensified. She smiled, a caricature of kindness. "Who is this precious little angel?"

Damen cast a dark glance of warning her way. "My daughter, and Ariana's." He nodded at Hakon. "Keep our prisoner far from my child, Hakon."

Lissa looked both shocked and hurt. "You cannot think I would harm a child?"

Hakon clamped his hand on Lissa and held her fast. "What is a child to a woman with no heart? Now, get moving!" He shoved her forward, but Fia stood unmoving.

"I cannot enter that place." Fia's normally calm voice quavered, not with fear, but with horror and loathing, and dread. Only she had made no effort to free herself from the Automon shell. "I cannot. . . ."

Damen went to her. "There is no need. If you prefer, wait here. . . ."

Fia collected herself and straightened. "No. It's all right. I don't know what afflicts me. I will go with you."

Damen hesitated. "If you're sure. . . ."

"I am sure."

He went to the door and ran his hand over various panels.

He eyed Lissa, but she shook her head and began to cry. "Don't go in there! You'll kill us all!"

Ariana bent to examine the entrance panel. "I don't see how it opens."

Fia stepped forward, then pushed a grid seemingly at random. The huge door slid slowly open. A blinding pale light struck their eyes and they winced and turned aside. Damen and Ariana entered together, Elena holding Ariana's hand. Hakon yanked Lissa through the door. Fia came last, and Nob closed it behind them. Ariana closed her eyes to block the light, but a wave of sick pain struck her so hard that she nearly crumpled. "It is here. The presence, the sorrow . . ."

"Yes, it is here." Damen's voice came low as if torn from deep inside him. "Look."

Ariana opened her eyes. At the center of a high-ceilinged grey room was a clear cubicle, and within the cubicle lay the form of a man, if man it could be called. He was curled in a fetal position, and his skin was pale, almost translucent, as if every cell of his being had been drained to a point hovering on death. Compelled beyond horror, Ariana approached him, and she saw that he was living.

Nausea overwhelmed her and she nearly crumpled with pain. Damen held her shoulder, but he, too, seemed too stricken to speak. Tears spilled to his strong cheeks, and he bowed his head. "Behold the King."

A sob welled in Ariana, but Elena released her hand and moved to look at the frail figure. "His ears. His ears are pointed."

As Elena spoke, Fia swayed and would have fallen, but Hakon dropped his hold on Lissa to catch her. She sank to her knees, overcome, and Lissa backed against the wall. "You have to get out of here! It can destroy us all!"

Damen looked at her with loathing. " 'It?' Do you call the High King of Gyandorath 'it?' " He growled the word, but Lissa's eyes darted, then fixed on his in a final plea.

"I knew nothing of this, I swear. Camron has forbidden me from entering this place. I just knew it was dangerous, to all of us. Surely you can see that my captivity has been much worse?"

Damen assessed her, and his lip curled in a dangerous anger. "For a creature kept in captivity, you have thrived remarkably well. The king, it seems, has not."

Lissa started to cry again, her eyes swollen and red as if genuine emotion assailed her. "I've been a slave here! Commander Mallik has used me, Damen, brutally, in a manner that I know would appall a man with such a sensitive heart as yours. I believed that he loved me, but I was just a conquest, a toy for his amusement and pleasure. I knew nothing of this, I swear!" She was crying as if in genuine emotion, but Damen turned away, disgusted.

"You used each other. Neither of you is capable of anything else."

A strange sound broke the low hum of Hel's core. From the king's cracked, dry lips, a voice emerged. "*Si liegt. . . .*" It came so weak that Ariana could barely hear him, but Fia sucked in a deep breath, then struggled to her feet. She trembled, but tore off her Automon helmet and freed herself from the shell's body. She stumbled to the king's side, then struggled to remove the cubicle glass. Damen, Hakon, and Nob lifted it off his body. It was entangled with hundreds of thin tubes, and though none touched the king's body, they seemed connected to him, and on a deeper level they actually pierced his flesh.

Fia's voice quavered, but she answered the king in his own tongue. "*Si liegt?*" As Ariana watched, astounded, Fia began to speak to him. The king opened his eyes. They were so pale that color hardly remained, but once, the shade might have been blue. As he focused on Fia's face, a power returned to him, faint, but alive. He tried to move, but his paralyzed body refused.

His voice came in a cracked whisper, but his eyes glowed when he looked at Fia. "*Onwyn an Anfia-dori. . . .*"

Ariana's breath caught, and she glanced at Damen. "'*Anfia*' . . . Fia."

Fia spoke with the tortured king softly, and the emotion

came so acute and so exquisite between them that Ariana sank to the floor with its weight. Elena leaned against her, her face plaintive, the wonder of a child that reaches beyond horror. Damen stood beside Hakon, and both were crying. Finally, Damen spoke. "What does he say, Fia? Is he the king?"

Fia struggled to regain herself, to respond. She answered, but her gaze remained fixed on the king. "He is the High King of Gyandorath, Prince of the Daeron. . . ." Tears spilled to her cheeks. "He is my brother."

Ariana cried softly and bowed her head, but Fia continued. "He speaks the language of the Daeron, which I recognize, though I do not know how, or why I recall it so fully. He understands our speech, but cannot speak it well himself, and he is too weak to remember what he learned."

Ariana met Damen's gaze across the room, and felt his pain blended with her own. "Why is he here?"

Fia exhaled a slow breath. "He says we were taken when we were children—I was a baby, and he was three years old. We were taken by Mallik and a force that had invaded Gyandorath. Mallik brought my brother here, and I was left in captivity, until Mallik had fully established this station. Then I was sent to the malloreum colony in hopes I would be lost."

Ariana gazed up at Fia, her heart aching. "Why did they let you live?"

"Apparently, they feared to kill me because of the power an Automon assault might have released inside me. Mallik assumed the barbarian tribesmen would destroy me—he knew that when able, a Daeron female will fight to the death rather than submit." She paused, fighting for composure. But then she turned to where Lissa stood. Bright fury glittered in Fia's blue eyes and she took a step toward her. "He says this woman lies. She knew he was here." Fia took another step, and Lissa recoiled.

"It's a lie! I knew nothing!"

The glow that had always emanated from within Fia

shone brighter as if flamed by the power of her will. "*Nothing?* You put him here!"

Lissa paled, but the truth showed on her face. "How can you say that? This poor creature's condition grieves me more than anyone!"

Hakon glared at her. "Your tears are what they have always been, for yourself. You feel nothing, because nothing of you is real."

Fia's glittering eyes fixed on Lissa, fired with deep anger. "Before this female arrived on Hel, Mallik kept my brother as a prisoner, draining his power for command over the Automon, but he had some limited freedom here, at least, and Mallik was not unkind nor cruel. He even spoke of my brother like a son, and always claimed they worked together for the benefit of all. For a while, my brother believed him, and allowed himself to be drained."

Ariana rose to her feet and looked down at the king. He looked like a child, shrunken and drawn, and yet, still possessing the mystic beauty of the Daeron. He might have been a tall man, long-limbed, graceful, but his life had been torn from him, leaving him like a core of himself, raw and defenseless against his invaders. "What power does he have over the Automon?"

"The Daeron created the Automon as robots and helpers. The High King holds the combined energy of all our people, and he controls the Automon by his essence and life force. That is why we felt sorrow emanating from the Automon. We felt his pain, his sorrow." Fia paused and contained her emotion. "Many generations ago, Mallik's people invaded the Realm of the Daeron and held its High King captive. They turned the Automon into weapons and took over the rest of the Gyandorath System. At that time, they began the malloreum colonies operated by Automon. My people were powerless to stop them."

Hakon's brow furrowed. "But why, if the Daeron are as powerful as legend tells?"

"I do not know, for my brother says Mallik's people had

no power akin to the Daeron. But Mallik betrayed even his own people by stealing my brother to seize all that power for himself. He took me so that another of his kind couldn't supplant him. But why the Daeron are subjugated thus, I do not know."

Hakon glanced at Ariana. "This may be an area where the Intersystem can offer assistance."

Ariana nodded, then gazed down at the stricken King. "So Mallik couldn't let him die . . ."

Fia's voice came low. "No . . . And in this condition, he might be kept alive for many ages." She stopped, overcome, but Hakon touched her shoulder gently.

"Did you tell him we have come to free him?"

"Yes."

The High King spoke again, and Fia abandoned Lissa to lean over him, listening and speaking in that strange, mystical tongue. As he spoke, she wept, then bowed her head before relaying what he said to the others. When she looked up, all pain showed in her beautiful face. "He says there was another. She was called Kaila. . . ."

At this, Lissa recoiled like a snake to the corner of the room. "It was he who murdered Kaila! That is why Camron placed him here—he is a threat to us all!"

Fia ignored her. "Kaila arrived with *her*." She pointed at Lissa, but could not speak her name. "At first, Kaila was loyal and devoted, accepting all this female did. Kaila believed her when she claimed she had fallen in love with Mallik, and that her sensitive nature was simply subservient to Mallik's dominant will."

Lissa tried to approach Damen, but he glared, so she approached Ariana instead. "You know how much I loved Kaila. She understood how much I had suffered, that I was too fragile to endure our captivity. You're so much stronger than I am. Even now, despite all Damen has done to hurt you, you refuse to let him go." Tears bubbled in Lissa's big eyes and dripped to her cheeks. Her voice shook with pain and she looked like a wounded animal cornered by bloodthirsty hunters. "I know you're angry to learn that I care for Damen, too, Ariana, but I can't help how I feel. Feelings have always dominated me. You know that."

Ariana hesitated. Had Lissa's feeble will been dominated by the powerful Mallik? Had Ariana's own fury blinded her to Lissa's misfortune? Then she turned her gaze to the High King, and her heart quailed. She spoke slowly, recalling Damen's words from Valenwood. "You play the victim while holding the sword."

Though Ariana defied her, just her response alone seemed to empower Lissa. "You don't understand. It was Camron. . . . He deceived me about everything. He said that he loved me, but all he wanted was sex. . . ."

"Ha!" Fia waved her slender fist at Lissa, and Lissa backed away. "She paints herself as the victim, but that is not the story my brother tells. With Mallik at her disposal, she became ever hungrier for power. It was she who insisted that the Automon expand toward the Intersystem, and she who sought allegiance with our Dark Sun Fleet. She used my brother's power to achieve her goals, sending more and more Automon forth, and in doing so, reduced him to this condition."

Lissa breathed in sharp gasps and her face reddened with anger. "He . . ." She pointed at the fallen king. "He is saying only what Mallik told him to say, to blame me rather than himself! It is Camron who desires control over the Intersystem, not I."

Again, Fia ignored her denial. "Her control over Mallik was complete, and whatever he felt for my brother had no weight against her manipulation. She fanned his conceit and desire to inflict order on others, and together, they drained my brother to a point where life became torment. Kaila befriended him and they fell in love, and at that point she saw her beloved friend for what she truly was. Risking everything, Kaila tried to save him, but apparently, this demonic female intuited Kaila's heart. . . ." Fia's voice cracked, and a single tear emerged on the High King's cheek. Fia looked up, her face stricken, but calm. "Their attempt to escape was thwarted, and Kaila murdered—here, before my brother's eyes, while this woman watched."

Lissa choked on her fury. "This is madness! He lies to destroy me! It is he who chose this center because he desires to spread his control across the universe!" Lissa's voice came shrill, but no one would look at her.

"After Kaila died, his life sank into darkness. They drained him to the utmost, so that he became as you see him now, on the edge of death, loathing life." Fia paused, then looked to Ariana. "He says also that this woman boasted of thwarting your escape with Damen from the Dark Sun colony. It was she who first betrayed you, Ariana, because she wanted Damen for herself."

Lissa screamed as if she could endure no more. "None of this is true! Why would I do such an awful thing? I wanted to escape as much as Ariana!"

Hakon crossed the room, and for an instant, Ariana thought he might kill Lissa then and there. Ariana had no will to stop him. But Hakon stopped before Lissa and his blue eyes glinted as he faced her. "Look at you! Nothing matters but what you want. This man who lies broken is more real than you. You and your dormant lover drain from him what you don't have in yourselves." He waved his hand indicating the station. "You're like this space station, the aptly named Hel. It's a mockery of a real world, devoid of color, and the core on which it thrives is the life of another. But I say to you, Lissa, you are more a prisoner than he ever was, a prisoner of your malice, envy, and hatred."

"All I've done is for love!"

Hakon laughed. "For love? For what? For Damen?"

Lissa turned away as if her heart had been laid bare, but Hakon laughed again. "Your love comes from lust, and your lust from sexual jealousy—nothing more. You sicken me. You've hunted down all this power, rolled around in it like a hyppo in mud, and for what? Because you lust after someone else's lover? All I saw in you during our Academy years has come to the surface. You can never have anything of your own, because you will always desire someone else's treasure. All you want is to hurt those more powerful, like this young king, like Ariana whom you have spent your life trying to destroy."

Lissa sobbed. "You have always hated me, Hakon." She paused to sniff. "I never wished any ill upon Ariana. I admit that I have feelings for Damen. . . ."

"You have feelings for no one or nothing but yourself. Ariana has everything you lack, because she is real, something you hate more than all else, because it eludes you utterly."

Lissa ran to the door and banged at the panel, but Nob stopped her, his gentle face hard with loathing. "You're not going anywhere."

"You are all so cruel! Ariana, how could you let them do this to me?"

Ariana looked at her and saw through every veneer Lissa had ever concocted. She gave no answer. At last, she understood that any answer, any response at all, gave Lissa what she wanted, and that was access into Ariana's thoughts and feelings. *Control.* She turned away from Lissa and laid her hand on the king's cold forehead. "Tell him we will set him free."

"You can't ignore me!" Lissa lurched toward Ariana, but Hakon shoved her away.

"It seems your voice has lost its power. Once someone has seen what you really are, you can no longer deceive them."

Fia spoke to her brother, and he smiled. He raised his pale arms, then with all the effort of his soul, sat up. He gripped Fia's hands, then spoke, and she bent to touch her forehead to his. As the others watched, a great light swelled up within the king's body, met with a light that emerged from Fia's heart. The light became a ball of energy that hovered between them, shone brightly, then passed into Fia's chest. She trembled violently as its power spread through her, but when she straightened, it was a queen who faced them, and no longer a child.

Ariana went to her and took her hand. "What happened? What did he do?"

"My brother has passed into me the power of the Kingdom of Gyandorath. I am now its queen." She didn't speak with her former youthful glee at importance, nor did she relish the title. It was a statement of whom she was, not whom she desired to be. A slight smile formed on her lips as she turned to Damen. "The power of the Automon is now at your command, my captain and father. How would you have me direct them?"

Damen hesitated, then shrugged. "Have them dismantle this station, before Mallik has a chance to escape."

Fia tilted her head back and seemed to enter a waking trance. Her eyes glazed over and the power swelled around her. "It is done. We must be swift, for they will soon comply."

Hakon went to the king to lift him, but the king shook his head, then held up his fragile hand. "Nein. . . ." He spoke softly to Fia.

Fia winced when he spoke, but translated his words. "He says his life is over, and tells us to go."

"No!" Elena left Ariana's side and ran to the king. She climbed up on his cubicle beside him. He smiled when he saw her, then touched her head.

He spoke again, and tears fell again to Fia's cheeks. "He says you give him joy, small sister, and it heals his heart to see you. He hopes you will live well."

Elena shook her head, and though she was crying, too, she placed her fingertips on the king's forehead and spoke in the Ellowan tongue. "Yield to me, and I will heal you." She paused, but the king lay down, weakened. Elena refused to give up, and spoke more forcefully. "Yield to me, and I will heal you!"

Ariana went to her and touched her shoulder. "You must respect his answer, Elena. It is at the core of all healing that the soul has this right."

"No! He will yield!" Elena was crying now, but she released the king and fell into Ariana's arms. "He deserves to live."

Even as she spoke, the king exhaled and then faded into death. Fia kissed his forehead, followed by Ariana and Hakon, and then Damen. "Sleep well, good king. May you be at peace."

Elena sobbed and Ariana gathered her into her arms. "He is free now, damanai."

Elena shook her head, and Carob regained his position on Elena's shoulder and spoke in the gentlest voice Ariana had ever heard the lingbat use. "Look there, young sprite, and you can see him still. . . ."

Elena looked at Carob, her small face streaked with tears. She pointed at the king's still body. "He lies there, unmoving."

Carob leaned toward her. "His spirit flies above us."

"I don't see him, Carob." Elena paused, and Ariana studied the small bat with wonder.

"You really see him, don't you, Carob?"

"Of course, I do! Lingbats have superior vision. His being has shifted to the Other Side, and dwells there now, free. His mate is with him, the one who died before. They are together, and they will pass on, and now they can grow stronger so that the dark souls like Mallik and that Nirvahdi female can't touch them. While the living grieve, know they are free and they are safe, and joy has returned to them so that the sorrow is no more than a distant memory. Already they have forgiven their enemies and grown stronger themselves, yet their foes will be haunted by the pain they have caused until they face what they have done."

Lissa screamed, a rage of fury as if Carob's words attacked her. She slammed against the door, and this time, Nob allowed her to break free. She raced from the room as Damen turned to the others. "We will leave her to her rightful torment. I trust it will follow her long past her death. But we must leave this place."

Fia nodded. "And soon—the destruction has already begun." She paused and looked to her brother. "I know he is

346

gone, and his body is only a shell. But I don't wish to leave him this way."

Hakon picked up the king's lifeless body and held it against his chest. "We will bring him with us, and lay him to rest on a world filled with life, in the deep woods and in the soil."

Fia met Hakon's gaze and her whole being seemed to soften. "Thank you."

Pip jumped from Hakon's shoulder onto Fia's head. She startled, but he worked his way to her shoulder and looked her in the eye. "You'll be a wise queen, Miss, because your heart is strong, even if the outside's covered in frost."

Pip spoke with more authority than usual, and Ariana realized that though the young lingbat seemed high-strung and vulnerable, he shared Carob's ancient wisdom.

"We're lucky to have you with us, Pip. Thank you." Pip looked up at Ariana. "I know that, Miss. You're welcome."

Damen picked up Elena and carried her to the door. The others passed through, but Ariana stopped and looked up at him. "The power the king gave to Fia will bring down this evil place, but the power in you, my love, has set a great soul free."

Damen smiled through his tears. "I am free, too, Ariana." He paused, and his smile grew. "Let's go *home*."

They ran back along the grey corridors. They passed the Automon at work, tearing apart Hel with the same methodical precision that they did everything. Though Fia had power over them, they paid no attention when she went by, nor did they notice the dead king who had for so long supplied them with his life force.

They came to the hanger deck, and saw Lissa screaming at Mallik. He stood clutching a large, black console as if it held everything that he'd ever valued. Damen stopped, and Nob aimed his rifle. "Should I shoot, sir? Deserve it, they do."

"Let them determine their own fate, Nob. They're not worth your effort."

His words reached Lissa, and it was the final defeat. Hate filled her like a cloud of red fury and crackled in her eyes, directed not at Damen nor Hakon, but at Ariana. "You self-ish witch! Look what you've done to me! You've taken all that should have been mine! You've destroyed everything!"

Mallik reached for her, not out of compassion or love, but simply as a reflex to control her motions. Lissa burst away from him and raced toward the hangar. She jabbed at a panel, which opened into the pressure room. Its door closed behind her. Through a window, they watched in hor-ror as she opened another door into space. The nothingness of space devoured her and sucked her into its void, and she was gone.

Mallik stared in disbelief as he clutched his console. He noticed the king in Hakon's arms and his brow furrowed. "He is dead, then?"

Damen walked toward him. "He is free. But as long as you try to hold power over others, you will remain en-slaved."

Mallik gripped his black console tighter. "I don't need him for control! This station is mine. I will regain control!" With that, he hurried from the hangar, heading back toward the command center where all his great plans had once been laid. He would stay in his great station as it crumbled around him.

Damen sighed and took Ariana's hand. "People choose their own fate. Let us choose ours with more wisdom, based not on what we have lost, but on how much we love."

In the death throes of Hel, he bent to kiss her mouth, and for an instant, all she felt was the eternal love that bound them. Then they ran together into Hakon's ship, and the Lord of the Dark Sun went home.

Chapter Thirty-one

Damen stood by the Altar of Beginning, and the morning sun shone full on the Temple of Ariana. The great leaves of tropical trees swayed gently overhead, casting magical shadows over the eternally shifting crystal columns, and the gold of the Beginning Symbol glittered like fire. Hakon stood beside him. Somehow, they had become friends, though Damen wasn't sure when the change had occurred.

His people lined the temple, inside and out, speaking softly and happily as they awaited the ritual that inspired Damen's first creation. Near the front, Arnoth of Valenwood stood with Sierra. Dane moved through the crowd, Carob and Pip both perched on his shoulders, with his tiny, exquisite wife at his side. The ambassador Seneca had come, too, bringing his wife, who was Dane's sister. The rest of Ariana's family, her brothers and various relatives from Valenwood, were mixed in with Damen's people. Damen's crew held fast near Arnoth, the closest thing Damen had to family. Nob grinned from ear to ear, though Graff seemed more interested in Seneca's youngest daughter.

Stobie Piel

Damen had planned this day for ages. Each moment had been divined in his thoughts while he worked on the building of the temple. But as he waited for Ariana's arrival, his heart throbbed with something close to panic. He fiddled with his hair, then adjusted the narrow braid decorated with shells and crystals. If he'd overdone . . . or perhaps might have added more . . .

Hakon elbowed him, and he turned.

Elena stood at the temple's entrance, at the bottom step, flowers in her hair and Damen's crystal shard around her neck. She puffed a quick breath, then commenced marching slowly through the guests, who hushed and parted for her entrance. Fia stepped up behind her, tall and beautiful and elegant. Like Elena, she wore a shimmering dress in the same material Ariana had worn for their first feast together. Hakon gasped at the sight of her, and for the slightest second, it seemed she paused, then moved onward.

Last, Ariana came, and Damen stood transfixed at her loveliness. Her long hair flowed behind her, rippling like dark waves in the sun. She wore a light circlet of silver and crystal over her brow, and her gown floated as she moved, as if the wind itself carried her to him.

Her gaze never shifted from his face and tears glittered like crystals in her eyes as she approached him. Damen looked at her, and he saw the girl she had been when they first met, terrified and defiant, her heart unveiled. He remembered her standing outside his door on the ship, nervous but ready to love him. He remembered her trust when he led into the heart of evil, and freed its soul on the space station.

Slowly, mesmerized, Damen held out his hand. Wisdom and understanding sparkled in her beautiful eyes, not the innocence of a young girl, but the knowledge and passion of a grown woman who lived in accord with her deepest and truest soul. Ariana placed her hand in his and they faced each other before the Altar of Beginning.

She spoke first, softly with the gentle inflection of the Ellowan tongue rich in her voice. "I have come to you through all fear and all doubting. I open my life to you forever more, and share with you all that I am."

Damen looked into her eyes and his nervousness faded beneath the power of their love. "When I first beheld you, I was the core of a man. I looked into your heart and found the reflection of my own. All that you are fascinates me, and I place all that I am in your hands."

The Zimdardri ambassador stood behind the altar, her long hands crossed over her heart, her head bowed as she witnessed their vows. She looked up across the crowd, then turned her turquoise eyes directly to the sun. She shifted her gaze to Ariana and Damen, then bowed.

"On behalf of all those who witness this sacred wedding of two souls into one, I honor you both for melding your union before us. Around you, I see the white light that is love, the force which bonds us all. In you, Damen of the Dark Sun, I see the strength of your purpose, the wisdom and force of your independent nature. In Ariana of Valenwood, I perceive your grace and sensitivity. Together, separate, you are joined by one heart. Torn asunder by the storms of your lives, you are rejoined by this love that surpasses all other forces. May this love carry you in bliss and to the betterment of all! Now, after the manner of the Dark Sun People, plight your troth and marriage."

Facing Ariana, Damen took her right hand in his right hand, then crossed his left over and took her other hand. Where their hands joined, he saw a glow, warm, as if the energy between them made itself visible. It faded, but he knew it had been there all along.

She looked up at him, her face aglow with love. He bent to kiss her, but she rose up on tiptoes and kissed him first. He swept her up in his arms and lifted her off her feet, and they kissed until his people erupted in joy and laughter. Damen released her, then picked up Elena. She hugged him and kissed his cheek, but she seemed too excited for words. Then Damen turned to his people and held Ariana's hand above his head. She glanced at him uncertainly, but the force and power of the barbarian king he had been flowed strong in his veins, and when he spoke, it was with words he had dreamed of speaking since he first saw her.

"Ariana, Queen of the Dark Sun!"

"What is it, little one? Are the hyppos unhappy in their new home?" A day of feasting and joy had passed into sunset, and Damen had known more joy than he'd ever imagined possible. But Elena sat by the river's edge where it flowed past the city of Ariana-annai, and looked despondent despite the large creatures floating blissfully in the newly-muddied water.

"No . . . The hyppos are very happy. They have already eaten all the eplar fruit I threw to them. Grandpapa was wise to bring them here, because the waters in Valenwood were too cold."

"Then what troubles you?"

She hesitated as if reluctant to open her heart. Damen seated himself beside her, cross-legged, and waited. Elena sighed. "It's just . . . well, I was thinking that even though the hyppos like their new home better, Vender must be very sad because he will miss them."

"Ah . . . I see. Well . . ."

A bright voice interrupted them. "*He* won't be sad, because *he* is here!"

Elena and Damen turned in surprise. Ariana led Vender to the river, and he bounced with excitement when he saw the hyppos in the water. Elena hopped up, her eyes wide with happiness. "What are you doing here?"

Vender released Ariana's hand and went to Elena. He assessed her shimmering dress, then nodded in approval. "You look like a princess in that dress." Vender stopped, embarrassed. "The hyppos think you look pretty." He paused again and looked idly around. "We arrived too late for your parents' wedding, but guess what? My family is moving here with the hyppos! You know something about hyppos, Ellie, but we're bringing a lot more to other parts of this island, and your father invited us to live here, too."

Elena was speechless. Ariana smiled at Damen, and he

took her hand. Vender waded down to the water, then nodded appreciatively. "This is good. The water is much warmer here than in Valenwood."

Elena waded in beside him. "Even so, the hyppos look a little bored."

Vender's brow furrowed. "We can put on a show for them, like we used to do in Valenwood, and then they will feel more at home."

Elena peered at Damen. "Is it all right, Papa, if we play for awhile?"

Damen shrugged. "If the hyppos require entertainment, who I am to stand in their way?"

The children headed off to rehearse, and Damen slipped his arm around Ariana's waist. She snuggled close beside him, then kissed his shoulder. "This has been the most beautiful day of my life." She paused, then moved to kiss his neck. "Though I have spent the latter half of it imagining the night to come."

Damen's pulse quickened. "As have I, my lady." He moved to kiss her, but someone coughed loudly, and Damen looked up to see Dane Calydon and Arnoth standing behind them.

Damen started to rise, but Arnoth motioned them down, and the two men seated themselves beside Damen. Dane looked happy. "So, young pirate, you have taken a queen, and welcome even the esteemed hyppo into your realm! A good day has been had, I'd say."

Damen glanced at Arnoth. "I trust you have forgiven me for defying your order and departing your realm?"

Arnoth looked casual and content. "No . . . No, not really." He stopped and shrugged. "But I knew you would." His dark eyes twinkled with a light Damen hadn't seen before. "I don't normally leave the Intersystem port unguarded, you know."

Damen hesitated. "No. I didn't know."

Dane reached over and slapped Damen's knee. "He's too stubborn just to tell you to get on with it. You got as good a 'go-ahead' from Arnoth of Valenwood as anyone ever has, trust me! We understand now that had the Intersystem joined you, you would never have gotten close enough to save the High King and dismantle the Automon."

Ariana nodded vigorously, then beamed up at Damen. "You told me once that you had to get close enough to the dragon to find its heart. Did you know about the king?"

"No, but I knew there was something captive, something real at the heart of the Automon empire. And I knew it wasn't Mallik. I had to get close to him in order to find the one he was using."

Dane patted Damen's shoulder. "It was well done. Impressive enough for Arnoth to recommend you on the Intersystem High Council."

Damen's mouth dropped and Ariana held her breath. "Assuming I agree to unite my people with the Intersystem, what would motivate you to offer me a place on the High Council?"

Arnoth frowned as the fattest hyppo shoved its mate aside and devoured a large leaf, apparently without chewing. "How fat is too fat, I wonder?"

Damen smiled. "Don't let Elena hear you say that."

Arnoth smiled, too. "Actually, it was the Zimdardri ambassador who has abandoned her seat, leaving an opening that we hoped you might fill."

Dane exhaled a breath of relief. "Thank the stars she's gone! Swept in and commandeered your wedding, then left before the feasting was over."

"The feasting, boy, has just begun!" Carob bounded toward them, Pip at his side, and both gazed at the river bank with wide, eager eyes. "Even the swamps of Keir don't offer such riches! Look, lad, at that plump slug easing its way over the grass!"

Pip squealed. "Look? I can do better than that!" The smaller bat hurtled itself over the grass, landed on the bug and devoured it with a loud chomp. Damen grimaced and Ariana shuddered, but Dane nodded happily.

"Sounds tasty!"

Arnoth eyed him with misgivings. "You frighten me, Thorwalian."

Carob cranked his head around, proud. "In no time, he'll be one of us!"

Dane winced. "Now I'm frightened." He lay flat on his back to look at the sky. "Anyway, the Zimdardri has left with her mate. She's decided to 'explore the wonders of the galaxy in its most primal element.'" Dane propped himself up. "Guess how?"

Damen met Dane's eager gaze. "She's headed off to witness a Tyrikan tournament."

Dane's face fell. "How did you know? Did she tell you that?"

"No. But I had a feeling."

Ariana looked between them, mystified. "How odd!" She glanced around. "Where's Hakon?"

Dane's eyes twinkled. "He's arguing with the lovely but tyrannical Fia about which of them should lead the mission to Gyandorath. Hakon feels it's his role as the premier pilot of the Intersystem fleet, but Fia insists that the rightful heir to that mystic realm should have command."

Ariana's brow furrowed. "Why can't they have joint command?"

Damen and Dane both eyed her doubtfully. Damen shook his head. "You don't know Fia if you think she'll share command with anyone."

Dane huffed. "Or Hakon."

Ariana pondered this and sighed. "I suppose you're right, but I couldn't help noticing that they find each other intensely interesting."

Dane grinned. "Should be quite a journey. Think I'll have to send a bat or two along with them, so that I get a full report when they return."

Fia had entered the Intersystem elite as easily as she once led a group of pirates. She was ready for adventure, but Damen would miss her. They had laid her brother to rest here on Damen's world, surrounded by the beauty of life that he had never known. Fia had changed since learning her true heritage, though she wasn't yet in full command of her Daeron powers. With that force, however, she had contacted the Automon on all the remaining colonies and learned the whereabouts of each. Damen and Ariana had freed them, and found to their surprise that the Automon had not only stopped working the miners, but had improved their feeding and clothed the tribe in a manner suiting Fia's restrained taste.

Dane nodded at Arnoth. "We were also impressed by your handling of the now defunct malloreum mines."

Ariana placed her hand on his arm and seemed proud. "Even I expected you to keep control of them."

Damen angled his brow. "I, and all my people, have had enough of malloreum. We thought the Border Territory inhabitants might enjoy the pursuit of wealth more, and it seems we were right. Every deserted colony is now crawling with pirates."

Ariana shook her head. "An ugly scene, I'm sure."

Dane shrugged. "It will work itself out. Let those who desire wealth learn its true value, in their own way."

Arnoth didn't argue, but he sighed as he resigned himself to the inevitable conflict of greed. He eyed Damen. "What do you think of taking a seat on the Council?"

Damen turned to Ariana, but her face was knit doubtfully. "What do you think, Ariana?"

"I think you would be wonderful, of course. It's just that. . . . Well, the Zimdardri ambassador was the only female on the High Council, though in the greater council, women outnumber the men. It doesn't seem right to have no woman. . . ."

Arnoth huffed. "Then I beg you to remember, my child, that previous to mine, the past seven High Councils have been made up of almost exclusively female ambassadors."

"I suppose that's true. . . ."

Damen studied her face. "It might be that you, my love, would be a better ambassador than I."

She gazed up at him, but she shook her head. "I have other things in mind for my life, Damen. I've been writing hyppo adventures for Elena, and I am finding that very engrossing. And, of course, I'm pregnant. . . ."

He gasped, then caught his breath and reached to touch her as if she might break. "But that's not possible. . . . I have . . . well. . . ." He glanced at Arnoth, reluctant to divulge such personal matters.

Ariana looked casual. "The implant you told me about? Yes, I wondered about that, too. But I'm pregnant."

Arnoth's brow arched. "You trusted an anti-conception implant? Those might work for a few years, if you're lucky. As a matter of fact, I purged it from your body when I healed you. The Automon blast had dislodged it and it wasn't working, anyway."

Ariana cast a quizzical glance at her father. "You might have mentioned that fact, Papa."

Arnoth rose to his feet and glanced back toward the city. "I wanted more grandchildren! Come along, Dane. There's wine to be had, and our wives will be getting into trouble without us."

Dane got up, too, called to the lingbats and the children, and together, they headed back to the city. Pip perched on Vender's head, and Carob had settled on Elena's shoulder, regaling them all with tales of his latest conquest. Damen watched them go, then turned to Ariana.

For a long while, he just stared. A balmy, sweet breeze swirled her hair across her face and she bit her lip waiting for his reaction. He realized he was trembling.

"Are you all right, Damen? I should have told you more carefully, but it just popped out."

Tears clouded his vision, pure from a heart that had endured pain and loss, and then found itself stronger and more filled with love than he'd ever dreamed possible. "Impulsive . . ." He took her hands and kissed them. "I can take care of you, feed you, bring you all that you need, and you don't have to do anything. All the things I should have done when you were pregnant with Elena, I will do for you now."

Ariana smiled, a seductive light in her eyes. She caught his long hair in her fingers and then edged him onto his back. She gazed down at him and his blood turned to fire. "All that I need is you." She bent and softly kissed him, played with his lips, then slipped her tongue over his. She kissed his neck. Damen wrapped his arms around her, and whispered against her hair.

"Then, my dearest love, that's just what I will give."